THE DEVIL'S CROSSING

THE DEVIL'S CROSSING

A PREACHER & JAMIE MacCALLISTER WESTERN

WILLIAM W. JOHNSTONE

AND J.A. JOHNSTONE

PINNACLE BOOKS
Kensington Publishing Corp.

www.kensingtonbooks.com

PINNACLE BOOKS are published by

Kensington Publishing Corp.
119 West 40th Street
New York, NY 10018

All Kensington titles, imprints, and distributed lines are available at special quantity discounts for bulk purchases for sales promotion, premiums, fund-raising, educational, or institutional use.

Special book excerpts or customized printings can also be created to fit specific needs. For details, write or phone the office of the Kensington Sales Manager: Attn.: Sales Department. Kensington Publishing Corp., 119 West 40th Street, New York, NY 10018. Phone: 1-800-221-2647.

PINNACLE BOOKS, the Pinnacle logo, and the WWJ steer head logo are Reg. U.S. Pat. & TM Off.

First Printing: May 2022
ISBN-13: 978-0-7860-4882-3

ISBN-13: 978-0-7860-4883-0 (eBook)

10 9 8 7 6 5 4 3 2 1

Printed in the United States of America

Chapter 1

The Sweetwater River, July 1852,
in what will one day be Wyoming

Ethan Prescott hipped around in the saddle, raised his hand in a signal, and bellowed, "Hold it! Hold it! Stop where you are!"

The lead wagon was about twenty yards behind him. The driver, Frank DeVries, who was the captain of this wagon train, hauled back on the reins and brought the big, canvas-covered Conestoga to a halt. The trail was fairly narrow here, with thick brush on both sides, so the drivers of the other wagons stretched out in a line behind him had no choice but to halt as well. One by one, they lurched to a stop.

Prescott turned to the young man riding beside him and said, "Go down the line and tell the leaders I want to see them up front."

"Yes, sir," Tom Linford said. He was in his early twenties, lean, bronzed, at home in the saddle, and proud of his job as a scout for this wagon train. Prouder still to be working for the well-known wagon-master Ethan Prescott. He nudged his heels against his mount's flanks and headed along the line of wagons, pausing to speak to several of the men who had been elected to form a council that advised Prescott and DeVries.

He also slowed just long enough to trade a quick smile with Alma Stockton as he passed the wagon belonging to her family. She was beside her father on the seat, her sun bonnet shading her face but failing to hide the sparkle in her eyes or the blond curls that peeked out from under the bonnet. She was the prettiest girl Tom had ever seen, and she had consented to let him come courting of an evening.

Tom delivered Prescott's message to the half dozen members of the council. Some of them grumbled as they climbed down from their wagons and began trudging along the trail to join Prescott and DeVries by the lead wagon. Figuring that he needed to know what was going on, too, Tom rode back up there, drawing glares from the men on foot as he passed them.

This was the first wagon train he had helped guide along the Oregon Trail, so he wanted to learn as much as he could from Ethan Prescott, who was an old hand at these journeys. Prescott's first trip over this long trail had been more than ten years earlier. He was one of the most experienced wagon-masters in the business, so there was no one better to teach Tom Linford what he needed to know.

Frank DeVries passed around a jug when all the men had gathered. The whiskey had been brought along mostly for medicinal purposes, and as captain, DeVries kept their entire store of it in his wagon and doled it out only as needed, or for quick nips like these when serious talking had to be done.

Tom held the reins of both his and Prescott's mounts

as the wagon-master pointed along the Sweetwater River. The stream lay just ahead of them, its water sparkling in the sun.

"That's the Sweetwater," he said. "We'll follow it for quite a ways. But to do that, we have to go through there."

His finger moved, sweeping along the river's course to where it flowed through a range of rugged hills.

"You can't see it from here," Prescott continued, "but where the river cuts through those hills, the terrain gets pretty rough. Most of the way, the trail's only wide enough for one wagon at a time."

DeVries said, "I don't see why that's a problem. We normally travel in single file, don't we?"

"Yeah, but we can swing the wagons out and form up into a circle if we need to, even when the brush kind of hems us in like it has been for the last few miles. Up there in the Narrows, we won't have that option most of the time. We'll have the river on one side of us, granite bluffs on the other, and like I said, just enough room for one wagon. No place to go if there's any trouble."

"The Narrows," repeated one of the men. "That's what people call it?"

"Some do," Prescott replied with a shrug. "Some call it Three Crossings, or the Triple Crossing, because we'll have to ford the river at least three times to get through there." He paused. "And here lately, some folks have taken to calling it the Devil's Crossing."

DeVries laughed and said, "That certainly sounds ominous. Is it really that bad, Ethan?"

"The crossings themselves can be pretty difficult, depending on how high the river is and how fast it's flowing. On some trips, when there's been a lot of rain upstream, the wagons have had to stop and wait for the water to go down."

"We don't want to do that," spoke up Jethro Calhoun, a weedy pilgrim whose beard and mustache always seemed to have bare patches. "We got good land waitin' for us in Oregon, and we need to get there and start workin' it. If we can get a crop of some kind in before next winter, even a small one, it'll sure help us get through."

"I know that," Prescott said, nodding. "All those difficulties are just the regular ones, though, that hundreds of wagon trains have faced coming through here in the past. What's changed lately is that rumors have started circulating of an outlaw gang operating in these parts."

"Outlaws!" Frank DeVries exclaimed. "All the way out here in the middle of nowhere?"

"We may be a long way from civilization, but that doesn't mean this is unspoiled wilderness. I reckon there'll always be predators, no matter where you go, and a group like yours . . . well, you make pretty tempting prey."

Prescott looked around at the circle of dismayed faces and went on, "Think about it. Not only are you carrying plenty of supplies that can be stolen and sold or traded elsewhere, but some of you also brought along all the cash you could gather up in order to help you get started in your new homes. Add everything together, and there's a considerable amount of loot to be had here."

"So you believe these bandits are going to attack us?" asked DeVries.

With a grim look on his ruddy, white-mustached face, Prescott said, "I just don't know, Frank. I looked into it before we started, because I knew our route would take us through here. They're not hitting every train, only some of them. But is there a chance we'd be one of the unlucky bunches? Sure there is."

The members of the council looked solemn and downright scared, Tom Linford thought as he glanced around at them. He didn't blame them; Mr. Prescott's words were mighty worrisome. He thought about what might happen to Alma Stockton if bloodthirsty desperadoes attacked the wagons, and the possibility was like a cold fist closing uncomfortably on his belly.

DeVries said, "From the sound of it, those hills up there and that narrow passage would be a good place for outlaws to lie in wait, sure enough. But what are our options? Is there another route we can take?"

Prescott nodded and swept a hand toward the south. "There is. We can swing that way and go around the hills. It's farther, and that's not the only problem. People call it the Deep Sand Route, for a good reason. There are miles of soft, sandy ground that we'd have to cross. Your mules and oxen will wear themselves down to a nub pulling those heavy wagons. They'll be so worn out by the time you get around the hills that you'll have to stop for a while and let them rest and recover before you can go on. You should be safe from outlaws, though. It's open country all around, without any really good places for an ambush."

"But if it's farther that way to start with," said Calhoun, "you throw in the sand slowin' down the livestock and then the need for them to rest . . . just how long will it delay us if we follow that so-called Deep Sand Route?"

"Two weeks," Prescott said heavily. "At least. Maybe longer."

Calhoun shook his head. "Then I vote no, if it's a vote

that we're takin'. We got to get to Oregon, dadblast it! Like I said, we got land to work."

"Now, hold on, Jethro," said DeVries. "If it's too dangerous to go through this . . . this Devil's Crossing, maybe we'd be better off in the long run going around it. If we all get killed by outlaws, we'll never get to Oregon!"

"You heard what Prescott said," Calhoun argued. "There ain't no way of knowin' if those bandits are even around here. We could make it through just fine and save two weeks. That's two more weeks to get a crop in."

One of the other men asked, "How does the river look, Mr. Prescott? Do you think it would give us any trouble if we followed it? Would we be able to ford it all right?"

"From what I've seen of it, the teams and the wagons can handle the crossings themselves without any more trouble than normal. Which, I'll remind you, can be pretty tricky at times."

"But you've taken wagon trains through there before, right?"

Prescott nodded and said, "Dozens of times."

"Have you ever lost any wagons?"

"As a matter of fact, I haven't. Not to the Narrows. But there can always be a first time," the wagon-master added.

DeVries looked at the other men and asked, "What do you think, fellas? Should we risk it?"

"What do you think, Frank?" another man said. "We elected you to be captain. You're the most levelheaded of the bunch."

DeVries rubbed his chin and frowned. He and Prescott had become friends during the journey, so he used the wagon-master's given name as he asked, "Are you saying you *won't* take us through this Devil's Crossing, Ethan?"

"Not at all," Prescott replied without hesitation. "Part of my job is to make decisions, sure, but where something like this is concerned, the whole group ought to be in agreement, at least within reason. There's just no way of knowing how much of a risk it would be, so I'll abide by whatever you decide."

"Go on through," Calhoun said with a curt gesture toward the hills. "It'd take too blasted long to go around."

One of the men said, "If the other route is as hard on the livestock as Mr. Prescott says, we might actually lose some of them by going that way."

He looked at Prescott for confirmation. The wagonmaster nodded and said, "Could happen."

"I agree with Jethro," the man said. A couple more nodded, and another said, "So do I. That's too much of a delay."

Frank DeVries nodded slowly and said, "I'll go along with the others. I think we want to risk following the river and going on straight through the hills."

"That's what we'll do, then," said Prescott. "You fellas can go back to your wagons. We'll rest the stock for a few more minutes, water them at the river, and then move out. We can put a few more miles behind us today and start through the hills fresh tomorrow."

The other men talked a few moments among themselves, then started back to their vehicles. DeVries said, "I hope we made the right decision, Ethan."

"So do I, Frank. So do I."

Prescott jerked his head to Tom Linford and walked toward the river. Linford followed, leading the two saddle horses.

As the animals drank, Prescott stood hipshot, gazing

toward the hills. Linford hesitated for a moment, then said, "I notice that we didn't get a vote back there, Mr. Prescott."

The older man chuckled. "That's because you and I are just hired hands, Tom. Those men back there are wagering everything they have, including their families, on this new start they intend to make in Oregon. The two of us, we don't really have any stake in this."

"No, sir," said Linford. "I suppose not."

Only our lives, he thought.

Chapter 2

A half hour later, the wagons once again began their slow, rocking, lurching journey westward, now rolling along the southern bank of the Sweetwater River toward the hills. While they were stopped, resting and watering the stock, Tom Linford had taken advantage of the opportunity to talk to Alma Stockton.

"You and the other men seemed to be having such a serious discussion," she said. She was shy and didn't look directly at him as she spoke. "What were you talking about?"

"Oh, Mr. Prescott was just telling us about a couple of different ways we can go from here." He didn't explain that he had just stood there listening. He hadn't actually *discussed* anything.

"What did you decide?"

He hadn't decided anything, either. As he had said to Prescott, they didn't get a vote. But he didn't want to get into that with Alma, so he just said, "We're going to follow the river."

"Well, that seems reasonable to me. Rivers are usually the best routes, aren't they?"

"Usually," Linford agreed.

He debated with himself whether to tell her what Prescott had said about the threat of outlaws. Before their meeting broke up, the members of the council had decided *not* to spread the word among the others, for fear of starting a potentially needless panic. Linford wasn't bound by that decision, though. If he didn't get any voice in the way they did things, he wasn't going to worry too much about abiding by their rules.

When you came down to it, though, he didn't want to worry Alma for no reason, so he said, "Your pa knows to keep his eyes open all the time, doesn't he?"

Alma looked at him now, a tiny frown prettily creasing her forehead. "Of course. Mr. Prescott and Mr. DeVries always tell everybody to be watchful."

"Good."

"Why did you ask that, Tom?"

"No particular reason," he lied. "I just figured it's a good idea. The train's been lucky so far, but you never know when trouble might crop up."

"No, I suppose not." She started to turn away, then paused. "Tom . . . why don't you come to our wagon for supper tonight? We have beans soaking, and Mama made fresh bread this morning."

He smiled and said, "That sounds good. And I'd sure enjoy the company."

She looked down again. "So . . . so would I."

She sure was shy. He had a sudden urge to lean down and kiss her on the cheek, but he kept a tight rein on the impulse. If he did that, he'd probably startle her so bad that she'd bolt like a runaway mule.

Although that wasn't a good way to think of it, he told

himself as Alma moved off to help her ma with something. She wasn't anything like a mule. More likely she'd fly away like a pretty bird . . .

"What have you got on your mind?"

Ethan Prescott's deep voice cut into the young man's thoughts and scattered them. He shook his head and said, "Oh, nothing important."

Prescott grunted. "Yeah, I'll bet. I've seen looks like that on the faces of young men before. You're sweet on one of the girls in this wagon train. You'd better be careful or her pa will dust the seat of your britches with buckshot, and I won't do a blasted thing about it except stand there and laugh at your little predicament."

"I'm not going to do anything to make somebody come after me with a shotgun."

"You'd better remember that. And there's a preacher among those pilgrims, too, if there's any marrying to be done. You'd best not be forgetting about *that*."

Linford felt his face burning. "Won't need no preacher," he said shortly.

"Good. Now ride on ahead and see how the river looks."

Linford swung up into the saddle and heeled his horse into motion. He followed the Sweetwater, his mount loping along until the wagons were almost out of sight behind him. His head moved almost constantly as he swung his gaze from side to side, searching intently all around for any signs of potential trouble. As he had told Alma, they had been lucky so far, but vigilance went hand in hand with luck.

Nobody was going to sneak up on them as long as he was scout and had anything to say about it.

* * *

They drew the wagons into a circle and made camp that evening while they were still out on the plains, a few miles short of the hills. Tom Linford had supper with the Stockton family—Alma, her ma and pa, and her two little brothers. The fare was the same as always, beans cooked in an iron pot, bacon fried up in a big pan, bread that had been baked that morning in a Dutch oven, all washed down with strong black coffee, even for the kids. There was one extra treat, some dried fruit. Linford didn't know if that was on account of him being a guest, but he enjoyed it.

The whole evening was enjoyable. He and Alma were never alone, but they were able to sit next to each other on the lowered tailgate of the wagon and converse in low tones. Neither said anything of any consequence, just idle talk about the journey so far and the family's plans for their new farm in Oregon, but it was the intimacy that counted. Linford curled up in his bedroll that night with thoughts of blue eyes and blond curls filling his head.

All that was forgotten early the next morning, when Linford was up before the sun, getting his horse ready to ride. Ethan Prescott was up even earlier, though. Nobody beat the wagon-master when it came to working hard. First to start and last to quit, that was Prescott.

The wagon train reached the hills in late morning. During a pause before they started following the winding trail, Prescott told Frank DeVries that he hoped to get through the challenging passage and make camp that evening on the far side of it.

"Can we do that?" asked DeVries.

"If nothing happens to delay us." Prescott's mouth

tightened. "I'd just as soon not have to stop where we're stretched out with no place to go. Just in case."

He didn't have to say in case of what, thought Linford. He knew what Prescott meant. That would make them an even more tempting target for bandits.

As he and Prescott rode a short distance in front of the wagons, the young man kept his eye on the beetling brow of the hillside. It kept looming closer and closer to the trail, the farther into the hills they penetrated.

Another couple of miles fell behind them, then Prescott reined in and nodded toward the trail in front of them. A hundred yards ahead, it petered out into the steep, rocky hillside.

"This is as far as we go on this side," Prescott announced. "The wagons will have to ford the river."

He pointed, and Linford looked across the stream. There was room on the other side for the wagons to travel.

"How far does the trail run over there?"

"A couple of miles," said Prescott. "Then we'll have to cross back to the south bank. There'll be one more ford after that, which will leave us on the north bank. We can go on from there without any more crossings, unless things have changed since the last time I came through here."

"It doesn't seem that bad so far," Linford commented.

"We're just getting started," Prescott said. He turned in the saddle to wave at Frank DeVries, who had already halted his wagon without being told to. "It's close enough to midday that we'll stop here for a little while to let folks eat and rest the livestock."

"You want me to pass the word?"

"Sure, go ahead. Thanks, son."

It made Linford feel good to have Ethan Prescott call him son.

The women in the wagon train were in the habit of saving back some of the food from breakfast so it could be eaten cold for the midday meal. If there was time, they brewed coffee to go with it. In this case, though, there was plenty of good river water right there a few steps away, so the pilgrims filled their tin cups and drank it down. Even though it was summer, these streams that flowed down from the mountains still ran clear and cold, fed as they were by snow melt.

Linford would have sought out Alma Stockton to spend a few minutes with her, but Prescott called to him and motioned for him to follow. The two men rode into the river, letting their horses pick their path, feeling out the bottom as they went along.

"Feels pretty solid right here," Prescott opined. "And the water'll only come up to the wheel hubs, so there shouldn't be any trouble with wagons starting to drift. Plenty have crossed here in the past."

"You must know just about everything there is to know about this part of the country," said Linford.

Prescott snorted. "Not hardly. There are other wagon-masters who've been at it even longer than I have, like my friend Simon Lash, and before them, other men were out here. I'm talking about the fur trappers, the mountain men. They were the first white men to explore these parts. Fellas like John Colter, Jim Bridger, Kit Carson." Prescott grinned. "You ever hear tell of a man called Preacher?"

"Preacher," repeated Linford. "Yes, I think so."

"Preacher's been over every foot of ground west of the Mississippi, they say, and probably knows it better than any other man alive. I've crossed trails with him a few times, and it was a real honor every time I did."

Linford had trouble comprehending that a veteran frontiersman such as Ethan Prescott would feel in awe of any other man, but he could tell that Prescott was sincere.

"Maybe I'll run into this Preacher sometime," he said. "Is he an actual minister?"

Prescott threw back his head and laughed. "Not hardly. But you can ask him to tell you the story of how he came to be called that. It's a pretty famous tale out here."

"Yeah, I reckon I'll do that," Linford said. He had the feeling there was more to it than what Prescott had told him, but he didn't press the wagon-master for details.

Satisfied that this was a good place to ford the Sweet-water, Prescott turned back to the wagons after telling Linford to go on ahead and take a look around on the other side of the river. Linford did so, riding along the trail until he was out of sight of the ford. It began to narrow down again, just as it had done on the south side, and as he rode around a bend, he saw a sheer, towering granite bluff crowding close to the water. The trail was still wide enough for a single wagon, and it ran fairly straight for as far as Linford could see, which was a little unusual in this country where most paths twisted and turned quite a bit.

He saw something else that made his eyes widen. The face of that granite bluff was covered with names. Hundreds, maybe thousands of names. Some written with hunks of charcoal, others daubed in axle grease. They ranged from crude, barely legible printing in block letters to elaborate, flowing script. Covering the rock wall for a hundred yards or more, they were crowded onto the rock from the ground up to as high as a tall man could reach while standing on a wagon seat. Some were faded with time, while many others looked relatively fresh and new.

Linford knew he was looking at a record of the thousands of immigrants who had passed along here, bound for Oregon. He had seen similar places, back along the trail, where names were scrawled on rocks, but this was the most impressive such display he had come across so far on the journey. There was no way of knowing who had first given in to the impulse and written his or her name here, but others had seen it and thought it was a good idea. Time had passed, and the river of immigrants had flowed on, much like the Sweetwater, only in the opposite direction.

As Linford stared at the names, he wondered how many of those people had made it to their destinations . . . and how many were lying alongside the trail in graves with markers that would collapse and decay and vanish, just as the graves themselves would flatten and new grass would grow, and flowers would bloom on them in the spring so that no one would ever know someone with dreams and hopes and passions lay there, slumbering forever alone and forgotten . . .

Linford took a deep breath as he shook himself out of his reverie. Maybe Mr. Prescott would allow the wagons to stop here long enough for folks to add their names to the bluff. He thought about Alma writing her name on there, and if she did, he intended to add his right underneath it, so that from now on, anybody who passed along here might see the names and think that they were linked.

That put a smile on his face, and he was still smiling when he heard three shots fired one right after the other, the reports echoing along the canyon between the hills in the universal signal for trouble.

Chapter 3

The trail beside the name-covered bluff was plenty wide enough for a horse to turn around, so Linford wheeled his mount sharply and jabbed his boot heels into the animal's flanks. The horse leaped into a gallop that carried him back along the riverbank toward the ford.

More shots blasted, a ragged volley, followed by a rolling wave of gun-thunder that echoed so loudly in the canyon it seemed like Linford's head would explode from the racket.

Or maybe that was the blood pounding inside his head, he realized as he felt his heart slugging so hard in his chest that it seemed on the verge of bursting from his body.

The gunfire continued, and with every brief pause, Linford heard men shouting and women screaming.

Alma.

He told himself not to think of her, just to get back as fast as he could so he could help fight off the outlaws.

Linford had no doubt in his mind that was what was happening. The wagon train was under attack by the desperadoes Prescott had warned the council about. The raid had taken place even sooner than Linford thought it might.

The bandits must have struck while the wagons were fording the river. The drivers of the vehicles in the water would have nowhere to go. Those already on the north bank or still on the south bank wouldn't be able to fort up in a circle, either. There wouldn't be enough of them.

At least those immigrants could take cover under their wagons. Those in the stream wouldn't even be able to do that without submerging themselves in the cold water.

The Stockton wagon was just about in the middle of the train. Linford had no way of knowing how far along the crossing had been when the outlaws struck.

Alma might already be—

He stopped that thought from forming fully in his head. He wasn't going to allow himself even to think it.

Linford leaned to the right and left to balance himself as his horse took the bends in the trail at breakneck speed. The gunfire continued hammering through the air, so fast and loud that it sounded like a battle in wartime. At least, Linford imagined a battle would sound like that. He had never been in one, had never fired a shot in anger.

His mouth was so dry and puckered it felt like it was going to close up in his face and go away. He thought he caught the tang of powder smoke in the air, but he could have imagined that.

The trail had widened considerably, so he knew he was getting close to the ford. He swept around another bend, and suddenly the terrible scene unfolded before him.

Four wagons were on the north bank, another six were in the river with water swirling around the wheels and the legs of the livestock, and the rest of the wagons were still on the south bank.

The Stockton wagon had been the last one to enter the river. It was only a few yards from shore. It would have been easy enough for Alma and her family to jump down and wade clear, but it also would have been suicidal because of the bullets flying through the air all around the wagons. They would be better off hunkering down behind the vehicle's thick sideboards.

Linford didn't see Alma or any of the others, but as he hauled back on his horse's reins, he saw the barrel of a rifle stick out from under the canvas cover at the back of the wagon. Flame and gray smoke spurted from the weapon.

Men on horseback swarmed around the wagons, firing pistols and rifles. Linford's first, shocked impression was that they looked like animals, but then he realized they were all wearing long, shaggy buffalo coats, despite the fact that the day was a warm one. Felt hats with broad, drooping brims obscured their features, which were further concealed by bandannas tied around the lower halves of their faces.

Several men lay facedown in the river, floating and drifting slowly. Wagoneers who had been shot off their vehicles, Linford realized. He didn't see any female bodies, only male, so maybe Alma was still all right.

For a second, his anxious gaze searched for Ethan Prescott. He didn't catch sight of the wagon-master anywhere.

Only a few heartbeats had passed since Linford rounded the bend and reined in, but the time seemed longer than that. He couldn't stand by and do nothing. He was armed with a Colt Navy revolver and a Sharps carbine. He hauled the carbine from its scabbard strapped to the saddle as he swung down.

The Sharps was a heavy weapon. Linford pulled the horse around so the animal was between him and the battle. He rested the carbine's barrel on the saddle and spoke softly to the horse so it would stay still and steady. The gunfire and the smell of powder smoke in the air had the mount a little spooked, but it calmed as Linford rested his cheek against the smooth wood of the carbine's stock and eared back the hammer.

He knew the horse wouldn't stand still for long, so as quickly as he could without rushing, he drew a bead on one of the buffalo-coated outlaws. In those thick garments, they bulked larger than life. Linford settled his sights on a man who was facing away from him and firing toward the wagons.

The thought that he was about to shoot a man in the back never crossed his mind.

He took a deep breath, held it, and the whole world seemed to go still. Linford squeezed the trigger, and the Sharps went off with a tremendous boom and a kick that sent him reeling back a step. The horse jumped to the side, startled by the shot.

Linford blinked to clear the smoke from his eyes and saw the outlaw he had targeted slowly toppling off his horse. Something looked odd about the man, though, and after a split second, Linford realized what it was.

The man's head was pretty much gone, and blood fountained up from the stump of his neck. The horrified youngster felt relief when the corpse splashed into the river and he couldn't see it anymore.

Linford had aimed for the biggest part of the outlaw's body and tried to place his shot right in the middle of the man's back. Instead, the .54 caliber round must have gone high. It could have missed entirely, but luck—good for Linford, bad for the outlaw—had guided it right to the back of the man's head. It was an amazing shot, the likes of which Linford might not ever make again.

He couldn't think about that now. He grabbed the skittish horse's reins, rammed the empty Sharps back in its sheath, and practically leaped into the saddle again. Then, holding the reins in his left hand, he used his right to pull the Colt Navy from its holster and banged his heels on the horse's flanks. He charged into the fracas, waiting until he got closer to open fire with the revolver.

Something hummed past his ear. That was a bullet, he realized, coming close enough for him to hear it. He had nearly gotten *his* head blown off just now.

But he was still alive, still in the fight, and he headed for the lead wagon, knowing he was likely to find Prescott somewhere around there. Part of him wanted to charge directly to the Stockton wagon, but he figured he could do more to help Alma and her family in the long run by helping Prescott rally the immigrants to fight off the attackers.

One of the outlaws spotted him heading in that direction and moved to intercept him. Linford saw orange muzzle flame geyser from the man's gun. He ducked low in the saddle and thumbed off two shots from the Colt Navy. The outlaw's horse suddenly collapsed, its front legs folding up as if they had been jerked out from under it. The rider sailed over the dying animal's head, his buffalo coat flapping wildly behind him like a grotesque pair of wings.

He crashed to the ground, rolled over and came up on his knees, obviously stunned and groggy. His hat had come off, revealing a shock of dark hair, but the bandanna still covered his nose, mouth, and chin.

With hooves pounding nearby, he looked up just in time for Linford to shoot him in the chest while racing past. The .36 caliber bullet smashed into the outlaw and knocked him over backward. Linford didn't even glance at the dead man as he rode by.

He was close enough to Frank DeVries' wagon to see the crumpled shape lying on the floorboards of the driver's box. Linford groaned when he spotted the spreading pool of crimson in which the man lay. He recognized DeVries' clothing. The wagon train's captain was either dead or the next thing to it.

Another mounted outlaw lunged around the back of the wagon and fired at Linford. The young man's hat flew off his head. Again, he had come mighty close to dying. He had two shots left in the Colt. He jerked the weapon up and triggered one of them. The outlaw twisted in the saddle. Linford had hit him.

The bandit didn't fall. He threw a wild shot at Linford, wheeled his horse, and galloped away, not wanting any more of the fight right now. Linford rode around the wagon, still looking for Ethan Prescott.

Another groan escaped from his lips as he saw the wagon-master's horse on the other side of the vehicle, lying on its side with blood pumping from a wound in its neck. Prescott wasn't there, though. With his horse shot out from under him, he was probably somewhere in the melee, fighting from the ground.

Linford yanked his horse around again and splashed

into the river. Water droplets flew up around him and the horse and sparkled in the afternoon light. Under other circumstances, they would have been pretty.

There was so much confusion—masked raiders on horseback lunging here and there, clouds of powder smoke rolling through the air—Linford couldn't even make a guess how many attackers there were. It was a large group, he knew that. He had killed two and wounded another, but that probably wouldn't make much difference in the long run.

He pounded through the water, determined now to reach the Stockton wagon and protect Alma to his last breath. Maybe if the immigrants put up enough of a fight, the outlaws would decide the price was too high and break off the attack. That was the only real hope, so Linford clung to it.

He kicked his feet free from the stirrups, and as he came alongside the Stockton wagon, he leaped from the saddle to the driver's box. One of the oxen in the team was down in its traces, killed by a stray bullet. The other three animals stood there, unable to move.

The wagon shifted when Linford landed on the box. A pistol barrel poked out from beneath the arching canvas cover. Linford looked past it and saw Alma's pale, horror-stricken face as she aimed the gun at him, no doubt thinking that he was one of the outlaws.

"Alma, it's me!" he shouted. "Don't shoot! Don't shoot!"

Alma's blue eyes were enormous with shock and fear already, but they widened even more as she recognized him. "Tom!" she cried. "Oh, Tom!"

The pistol started to sag, but then, abruptly, she jerked it up again and flame stabbed from its barrel. For a split second, Linford thought she had fired at him, but then he realized the bullet had whipped past him. He jerked his head around and saw one of the outlaws toppling from his saddle to land in the river. He must have been drawing a bead on Linford's back when Alma shot him.

She dropped the gun and reached for him. He holstered the Colt and caught hold of her, pulling her halfway out of the wagon as he tightly embraced her. He looked over her shoulder into the shadows of the wagon bed, under the canvas cover. Her mother was sprawled halfway over the raised tailgate, motionless. Linford knew she was dead as soon as he saw her.

Alma's father lay on his back, his chest rising and falling raggedly as one of his young sons held a folded cloth on his chest and pressed down on it. The cloth was turning red rapidly, however, as Stockton's blood drained from the wound. Linford didn't see the other little boy.

He clung to Alma, cradling her against him, saying, "It'll be all right, it'll be all right," over and over. Then he heard a thud and felt her jerk in his arms. Her head went back and their gazes locked. Terrible pain and realization filled her eyes. Linford screamed, "Nooooo!" as she sagged in his embrace. A warm wetness covered the hand he pressed to her back.

"Tom . . ." His name came from her lips in a sigh, and then she was gone, the life fading from her eyes as they rolled up in their sockets. Linford hugged her against him even harder, but it did no good, of course. Scalding tears stung his eyes as he lowered her carefully to the wagon bed behind the seat.

Shouting incoherently in rage, he turned and jerked the Colt from its holster once more. He saw a rider in a buffalo coat aiming a rifle at him and fired his last shot at the same instant as the outlaw's rifle blasted.

Tom Linford never knew if his bullet found its target or not. A tremendous blow slammed into his head. He pitched off the wagon to land in the river. He barely felt the water's icy chill for a second, and then a greater coldness swallowed him whole.

Chapter 4

Linford choked, sputtered, spit out the water that came up his throat. Spasms shook his entire body. More water slapped him in the face, filling his nose and mouth. He shook his head from side to side, trying to get away from the flood, and the movement made the top of his head fly off.

That was what the pain felt like, anyway—his skull had cracked completely in two, and he had lost part of it. As he gasped in agony, his arms and legs worked involuntarily, as if some instinct commanded him to get out of the water. He crawled a few feet and collapsed. He was too weak to hold his head up. Sharp rocks gouged into his face.

That pain was nothing compared to the throbbing torture in his head. Gradually, over a span of time that might have been a minute or an hour for all he knew, he realized that he was alive, his heart was beating, his head was relatively intact, and that drumbeat of misery was his pulse.

His hands scrabbled on the rocks, found purchase. He pulled himself forward again. Eventually, he began to comprehend that he was out of the river, lying on the bank.

Something bumped his shoulder. Something alive.

Instinctively, Linford flinched away from that unknown touch. It might be a danger, something that wanted him dead. Then it bumped him again, and he heard a soft, snuffling sound and felt warm breath against his face.

He forced his eyes open. For a moment, they refused to focus. When his vision began to clear, he found himself looking up into a long, familiar face. His horse nudged his shoulder again and nuzzled his jaw.

Linford reached up with a shaking hand. It took him two tries to grab the horse's headstall. The horse tried to pull away. Linford held on in desperation, and with the horse's help, he lifted himself to his knees.

From there he was able to catch hold of the dangling reins with his other hand. The horse whinnied, obviously unhappy about what was going on. Linford muttered something. The animal seemed to relax slightly at the sound of his voice. He said, "Easy . . . Easy, fella . . . Don't run off . . ."

If the horse bolted, Linford wouldn't be able to hold it. He didn't have nearly enough strength for that. And if it ran off, he couldn't catch it.

In the back of his mind was the thought that he was going to need the horse if he intended to survive. His brain might barely be functioning, but he knew that much.

He made it to his feet and leaned against the animal while his madly spinning senses slowly got back to normal. The pain in his head receded somewhat. He moved his left hand to the saddle horn, got a firm grip on it, then gingerly explored the area above his right ear with the fingertips of that hand. He found a sticky, swollen welt and knew that was where a bullet had creased him, banging his head on the side of the wagon and knocking him unconscious, as well.

The outlaw who had shot him must have figured he was dead. It was pure luck the man hadn't riddled him with bullets to make sure of it.

Linford drew in several deep breaths. He lifted his head more and looked around.

He wished he hadn't.

He was a short distance downstream from the ford where the wagon train had been crossing the Sweetwater. Most of the wagons were still there, but it looked to Linford like a few of them were missing. The outlaws must have piled their loot into those vehicles and driven off with them. The wagons that remained no longer had teams hitched to them. The bandits had taken the surviving mules and oxen, as well. They had stolen anything and everything that might be valuable to them.

Which meant they had left behind the dead.

Bodies floated in the water and littered both banks of the river. Men, women, children . . . all slaughtered, cut down cruelly and ruthlessly.

Including Alma, Linford remembered as a sob wracked him and set off a fresh wave of pain in his head. She was gone. She had died in his arms. He was certain the rest of her family had been killed, too.

When he felt strong enough to move around again, he tied his horse's reins to a bush so it wouldn't wander off and waded into the water to start retrieving the bodies. He had to stop and rest fairly often, but as the afternoon waned, he managed to haul all the people he could find out of the water and onto the south bank, which was where he had washed up.

He knew there had been exactly eighty-seven immigrants in this wagon train, not counting himself and Ethan Prescott. He found sixty-three bodies, leaving twenty-four unaccounted for. Some of them could have floated farther downstream before hanging up on a rock or a branch sticking out into the water. When he realized that most of the missing were women or girls, his guts twisted. The outlaws had taken prisoners with them, to use the captives for their own pleasure before selling or trading them somewhere. There weren't any real settlements this far west, but there were isolated trading posts where women could be forced into lives of prostitution. The owners of such places wouldn't care where they came from.

Alma had been spared that fate. Her body was among the ones Linford pulled out of the river, along with her mother and father and the brother he had seen earlier. Where the other brother had gone, what had happened to him . . . Linford just didn't know.

He also didn't find Ethan Prescott's body. It was one of the corpses that had floated off downstream, Linford decided.

The thought of digging more than sixty graves was almost more than Linford could bear. The shape he was in, it was more than he was physically capable of. Just dragging the bodies out of the river had almost done him in.

Yet he couldn't leave them for the scavengers, either. Not Alma or the other members of her family, and if he couldn't turn his back on them, he couldn't do that to all those other innocent people. Even though he wanted to collapse, he started looking through the wagons, hoping to find a shovel that the thieves had neglected to steal or something else he could use to dig. It might take him days to accomplish it, but he would do the right thing.

Instead, he found several cans of coal oil, which people had started burning in lanterns in the past few years. He held one in his hand and looked at it for a long moment before sighing in resignation.

He was able to pile all the bodies in four wagons that still stood on the south bank. He made sure that Alma, her parents, and her brother were together in one of the wagons. By the time he was finished, he was staggering with exhaustion.

But there was still more grim work to do. He splashed coal oil on the sideboards of the wagons and on the bodies inside them. He used every bit of the stuff and tossed the empty cans aside. His matches had gotten wet when he fell in the river, but he carried a little pouch with steel and flint in it, so he was able to gather some dry brush and build a small fire.

Then, using burning branches, he lit every wagon.

The flames caught and spread quickly. Tendrils of black smoke began to coil and gather into clouds. Linford backed away, grimacing as a terrible smell drifted to him.

He had one more thing to do, he told himself. He found a little pot of axle grease hanging under one of the other wagons and took it and several branches with him as he mounted up. The smell coming from the burning wagons had spooked the horse again, but it settled down once he was in the saddle. He looked one last time at the blazing vehicles, then turned and rode up the canyon.

He didn't stop until he reached the granite bluff where all the names were written. He rode along it and reined in when he came to a clear space. The light was fading now. The sun had dropped behind the hills to the west. But enough reddish-gold illumination remained in the sky for him to see what he was doing as he used one of the sticks and the axle grease to print Alma's name on the rock. He was careful and made sure what he wrote was legible.

Below her name, he wrote those of her parents and brothers. He didn't put his own name. He didn't feel that he had the right to. Instead, he wrote Ethan Prescott's name and Frank DeVries' and every other name he could recall. He was sure he was forgetting people, but he didn't keep count. He just wrote down the ones he could remember and figured the others would forgive him.

They hadn't made it quite this far, but he thought they deserved to have their names here anyway. In time, what he was doing here would fade. It might vanish entirely. But for a while, these people who had dared it all and risked everything would not be forgotten. Every time somebody else passed along this trail, the names would be there.

Linford didn't stop until it was too dark to see what he was doing, and by then he couldn't come up with any more names. He threw away the stick he'd been using and the nearly empty pot of grease and tugged his horse's reins from underneath the chunk of rock where he had left them. Utterly weary, he climbed into the saddle and nudged the mount into motion.

The afterglow of the sunset was just about gone now as Linford rode west along the canyon. But an orange hue tinted the sky to the east as flames continued consuming the wagons and their grisly contents, there beside the Devil's Crossing.

Chapter 5

"Watch where you're going, old man."

Preacher stopped and looked back over his shoulder. The harsh, angry voice came from behind him. He had almost run into several men as they emerged from a saloon, but with a nimble agility that belied his years, he had stepped around them and avoided a collision.

"You talkin' to me?" he asked in a mild voice.

"You're the only old man here, aren't you?" demanded the middle member of the trio.

Their clothes told Preacher they weren't frontiersmen. The frock coats, vests, and tall silk hats marked them—probably—as gamblers. Although they might be some other sort of bottom-feeders whose goal in life was to cheat, hoodwink, bamboozle, or otherwise get their greedy hands on money they hadn't worked for.

A lot of those types could be found in Independence, which had been the jumping-off point for nearly all westward migration for more than a decade and a half. The Oregon Trail started here, as did the Santa Fe and California Trails. Preacher had traveled all those routes more than once; of course, it was mighty difficult to find *any* place west of the Mississippi where Preacher hadn't been more than once.

Most folks didn't have that sort of experience, though. Thousands of people came through Independence every year, bound for new starts, and the vast majority of them were babes in the woods when it came to frontier life. Easy prey for varmints like these three, in other words.

Preacher wondered briefly just how much trouble the law would give him if he pulled the two Colt Dragoon revolvers he wore and filled them full of lead. That was what he'd do if he'd come across three venomous snakes coiled up and ready to strike. He didn't really see much difference.

The authorities probably wouldn't agree with that, however, and he didn't have the patience for a lot of folderol and foofaraw. So he said, "I don't reckon there was any harm done either way, so I'll bid you fellas a good evenin'."

"You will, will you?" jeered the spokesman. "The way I see it, you nearly ran into us, so I think what you should be doing is giving us an apology."

"That's what you think, do you?"

One of the other men said, "Oh, let him go, Hartford. He's just a simple-minded old-timer."

"That's right," added the third man. "Anyway, you're just mad because Georgiana is booked up for the entire night and you won't be able to spend any time with her."

The one called Hartford snapped, "Don't be ridiculous. I've never wasted a second's time being upset over any woman, let alone some painted harlot."

"Then let's go," said the second man. "There should

be a game getting started at the Winston House. Maybe we can still get in on it."

Hartford sighed and said, "I suppose you're right." He started to turn away, and the others would have followed him.

A contrary notion welled up inside Preacher. He ought to be old and wise enough to ignore it, he told himself.

But instead, he drawled to the man's back, "Hope you have better luck with the cards than you did with Georgiana, mister."

Hartford stopped short, stiffening. The other two paused, as well. Hartford swung around, glared at Preacher in the light that spilled through the saloon's front windows and door, and said, "You've got a big mouth, old man. I think I need to shut it for you."

"Come ahead," Preacher told him.

One of the other men put a hand on Hartford's arm. "Forget it, Jack. He's too old. You're just going to get in trouble if you hurt him."

"That's right," Hartford's second companion said. "I mean, look at him. He's practically decrepit."

Preacher's mouth curved slightly under the graying mustache. He knew what he looked like. He was in his early fifties, but the life he'd led had weathered and seasoned him, putting plenty of gray and silver in his hair and making the skin of his face resemble well-tanned leather. Tall and lean, he didn't look all that strong, but immense power was packed into the corded muscles of his wolfish frame. He wore high-topped black boots, canvas trousers, a buckskin shirt, and a wide-brimmed, flat-crowned brown hat. Two cartridge belts, each with an attached holster, were buckled around his trim hips.

A walnut-butted Colt Dragoon revolver rode in each holster. A sheathed hunting knife with a long, heavy blade also hung from one of the belts.

If Hartford and his friends saw those weapons, they ignored them, concentrating instead on the silver in Preacher's hair and the wrinkles on his face. They had no idea who they were facing.

Hartford shrugged off the restraining hand, growled, "I don't care," and lunged at Preacher, swinging a big right fist.

With such grace that it didn't look as if he were moving fast, Preacher stepped aside so that Hartford's blow missed him by a good six inches. Thrown off balance, Hartford stumbled forward, putting him in perfect position for the left that Preacher hooked into his belly. The punch didn't travel very far but had enough force behind it that Preacher's fist sunk almost to the wrist in his attacker's midsection.

Hartford gasped and doubled over. His fancy hat fell off. Preacher whipped his right hand up and around and brought the edge of it crashing down on the back of Hartford's neck. The blow drove Hartford to the boardwalk. His face struck the planks with an ugly crunch. He curled up in a ball and whimpered in pain.

One of the other men cursed and said, "Get him!" They both charged at Preacher.

He didn't wait for them to reach him. He stepped past Hartford to meet them. His hands dipped and came up with a Dragoon in each fist. He clubbed the nearest man with the left-hand gun, crashing it against the side of his head. The man went down as if every muscle in his body had been disconnected suddenly.

At the same time, Preacher raised the other revolver and thumbed back the hammer. The third man skidded to a frantic halt as he found himself staring down the Dragoon's barrel from a distance of six inches. From that perspective, it must have looked as big around as a cannon.

"I've got this gun rigged so it don't take much of a trigger pull," Preacher said in a conversational tone. "If it was to go off right now, I don't reckon there'd be much of your head left, son. So you might ought to just back away."

The man did so, half-lifting his hands to show that he no longer meant any harm.

"We . . . we're sorry, mister," he stammered. "Hartford was in a bad mood, but we didn't mean any real harm, I swear—"

The man's gaze darted past Preacher toward the fallen Hartford. For a split second, Preacher thought it was a ruse, a trick to try to get him to turn around.

Then he heard the metallic sound of a gun being cocked.

He should have made sure Hartford was out of the fight for good, he thought as he started to wheel around so he could bring the left-hand gun into play while still covering the third man.

That didn't prove to be necessary, because another figure stepped swiftly out of the shadows along the street and kicked the gun out of Hartford's hand. Hartford cried out in pain and clutched his wrist. That hand hung at an odd angle, indicating that the wrist was broken.

The newcomer stepped back and drew a pistol. He pointed it at Hartford and said, "Be thankful I didn't kill you, friend. It would have been quicker and simpler."

A few feet away, Preacher watched the third man from

the corner of his eye. When the man shifted, Preacher wiggled the barrel of the Dragoon aimed at him and said, "Be careful there, son. You don't want to make me nervous right now."

The man gulped and stood as still as possible.

The newcomer prodded Hartford with a booted foot and said in a crisp, authoritative tone, "All right, on your feet, you scoundrel. There's nothing wrong with your legs. Scurry off like the vermin you are." He blew out a disgusted breath. "Trying to shoot an old friend of mine in the back. Disgraceful. What's this town coming to when they allow people like you to wander around?"

Groaning, Hartford struggled to his feet. His nose was swollen and bloody from landing on his face a few minutes earlier. He had to reach out with his uninjured hand and grasp one of the poles that held up the awning over the boardwalk.

Preacher told the third man, "Pick up your friend and get outta here, too." He nodded toward the sprawled figure of the man he had clubbed senseless.

"Sure. Sure, mister." The tone of the third man's voice made it clear that he believed Preacher was loco. Dangerously loco.

Grunting with the effort, he got his hands under the unconscious man's arms and lifted him. Then he backed away, dragging the limp burden. Hartford staggered after them.

"Give me a hand, blast it," said the third man. "It's your fault this happened."

"I'm hurt," whined Hartford.

"You still got one hand."

Hartford tucked his right hand inside his vest and

reached down with his left to grasp one of the unconscious man's ankles. Between him and the third man, they dragged him away.

The newcomer holstered his gun and sauntered along the boardwalk to join Preacher. The mountain man thought he had recognized the cultured voice that retained just a hint of a British accent. When the newcomer came into the light, that confirmed Preacher's hunch.

"Howdy, Simon," he said.

Simon Lash was younger than Preacher, probably in his late thirties, but he had the same sort of weathered look that said he had spent most of his life in the open. He was clean-shaven except for a thin brown mustache above his expressive mouth.

Lash was dressed similarly to Preacher, only his trousers were buckskin, too, not canvas, and his hat had a curled brim and slightly taller crown. He had only one holstered revolver belted around his waist. It had ivory grips on the handle, rather than the plain wood on the butts of Preacher's guns. A scarlet neckerchief was knotted around Lash's throat, too.

"I'm obliged to you for the help," Preacher went on. He grinned. "Still as big a dandy as ever, I see."

Lash returned the grin. "Nothing wrong with a man trying to make a good impression on the ladies by being well-dressed and mannerly."

"You always did fine with the ladies, I'll grant you that."

Lash's expression grew more serious as he looked in the direction Hartford and the other two men had gone and said, "What do you think the chances are that those three will return and attempt to settle the score, probably by trying to shoot us in the back from some dark alley?"

"Can't rule it out," said Preacher. "Maybe we'd best go somewhere and get a drink so they'll have more trouble findin' us."

"That's exactly what I was about to suggest. Somewhere private, since I have something important to discuss with you."

"Important?" Preacher repeated with a puzzled frown.

"That's right. Meeting you this way is a very happy co-incidence. Actually, I was thinking about asking around to see if I could find out where you were."

"What is it you want from me, Simon?"

"What I'd like," said Simon Lash, "is for you to assist me in tracking down and killing some men who are badly in need of killing."

Chapter 6

Simon Lash had been born into a wealthy, aristocratic family in England. Unfortunately, he had an older brother, which meant he would never inherit the family's riches, estates, or titles. With that avenue closed off to him, he had joined the East India Company and wound up soldiering. At least, soldiering was what he had assumed he would be doing, as he had told Preacher during previous conversations.

Instead, he had found himself smuggling opium for the Company. Disliking the trade and all the sordidness that came with it, he had deserted, crossed the Himalayas, traveled through China, worked his way to Spanish California on a ship, and from there made his way to Missouri, where he began working as a scout on the first wagon trains to make the journey over the Oregon Trail in 1837. Soon, he had been *leading* those wagon trains, and by now there was no more respected wagon-master in the business.

Preacher had asked him once if he worried about the East India Company coming after him for deserting. Lash had laughed and said, "I gave them so much trouble while

I was in India that I'm sure they were quite happy to be rid of me. Besides, I went by another name then. I adopted the one I use now not because I want to hide, but because I don't want the shame I caused ever coming back to trouble my family."

"Anybody who knows you wouldn't be ashamed to have you as kinfolks."

"I appreciate that sentiment, Preacher, but you don't know what it's like in England."

Preacher agreed with that. He didn't want to know, either. He had met quite a few Englishers, had gone up the Big Muddy with some lords and ladies once upon a time, and as far as he was concerned, they were strange birds.

He liked and respected Simon Lash, though, so he was interested to hear what the man had to say as they leaned back in their chairs at a table in the rear corner of a tavern and sipped the beers a buxom young woman had brought them.

Lash got right down to business. "Do you remember Ethan Prescott?"

"Sure," Preacher said, nodding. "He's been leadin' wagon trains out to Oregon almost as long as you have. I've met him a few times. Seems like a good solid fella."

"I hate to be the one to tell you this, but Ethan is dead."

Preacher drew in a deep breath and frowned. He didn't doubt for a second what Lash had just told him. Simon Lash wasn't the sort to make a mistake about something like that.

Instead, he asked simply, "What happened?"

"Last summer, outlaws attacked the train he was leading, killed all the immigrants except for the young women they carried off to sell into a life of squalid slavery, and looted the wagons."

"Where was this?"

"At what people have started calling the Devil's Crossing. You probably know it better as the Three Crossings of the Sweetwater. This wasn't the first wagon train that's been attacked there. I've asked around, and two other such atrocities were carried out last summer."

Preacher nodded slowly. "Yeah, I know the place. The Devil's Crossin', eh? Well, based on what you just told me, that sounds pretty accurate. I've been sort of busy lately and hadn't heard about those attacks. But if the bandits wiped out ever'body except the gals they carried off, how do you know about it? Somebody come along and find what was left, then figure it out from that?"

Lash shook his head and said, "Actually, there was one survivor. Not one of the immigrants, but rather a young man who was working for Ethan Prescott as a scout. He was wounded but made it to Oregon, where he was laid up for a long time recovering from his injury. From there he went to Fort Benton, caught a steamboat, and came back down the Missouri River to St. Louis, where, after arriving a few weeks ago, he sought me out and told me what happened. He knew that Ethan and I were friends and thought I might be the man to do something about it." Lash's mouth tightened into a grim line. "I am."

For several seconds, Preacher considered the tale Lash had told him, then said, "You trust this youngster?"

"I do. He's here with me in Independence. I'd like to introduce you to him and let you hear his story for yourself."

Preacher regarded Lash with a slightly suspicious

narrowing of the eyes and asked, "Why do you want me to hear about it?"

"I told you. I could use your help to make sure justice is done."

"You're goin' after those outlaws?"

"Actually," said Lash, "I had already agreed to guide a wagon train leaving Independence around the first of May. I intend to fulfill that commitment. But there's a chance those brigands will target it, too, and if they do, I'd like to strike back, track them to their lair if necessary, and destroy them. The chances of doing that will be better if you come along."

"I don't reckon I'd change the odds that much," scoffed Preacher. "I'm just one man."

Lash chuckled and said, "That's true, old friend, but let's have no false modesty. When it comes to battling villains, you're worth twenty men or more."

Preacher swallowed some beer and sat there frowning. Finally, he said, "I ain't makin' no promises, but I reckon it won't hurt to listen to what the young fella has to say."

"I'm glad. He's staying at the same hotel I am. Perhaps you're there, as well? The Fuller?"

Preacher shook his head. "I've been sleepin' in the hayloft at the stable where Horse and Dog are stayin'. That's always been good enough for me."

"All right, come along with me. Have you had supper?"

Preacher shook his head. "Was on my way to hunt some grub when I ran into them troublesome varmints you helped me with."

"Then we'll eat in the hotel's dining room, and Tom can join us. That's his name. Tom Linford." Lash clicked his tongue sympathetically. "Poor lad. Not only was he wounded, but he was smitten with a girl whose family was part of the immigrant group. She was killed in the attack. Died in Tom's arms, in fact."

"And he's goin' over the trail with you when you leave for Oregon?" Preacher guessed.

"That's right."

Preacher nodded. He didn't say anything else, but he resolved that if he threw in with Simon Lash, he would keep a close eye on this Tom Linford.

Sometimes a man with a big-enough score to settle was a danger not only to those he was after but also to himself and those around him. The lust for revenge could make a fella blind . . . and careless.

The hour was a little late, so the dining room at the Hotel Fuller was only about half-full. Preacher and Simon Lash took one of the tables, ordered coffee, and then Lash went upstairs to fetch Tom Linford.

He came back with a gaunt young man whose brown eyes looked haunted. Those eyes, along with the pallor of his face, showed the ordeal he had been through. But there was strength in his grip as he shook Preacher's hand and gave the mountain man a curt nod.

Linford ordered coffee, too, and Lash told the waitress to bring them all steaks, with the usual trimmings. When Linford protested that was too much, Lash said, "Nonsense, my boy. You have to eat a hearty diet if you ever want to regain your full strength. And I know you *do* want that."

"Yeah, I do," admitted Linford. He looked at Preacher

and went on, "I suppose Mr. Lash told you about what happened."

"Yep, he did. But I'd be obliged if I could hear it from you, too, son, since you were actually there."

"I was," Linford murmured. "No matter how much I wish I hadn't been . . . no matter how much I wish it was all just a terrible dream, a nightmare . . . I was there, and it was all too real."

"Tell me about it," said Preacher.

It was a harrowing tale, interrupted briefly when the waitress brought their coffee. Preacher listened intently, taking in all the grim details as Linford supplied them. The young man's voice caught now and then, but he stayed surprisingly calm and impassive as he told the story. Preacher supposed he had recounted it enough times by now that the pain it stirred up had dulled somewhat.

When Linford was finished, Preacher looked at Simon Lash and asked, "You say this has happened other times?"

"Half a dozen, at least," Lash replied with a nod. "And Tom, here, is the only witness who has survived to give us a description of the outlaws."

"Does that mean anything to you?" asked Linford. "The fact that they wore those buffalo coats and were masked?"

Preacher shook his head. "No, I don't recall ever hearin' about a gang like that. But I reckon it's just to make them harder to catch, in case somebody got away, like you did. With those thick coats and masks, nobody would have any idea who they were. They could scatter across the frontier and nobody would ever know the difference. Then, when it was time to hit another wagon train, they'd get back together."

"An arrangement such as that would require some organizing," Lash commented.

"Yeah, it would. Somethin' else I was thinkin' about . . . Plenty of wagon trains must've gone on up the trail without gettin' hit. Why is that?"

Lash said, "You're right. A lot more wagon trains *weren't* attacked than were. The ones that were targeted were known to be carrying quite a bit of money and valuable goods." He cocked his head to the side. "You're thinking what I'm thinking, aren't you, Preacher?"

"That somebody's been tippin' off the gang? Seems likely. All they'd have to do is keep an eye on the trail and watch for a signal that'd tell them which bunch of wagons to jump."

"Wait a minute," said Linford. "That would require someone who's traveling with the wagon train to give the signal."

"That's right," Lash said. "An inside man, so to speak."

Preacher looked at Linford and said, "Think back to when you were with that wagon train. Was there anybody who struck you as the sort of fella who might throw in with a bunch of outlaws and killers?"

Linford shook his head. "No, I can't imagine anybody . . . Wait a minute. When Mr. Prescott got the immigrant leaders together and talked to them about whether we should go through the Devil's Crossing or follow what he called the Deep Sand Route, there was one man who was really determined that we ought to stay with the river. He spoke up right away, and he convinced the others that he was right. His name was Jethro Calhoun."

"Here's the important question, Tom," Lash said as he

leaned forward. "When you gathered the bodies after the massacre, was this fellow Calhoun among them?"

A pained look came over Linford's face. "Let me think. That was quite a while back . . ." He drew in a deep breath, and his voice strengthened as he went on, "No. No, I'm convinced that his body *wasn't* there. But I didn't think anything of it at the time. There were quite a few bodies I wasn't able to recover. I was convinced that they floated downstream, or maybe some of them crawled off in the brush to die and I didn't find them. I . . . I should have looked farther . . . should have gone downstream to see if any of them had washed up, but I was so tired and in such bad shape to start with . . ."

Lash reached over and gripped the young man's upper arm. "No one would ever think less of you because you didn't do that, lad. Most men, if they'd been as badly hurt as you were, would have simply ridden off and left those poor people as they were."

"I couldn't do that," Linford muttered. "Alma was there, and her folks, and one of her little brothers . . . I never found the youngest one . . . I never found Mr. Prescott, either. I hated to leave . . ."

"You did what you could, son," Preacher told him. "Nobody can do more'n that."

"This man Calhoun," Simon Lash went on. "Was he the sort you might suspect of being in league with brigands?"

"Who can say about something like that? He was never friendly. He was traveling by himself, and he kept to himself. Didn't have any close friends among the other immigrants, as I recall. But I never thought anything about that at the time."

"There's no reason you would. But the fact that his

body was missing, and he argued for you to follow the Sweetwater instead of taking the other route, those things could be regarded as suspicious."

Preacher said, "The other fellas who voted on the route, they were all killed?"

Once again, Linford had to cast his memory back to that horrible time, but after a few moments, he nodded.

"They were," he said. "I just made a list of them in my head, and I found the bodies of all of them except Mr. Calhoun."

Lash looked at Preacher. "That's not proof, of course. Not that would stand up in a court of law."

"This ain't a court. And it sure adds some weight to the notion that the gang plants inside men with the wagon trains who let 'em know which ones to hit."

"That does seem like a feasible theory," agreed Lash. He turned to Linford and continued, "You may be wondering why we're discussing this with Preacher."

Linford shook his head. "Not at all. Mr. Prescott told me about you, Mr. Preacher."

"Just Preacher," the mountain man said. "No mister."

For the first time since he'd met the young man, Linford smiled faintly.

"Yes, Mr. Prescott told me to ask you about that name, if we ever crossed trails. Right now, though, I think it's enough that I understand Mr. Lash wants you to come with us."

"You're goin' back up the Oregon Trail?"

Preacher already knew the answer to that question, but he wanted to see what Linford would say.

"Wouldn't you, if you were in my position?"

"More than likely, I would," Preacher admitted. "But what if those outlaws don't attack this wagon train?"

"Then I'll come back here and get a job as a scout with another one. Sooner or later, I'll come face-to-face with those killers again, and it'll end differently next time."

Linford's voice held quiet determination and confidence. Preacher still didn't know if he could keep his thirst for vengeance in check if he needed to, but at least that seemed possible.

"How about you, Preacher?" asked Lash. "Are you willing to join us?"

"I'm leanin' in that direction, but I still need to ponder on it a mite more." Preacher nodded toward the waitress approaching, carrying a big platter with their meals on it. "And right now we got some grub to dig into."

As they ate, he thought that if they were really going up against odds as dangerous as the bloody encounter Tom Linford had described, they really needed something else on their side. A secret weapon, so to speak.

And Preacher knew just the man for the job.

Chapter 7

Jamie Ian MacCallister saw the men coming long before they reached the ranch house. It was said of Jamie that he had the eyes of an eagle, and he had proven the truth of that many times.

Moving with graceful ease and strength, he swung the saddle he carried onto the top rail of the corral and told his youngest son Falcon, "Head on in the house and tell your ma that company's on the way."

The blond teenager looked around. "Really? I don't see anybody."

"They're there," said Jamie. "Now do like I told you."

Something about his father's tone of voice must have warned Falcon that this was serious. He started to trot toward the big ranch house, but halfway there he paused and looked back at Jamie.

"Is this gonna be trouble?"

"Don't know yet," Jamie replied.

"Well, if it is, I want in on it."

Of course he did, thought Jamie. Falcon was pretty much man-sized already, and he had inherited not only the MacCallister wanderlust but also the proddy streak.

MacCallisters didn't hunt trouble—well, not often, anyway—but they sure as blazes never backed away from it.

The thing of it was, Falcon was capable of handling whatever life threw at him. He was big, good with his fists, and could draw and fire a gun with the sort of speed and accuracy that would rival Jamie someday. Already, he was faster on the shoot than most men.

But he hadn't been blooded yet, not really tested under fire. By the time Jamie was Falcon's age, he had seen more than his share of violence and death. He had tried to protect Falcon from that, at least to a certain extent, not because Jamie thought Falcon couldn't handle it, but because that was what Kate, the boy's ma, wanted. It was natural for any mother, even one as feisty and capable as Kate, to want to protect her offspring.

The day was coming, though, probably not too far in the future, when they wouldn't be able to do that with Falcon anymore. But maybe it didn't have to be today, Jamie told himself as Falcon disappeared into the sprawling house. Maybe not today . . .

He had spotted the riders, half a dozen or so of them, coming down one of the hills that formed MacCallister's Valley, a wide, lush slice of heaven here on the Colorado frontier. They moved in and out of the thick growth of pines so that it was difficult to get an exact count or make out any details about them. But there wasn't a real trail up there, so unless they were lost, they weren't ordinary pilgrims.

That didn't mean they were up to no good . . . but Jamie hadn't lived more than four decades of an adventurous life by being careless.

He moved with catlike grace toward the house, a big, broad-shouldered man with a thatch of graying brown hair and a mustache of the same color. He looked strong, and he was. Not many men could last even a few minutes in a hand-to-hand battle with Jamie Ian MacCallister, let alone stand a chance of defeating him.

A long-barreled Walker Colt revolver rode in a holster on his right hip. Weighing almost five pounds, the gun was heavy enough that it required a strong man to wield it. In Jamie's capable hand, it seemed much lighter than that. He could draw, aim, and fire in less than the blink of an eye. No one on the frontier was faster or more deadly.

As he went up the steps to the ranch house porch, Kate emerged from the house carrying a shotgun. A blond beauty who looked younger than her years, she and Jamie had been pulling in double harness since they were barely full grown. Most folks figured a couple ought to be older than that before getting married, but seldom had a man and woman been more perfectly matched than Jamie and Kate MacCallister.

She leaned the shotgun against the wall beside the door, reached back inside the house, and hefted a Sharps carbine that she passed into Jamie's waiting hands. He smiled and said, "Falcon told you we've got visitors, I reckon."

"He did. I figured we needed to be ready for them." She returned his smile. "I put a pot of coffee on to boil, too, if they're friendly."

Jamie patted the smooth wood of the carbine's stock and nodded toward the shotgun. "And these if they're not friendly."

"That's right, Pa," Falcon said as he stepped out of the house, also with a Sharps in his hands.

Jamie glanced up the trail leading to the ranch headquarters. The strangers had reached it and were riding slowly toward the house, about three hundred yards away.

"Get back inside, son," he said. "You can help from there if you need to."

"Ma's the one who should go inside," argued Falcon. "I need to be out here where I can see what's going on."

Jamie was about to issue the order again when Kate surprised him by saying, "Maybe he's right."

Jamie narrowed his eyes as he looked at her. "You think so?"

"I wouldn't have said it if I didn't . . . would I?"

She was right about that. Kate MacCallister didn't mince words. It wasn't in her nature.

She went on, "If they're looking for trouble, they're more likely to change their minds and ride away if they're confronted with two big, dangerous-looking men."

Jamie could tell that Falcon liked hearing himself referred to as a dangerous-looking man.

Kate went on, "There's another shotgun right beside the front window. I'll be there in case I need to take a hand. I'll leave this one out here in case you need it."

"All right," Jamie agreed. He turned to his son. "If the ball starts, you hit those planks and do your shooting from there."

"Sure, Pa," Falcon said easily. Jamie wasn't sure if he would follow that order or not, but it was too late to brood about such things, even if he'd been the brooding sort—which Jamie Ian MacCallister definitely wasn't. The riders were only fifty yards away now. Jamie tucked the Sharps under his arm, stepped to the edge of the porch, and waited for them as he heard the front door close behind Kate. Falcon was about ten feet to his left, with the door between them—and the shotgun leaning against the wall.

The riders loped up easily and reined in their mounts. Jamie saw that his initial estimate had been correct: there were six of them. Their leader, or at least the man who urged his horse slightly ahead of the others, was in his thirties, lean and beard-stubbled, with a slight cast to his left eye.

Despite his somewhat sinister appearance, though, the smile he gave Jamie appeared friendly and sincere. "Howdy," he said. "Would you be Jamie MacCallister?"

"I would be," replied Jamie.

The stranger chuckled. "Thought so. I was told that Jamie MacCallister was a big son of a gun, and I haven't run across too many fellas bigger than you, friend."

Jamie didn't figure they were friends yet, but he let it pass and asked, "What can I do for you?"

"My name is Pendleton. Dodge Pendleton. My friends and I are looking for work, and we were told you have the biggest ranch in these parts. Shoot, practically this whole valley belongs to you, doesn't it, Mr. MacCallister?"

"It does. But I'm not looking for ranch hands right now. Got plenty in my crew already."

Dodge Pendleton looked around pointedly and said, "I don't see anybody except you and this youngster."

"My son, Falcon. And my men are all out on the range,

working, where they ought to be this time of day. I just rode in, myself. Been out giving the boys a hand."

"So it's just you and the boy here, eh?" mused Pendleton as he leaned forward in the saddle as if easing weary muscles.

Before Jamie could answer—and likely tell Pendleton that it was none of his business who was here—one of the other strangers spoke up, saying, "I thought I saw somebody else here on the porch while we were ridin' in, Dodge. Would've sworn it was a woman. Nice-lookin' one, too."

"That was my ma," Falcon snapped. "You don't need to be talking about her, mister."

Pendleton said, "Take it easy, son. My friend here didn't mean anything by what he said. Just stating a fact, that there's a lady here, too. But that's none of our business."

"That's right," Jamie said. "It's not."

"I heard you raise some mighty nice horses, Mr. Mac-Callister," Pendleton went on, and Jamie thought that now they were getting down to it. "If you don't have any work for us, we'd better be moving on, but to do that, we really need fresh horses. You might have noticed that the ones we're riding are a little played out."

"I noticed," Jamie said. "Probably decent mounts if they were rested up, though. I can sell you some horses, and I'll give you some in trade for those animals."

"Well . . . you see, we sort of figured on taking these horses with us, to use as spare mounts, you know. So we can switch out with the ones we get from you."

Jamie nodded. "Spare mounts come in handy . . . when you're being chased."

"Problem is, we don't have any money to buy any horses from you."

"That is a problem," Jamie agreed.

"Oh, hell, Dodge!" one of the men burst out. "Let's get on with it!"

And he grabbed for the gun on his hip.

Jamie could have gone for that man first, but he figured Dodge Pendleton might be the bigger threat in the long run. So he shifted his grip on the Sharps and blew a fist-sized hole through Pendleton's chest while the man was still trying to claw his gun out of its holster. To Jamie's left, Falcon's Sharps boomed, and the man who had started the ball by drawing toppled out of the saddle before he could get a shot off. A considerable chunk of his head was missing when he hit the ground.

Jamie threw the empty carbine at a couple of the other men, who flinched away from it involuntarily. That gave Jamie plenty of time to palm out the Walker Colt. He cocked the revolver as it came up. Flame spurted from the muzzle of the nine-inch-long barrel. The .44 caliber ball thudded into the chest of another man who was trying to draw. He rocked back in the saddle and threw both arms wide, then fell forward on his horse's neck. The animal spooked at the racket and smell of blood, crow-hopped a couple of times, and then bolted. The dead man slid out of the saddle, but his right foot caught in the stirrup and the horse dragged him along the trail with dust swirling up behind them.

Jamie swung the Colt to his left as a shot ripped out from one of the remaining would-be horse thieves. The bullet came close enough that Jamie felt the wind-rip of its passage close to his head. He didn't give the man a chance to fire a second shot. The Colt roared and bucked against Jamie's palm.

Just as Jamie squeezed the trigger, the horse on which his target was mounted jumped to the side, so instead of the shot going into the man's chest as Jamie intended, the .44 round shattered his right shoulder. He screamed and dropped his gun. His horse bolted, too, but he managed to stay mounted. He was out of this fight, though.

That left two of the enemy. From the corner of his eye, Jamie saw that Falcon hadn't dived to the porch floor after firing his shot, as Jamie had told him to do. Instead, the youngster had dropped the Sharps and wheeled to scoop up the shotgun. He went to one knee, brought the shotgun to his shoulder, and fired one barrel. The load of buckshot shredded the chest of another horse thief and punched him right out of the saddle. Smoothly, Falcon shifted his aim, but before he could touch off the second barrel, Jamie's Colt blasted again, and the final man twisted as the bullet tore through him. He toppled to the ground and didn't move.

"Well, looks like that'll just about do it," Jamie said as the echoes of gun-thunder began to die away. "You all right, son?"

"Yeah, none of 'em even came close to me," Falcon said as he came to his feet. He was uninjured, but he was breathing hard and looked a little shaken. "That was sure loud . . . and fast . . ."

"That's the way gunfights are," Jamie told him. "Most of the time, they're over before you know it, and while they're going on, they're usually mighty confusing. That's why you have to stay calm and keep your wits about you."

Jamie paused. "Looked to me like you did a good job of that."

Kate hurried out of the house. "Is it over?" she asked.

"It is," said Jamie. "One of those fellas got away, but he was hurt pretty bad and I don't think he'll be back."

"I don't know, Pa," Falcon said, taking Jamie by surprise. "Here comes somebody else along the trail, and he looks like he could be hunting trouble, too."

Chapter 8

Jamie turned to look where Falcon was pointing and saw a rider ambling along the trail on a big, rangy gray stallion. The newcomer was leading another horse that had a grim, familiar shape draped over the saddle. A large, shaggy cur that looked as much like a wolf as a dog trotted alongside the rider.

Kate lifted a hand to shade her eyes as she peered at the man approaching on horseback. She said, "Is that . . ."

A grin broke out on Jamie's rugged face. "It is," he said. "I figured that much as soon as I recognized Dog and Horse."

Falcon let out a whoop. "That's Preacher, ain't it?"

"Isn't it," Kate corrected him. "Just because the smell of powder smoke is still in the air doesn't mean we can't speak correctly."

Jamie and Falcon traded a glance and chuckled.

Preacher was close enough now that they could make out the mountain man's craggy features. He rode on, not getting in any hurry despite the bodies scattered around the ranch yard in front of the house. When he finally reined to a halt at the foot of the steps, he took off his hat, nodded politely, and said, "Afternoon, Miz MacCallister. Looks like you've already had some company come callin' today."

"More company is always welcome when it's you, Preacher," she told him. "And you really need to call me Kate."

"Why, sure thing, Kate." Preacher turned his attention to Jamie. "Had yourselves a little set-to here, from the looks of things."

"These fellas had their minds set on stealing some horses from us," explained Jamie. "We talked 'em out of it."

Preacher grunted. "Permanent-like, I'd say. One of 'em got away, though."

"He did," Jamie allowed. "Galloped off in the same direction you came from. His shoulder was busted to pieces, so I figured he wasn't really a threat anymore."

"Yeah, he raced past me, still bleedin' to beat the band. Don't reckon he's stopped yet, unless he fell off and died."

Jamie nodded toward the other horse. "Who have you got there?"

"This one was dead when I found him. Had his foot hung up in a stirrup and had been dragged a ways. That's why I wrapped him up in a blanket before I slung him over his saddle to bring him back." Preacher glanced at Kate. "He ain't a pretty sight. Not fit for a lady's eyes."

"My sensibilities aren't as delicate as those of most ladies," she said, "but I appreciate the gesture anyway, Preacher. Falcon, go out to the barn and fetch a shovel. You'll have some digging to do."

"Me?" said Falcon. "You mean I have to dig graves for these horse-thievin' varmints?"

"Horse thieves they may be," Jamie said. "Good chance

they stole the mounts they were riding. But they're dead now and we'll lay them to rest with at least a little respect."

Grumbling, Falcon went down the steps and started toward the barn. Preacher stopped him by calling after him, "Hey, sprout, did you get in on this little fandango?"

Falcon looked back and said, "I killed two of them."

Preacher nodded. Falcon went on to the barn. When he was gone, Preacher said to Jamie and Kate, "He's puttin' up a brave front right now, but he's liable to wake up in a cold sweat tonight. Sendin' a couple of hombres across the divide, even scum like that, takes some gettin' used to."

"If he needs to talk about it, he will," Jamie said. "And we'll be here to listen to him."

"Well . . . at least his mama will."

"Oh, no," Kate said. "You've come to drag Jamie off to some adventure again, haven't you, Preacher?"

"Got a mite of business to talk over with him," the mountain man admitted.

"You might as well do it inside. And I have coffee brewing. Get down from that horse and come on in."

"Don't mind if I do," said Preacher, grinning.

Preacher stayed for supper and spent the night, of course, since it was a good ways back to the nearest town. After hearing all about the attacks on the wagon trains, Jamie promised Preacher a decision by the next morning on whether he would accompany the mountain man back to Independence.

"That was a mighty long way to ride just to ask me to come with you," Jamie commented as they stood on the front porch after the evening meal, looking out at the starry night.

"Had to travel pretty fast, too, to get here in time to make it back to Independence 'fore Simon leaves with that wagon train. I figure we've got just about enough time if we hurry."

"I'll bear that in mind," said Jamie, nodding slowly. "You won't be leaving before morning, anyway, so I thought I could take that long to mull it over and find out what Kate thinks."

"She won't try to stop you. She'll just say for you to do what you think is best."

"I know. But I owe her the consideration of asking her." Jamie chuckled. "Who knows, one of these days she's liable to tell me I've gone loco and I'm too old to go gallivanting off on adventures."

"Shoot, you ain't even close to that! I'm ten years older'n you, and I'm still hale and hearty."

"Yes, but you'll still be rousting around when you're eighty, Preacher."

The mountain man grinned. "I sure hope so."

Both men straightened from their casual poses leaning on the porch railing as the sound of approaching hoof-beats drifted to them on the night air. They didn't draw their guns, but their hands hovered near the holstered revolvers.

"Some of my crew haven't come in yet," Jamie said quietly, "so that could be them. On the other hand, one of those would-be horse thieves got away. He might be coming back with some friends."

"If he is, I reckon he'll get the same sort of welcome he did earlier," said Preacher.

"Hello, the house," a voice hailed a moment later. The hoofbeats stopped as the riders reined in.

Jamie relaxed and said, "I know that voice."

"I think I do, too," Preacher said, sounding a little perplexed.

"You ought to," Jamie said, then called, "Come on in, Roscoe."

The man who had spoken before said, "See you later, boys," and from the sound of the hoofbeats, several riders veered off to the side while one came straight on toward the house. He rode into the light that spilled through the windows and the open door.

Even on horseback, it was easy to see that he was a big, bulky man with a bushy black beard. The growth couldn't completely conceal his craggy features. His hat was shoved back on long, tangled black hair. He wore canvas trousers and a homespun shirt that bulged with the muscles of his arms and shoulders. A holstered revolver was belted at his ample waist.

"Howdy, fellas," he said as he brought his horse to a stop in front of the porch.

"Lomax, you ornery old cuss," Preacher greeted him. "What are you doin' here? Last I heard, you were bullwhackin' a train of freight wagons bound for Santa Fe."

Roscoe Lomax grinned and said, "I got those wagons to Santa Fe and then decided to amble up this way to visit with Jamie for a spell. I didn't know the old varmint was gonna put me to work on his ranch!"

Lomax, a veteran bullwhacker with a reputation for drinking, fighting, and cussing, had taken part in the last bloody little jaunt involving Jamie and Preacher. He and Jamie had started off as enemies but became staunch friends through shared danger. He still had trouble controlling his temper at times, but the big grin on his face as he spoke made it clear that he was just joshing Jamie, not trying to pick a fight.

"Roscoe wanted to know what it's like to be a rancher," Jamie explained. "So I figured the best way to show him was to get him involved in the day-to-day work. That way he can decide whether he wants to keep on being a bull-whacker or maybe someday get a spread of his own."

"And I've sure learned! Ownin' anything is too blasted much work. I'll keep hirin' on to crack a bullwhip and cuss critters, thank you 'most to death."

"Hmmm," Preacher said with the air of a man to whom an idea has just occurred. "Why don't you light and set a spell, Lomax? I got a job you might be interested in."

Jamie looked over at the mountain man and said, "Now that's a good idea. We could use another good fighting man on our side."

"That makes it sound like you done made up your mind and don't need until mornin'," said Preacher.

"Well . . . let's just say I'm leaning one way more than the other."

"Let's just say the both of you tell me what in blazes you're talkin' about." Lomax swung down from the saddle and looped his horse's reins around the porch railing.

"Have you ever been part of a wagon train, Roscoe?" Jamie asked. "The immigrant kind, I mean. I know you've gone along with a lot of freight wagons."

"No, but it ain't that much different, I suppose," Lomax replied as he propped a booted foot on the bottom step. "Except there's more *people*." He made a face. "Been my experience that human folks are usually harder to get along with than mules and ox critters."

"I can't argue with you about that," Preacher said. "I get along better with Horse and Dog than any two-legged varmints I've ever been around." He grinned at Jamie. "Although you're tolerable most of the time, old son."

Jamie grunted. "Thanks . . . I think. Anyway, Roscoe, Preacher's got a story to tell if you want to hear it."

"I'm all ears," Lomax said.

"Yeah, but I'm naturally too polite to point that out," the mountain man said. "I'll tell you all about it."

Lomax licked his lips. "I might be able to listen better if there was a jug involved."

"I'll see what I can rustle up," Jamie said.

Chapter 9

Independence, Missouri

Preacher, Jamie, and Lomax arrived barely in time to join the wagon train, which reached Independence the night before it was scheduled to roll away from the jumping-off point. But they made it, and Simon Lash was glad to see them.

He pumped Preacher's hand and said, "Thank goodness you got here when you did. We're leaving first thing in the morning. I would have had to depart without you if you hadn't arrived. We have plenty of time to reach Oregon while the weather's still good, but now that the train is assembled and ready, everyone is anxious to get started."

"Can't argue with 'em about that," Preacher said. "They're ready to get where they're goin' and make those new starts in life they're after." He gestured toward his two companions and went on, "Simon, this here is Jamie MacCallister and Roscoe Lomax."

They were standing under some trees about a quarter of a mile from the vast, open stretch of ground where the wagon train had assembled. The large, sturdy vehicles had been ferried across the Missouri River already for this final gathering before the journey began.

It was early evening, and shadows had begun to gather quickly. That was good, because Preacher had a good reason not to want to call attention to this meeting.

Lash extended his hand to Jamie and said, "I've heard a great deal about you, Mr. MacCallister. You're as famous a frontiersman as Preacher here."

"I don't know if I'd go so far as to say that," Jamie replied as he gripped Lash's hand. He chuckled and added, "As he likes to point out, he's ten years older than me, so he's had a head start."

"Even so, I'm surprised we've never met before."

"The frontier is a big place."

"But surprisingly small at times."

"It can be," allowed Jamie.

Lash turned and shook hands with Lomax, who said, "You ain't never heard of me, Mr. Lash. I'm a plumb nobody compared with these two."

"Roscoe is a bullwhacker and a good hand with wagon teams," Jamie said. "And a good hand in a fight, too. It seemed like he might be a good man to come along with us."

"That strikes me as an excellent idea," agreed Lash. "In fact, later I want to introduce you to a member of the group named Edmund Farrington. He owned a general mercantile store back East but has decided to try his luck by opening a new store in Oregon. But he's taking a great deal of his inventory with him so he'll have stock as soon as he gets there. Five wagonloads, in fact."

Lomax let out a low whistle. "That's a heap of goods, all right."

"He has drivers for all the wagons, but he's been fretting that he needs someone to take charge of the whole operation, make sure the vehicles and the stock are sound and well cared for and the drivers capable, things like that. His experience is in running a store, not in picking up and moving one across the country."

"Yeah, I could handle a chore like that. I've taken plenty of freight wagons along the Santa Fe Trail. This'll be a different trail and different country, but a lot of the work is the same."

"And that will give you a good excuse to accompany us. I don't know if Preacher told you, but we suspect the outlaws may have planted a confederate among the immigrants to alert them when to strike. They do this from time to time so we're never sure which wagon train but better safe than sorry."

Lomax nodded. "Yeah, he mentioned somethin' about that." A scowl made the bullwhacker's normally intimidating visage even more formidable. "It'd take a mighty low-down snake to do a thing like that."

"Indeed." Lash turned to Jamie. "You, of course, will serve as a scout along with Preacher and myself, Mr. MacCallister—"

Jamie shook his head to stop the wagon-master. "Call me Jamie," he said. "None of this Mr. MacCallister business. And I'm not going along with the wagons."

Lash looked surprised. "But I thought that was the whole point of Preacher's hasty trip to Colorado."

"Jamie's comin' along," Preacher said, "but not with the wagons. You see, since those outlaws may have themselves a fella workin' on the sly, we ought to, as well. Jamie's gonna follow the wagon train but stay far enough back that he can get a good look at the country all around us. That way, if anybody's doggin' our trail, he'll spot 'em before they can pull anything and try to give us some warnin' so that we can give them bandits a lot hotter reception than they're expectin'.'"

Simon Lash rubbed his chin and frowned in thought for a few seconds before nodding. "That sounds like an excellent idea. That's why you wanted to talk here in the shadows, away from the wagons, so that no one will see Jamie and know that he's part of our group."

"That's about the size of it."

Lash turned to Jamie. "You'll be out there on your own," he said, "stalking a band of ruthless killers. That might turn out to be an extremely dangerous assignment."

"Seems like it's a risk worth taking," said Jamie.

"Very well. Strategically, it strikes me as a sound tactic. Just keep your eyes open."

Preacher laughed. "Jamie's like me. He ain't lived as long as he has by bein' careless."

"Tomorrow morning, then," Lash said with a decisive nod. "The wagons roll at dawn."

Since Jamie wasn't going to be traveling with the immigrants, and since his involvement in the affair needed to be kept a secret from them because there was no telling who might be working with the outlaws, he and his horse faded off into the night without getting any closer to the camp. He would make a lone camp elsewhere.

Simon Lash took Preacher and Lomax with him, though, as he returned to the people he had agreed to guide west.

Once they were in camp, Lash led them directly to one of the wagons and rapped on the closed tailgate. A hand pushed aside the canvas flap that covered the opening at the back of the vehicle, and a mostly bald head stuck out.

"Oh, it's you, Mr. Lash," the man said in a rather high-pitched voice. "What can I do for you?"

"There's been a stroke of luck, Mr. Farrington. I've found a man to take charge of your wagons for you." Lash gestured toward Lomax. "Meet Roscoe Lomax. He's a seasoned veteran of the Santa Fe Trail and has been part of many wagon trains carrying freight to New Mexico Territory, even while it was still part of Mexico. He's agreed to go along and make sure your wagons and all your stock make it to Oregon safely."

"Oh!" Farrington threw a leg over the tailgate, swung himself out of the wagon, and hopped to the ground quite agilely for a middle-aged storekeeper. He grabbed Lomax's hand and pumped it. "I'm very glad to meet you, Mr. Lomax. This is a big undertaking for me, and you don't know how worried I've been about it. I mean, it's not everyday that a fellow uproots himself and moves his entire existence clear across the country!"

"No, I, uh, reckon not," said Lomax as he shook the smaller man's hand. He was a head taller than Edmund Farrington and probably eighty pounds heavier. "But I'll do my best to make sure it all goes smooth for you."

"Well, now," said Farrington, "there's still the matter of your fee to be discussed before the arrangement is settled. What would you say to . . . a hundred dollars?"

Lomax's bushy eyebrows rose. "I'd say those were pretty good wages." He squinted. "You wouldn't want to see your way clear toward slippin' me a little in advance?

I mean, we ain't leavin' until tomorrow mornin', and I'm bettin' there are taverns in Independence . . ."

"No drinking the night before departure, Mr. Lomax," Lash said briskly. "A little rule of mine. A tradition, you might say."

"That's all right, I reckon," Lomax said, sounding more than a little disappointed.

Farrington turned to Preacher and said, "And who might you be, friend?"

"Name's . . . Arthur," Preacher replied after only a split second's hesitation. He and Jamie had discussed the matter on the way to Missouri and decided that it would be better for Preacher to travel under a different name. His real name, in this case, although he hadn't used it regularly in many years. Lomax wasn't well enough known to spook the outlaws, but knowing that the famous mountain man called Preacher was along on the journey might cause them to hesitate before attacking the wagons.

Which was a double-edged sword, of course. They wanted to get the wagons and the immigrants through to their destination safely, but at the same time, the destruction of the gang preying on people traveling on the Oregon Trail was a vital goal, as well. If the outlaws were scared off, Preacher, Jamie, and Simon Lash would have to start over in their quest.

And Tom Linford, too. The young man had made it quite clear that he wouldn't rest until he had avenged that massacre at the Devil's Crossing, no matter how long it took.

Preacher went on, "I've signed on to give Simon a hand with the scoutin'. Between him, me, and that young fella Tom, you folks won't have to worry about not knowin' where you're headed."

"Is that right?" said Farrington. "Been to see the elephant, have you?"

Preacher chuckled, not having expected to hear that phrase come out of the little storekeeper's mouth. "A time or two," he said dryly.

"I thought perhaps you wouldn't mind gathering the leaders of the train, Edmund," Lash said. "I'd like to introduce all of you to Arthur and Roscoe."

Farrington bobbed his head. "Sure, I can do that. In the meantime, I'm pretty sure the coffee's still on at the main fire."

"Well, it ain't like visitin' a tavern," said Lomax, "but I reckon it's better than nothin'. I could drink a cup of coffee right now."

Farrington scurried off to assemble the wagon train's leaders while Lash, Preacher, and Lomax ambled toward the main campfire, which was still burning brightly. A number of people were gathered around it, talking animatedly in small groups.

Lash went up to an attractive woman with hair the color of honey and said, "Good evening, Mrs. Bradley. I'm told there's still coffee . . . ?"

"Of course," she replied. "I'll fetch cups for you and your friends." She looked at Preacher and Lomax and added, "Are you gentlemen joining the wagon train?"

"Uh, yes'm, we are," Preacher replied. He got a better look at the woman in the firelight, and he liked what he saw. The glow struck reddish highlights from her thick hair and revealed deep brown eyes. Her body had the lithe slenderness of youth, but at the same time, her eyes had lines of character and determination around them that did nothing to detract from its beauty. The smile lines around her mouth testified that she also had a sense of humor, perhaps even one that could be slightly bawdy at times.

However, Preacher had heard it plain as day when Lash called her Mrs. Bradley, so he supposed she had a husband somewhere around here, too. Because of that, he merely smiled and nodded politely when he answered her question.

"Good," she said. "You both look very capable, if you don't mind me saying so, and we can always use more capable men since we're setting out across the wilderness." She smiled. "Let me get that coffee."

She walked off toward the fire. Lomax watched her go with open admiration in his eyes and rumbled, "That there's a mighty fine-lookin' woman."

"Yeah, but she's married, so don't go gettin' ideas in your head," Preacher cautioned him.

"Actually," Simon Lash said with a smile, "Mrs. Bradley's husband passed away a year ago. They had already started making plans to move to Oregon, so she decided to go ahead with it. She says that's the best way to honor his memory."

"So she's a widow," Lomax said with a smile that threatened to turn into a leer. "Could be she's missin' the comfortin' touch of a man."

"Could be you'd best hush," snapped Preacher. "Here she comes."

She had filled three tin cups with coffee and brought them over to the men, carrying two of the cups in one hand. "Here you are," she said as they carefully took the cups from her. "That just about emptied the pot, so it should be pretty strong."

"That's fine with me," Preacher said. "I like my coffee strong enough to get up and walk around on its hind legs."

"Thank you, Constance," Simon Lash said. He sipped the hot brew and added, "Not bad at all."

Constance Bradley looked at Preacher and asked, "Do you have a wagon of your own, Mister . . . ?"

"Just call me Arthur," Preacher said. "And no, I'm gonna help Simon with the scoutin'."

"And I'm Roscoe Lomax. I'll be doin' some bull-whackin' for a little fella name of Farrington," Lomax added without waiting to be asked.

"Oh, I'm glad Mr. Farrington found someone to give him a hand. He's a dear man."

"Edmund is gathering up the train's leaders," Lash explained, "so that I can introduce Arthur and Roscoe to them. Have you seen Tom Linford this evening?"

Constance's face grew solemn. She nodded toward the far side of camp and said, "He was over there the last time I saw him. He came back from town a little while ago. He looked for you, but you weren't around just then. I gather he heard something in Independence that disturbed him."

"Oh? What was that?"

"Word of a wagon train that was attacked by bandits." Constance shook her head sadly. "The rumor is that the entire train . . . everyone that was a part of it . . . was wiped out."

Chapter 10

Preacher, Lash, and Lomax went to find Tom Linford after thanking Constance Bradley for the coffee. The young man was at the center of one of the groups Preacher had noticed earlier. He sat on a wagon's lowered tailgate with a grim look on his face.

"Excuse me, friends," Lash said to the gathered immigrants. When the crowd parted and allowed the newcomers to step up to Linford, the wagon-master went on, "Hello, Tom. I hear that you were looking for me earlier."

"That's right, Mr. Lash. I went into town to pick up a few more boxes of ammunition, and folks in the store were talking about . . ." He stopped and had to swallow hard before continuing. "Talking about how some men had ridden in with the news of another wagon train massacre. They were trappers on their way back from the mountains, and they came through the Devil's Crossing. There was fresh . . . evidence . . . of what happened."

"Blast it," Lash said quietly. "There were no survivors?"

Linford shook his head. "No, sir. Not that I heard about."

Lash sighed and clapped a hand on the young man's shoulders. "I'm sorry, Tom."

One of the immigrants spoke up, saying, "Maybe we ought to call off the whole thing. I don't want to take my family into danger like this."

"That's your right," Lash told him, "and I certainly understand why anyone would feel that way. But I'm going to do everything in my power to see that *this* train makes it through safely to Oregon. And while I don't wish to boast, I'd remind you that I have a good record in that regard."

"A perfect record," said another man. "You haven't ever lost a wagon train, have you, Mr. Lash?"

"No, Mr. Carrothers, I haven't," Lash replied. "I wouldn't call it perfect, because a few wagons have been lost on the way, and we've had to bury a few people along the trail, too. A considerable amount of risk exists in a journey such as this, there's no point in denying it. But losing an entire wagon train . . . No, that's never happened on my watch."

"Good enough for me," declared Carrothers.

Edmund Farrington walked up with several men following him. "Mr. Lash, I did like you asked," he said. "I fetched Captain Kemp and the other leaders, except for Jake, and he's here already."

He nodded toward Carrothers.

"Gather 'round, men," Lash told them. "The rest of you, please go back to your wagons. I know the news has upset you, and I don't blame you a bit. But things will look brighter in the morning, I promise you. They always do at the start of a great journey."

Some of the immigrants were muttering as they walked off, but at least it looked as if Lash wasn't going to have a mutiny on his hands, thought Preacher. Folks who were willing to set off on a long trip across the country like this had to have a considerable amount of fortitude to start with. They knew it would be risky, and they were willing to run those risks or they wouldn't have come to Independence and joined the wagon train in the first place.

Lash said to the men who were still gathered around the wagon, "Thank you for coming, gentlemen. I want to introduce you to two new members of our company, most likely the final two additions we'll have since we're leaving early in the morning. This is Arthur, an old friend of mine who's agreed to help with the scouting, and Roscoe Lomax, who's going to assist Edmund with his freight wagons. Arthur, Roscoe, this is Wesley Kemp, who's been elected as the train's captain."

Kemp was a broad-shouldered, well-built man in his thirties with dark hair, a mustache, and a cleft chin. He clasped the hands of Preacher and Lomax in turn and said, "It's a pleasure to meet you." He nodded to a man who stepped up beside him and added, "My brother Harrison."

Preacher could see the resemblance between Wesley and Harrison Kemp. Harrison was a few years younger and clean-shaven, so it wasn't difficult to tell them apart even though they did look like brothers.

"And this is Cornelius Russell," Lash continued, nodding toward a slender, graying man in his forties who wore spectacles. "Mr. Russell used to teach literature and philosophy at one of the universities back East."

Preacher almost blurted out that one of his best friends, the diminutive mountain man known as Audie, was also a former professor, but he caught himself and didn't say anything. It was well known on the frontier that Audie and the giant Crow warrior Nighthawk were good friends with Preacher, and he was supposed to be Arthur now, not Preacher.

Instead, as he shook hands with Russell, he said, "That's mighty interestin'. Where we're goin' won't be much like a classroom, though."

Russell smiled faintly. "I hope not. I'm looking for a change in my life, not more of the same thing."

"I know what you mean. I've always been a mite on the fiddlefooted side, myself."

Lash also introduced Preacher to Stephen Millard and Adam Gideon, who completed the circle of leaders from the wagon train. Half a dozen men, plus Wesley Kemp as their captain, who made the decisions for the group of immigrants, which numbered slightly more than a hundred men, women, and children.

Wesley Kemp said, "Will we still be leaving first thing in the morning, Simon? I suppose you've heard that we had some disturbing news this evening."

"Yes, the wagons will roll at dawn," Lash said without hesitation, his voice firm and decisive. "I've heard about the attack on the other wagon train—"

"Attack?" Adam Gideon repeated. He was an excitable young man with dark, curly hair. "It was a massacre, Mr. Lash! Everyone was wiped out. No survivors!"

"That's true, as far as we know," Lash admitted. "But we're a large, well-armed group, and I believe any bandits will think twice before they dare to bother us."

"Maybe it wasn't outlaws," Cornelius Russell suggested. "It might have been Indians."

From where he still sat on the lowered tailgate, Tom Linford said, "It wasn't Indians, at least according to what I heard. There was no sign of . . . mutilation."

Preacher could have pointed out that Indians didn't always scalp their victims, but he kept that thought to himself. Anyway, given the history of the situation, it was more likely outlaws were to blame for the atrocity, although some of them could have been Mexican or half-breeds or even full-blood Indians. The gang wasn't necessarily made up entirely of whites.

"Well, I, for one, have faith in our wagon-master," Wesley Kemp said. "If Simon believes the risk is worth running, then so do I."

"None of us are talking about backing out," Jake Carrothers said.

Edmund Farrington nodded and said, "My wagons will be ready to roll first thing in the morning. Isn't that right, Mr. Lomax?"

"It durned sure is," Lomax declared. "And call me Roscoe, boss."

Farrington grinned as he said in his high-pitched voice, "I'll do that, Roscoe. I think we're going to make a formidable pair, you and I."

"I, uh, don't doubt it," Lomax rumbled.

"All right, gentlemen, everything seems to be settled," said Simon Lash. "We proceed as planned. So now, I believe we should all try to get a good night's sleep. Tomorrow we're going to need all the rest we can get tonight!"

Simon Lash bunked in Cornelius Russell's wagon, when he didn't sleep out under the stars. The two well-educated men had formed a friendship based on that. Russell told Preacher that he could pitch his bedroll in the wagon, as well, but the mountain man said, "I'll just crawl under it anytime it rains, if that's all right with you fellas. I like bein' in the open air as much as I can. Right now I'm gonna go check on my trail pards before I turn in."

Horse and Dog were going along with him on the journey, of course. The rest of the saddle stock was gathered in a rope corral just outside the camp, but Preacher hadn't put the big gray stallion with them because he didn't always get along that well with other horses. Instead, he was picketed not far from the corral, and Dog was with him. Preacher cut across the camp and headed in that direction.

The wagons weren't pulled in a tight circle as they would be while camping on the trail, but they were grouped in a loose ring with the oxen and other livestock in the center, as well as the main campfire and a few smaller, scattered cooking fires. Preacher had to pass through that ring to reach the makeshift corral, and as he did so, from the corner of his eye he spotted movement in the shadows on the far side of the wagons.

He stopped where he was, also in shadow, and waited to see who was still out and about as the camp was settling down for the night. Somebody bent on the same errand he was, checking on the horses, he supposed was most likely.

But his keen hearing picked up a soft swooshing that he recognized as the sound of a woman's skirt as she hurried along. That sound stopped when the indistinct figure Preacher was watching also halted abruptly.

Then another shape moved through the darkness and merged with the first one. Unseen in the gloom, Preacher's mouth curved in a faint smile. He had almost stumbled into a rendezvous, and not the sort he was accustomed to, where all the trappers and mountain men got together once a year to trade, spin yarns, and raise hell. This was a two-person rendezvous—a man and a woman.

Not wanting to embarrass them by revealing that they'd been discovered, Preacher stayed where he was, silent and unmoving. He had considerable experience at that. Plenty of times, his life had depended on not letting folks know he was around.

After a minute or two, the merged shapes parted slightly. A woman's voice whispered, "Harrison, we shouldn't be out here. You know that. I . . . I wish you hadn't asked me to meet you . . ."

"But you did," the man replied. "You did meet me, Virginia. What am I supposed to make of that except that you want me as much as I want you."

The man's voice was vaguely familiar to Preacher, and the woman had called him Harrison, so it stood to reason he was Harrison Kemp, brother of the train's elected captain, who had slipped out here to spark some gal named Virginia. That was none of Preacher's business, so it would be fine with him when they got done with their kissing and went on about their business.

That didn't happen for several more minutes, and there was a lot of whispering and caressing going on while Preacher stood there in the shadows getting more impatient. He was on the verge of retreating a short distance, then stomping forward and clearing his throat to alert the sweethearts that somebody was around. That ought to make them withdraw discreetly.

Instead, before he had to take that drastic step, the woman said just loudly enough for him to hear, "I have to get back. Wesley's probably wondering where I've gotten off to. I told him I was going to the Keller wagon to visit with Mrs. Keller."

"The woman who just had the baby?" asked Harrison Kemp.

"That's right."

He laughed softly. "She's going to have her hands full, riding in a wagon all day with a newborn. I don't envy her."

"She has children, so I *do* envy her, I suppose."

An uneasy silence followed that statement. Preacher got the feeling Harrison Kemp didn't know how to respond to it, so he just didn't say anything. After a moment, he cleared his throat and said, "Good night, then. I . . . I'll see you again."

"Of course, you will. I'm married to—"

"That's not what I meant, and you know it," Harrison Kemp broke in. "I have to be with you, Virginia."

"You know that's impossible." The woman's voice was starting to get an angry edge to it. "This is wrong, and we're not going to keep doing it."

"We didn't *do* anything."

"Other than sneak around behind your brother's back and . . . and . . ." She drew in a sharp breath and went on in a tone that brooked no argument, "Good night, Harrison."

"Good night, Virginia," he responded, sounding more than a little sullen. The shapes broke apart completely and drifted off into the darkness.

Preacher rasped the fingertips of his right hand on his bristly chin and frowned. It was clear from what he had overheard that Harrison Kemp was sweet on his own brother's wife, and evidently she returned the feeling, at least enough to meet Harrison in the darkness and let him kiss her for a while. They had parted company with some hard feelings, though, so maybe that would keep them apart for the rest of the journey west.

Preacher hoped that would be the case. Where they were headed, everybody needed a clear head in order to concentrate on what was necessary to stay alive and reach their destination. A bunch of emotional uproar was just a distraction that could prove costly.

Funny, though, how with that thought in his head, his own mind went back to the pretty widow, Constance Bradley, and the way he'd felt when Roscoe Lomax took an interest in her. Could be he'd experienced a little jealous moment of his own.

Preacher shook off that idea and moved on, resuming the errand that had brought him out here, checking on Horse and Dog. He knew they were like him, ready to get started on this epic and quite possibly dangerous westward journey.

Chapter 11

Preacher had no trouble waking whenever he wanted to. He had developed that ability early on, after leaving the family farm and heading west. He slept under a tree near the camp, with Dog lying at his side and Horse not far away. He threw off his blankets when the approaching dawn was just a faint gray glow in the eastern sky.

When he walked into camp, some of the immigrant women were stirring embers and rekindling fires that had burned down overnight. Flames began to dance here and there. Within minutes, the smell of coffee brewing drifted through the early morning air. Men climbed out of wagons, stretched, yawned, and pawed at their sleep-tousled hair. The wagon train was waking up and coming back to life.

Preacher found Simon Lash hunkered on his heels next to one of the small fires, watching intently as the flames heated a coffeepot. Constance Bradley emerged from a nearby wagon, carrying a frying pan and a slab of bacon. In a white, long-sleeved shirt and a long brown skirt, she looked better than she had any right to at this hour.

She smiled at the mountain man and said, "Good morning, Mr. Arthur. I hope you'll join Simon and me for breakfast. I'm afraid the biscuits are left over, but the coffee and bacon will be fresh."

"Sounds mighty good to me," Preacher told her. "I'm obliged for the invite."

Still smiling, Constance knelt by the fire and put the pan on the flames to heat as she unwrapped butcher paper from the bacon. "Did you sleep well?" she asked.

"Uh, yeah, I reckon so," Preacher replied. "I pert near always do." He chuckled. "Clean livin' and a clear conscience are responsible for that, I reckon."

He saw admiration in Simon Lash's eyes as the wagonmaster watched Constance preparing breakfast. That made Preacher feel even more that he shouldn't be jealous. Constance probably had a number of admirers among these immigrants. A woman like her would always have her choice of suitors, especially on the frontier where females could be scarce—especially attractive, unattached ones.

And even though she had impressed him, he wasn't in the market for a wife! No woman could ever be a comfortable permanent fit in the way he had chosen to live his life, he believed.

When Constance stepped back into her wagon for a moment, he put those thoughts out of his head and quietly asked Simon Lash, "Have you been postin' guards at night?"

"Yes, of course. Right outside of Independence like this, the odds of there being any trouble are almost nonexistent, but it never hurts to be careful. I mean to impress upon everyone the added importance of vigilance as we proceed westward, however."

Preacher nodded. "Good idea. Every day, we'll be gettin' farther away from civilization, and the odds of somethin' happenin' will go up."

"I don't expect any attacks by the outlaws until we reach the Devil's Crossing, though," said Lash.

Preacher tugged on his earlobe and said, "There might be other problems along the way."

"Of course," Lash replied. "I didn't mean to imply that none of the usual dangers may be lurking out there, waiting for us. And we don't need to concentrate all of our attention on what might happen at the Devil's Crossing. Young Tom's story was quite harrowing, though."

"Yeah, that's for dang sure," Preacher agreed. His mind went back to the things that had occupied his thoughts a few moments earlier and added, "That Missus Bradley is a mighty fine woman."

"Indeed she is," said Lash.

"I noticed Roscoe seems to think so, too. If you're interested in her, though, I don't mind tellin' him to back off . . ."

"There's no need for that," Lash said with a smile. "Constance is quite attractive, of course, and I always admire a strong woman. But she's going to make a new life for herself in Oregon, and the day that I'll be ready to settle down is far in the future." He shook his head. "No, I already regard her as a friend, but that's the extent of it. So if Mr. Lomax has any notions . . . or for that matter, you yourself—"

"Nope," Preacher said. "I ain't nowhere near ready to

settle down, neither." He sniffed the air and changed the subject. "Smells like that coffee's ready."

A few minutes later, while Preacher and Lash were enjoying the coffee and eating biscuits and bacon, Tom Linford came up and joined them. The young scout still had a haunted look to his face, but he had filled out some and regained more of his strength since Preacher had first met him more than a month earlier. He had a holstered revolver and a sheathed knife attached to the belt around his lean waist.

Linford didn't know the part that Jamie MacCallister was going to play on their journey; only Preacher, Lash, and Roscoe Lomax were aware of that. He said, "I'd like to take the point with you today, Mr. Lash, if that's all right."

"Of course, Tom. When we get farther up the trail, you and Preacher will be ranging a good distance ahead most of the time. I'm counting on the two of you to be my eyes and ears."

Linford grunted. "That's what Mr. Prescott said, but it didn't do him much good, did it?"

"That's in the past," Lash said in a firm but gentle voice. "We can't change it, but we can put it behind us, at least to a certain extent."

"You're right," Linford said with a nod. "Brooding about what happened isn't going to change anything."

"No, it won't."

"Neither will killing every single one of those low-down snakes who were responsible for it . . . but that's not going to stop me from trying, if I get the chance."

* * *

A short time later, when breakfast was finished and an arch of reddish-gold light appeared on the eastern horizon, the immigrants began packing away everything and hitching their teams to the wagons. While Preacher was walking around the camp, watching the preparations, he spotted the Kemp brothers backing a pair of oxen into their traces alongside the tongue of a large, canvas-covered wagon.

"Mornin', Cap'n," Preacher said with a nod to Wesley Kemp. He extended that to the other brother and added, "Mr. Kemp."

"Hello . . . Arthur, was it?" Wesley Kemp said.

"That's right."

Before either of them could say anything else, a woman poked her head out through the opening behind the driver's box and said, "Wesley, I need some help moving one of these crates."

"I'm busy now, Virginia," snapped Kemp. "Can't you see we're hitching up the team?"

She frowned. She was younger than Kemp, probably in her late twenties like Harrison, and had dark hair gathered under a sun bonnet. The brightening light revealed that she had a pretty, heart-shaped face Preacher hadn't been able to see the night before when he happened on her and Harrison in the shadows just outside the camp.

Preacher said, "I can spell you on this chore, Cap'n, if you need to give the missus a hand."

"That's not necessary. She can wait. Come on, Harrison, let's get this done. We don't want the wagon train leaving without us!"

"They're not going to leave without us," Harrison Kemp said. "You were elected captain, remember?"

"All the more reason to set a good example and be ready to go when the time comes. Now, let's wrestle these brutes into place."

Preacher nodded and moved on, thinking that he could understand why Virginia Kemp might turn to her brother-in-law for a little comfort. Wesley Kemp seemed to be a mite full of himself, and short-tempered, to boot.

Not far away, the mountain man saw Roscoe Lomax helping several other men get teams hitched to Edmund Farrington's wagons. Farrington stood off to the side, watching the effort with a slightly anxious expression on his round face.

"Good morning, Arthur," he greeted Preacher.

"How's Lomax workin' out so far?"

"Thank goodness he came along when he did! The whole process of getting ready to travel has gone much more smoothly this morning than it did all the other mornings when we were coming out here to Independence. Roscoe seems to know exactly where to move those beasts and when to prod them . . . and what, uh, colorful names to call them."

Preacher laughed. "Yeah, ol' Roscoe's been known to cuss a mite while he's workin' with livestock."

"I'm afraid I may have to ask him to control the impulse, if that's even possible. I mean, there are children within earshot. There's a limit to what strong language they should be exposed to."

"Well, you can give that a try if you want," said Preacher, "but I ain't sure how well it's gonna work."

"I was afraid you'd say that." Farrington paused, then added in a conspiratorial tone, "I also thought about asking him to teach me some of the more, ah, evocative words and phrases he uses. I didn't think I had led that much of a sheltered life, but evidently I have! Why, some of those things he yells at the oxen don't even seem possible."

"If you want somebody to teach you how to cuss, Roscoe's your man, all right."

"If he can help get those wagons and goods safely to Oregon, he can say whatever he wants to. And that's the . . . the dang-blasted truth."

Preacher grinned, patted Farrington on the shoulder, and said, "Yeah, you and him can work on that."

He continued circulating around the camp, saying hello to the men he'd met the night before and introducing himself to some of the other immigrants. He tried to size up the men, maybe get an idea of who might be working with the outlaws, but none of them struck him as the sort. Most of them seemed like hardworking family men who were eager to head for Oregon but at the same time worried about the safety of their families.

Preacher could understand that feeling, even though he had no real family of his own and hadn't for many years. Probably some of his relatives were still alive, somewhere, but he hadn't returned to his boyhood home in a long, long time and had no plans to do so.

He did have one son that he knew of, and a couple of grandkids, and since he'd wintered with various tribes numerous times as a young man, he might well have other offspring he was unaware of. He tried not to let his thoughts go down that rabbit hole too often, though.

There *was* one hombre who made the hair on the back of Preacher's neck stir slightly. When Preacher introduced himself, the man said his name was Jesse Willis. Preacher had no reason to doubt that, but over the years he had developed a sense for when somebody was lying and it told him Jesse Willis might not be telling the truth. Willis was traveling alone. He told Preacher that when the wagon train reached Oregon, he intended to open a black-smith shop.

That might well be true, but Willis didn't *look* like a blacksmith. He was tall, lanky, and rawboned, not the muscular sort of man who usually worked with hammer and anvil, bellows and forge. But he had ropy muscles in his arms and shoulders, and as long as he possessed enough strength to wield a hammer, that was all that was required.

He wasn't overly friendly or forthcoming, either. Preacher practically had to pry information out of him. He was going to reserve judgment about Mr. Jesse Willis, Preacher decided—and try to keep an eye on the man as they were heading west.

The sun hadn't made its appearance yet, but it wasn't far below the horizon as the wagons lined up. Preacher had saddled Horse by then, and he loped along the column with Dog trotting beside him. He counted twenty-eight wagons. Most had men handling the reins, but on a few of them, women perched on the driver's box and were ready to get the teams moving.

One of those was Constance Bradley. Preacher smiled and pinched the brim of his hat to her as he rode past. She returned the smile and gave him a little hand wave to go with it.

Four outriders on horseback flanked the wagon train on each side. They were armed with pistols and rifles. Preacher would have preferred more, but he and Lash had to work with what was available. It would have taken an army escort, a whole troop of dragoons, to ensure the wagon train's safety, and the army just didn't have that kind of manpower to spare. To a large extent, anybody daring to cross the plains and the mountains was on their own.

Preacher reached the front of the wagon train. As the elected captain, Wesley Kemp had the honor of having his wagon first in line. The seat was wide enough only for the driver, so Virginia Kemp wasn't sitting beside her husband. Preacher spotted her peering out over Kemp's shoulder, though. She was looking at something off to the side, and when he glanced in the same direction, he saw that Harrison Kemp was one of the outriders. Harrison sat his horse about forty feet away as he returned the look Virginia was giving him.

They needed to be careful about that, Preacher mused. If Wesley Kemp hadn't been so self-absorbed, he might have noticed the way his wife and his brother were making eyes at one another. It would take a blind man— or a fool—to miss it.

Preacher nudged Horse alongside Simon Lash and Tom Linford, who sat their mounts twenty yards ahead of the lead wagon. Lash asked, "How do things look to you, Arthur?"

"Everything's in good shape, as far as I can see, and so are those pilgrims. But they ought to be, since they're just now gettin' started. They ain't had time for the hardships to start pilin' up on 'em."

"Some of them had rough trips getting here," said Lash, "but they've had time to recover from that, and so have their animals. We should make good progress today."

"But it'll slow down a little more every day," Linford

cautioned. He made a face. "Although I reckon I shouldn't be telling you that, Mr. Lash. You have a hundred times more experience at these things than I do."

"Perhaps, but I value your opinion, Tom, as I do yours, Arthur. Please, both of you, don't hesitate to speak up any time you feel that you ought to."

"I ain't never been accused of bein' shy about speakin' my mind," Preacher said with a smile. "Don't figure I'll start now."

Lash returned the smile and said, "I appreciate that." He turned his horse, lifted himself in the stirrups, and gazed intently back along the line of wagons. The sun was beginning to edge above the horizon.

Lash took off his broad-brimmed hat, waved it in a big circle over his head, then turned his mount again and swept his arm down toward the west.

"Wagons . . . *hoooooo!*"

Half a mile away, on a slight, rolling rise, Jamie MacCallister sat on his horse and watched the wagons lurch into motion. His keen eyes followed them in the growing light as they rolled westward. It was a long way to Oregon, thought Jamie. Danger might not stalk them every foot of the journey . . . but the possibility of it was never far off.

He waited until the last of the wagons rocked and swayed out of sight before he heeled his horse into motion. As he rode easily, staying well behind and slightly to one side of the wagon train, his intent gaze roamed over the landscape all around them. He didn't see any signs of danger.

But it was waiting out there, somewhere in the hazy distance. Every instinct in Jamie's body told him so, and he had learned to trust those instincts.

When it finally came calling, he and Preacher would be waiting.

Chapter 12

Simon Lash's prediction was correct: the wagon train made good progress on the first day, covering a good twenty miles by the time Lash called a halt and told the immigrants to make camp.

Tom Linford had picked out the spot, and it was a good one. A creek trickled by, flowing south toward the Kansas River. It was large enough to water the stock but small enough that crossing it wouldn't be any problem for the wagons. The grass was lush and provided plenty of graze for the animals. The mood was very optimistic around the campfires that night, after a successful first day on the trail.

Preacher knew that wouldn't last. So did Simon Lash, Roscoe Lomax, and Tom Linford. The trick was to cover as much ground as possible before the problems set in, as they inevitably would.

However, as one day flowed into the next and one week became two and then three, the wagon train seemed blessed with extraordinarily good luck. They crossed the Kansas, Wakarusa, and Vermillion rivers on ferries that had been built to handle just such wagon traffic when millions of immigrants began heading westward. None of the streams were swollen enough by the spring rains to make those crossings difficult. The creeks they came to were shallow and could be forded without trouble. Previous wagon trains had worn down the banks so that those didn't present any obstacles.

It was almost like they had a Higher Power watching over them, Preacher mused as he rode ahead of the wagons with Dog ranging back and forth even farther out. He wasn't an overly spiritual hombre, but he believed in the Man Above, as some of the tribes called the Creator, and would take good luck from whatever source.

He also knew that they had Jamie Ian MacCallister keeping an eye on the wagon train. Preacher and Jamie had worked out a system by which Jamie would signal the mountain man if he saw anything suspicious. Preacher checked every evening for a thin column of smoke rising behind them, broken in puffs, Indian fashion. Such signals would be almost impossible to spot against the graying sky unless a person knew exactly what he was looking for—which Preacher did.

So far, there hadn't been any communication from Jamie. Preacher took that as good news. Of course, it was possible that something had happened to his friend, but he didn't really believe that. Jamie Ian MacCallister was as solid and invulnerable as a mountain.

Being out on the trail had been good for Tom Linford, too. Preacher hadn't known the young man before the tragedy that had struck at the Devil's Crossing, but other than the lingering haunted look in his eyes that was visible at times, Linford seemed hale and hearty once more. He was able to stay in the saddle all day and push himself as much as he needed to. Preacher felt an instinctive liking for the young scout, as did Simon Lash, who said as much to Preacher one evening as they hunkered on their heels next to one of the campfires, sipping coffee.

"Tom's a good man," Lash said. "I think he'll continue to be a good scout, and someday he might make a fine wagon-master."

"He sure might . . . if this whole thing of wagon trains goin' west continues long enough."

Lash frowned over his cup at Preacher. "What do you mean by that? Do you believe that attacks by outlaw gangs such as the ones we may face will bring an end to the wagon trains? Or were you thinking more of the Indians and their opposition to settlement?"

"Not either one o' them things, actually," said Preacher. "A while back, me and Jamie helped out the government on a little job that had to do with buildin' a railroad from one side of the country clear to the other. They might get around to doin' that, one of these days. If they do, folks can head west a lot faster and safer than travelin' in wagons like this."

"Yes, but will such a wild idea ever come to pass?" asked Lash. "It's difficult to believe that it could."

"Reckon we'll have to wait and see. One thing you can count on, though. Nothin' stays the same forever."

Lash grinned. "Except perhaps you, Preacher. You don't appear to have aged a day since I first met you several years ago."

"Maybe not, but I *feel* a mite older. Time catches up to all of us."

Lash nodded solemnly.

During the trip so far, Preacher had kept an eye on the

Kemp brothers when he thought about it. The situation involving Harrison Kemp and his brother's wife wasn't a major concern for the mountain man, but it *could* cause trouble to erupt if the illicit relationship was exposed. One day, while Tom Linford was scouting ahead, Preacher dropped back along the line of outriders until he came to Harrison Kemp. He turned Horse and fell in beside the man.

"How are you doin', Mr. Kemp?" he asked. "Holdin' up to the trip all right?"

"Yes, I'm doing fine. Being out in the open like this is very invigorating." Kemp grinned and lightly thumped his chest with a fist. "All this sunlight and clean air is wonderful. I've spent too much time cooped up in an office."

"What is it you used to do?"

Kemp's expression sobered. "I worked for my brother. He owned a wholesale supply business that manufactured parts and equipment for various factories. The company was quite successful, but keeping the books for it wasn't exactly exciting work."

"No, it don't sound like it would be," Preacher agreed. "What made him give it up?"

"One of his competitors offered to buy the business, and the price was good enough that Wesley didn't feel like he could turn it down. Then he got the idea of going west and starting over again in Oregon. He believes he can build a business that's just as successful out there, and if anyone can, it's my brother." Kemp's jaw tightened a little as he added, "Wesley always gets what he wants."

Preacher knew he probably ought to leave it alone, but he said, "Is that so?"

"Yes." Harrison Kemp drew in a deep breath. "Did you know there was a time when Virginia . . . my sister-in-law . . . was being courted by both my brother and myself?"

"No, I don't reckon I did."

Kemp shook his head. "No, of course you wouldn't. You don't know our family history. But it's true. As a matter of fact, *I* was the one courting her first. *I'm* the one responsible for the two of them meeting." He laughed, but there was no humor in the sound. "Life is funny, isn't it?"

"It takes some mighty odd twists and turns at times," agreed Preacher.

"Well, water under the bridge now, as they say. Virginia is married to Wesley, and I'm sure his new venture in Oregon will be a huge success."

"Maybe you could do somethin' else instead of workin' for him," the mountain man suggested.

"I suppose. Maybe I'll hunt bears or something."

Preacher laughed. "Well, if you decide to do that, let me know, Mr. Kemp. I might could give you a few pointers. I've tangled with a few of the varmints."

"Call me Harrison. And I'm not surprised that you've fought bears. You just look like a man who would have, along with, I don't know, mountain lions and Indians."

"There's a whole heap of things on the frontier that can kill you, all right. But if you keep your eyes open and your wits about you, most of the time you'll pull through all right."

"I'll keep that advice in mind."

Preacher could have suggested that he not mess with his brother's wife, either, along with bears and mountain lions, but he wasn't going to get that deeply involved in the Kemp family's drama. Harrison Kemp was a grown man and ought to know right from wrong by now.

Along with the Kemps, Preacher also kept an eye on Jesse Willis, but other than staying to himself and not socializing with the other immigrants, he didn't do anything out of the ordinary. If a man wanted to be sullen, that was his own business and didn't make him an outlaw, Preacher decided.

Ever since crossing the Vermillion River, the trail had run in a more northwesterly direction. Preacher knew that if they kept going that way, they would run right into the Platte River. Sure enough, late one afternoon, they came to the stream. Preacher, Lash, and Tom Linford reined in and looked out across the broad, shallow river as Wesley Kemp drove his wagon up to join them.

"What is this, gentlemen?" Kemp called from the driver's box as he hauled back on the reins and brought his team to a stop.

Lash turned his horse so that he sat sideways to the stream and waved an arm at it. "The Platte River, Mr. Kemp," he said. "A mile wide and an inch deep, some say. Another popular description is that the water in the Platte is too thick to drink but too thin to plow."

Indeed, the river looked as if it could be a formidable obstacle to a wagon train like this. Wide, shallow, cut by numerous channels and dotted with sandy islands, crossing it could be a very treacherous process. Just the mud was bad enough and could bog down a wagon's wheels in a hurry. Besides that, patches of quicksand out there could suck down men and animals and swallow them whole.

"How in the world will we get across?" Kemp asked.

As usual, Virginia looked out from the wagon, over his shoulder. "Wagons can't ford that!"

"Actually, they can, as long as they follow a carefully laid out path," Lash replied. "The problem is that the condition of the riverbed is constantly changing, so each time a wagon train comes along, the river has to be explored and a new route decided upon."

"Who's going to do that?" Kemp wanted to know.

Preacher said, "I reckon I will. Or rather, Horse will. Whether it's fordin' a river or climbin' a mountain, this old fella's mighty good at pickin' a path he can follow safely."

"But a wagon weighs a great deal more than a horse," Kemp pointed out. "Just because you can get across doesn't mean we can!"

"Well, there *is* a certain amount of luck and hope involved, I'll grant you that."

Lash said, "Don't worry, Mr. Kemp. I've brought dozens of wagon trains through here. Between us, Arthur and I will be able to find a safe route."

Kemp sighed and nodded. "I suppose we'll have to put our trust in you. That's what we're paying you for, after all."

"Indeed." Lash nodded to Preacher. "Go ahead. I'll follow and try to gauge how much leeway we'll have."

Preacher nudged Horse into motion. The stallion stepped down off the low bank into the muddy water. Dog started to follow but stopped and whined a little.

"Stay here," Preacher told the big cur. "You can come across on one of the wagons later. I'll tell Roscoe to be sure and fetch you."

Dog sat down and looked like he'd understood every

word Preacher said. The mountain man had never been convinced that he didn't.

Preacher and Lash proceeded carefully into the river. The wagon-master rode about ten feet behind Preacher and ten feet to the right. Horse picked his way slowly and carefully through the stream. Preacher could tell how soft the bottom was by how the stallion's hooves sank into it. From time to time, he guided Horse away from a particularly soft area and urged the stallion to find firmer footing. Behind him, Simon Lash adjusted his route accordingly.

By the time they reached the middle of the river, they were well out of earshot of those still on the southern bank. Lash called to Preacher, "Do you see those clouds back to the west?"

"I see 'em," Preacher replied. "And I don't like the looks of 'em. Some mighty big storms can boil up on these plains."

"I know, and we don't want to get caught in one of those with all the wagons in the middle of the river."

"Let's go on and finish takin' our look-see, but if those clouds keep comin' in, we may want to wait until tomorrow mornin' to cross over."

"And if it rains a great deal and the river comes up, the route we're mapping out today may not be any good tomorrow," Lash said.

"Maybe not. We'll just have to do it again."

Preacher's eyes kept glancing toward the dark clouds building in the western sky. They climbed higher and higher until they swallowed the sun. The air went still and became oppressively heavy. After a few minutes of that, a wind struck. The day had been very warm, so the wind probably felt colder than it actually was. Even so, it had an undeniable chill to it. Also, it carried a scent that Preacher recognized instantly.

So did Simon Lash. He said, "That's it. We'd best get back to the wagons. Rain's coming, no mistake about it."

Preacher wheeled Horse around. Muddy water splashed up around the stallion's hooves. Lash turned his mount, as well, and the two men rode quickly back toward the southern bank, following the route they had mapped out in their brains so they wouldn't blunder into any quicksand.

"I can see the rain now," Preacher called over the rapidly building howl of the wind. "Looks like a solid sheet comin' down."

"What I'm worried about is a cyclone," Lash replied. "I've seen them before, out here on these plains, and they're terrible things. Absolute engines of destruction."

Preacher knew what the Englishman meant. A big enough cyclone could snatch a man and a horse from the ground and carry them hundreds of feet in the air. It might even pick up a heavy wagon and team. The members of the wagon train could only hope that one wouldn't come swooping along and smash into them.

Out here, there was no place to hide.

Chapter 13

The immigrants all clustered around the first couple of wagons as Preacher and Simon Lash pounded back up the riverbank. Tom Linford was still mounted. He said, "That storm blew up in a hurry!"

"Indeed it did," said Lash. He raised his voice and addressed the assembled travelers. "Everyone return to your wagons as quickly as possible. Don't circle them. Turn them so that the rear of the wagon faces west, in case of a cyclone. Swiftly now! The storm hasn't gotten here yet, but it won't be long."

The urgency in his voice as he issued the orders made the immigrants respond. No one questioned them or hesitated. Preacher rode along the line of wagons and saw Roscoe Lomax running back and forth, bellowing curses as he supervised the positioning of Edmund Farrington's freight wagons. Dog trotted along with him, staying with the burly bullwhacker as Preacher had ordered earlier. Lomax didn't care for dogs in general, having an instinctive fear of them, but he had learned to get along with Preacher's big cur.

Lomax stopped blistering the air long enough to glance

up at Preacher and say, "I've seen two or three of them twisters. They can be bad!"

"Maybe luck'll be with us," the mountain man said. "It has been so far."

And that fact actually made him worry even more, he realized. The odds were going to catch up to them sooner or later. It might well be today.

Again, Preacher told Dog to stay with Lomax, then resumed checking on the other immigrants. He reached Constance Bradley's wagon. She was in the process of turning the team of oxen to the east so that the rear of the wagon would be to the west, but the big brutes weren't cooperating very well. Preacher saw worry etching anxious lines in Constance's face.

"Hang on!" he called to her. "I'll give you a hand!"

He brought Horse alongside the leader and reached down to grasp the yoke attached to them with oxbows. He urged the stallion ahead and hauled hard on the yoke. That forced the team to turn to the right, the direction they needed to go.

Between Preacher's effort and Constance pulling on the reins, they got the oxen headed east, which swung the wagon around in the proper orientation. Preacher dismounted hurriedly and held his arms up to Constance on the driver's box.

"Come on!" he told her. "Better get down and crawl under the wagon. You'll be safer there!"

"Arthur, stay here with me!" she begged as she dropped from the seat and he caught her under the arms.

Preacher was about to tell her he couldn't do that because he needed to continue checking on the other pilgrims, but at that moment, the rain hit.

And it was like being struck by a giant, watery fist, combined with a million stinging blows. No preliminary drops of warning, just a hard wave of water that slapped into Preacher. Combined with the wind, the force was enough to stagger him. Constance would have fallen if he hadn't had hold of her.

Nothing else he could do now. Horse would take shelter and instinctively protect himself as best he could. Preacher would have to hope that Lomax would look after Dog. He urged Constance toward the gap between the wagon wheels on the vehicle's left side. He didn't say anything and neither did she as they dropped to their knees and crawled under the wagon.

The wind was blowing so hard that the rain was falling almost sideways, rather than coming straight down, so the wagon didn't protect them completely. However, they were already soaked to the skin, just from the few seconds they had been out in the full force of the storm, so getting wet didn't really matter. At least under the wagon, they could breathe without feeling like they were going to drown.

The wagon bed was high enough off the ground that Preacher could sit up if he bent forward a little. He did so and without thinking pulled Constance into his arms and onto his lap. She threw her arms around his neck and buried her face against his chest. He felt her breasts move against him as she heaved in air and shuddered.

"Oh!" she said, her voice weak. "Oh!"

Preacher tightened his arms around her and said, "Don't worry. It's gonna be all right."

Only the fact that their heads were so close together

made it possible for them to hear each other over the raging storm.

Preacher felt Constance's heart pounding. As he held her, that wild hammering slowed slightly. After several minutes, she lifted her head and looked into his eyes from a distance of only a few inches.

"Thank you," she said. Her voice was still a little shaky, but she sounded better. "I . . . I don't know what I would have done if you hadn't come along when you did."

"You would've been fine," he told her. "I ain't known you for all that long, but I recognize a mighty strong woman when I see one."

"No," she said. "I thought I was strong. I didn't fall apart when my . . . my husband passed away, but this storm . . . It's so incredible, such a . . . a force of nature . . ."

"Storms usually are," Preacher said dryly—the only thing remotely dry about either of them.

"I was about to panic," Constance went on. "I probably would have just run screaming into the storm and died if not for you." She hugged him again and pressed her cheek against his.

If a fella had to ride out a storm, thought Preacher, this wasn't a bad way to do it.

The earth shook a little under him as thunder crashed. He looked out from under the wagon and saw a bolt of lightning slam into the ground about a hundred yards away, followed instantly by another boom. He seemed to feel the air crackling around him and held Constance tighter. Lightning flashed again, not once but several times, the bolts clawing down from the sky like the spread fingers of a giant hand. Preacher couldn't tell the peals of thunder apart anymore. They blended together into one long, earth-shaking, tooth-rattling roar.

But even so, he heard something else, a rumbling sound that was different from the thunder. If anything, it sounded like trains he had heard during his visits back East where the railroads ran. He let go of Constance and said, "Stay here."

She clutched at him and exclaimed, "No! Don't go!"

Gently, he disengaged her arms from his neck and told her, "I ain't goin' anywhere. I just want to scoot over a mite so I can see out better. Hear that rumblin'?"

Her eyes widened. "Is that . . . ?"

"I don't know. That's why I want to have a look."

Constance didn't try to stop him as he turned and crawled to the rear of the wagon. From there he could look out to the west, along the southern bank of the Platte.

At first, he couldn't see anything except the blinding sheets of rain. Then the lightning popped and flashed again, and Preacher bit back a curse as he saw the massive funnel cloud about a mile away, curving and writhing from the clouds to the ground like a gigantic snake. There was something sinuous, almost graceful, about its deadly, inexorable advance.

Constance screamed. She had ignored him when he told her to stay where she was and had scrambled to the back of the wagon beside him. Preacher writhed around, caught hold of her, and dived to the ground, taking her with him. He lay on top of her, pressing her into the mud, as the cyclone's roar became deafening.

It seemed to go on forever. The ground shook, and so did Preacher. He could feel himself vibrating all through his body. The hair on the back of his neck stood up straight. Electricity crackled through him. It seemed as if at any second, he might blow apart from all the forces building up inside him.

Then the terrible sensations were gone. The ordeal ended so abruptly, it left Preacher gasping. The rain still pounded down, the wind still blew furiously, lightning slammed to the ground and thunder rolled. But that was nothing compared to what Preacher and Constance had just endured. That was just a bad thunderstorm, not the end of the world.

Preacher became aware that Constance had her hands on his shoulders and was pushing against him. The way he was lying on top of her, she probably couldn't breathe. He raised himself on his elbows and looked down at her as he asked, "Are you all right?"

She had to gulp down some air before she could answer. "Y-yes, I . . . I think so. Is it over?"

"Maybe," Preacher said. He rolled off her and sat up, then crawled to the side of the wagon this time so he could look out toward the north. He made out the vague shape of the next wagon in line, so he knew it was still there, but the heavy rain made it impossible for him to see anything else. He twisted around and checked the other side, but it was the same story over there.

The rain still sluiced down, but the lightning had begun to ease up. It wasn't striking constantly now. Preacher knew he needed to go out there and see what had happened to the wagon train.

A part of him dreaded finding out.

Waiting wouldn't make things any better, though. He told Constance, "Stay here. And I mean it this time."

"I don't want you to leave, Arthur." She swallowed hard. "But people may need your help."

"That's what I'm thinkin'."

"So I can't ask you to stay. Just be careful, all right."

"Don't worry. I think the worst of it's over."

He hoped that was the case. He tugged his hat down tighter on his head, since a gusty wind was still blowing, and crawled out from under the wagon.

The rain pounded against the hat and ran off its sagging brim in streams. Preacher gripped the wagon's sideboards to steady himself as he made his way to the back of the vehicle. The downpour had turned the ground into a sea of sticky mud.

They wouldn't be crossing the Platte today, he told himself. In fact, they might have to wait a day or two before they could manage it.

Lightning flashed and gave him a chance to study the sky for a split second. For a while there, it had turned almost as dark as night. Now, he saw some areas of lighter gray back to the west. That meant the clouds were thinning and the storm truly was passing. When he turned his head to look toward the east, the black clouds still hung there like beetling cliffs, but they were receding. He didn't see the cyclone anymore.

He let go of the wagon and moved out to the side so he could see better. When he did, a shape suddenly loomed up through the gray curtains of rain. A head lowered and bumped his shoulder. Preacher threw an arm around Horse's neck and hugged the stallion.

"You made it, you old varmint! I knew you would." He chuckled. "I reckon you could say the same thing about me, couldn't you?"

Horse nudged his shoulder again.

Preacher turned his attention to the wagons again. The rain still fell too heavily for him to see all of them, but the line of vehicles appeared to be unbroken in both directions as far as his vision reached. That was good. If some of them had been missing, it would be because the cyclone got them. Thankfully, that didn't seem to be the case.

He stepped back over to Constance's wagon and bent to speak to her as she waited underneath it. "You'll be all right now," he told her. "The worst of it's over, for sure. I'm gonna go see how ever'body else came through it."

She came to the edge of the protected area under the wagon and reached out. Preacher clasped the hand she extended to him. "Thank you," she said. "Thank you so much. I . . . I think I would have lost my mind if you hadn't been here, Arthur. You saved me."

"Well, I'm just, uh, glad I could help." Even soaking wet and plastered with mud, Constance Bradley was a mighty pretty woman, he thought. He was uncomfortably aware of how the sodden clothing clung to her body. He nodded to her, slipped his hand out of hers, and turned to start checking on the other members of the wagon train.

Despite the rain, people were beginning to crawl out from under their wagons. When Preacher saw them, he waved them back underneath the vehicles.

"Best stay under cover for a little while longer, folks. The lightnin' ain't as bad now, but it can still strike and out here on these plains, it don't take much to attract it."

The women grabbed their kids and pulled them back to shelter, but most of the men stayed in the open, anxious to check on their wagons and livestock. Preacher supposed he couldn't blame them for that.

He heard a familiar bark. Dog bounded up to him. Rearing on hind legs, the big cur put his front paws on Preacher's shoulders and licked him in the face.

"Dadgum it," the mountain man said, laughing, "I'm already wet enough. I don't need a bath from you, old-timer."

He was glad to see that Dog had made it safely through the storm. He hoped that meant Roscoe Lomax and the freight wagons belonging to Edmund Farrington were all right, too.

A few moments later, Lomax himself appeared. In his buffalo coat, he looked like a giant, soaked rat. He let out an exuberant whoop, grabbed Preacher, and pounded the mountain man on the back.

"You done made it!" said Lomax. "I was afraid that dang twister might've carried you off."

"It was so loud I thought it was fixin' to," Preacher said. "It was comin' straight at us. By the looks of things, though, it must've lifted up just before it got here."

He had seen that happen before. Cyclones were unpredictable things. They could turn sharply with no warning, rise and fall the same way. Preacher had known them to take giant hops across the landscape, sparing one location only to wreak havoc in another only a hundred yards away.

"How'd the wagons come through?" he went on.

"All right, as far as I could tell," said Lomax. "Some of the covers ripped loose part of the way but didn't blow off. The rain probably damaged some o' the goods, but it'll be up to Mr. Farrington to figure that out. Livestock all survived."

Preacher hadn't seen any killed or injured oxen or mules yet. Left hitched to their wagons, with the brakes set, the teams had had little choice except to stand there and allow the wind and rain to lash at them. The wagons were heavy enough that they had withstood the straight-line winds that blew through before the twister's arrival.

Simon Lash walked along the line, the thick mud tugging at his high-topped boots. He came up to Preacher, grabbed his hand, and pumped it.

"I'm quite happy to see you, old boy! That was a devilishly bad storm."

"Anybody hurt?" asked Preacher.

"Not that I've come across so far—"

A shrill scream cut through the fading rumble of thunder.

Chapter 14

Preacher, Lash, and Lomax turned toward the sound. It came from farther toward the rear of the wagon train. As the scream was repeated, they ran toward it as best they could. The thick, clinging mud slowed them down.

Several immigrants joined them in rushing to see what was wrong. They came up to a wagon and saw a woman bending over beside it, holding on to a man.

"Help me!" she cried. "My husband's hurt!"

"Step aside, Mrs. Thomas," Lash said to her in a firm voice. "We'll see to him."

Constance Bradley had appeared on the scene, as well. She took hold of the distraught woman's shoulders, said gently, "Come on, Hannah," and urged her out of the way.

Preacher and Lomax bent over. Each grasped an arm of the man who lay there facedown and motionless. Preacher's forehead creased in a frown as he saw the broken piece of wood protruding from the man's right side. He couldn't tell how deeply it was buried, but a large, dark stain discolored the man's coat around it.

"Turn him over careful-like," Preacher told Lomax.

They eased the man onto his left side and then rolled him onto his back. Preacher could tell by the way the fella's head lolled loosely on his neck that he was gone. The blank, vacant look in the wide eyes confirmed it.

"What in blazes happened?" asked Lash.

"That cyclone," said Preacher. "It picked up an old, jagged piece of a board from somewhere. No tellin' where, maybe from the debris of an old, abandoned wagon that got left behind on another wagon train. No way of knowin' how far it carried that board, neither, whirlin' around and around in that funnel, before it finally shot out with enough force behind it to drive it halfway through this poor hombre. Pure, dumb luck . . . and all of it bad."

"But . . . but that don't make no sense! Nobody could ever guess that was gonna happen. To have death just come outta nowhere like that, with no warnin' . . ."

Lomax looked absolutely stricken as his voice trailed off. Simon Lash put a hand on his shoulder and said, "A prime example of the sheer capriciousness of life, my friend. Best not to dwell too much on it. That way . . . lies madness."

The grieving widow dropped to her knees beside her husband and began to wail and sob. Constance knelt beside her, put an arm around her shoulders, and tried to comfort her. Preacher, Lomax, and Lash, knowing that they weren't really suited to such things, backed away and stood there looking uncomfortable.

That lasted only a few seconds before someone called, "Mr. Lash!" They turned to look and saw Tom Linford hurrying toward them through the mud. The young scout appeared to be uninjured, too, just soaked to the skin like everyone else.

"What is it, Tom?" Lash asked sharply.

"You'd better come back up to the front. It looks like Cap'n Kemp and his brother may try to kill each other!"

Preacher didn't know what had happened, but he would have been willing to bet a new hat that it involved Virginia Kemp.

Lash said, "Roscoe, keep checking on the wagons and help anyone who needs it. Arthur, I'd appreciate it if you'd come with me."

He and Preacher started toward the lead wagon. Tom Linford slogged along beside them. The thunder had faded to an occasional boom, and the rain had slacked off. It was quiet enough now that they could hear the angry voices ahead of them.

Preacher spotted the two struggling figures off to one side of the lead wagon. They weren't that far from the bank of the Platte. The river hadn't risen; it took a lot of rain to make a stream as wide as the Platte come up very much, but that might happen yet.

Covered with mud as they were, it was difficult to tell who the two combatants were, but Preacher had no doubt it was the Kemp brothers wrestling and slugging at each other. They weren't very good at fighting. They staggered back and forth, threw more punches that missed than landed, and generally looked inept in their battling.

Their anger was sincere, though. They were putting their hearts into it, even if they weren't doing much actual damage to each other.

Virginia Kemp stood to one side, shouting, "Stop it! Stop it, you fools! There's no reason for you to fight."

The brothers ignored her. They grappled together and lost their balance as their feet slipped in the mud. With startled yells from both, they fell into the river.

Nobody was going to drown in the Platte unless they landed facedown and were out cold, neither of which applied to the Kemp brothers. Thrashing and splashing and shouting, they broke apart and struggled to stand up. As they reached their feet, Simon Lash stood on the riverbank and said in a loud, commanding voice, "That's enough!"

He got through to them where Virginia had failed. He stood there, hands on hips, glaring at them. With so much mud on their faces, it was hard to tell, but Preacher thought they looked a little sheepish and crestfallen.

"What in blazes is going on here?" demanded Lash.

Wesley Kemp wiped mud from his eyes and nose and mouth. He had to spit a couple of times before he could talk. He said, "This is none of your business, Lash. It's a personal matter, nothing to do with the wagon train!"

"*Everything* on this journey has to do with the wagon train," Lash replied.

"This is family business," Harrison Kemp said, spitting and coughing as he forced the words out.

Virginia came up to the edge of the shallow water and said, "You're both insane. You have no reason to fight. Nothing happened, except we all almost died in that terrible storm!"

"His hands were all over you," Wesley Kemp accused. "I saw it with my own eyes!"

"What you saw was Harrison catching me so that I wouldn't fall when I slipped in the mud," Virginia insisted. "That's all."

"I don't believe you!"

"It's the truth," said Harrison. "Good grief, Wes, you can't honestly believe that I'd try to . . . to take advantage of my own sister-in-law!"

Even with the mud on Wesley Kemp's face, Preacher could see the sneer that twisted the man's features. Kemp said, "You wanted to marry her yourself, before she realized she'd be much better off with me. That has to gall you, Harrison. I can see how you might want to get back at me for that by pawing her while you had the chance."

"Wesley!" Virginia said. "Do you believe I would have allowed such behavior, even if it wasn't such a ridiculous thing to accuse Harrison of?"

"You didn't seem to be struggling to get away from him. In fact, if anything I'd say you appeared to be enjoying it."

"Enjoying—" Virginia stopped short and looked flabbergasted. "Have you lost your mind? We were almost *killed!* Didn't you see that cyclone? We all could have *died!* I wasn't even thinking about anything else."

Preacher figured that was true. If Wesley Kemp wanted to be mad about something, his wife and brother had given him better reasons than what had just happened here. Maybe Kemp sensed that. Maybe he had seen more in the past than he let on and had kept his feelings bottled up for a while. He didn't strike Preacher as the sort of man to do that, but anything was possible. Almost dying in a storm, as Virginia had pointed out, was enough to make somebody's carefully controlled façade slip.

"That's enough," Simon Lash said again. "Captain Kemp, Mrs. Kemp, Mr. Kemp, you'll all have to work this out among yourselves, but I expect you to do so without violence. And the rest of us certainly don't need the distraction. Now, if this fight is over, I need to see if anyone needs any *actual* help."

"It's over as far as I'm concerned," Harrison Kemp said. "I never wanted to fight in the first place."

"Then come along with us," Lash told him. "There's bound to be someone who could use a hand. Leave your brother and Mrs. Kemp to talk."

"I don't have anything to say," snapped Wesley Kemp.

"Neither do I," Virginia added in a cold voice.

"Well, come along anyway," Lash said to Harrison, who climbed out of the river with muddy water running off his clothes. The rain, falling gently now, had started washing him off already. It soon finished the job.

As Lash had said, there were people in the wagon train who needed help. A number of the canvas covers had come loose in places and were flapping away in the wind but still attached to their wagons. A few had torn completely free and blown away. New covers would have to be rigged for those vehicles.

The man who had been impaled by the flying chunk of wood was the only one who had died in the storm. Preacher thought they had been mighty lucky, overall. A few other members of the wagon train had been injured, but none seriously. A couple of mules were dead, apparently struck by lightning. Some of the immigrants had extra livestock, so replacements would be found for that team.

Preacher approached Jesse Willis and asked, "Need a hand with anything, Willis?"

"No," Willis replied curtly.

Preacher stood there for a moment then said, "Well, I'm glad to hear it. Maybe you can help somebody else."

"Their trouble is their lookout," Willis said as he turned away.

"Wait just a minute." When Willis paused, Preacher went on, "I understand that you're one o' them surly varmints who don't like to associate with other folks. That's your right. But when somethin' like this happens, it don't hurt for ever'body to pitch in—"

"I paid my fee to join this wagon train. That's all I owe anybody. Now I'm going to tend to my stock and maybe try to find a piece of ground that's not quite so muddy."

Preacher grunted. "Good luck with that." He shook his head and moved on. He didn't figure that trying to get through to Willis was worth more than one attempt.

There was no question about waiting at least until the next day to try to cross the river. It was already late in the afternoon by the time the storm finally ended and sunlight began to slant through a few cracks in the clouds to the west. Also, the ground was a sea of mud. Lash didn't order the immigrants to pull the wagons into a circle. It was best to leave them where they were, rather than risk moving them, which might cause them to bog down even more.

"We'll make sure there's a good guard posted," the wagon-master told Preacher. "Even though I don't expect any trouble from the Indians. They won't want to move around in this muck any more than we do."

"No, it's too muddy for 'em to dash around on their ponies the way they like to," Preacher agreed. "I reckon we're pretty safe . . . for now."

Campfires were out of the question, too. No wood dry enough for burning could be found.

It was going to be a long, dark, miserable night out here on the prairie.

Chapter 15

But even the longest, darkest, most miserable night eventually comes to an end. When the sun rose the next morning, Preacher saw no clouds in the sky. It was a pale, unbroken blue from horizon to horizon.

He sat on the lowered tailgate of Cornelius Russell's wagon and said to Simon Lash, who stood nearby, "It's gonna be a scorcher today, I reckon."

"That's good," the wagon-master replied. "The sun will dry the mud. Although it's also going to make for a very muggy, uncomfortable day."

Russell leaned against the tailgate and asked, "How does the river look? Did the rain make it rise? Will we be able to cross it today?"

"We'll have to wait and see about that," Lash told him, "but the water level doesn't appear to have gone up appreciably. It's more a matter of the ground drying enough to move the wagons without too much difficulty."

Preacher lifted his head and sniffed the air. "Is that coffee brewin' that I smell? How'd anybody get a fire goin' in this swamp?"

"I don't know," said Lash. "Let's go see."

Russell went with them as they followed their noses. It didn't take long to discover that the small fire was beside Constance Bradley's wagon. She had used a hoe to scrape mud away and form a reasonably dry surface on which she had arranged some broken pieces of wood and some torn-up paper that served as kindling. The flames were small, but they were enough to heat coffee.

"Where in the world did you find fuel for that fire?" Lash asked her.

"I busted up an old jewelry box and a few other things," Constance replied without looking up from where she knelt beside the fire, feeding into the flames small sticks from brush that had begun to dry out already.

"Not heirlooms, I hope."

She shrugged. "I figured it was more important that you men have some hot coffee this morning, after everything that happened yesterday." She glanced up at Lash. "Will we be able to cross the river and be on our way?"

"I hope so. We'll wait a few hours and see how things look."

Constance smiled. "Excellent. Fetch your cups, gentlemen. I'll see if I can heat some biscuits, too. We may have to make do with that for breakfast."

"Sounds mighty good to me," Preacher told her. Constance had cleaned up and wore fresh, dry clothes this morning. She was a mighty appealing sight. Made a man feel that despite everything that had happened, there might still be a little hope for the world, he mused.

Constance wasn't the only one who managed to get a fire going that morning. People were stubborn in the face of adversity. As the sun rose higher, activity bustled around the camp.

One of the chores was grim: the burial of Fred Thomas, killed by the flying chunk of wood. Several men had to carry the blanket-wrapped body to a rise about a quarter of a mile away. When they tried to dig a grave closer to the river, the hole quickly filled with water. The rise was high enough that that didn't happen. By midday, Thomas had been laid to rest with his wife weeping over the grave and most of the immigrants praying and singing a hymn after Simon Lash read from the Scriptures.

Later, Lash said to Preacher, "This isn't the first trailside burial service I've conducted, I regret to say. But there's always a price to be paid for any worthwhile endeavor." He sighed. "I have a feeling we haven't finished paying that price."

"I'd be mighty surprised if we had," the mountain man agreed.

Several times during the morning, he had looked back along the trail they had followed to this point, checking to see if there was any sign of Jamie MacCallister. Jamie had been a good distance away from the cyclone and the center of the storm, so he should have come through just fine, but it was hard to be sure about things like that, especially considering all the lightning bolts that had struck from the heavens. Jamie was a veteran frontiersman, though. He knew how to take care of himself.

Early that afternoon, Lash sought out Preacher and said, "Let's go check the river."

"Sounds good to me." Preacher took off his hat and wiped sweat off his forehead. "This heat's good for one thing. The ground's dryin' pretty fast."

They saddled their horses and rode out into the stream again, as they had done the day before. To get there, they had to pass the Kemp wagon. Wesley Kemp was standing beside the vehicle and gave them a curt nod. Preacher didn't see Mrs. Kemp, so he assumed she was either inside the wagon or visiting with some of the other immigrants. He didn't see Harrison Kemp, either.

He hoped those two hadn't sneaked off to get together again, only in broad daylight this time. That would be a mighty foolish thing to do.

And Wesley Kemp, for the first time Preacher had known him, was packing an iron today. He had a gun belt strapped around his waist and a Colt Navy rode in the attached holster. Preacher didn't think Kemp would shoot his own brother . . . but sometimes blood made hate run even deeper than it would have otherwise.

Once again, Horse led the way across the river, picking his path. Preacher trusted Horse's instincts. The leisurely crossing proceeded without any trouble. When the two men reached the north bank of the river and rode out of the water, Lash reined in and said, "I'll go back and tell everyone to get ready to move. I can lead them halfway across, and you can meet us in the middle and bring them the rest of the way while I ride back and forth to make sure no one strays from the safe course."

"Sounds good to me," Preacher replied with a nod. "Watch out for that quicksand."

With everything that had happened so far, he was going to be surprised if they got all the wagons across without somebody bogging down—or worse.

But that was exactly what happened. Preacher and Simon Lash led the immigrants across the Platte. One family volunteered their almost grown son to drive Mrs. Thomas's wagon. Tom Linford scouted back and forth along the north bank to make sure that no one tried to sneak up on them while they were busy with the crossing. A few of the wagons that had lost their covers in the storm hadn't replaced them yet, but on a sunny day like this, that didn't matter. What was important was that the wagon train had reached a milestone.

It had done so without being attacked, too. But they were still a long way from the Devil's Crossing . . .

Jamie MacCallister came to the fresh grave in late afternoon. He stopped, dismounted, and took off his hat as he stood for a moment beside the mound of freshly turned earth. From this rise, he could see the Platte stretching out before him, broad and swampy.

"I don't know who you were, mister . . . or ma'am," Jamie said quietly, "but I hope you rest easy here."

Jamie didn't know anyone with the wagon train other than Preacher, Simon Lash, Tom Linford, and Roscoe Lomax. He couldn't even imagine a world without Preacher in it. The mountain man seemed timeless, almost immortal.

That was foolish, of course. Preacher was as mortal as anybody else. With the adventurous life he led, the odds would catch up to him sooner or later. But not yet, Jamie's instincts told him. Not yet.

He swung up into the saddle and rode on, carefully fording the Platte.

The storm the day before had been one of the worst Jamie had ever experienced. He'd seen it coming, and when he came across an old buffalo wallow, he had ridden his horse into it, dismounted, and forced the animal to lie down beside him. They were just below the lip of the wallow, high enough not to drown if it started to fill with water from the torrential rain, low enough so that lightning wouldn't seek them out and any cyclones that came along ought to pass over them.

It had been a nerve-wracking few hours when the storm hit with heavy rain, near-constant lightning, and howling winds. Jamie could tell that he wasn't at the center of it, either. The wagon train appeared to be getting it even harder.

Finally, the storm had moved on. Jamie made camp where he was, knowing that the wagons wouldn't be going anywhere until the next day, at the very least. They might be bogged down alongside the river for several days.

By the middle of the next morning, however, the sun was blistering hot. Jamie figured that might dry the ground enough for the wagons to move. He got close enough to see them, barely, and watched all day as they slowly forded the river. Careful to shade the lens of his spyglass, he studied the group until he had spotted Preacher, Lash, Lomax, and Linford. Relieved that his four allies were still alive, he waited until all the wagons had crossed and moved on out of sight before he rode north toward the Platte.

After pausing at the gravesite, he forded the river himself and followed the well-marked trail. Even though the ground had dried considerably during the day, the wagon wheels had cut deep ruts in the earth.

As dusk settled down, Jamie spotted the glow of campfires about a mile ahead. He stopped for the night, too, but made a cold camp, as he did most nights when he couldn't find a good place to conceal a fire. Water and jerky made a sparse, unsatisfying supper, but that was better than nothing. He had stretched out with his head on his saddle to sleep when he suddenly sat up straight and sniffed the air.

Wood smoke. The scent was faint but unmistakable. It wasn't coming from the wagon train camp, either; the wind was wrong for that.

Somebody else was out here on these vast plains.

Jamie looked around, hoping to spot the flicker of a distant fire, but whoever had kindled it had done a good job of hiding the flames. He didn't see anything.

When he stretched out again and laced his fingers together on his belly, he gave a grunt of satisfaction. Maybe whoever had started that fire had no connection to the wagon train and was just some other lone traveler out here. But that was mighty unlikely, Jamie knew. Every instinct told him that somebody else was following the wagon train, which was just what he and Preacher and Simon Lash expected.

He still had to keep an eye on the wagons, but now he had another goal, too.

He wanted to find out who else was stalking those wagons and the immigrants they carried toward Oregon.

The Platte River divided into north and south branches a few days later. The wagons followed the north branch. It would take them all the way to Fort Laramie, Preacher knew, and after weeks on the trail, even that rough, rude outpost of civilization would be a welcome sight for the pilgrims.

Before they reached the fort, however, they would pass another landmark. Preacher was riding at the head of the wagon train with Simon Lash when he spotted an unmistakable shape jutting up from the mostly flat landscape several miles ahead of them. A slender spire of rough, eroded sandstone, it rose from a broad mound at its base.

Lash saw it, too, and said, "Chimney Rock! That's always a welcome sight, because it signifies that we've made significant progress toward our destination."

Preacher grinned. "You know what the Lakota call it, don't you?" He added a guttural term in the Sioux tongue.

"Yes, I'm aware of that," said Lash. "I also know that it refers to the male member of an elk, but I don't believe I'll be explaining that to our charges back there in the wagons. I'm afraid most of the ladies would be scandalized."

"Don't worry, Simon. I'll just call it Chimney Rock like everybody else."

Dog had been trotting along beside them. He let out a warning bark as a figure appeared on horseback, riding toward them.

"I see him, Dog," Preacher responded. "It's just Tom, comin' back from scoutin' a ways ahead."

Linford joined them and turned his horse so he could ride alongside Simon Lash. "I didn't notice anything suspicious up ahead," he reported. "It's good to see Chimney Rock again."

"I never get tired of it, or Independence Rock, or Hell's Gate or any of the other landmarks," said Lash. "On a journey such as this, each bit of meaningful progress is something to be celebrated."

"Yeah, that's what Mr. Prescott said." Linford's voice was sober as he spoke. Preacher knew he was remembering the attack and the massacre.

"It's men like Ethan who have made so much of the country's progress possible," Lash told him. "Without them, without their adventurous, pioneering spirit, this country would still be a nation huddling in less than half of the continent. Now, though, it stretches from sea to sea, and soon there will be Americans everywhere." He smiled. "As an Englishman, I suppose I should regard that as a rather dubious prospect."

"I'm American clear through," said Preacher, "and I ain't sure I like the idea of folks clutterin' up the frontier from one end to the other. The world needs some wild places left."

"As long as you're around, my friend, I'm sure the wild frontier will continue to exist. Besides," Lash pointed out, "as one of the first fur trappers to journey to the Shining Mountains, you bear some of the responsibility for opening up the American West."

"Don't remind me," Preacher said.

They rode along in companionable silence for a while, then Lash said, "I believe I'll drop back and check on the wagons."

"Good idea. Tom and me will keep takin' the point." Preacher glanced at Linford. "Unless you need a break . . . ?"

"No, I'm fine," the young scout said. "I'll stay up here with you."

Lash nodded and turned to ride back to the wagon train. The lead wagon was about a quarter of a mile behind them. Wesley Kemp was still driving it. His wife rode with him every day. Preacher hadn't spent a lot of time watching them, but he knew that things were still a mite chilly between them.

Harrison Kemp had taken to avoiding his brother and sister-in-law entirely, though. He spent most of his time with the other single men and took his meals with different families, as the outriders usually did. Preacher didn't know how things would work out when the Kemps reached Oregon—assuming that all three did—but he didn't care all that much, either.

The immigrant he had found himself thinking about the most was Constance Bradley. Sparks had flashed between them even before the storm. The danger they had shared then had only increased the attraction. Preacher knew he was never going to settle down, but if he'd been of a mind to, Constance was the sort of woman he would seek out . . .

Dog's sudden bark of warning jolted him out of that reverie. Something whipped past the mountain man's ear, coming close enough he felt it brush his skin. He recognized the soft flutter of an arrow cutting through the air and knew they were under attack.

Chapter 16

"Indians!" shouted Tom Linford as he jerked his horse to a stop. He pulled his Colt from its holster and twisted in the saddle, looking for a target.

Preacher had been halfway expecting something like this to happen. Most of the tribes out here on the plains didn't like the steady stream of immigrant wagons crossing their hunting grounds. They put up with the incursion most of the time because so many of the trains were large and well-armed, and Indians didn't like to fight unless they were confident they stood a good chance of winning.

But this group Simon Lash was leading, while larger than some, wasn't an overpowering force. The Lakota Sioux, whose territory this was, were fierce fighters and might be willing to take on a bunch this size.

No "might be" about it, Preacher amended as he saw more than a dozen warriors leap up from the low brush. They had had their ponies lie down with them where the mounts couldn't be seen. Now the ponies surged upright, as well. Some of the Indians loosed more arrows at Preacher and Linford, while others leaped onto the ponies and charged at them.

Preacher's Sharps hung from a couple of straps on the saddle. He snatched it up and brought it to his shoulder in one smooth motion. The heavy weapon had barely come level before it boomed and kicked against the mountain man's shoulder.

One of the Sioux screeched and flew backward off his pony, arms flung wide. He landed hard, bounced, and then lay in a limp, silent heap of lifeless flesh.

"Get back to the wagons!" Preacher called to Tom Linford. "Go!"

"What are you going to do?"

"Slow these varmints down! Now git!"

Linford whirled his horse and jabbed his heels in the animal's flanks. Preacher hung the Sharps back on its straps and drew both Colt Dragoons from their holsters. He carried them with the six-round cylinders fully loaded. The cylinders had pins built into them between each chamber that fit into a notch on the hammer, making accidental discharges unlikely as long as the hammer wasn't cocked.

Preacher's thumbs looped over those hammers and eared them back as he raised the guns. Dog growled and leaned forward in anticipation, but Preacher said, "Stay." Horse stood rock-steady beneath him, not in the least spooked by the earlier shot from the Sharps, the yipping and yelling from the Sioux, or the arrows that still flashed through the air around them.

The warriors were in range now. Preacher said, "Dog, hunt!" and squeezed the trigger of the right-hand Colt. Alternating shots as he shifted his aim, Preacher emptied both revolvers in a matter of heartbeats, and every time one of the dragoons roared, an attacker either sagged and dropped his bow or toppled off his mount completely.

The lead scything into their front rank in such swift, deadly fashion made the other Sioux think better of their attack, at least for the time being. With furious cries coming from their throats, they wheeled their ponies around and retreated.

Dog had caught one of the warriors, leaping high to knock him off his mount. The big cur had him down, fangs ripping and tearing. Blood spouted in the air from the Indian's torn and savaged neck.

Preacher pouched both irons, yelled, "Dog!" and pulled Horse around. Without any urging, the big stallion broke into a run toward the distant wagon train. Preacher heard more shooting, saw puffs of powder smoke from the wagons, and knew that they were under attack as well.

As he rode, he reached into one of his saddlebags and brought out a couple of fully loaded cylinders for the Dragoons. With a deftness born of long practice, he switched them out with the empty cylinders, one gun at a time, so that when he snapped the second Colt shut, he had twelve rounds ready to go again—and plenty of targets that he was closing in on fast.

He spotted Simon Lash and Tom Linford riding back and forth along the line of wagons, firing their pistols at the Indians. There hadn't been time to circle the wagons, so the immigrants would have to fight off this attack with the vehicles strung out. Lash had gone over the plan with them a number of times: in case of attack, the women and children would stay as low as possible inside the wagon beds, behind the thick sideboards. The men would take cover either inside the wagons or underneath them, behind the wheels, and use their rifles and shotguns as they tried to drive off the Indians.

As far as Preacher could see, that was what was happening. Groups of mounted Sioux warriors charged the wagon train from both sides, but they were forced back by the stout defense the immigrants put up. Preacher glanced over his shoulder and saw that the Indians who had jumped him and Linford were chasing him, eager to get in on the fight, too.

If they joined forces with the warriors attacking the train, that would give the Sioux a superior force. They would be able to spread out even more and push the attack from all sides.

Preacher wanted to prevent that if he could, so he hauled back on the reins, brought Horse to a skidding halt, and whirled the big stallion around. Now he was again facing the Sioux, who were closing in on him quickly.

He closed that gap even faster by charging right at them.

Guiding Horse with his knees, he fired right and left, the Colts booming in a wave of gun-thunder that rolled across the prairie.

The Sioux yipped in surprise as the apparently mad white man galloped into their midst. Preacher slammed shot after shot into their ranks. Again, warriors flew off their ponies as the mountain man's bullets crashed into them. Clouds of powder smoke and dust filled the air, stinging eyes and noses, blinding the Sioux so that they didn't know where to aim their arrows.

That wasn't a problem for Preacher. Surrounded by enemies, any way he fired he was likely to hit one of them.

Suddenly he broke free of the dust and was out in the

open again. He had fought his way through the war party and come out on the other side. Now he was behind them—and his Colts were empty.

He didn't let that stop him as he wheeled Horse and once again plunged into the thick of the Sioux. He lashed out to right and left with the heavy Dragoons and felt skulls crunch and shatter as he struck savagely with the guns. He holstered the right-hand Colt and grabbed a lance away from a dying warrior who swayed atop his pony with blood running from his ears and nose. Leaning over in the saddle to avoid an arrow that flew at his head, Preacher twisted and thrust the other way with the lance. The sharpened tip penetrated a warrior's belly. Preacher put so much strength behind the blow that the lance went all the way through and the bloody tip erupted from the man's back.

Preacher didn't take the time to wrench the lance free. He let go of it and guided Horse into a tremendous leap that ended when the stallion crashed into one of the lighter Indian mounts. The pony went down with a startled whinny. Its rider spilled off, and a split second later, Horse's steel-shod front hooves came down on his head, splintering bone and pulping brain. Horse bounded away from the dead man.

The Sioux attack from this direction was awash in chaos and confusion now. They must have been overcome with disbelief that one lone white man could kill as many of them as Preacher had. More than two dozen bodies lay on the ground, either unmoving or writhing in their death throes. If Preacher had taken the time to think about it, he might have been pretty impressed with himself. But that wasn't his nature, and he was just glad to see the remaining Sioux—nine or ten of them—break and run, galloping to the north as hard as they could while they howled in outrage.

Angry they might be, but they weren't foolish enough to continue battling the mountain man. More than likely, they were convinced Preacher was both touched and protected by the spirits.

Maybe that was true, he thought as he raced toward the wagon train again.

He had two more loaded cylinders for the Dragoons in his saddlebags. He switched them for the empty ones as he approached. Once again, he struck from an unexpected direction, hitting the Sioux from their left flank. This time, instead of emptying the Colts in a swath of death, he squeezed off his shots at a slower pace, picking his targets, concentrating his fire on the warriors who seemed to be the leaders. Most of the time, he was able to identify them by their elaborate feathered headdresses. After several fell to his shots, a group of warriors broke off their attack on the wagon train and turned to deal with this new and unexpected threat.

That proved to be a mistake for one of them, because he cried out, flung his arms to the sides, and fell on his pony's neck, driven forward by the rifle bullet that smashed between his shoulder blades. As the Indian slid off his racing mount, Preacher looked past him and saw Roscoe Lomax standing beside one of the wagons, waving a Sharps over his head to indicate that he had just fired that fatal shot. The burly Lomax was an unmistakable figure.

Preacher waved back, then turned his attention to the Sioux still charging at him. He had a few rounds left in each Colt, so he bored in on them, firing as he advanced. Arrows whipped around him, but Horse zigzagged so that he and Preacher were hard targets to hit. A few of the Indians had rifles they had taken from the white victims of previous battles, but although they made a lot of racket, they weren't particularly good shots. Only one bullet came close enough for Preacher to hear its high-pitched hum as it flew past his head.

Several more Sioux fell, driven off their ponies by Preacher's deadly accurate fire, and then the party that had attacked him scattered. He turned and headed for the wagons. Horse's legs flashed as he raced toward the vehicles.

The Indians were still attacking, but without the same ferocity and enthusiasm they had displayed only minutes earlier. Preacher had been in enough of these battles to know that they were starting to regret their decision to jump the wagon train. The price they were paying was too high for what they hoped to gain.

If the immigrants could muster a stiff defense for another few minutes, the Sioux would give up and flee. But the tide could still turn in their favor. As Preacher approached, he heard Simon Lash bellowing at the settlers to keep fighting as he rode back and forth, firing his pistol deliberately at the warriors.

Suddenly, Lash tumbled off his horse. Preacher bit back a curse as he rode hard toward the fallen wagon-master. Lash pushed himself up onto his knees. He had held on to his gun, but he pressed his left hand to his side as he swayed slightly and struggled to raise the weapon.

One of the Sioux whooped exuberantly and raced his pony toward Lash, clearly intending to ride right over him.

Preacher urged Horse on to greater speed. The big stallion fairly flew over the ground. Preacher angled toward the warrior headed for Lash. When he was close enough, he left the saddle in a diving tackle that carried him into the Sioux with a crashing impact that sent them both to the ground.

The landing was hard enough to jar Preacher and stun him for half a second. As he lifted his head, he saw the warrior leaping toward him, knife lifted in an upraised hand to strike. Preacher met the attack just in time, heaving himself up and grabbing the Sioux's wrist as the knife descended. He stopped the blade with its tip just short of his throat.

Preacher held off the knife while he rammed his knee into the Indian's stomach. The man grunted in pain and heaved against Preacher's grip. Preacher rolled on the ground so that he forced the warrior under him. The man hammered at Preacher's head and shoulders with his free hand, but Preacher ignored the blows, got both hands on the warrior's knife wrist, and twisted it as he pushed down with all his strength. The man might have saved himself by dropping the knife, but he didn't realize that in time. Preacher drove the Indian's own weapon into his throat, shoving it all the way through. Blood seemed to explode out around the blade. The Sioux jerked and spasmed as death claimed him.

Preacher pulled the knife free and scrambled to his feet. A few yards away, Simon Lash was trying to stand up. Preacher ran to his side and took hold of his left arm.

"Let me give you a hand," he said over the bedlam of gunshots, war cries, and screams.

He was trying to help Lash when the wagon-master

abruptly jerked his gun up and fired. Preacher looked over his shoulder to see a Sioux warrior spinning off his feet. The lance the warrior had been about to plunge into Preacher's back dropped to the ground.

"Much obliged," said the mountain man. "Reckon you saved my life, Simon."

"Just returning the favor," said Lash. "I'm all right. One of the devils creased me with a bullet, that's all."

Preacher had seen the red stain spreading around Lash's fingers as he pressed his hand to his side. Cornelius Russell's wagon was close by.

"Come on," he said. "The professor can patch you up."

They hurried toward the wagon. As they approached, Russell leaned out the opening at the back, drew a bead with the rifle he held, and fired. It seemed odd, seeing the studious, mild-looking former educator with a powder-grimed face and his thinning hair askew. Even more jarring was the whoop Russell let out, followed by, "Got him! Take that, you heathen!"

Then he saw Preacher helping Lash and set the rifle aside.

"Bring him here, Arthur!" he called. "I'll take care of him."

"That's what I figured," Preacher said. With his assistance, Lash climbed into the wagon. An arrow thudded into the tailgate while he was doing that and embedded itself in the wood. It hung there, quivering from the impact.

Lash sprawled in the wagon bed. Russell lifted his bloodstained shirt to check on the wound. Seeing that his friend seemed to be in good hands, Preacher turned away from the wagon and ran over to pick up the lance dropped by the warrior Lash had gunned down. Armed again, even if it was only with the lance and a couple of knives—his own and the one he had taken from another Sioux he had killed, which he had stuck behind his belt— he trotted along the line of vehicles toward the freight wagons owned by Edmund Farrington. He figured he would find Roscoe Lomax there.

Lomax was defending the freight wagons, all right. He was choking the life out of a warrior he had engaged in hand-to-hand combat. The man went limp as Lomax crushed his throat. Yelling incoherently, Lomax swept the dead man up, holding him by the throat and one thigh, and pitched him into the path of a mounted warrior trying to sweep in on the wagons.

The pony's front legs got tangled up with the corpse. The animal went down hard. The warrior on its back sailed through the air, screeching in alarm. That cry ended suddenly as Preacher stepped in and raised the lance. The Sioux's momentum drove the lance completely through him. Preacher hopped aside nimbly to let the dying warrior crash facedown to the ground.

Lomax roared a curse and then exclaimed, "Preacher! You're still alive!"

In the excitement, Lomax had forgotten that Preacher was using the name Arthur, but in the middle of this wild melee, Preacher didn't figure that made any difference. He looked at Lomax and saw that the bullwhacker had blood smeared on his face.

"You all right?" he asked.

"Me? Yeah, I'm fine! Got a few cuts and scrapes, but that's all. How about you?"

"Been lucky so far," Preacher said. "I got to go check on some other folks."

"Go ahead," Lomax told him. "Ed and me got this part of the wagon train taken care of."

Preacher saw Edmund Farrington leaning over the driver's box from inside the wagon, firing a pistol toward the Indians as he shouted curses in his high-pitched voice. Obviously, he had learned some colorful language from Lomax.

Grinning at that even in the midst of this terrible battle, Preacher hurried from wagon to wagon, being careful not to step in front of any of the immigrants firing rifles, shotguns, and pistols toward the Indians.

He came to Constance Bradley's wagon and hauled himself onto the driver's box. "Constance!" he called. "You in there?"

"Arthur!" she cried. She was lying on the floor of the wagon bed, but she scrambled up at the sight of him. He reached over the seat to wrap his arms around her as she leaned toward him.

"Are you hurt?" he asked as she pressed her smooth cheek against his bearded one.

"No, no, not at all. Just scared."

Preacher held her and was about to tell her that everything was going to be all right when a face twisted by hate appeared over the tailgate at the back of the wagon. The Sioux warrior the ugly face belonged to drew back the string of the bow in his hand and poised to launch an arrow straight into Constance's back.

Chapter 17

Preacher's Colts were empty, and he didn't have time to draw one of the knives and throw it. He did the only thing he could, flinging himself backward and dragging Constance with him. She cried out as they fell, but whether in pain or surprise, he couldn't say.

He sprawled half on the floorboards and half off, with her on top of him. Crimson began to stain the back of her shirt, but the shaft wasn't protruding from her body, so he hoped the worst the arrowhead had done was graze her as it flew past.

He felt the wagon shift and knew the warrior had just climbed into it. The man would be on them in seconds. Still holding tightly to Constance, he threw his legs up, jackknifed his body, and rolled to the side. He landed on the ground beside the driver's box, awkwardly but feet first, at least. He had his left arm around Constance's shoulders and his right under her knees, holding her like a groom would carry his bride across the threshold on their wedding night.

No time for thoughts like that. He lunged along the side of the wagon, bent and thrust her through the opening between the front and rear wheels, and dumped her rather unceremoniously on the ground.

"Stay there!" he told her.

He straightened just in time for the Sioux warrior to dive from the box and crash into him.

They went down and rolled across the ground. The warrior had a knife in his hand and tried twice to drive it into Preacher's chest, but the mountain man twisted aside just in time. The Indian slashed at Preacher's face. He knocked the blade aside by hitting the warrior's wrist with his forearm.

At the same time, he finally had a chance to draw one of his knives. He brought it up at an angle and felt the blade go into the warrior's body, scraping on a rib and then penetrating even deeper. The Sioux jerked as his eyes widened in shock and pain. He tried again to stab Preacher. The mountain man shoved harder on the knife in his hand. The Indian sagged and seemed to fold up on himself. Preacher pulled the knife free and shoved him aside. The man rolled onto his back and stared sightlessly at the afternoon sky.

Preacher looked over at Constance, who lay on her belly underneath the wagon. Her head was lifted and she was breathing hard, but she seemed to relax slightly as their gazes met.

Preacher pushed himself onto hands and knees and crawled over to join her under the wagon. She embraced him and said, "Thank heavens you're all right."

"I'm fine, but what about you? Looks like your back's bleedin'."

"I think something scratched me, just as we were falling out of the wagon. That was what it felt like."

"That was an arrow," he told her. "I knew you'd get shaken up a mite if I threw us both down like that, but better'n bein' skewered by an arrow, I reckon."

"Much better." She pulled the left shoulder of her shirt down, revealing naturally golden skin, and twisted her head to try to look. "I can't see . . ."

Preacher lifted the shirt and saw the bloody scrape a few inches down her back. "You'll be all right," he said. "It just needs to be cleaned and bandaged. No real harm done."

"Thanks to you."

"I'm just mighty glad I got here when I did."

Preacher realized that the shooting was dying away now. He didn't hear any more whoops or war cries. The swift rataplan of hoofbeats still filled the air, but it was fading. All those things taken together told him that the Sioux were retreating. It was possible they would regroup and come back to try again, but after all the men they had lost, it wasn't very likely.

"Stay here. I'll go find you some help," he said to Constance.

"No, I'm coming with you," she said. "I'm not hurt very badly. I can help some of the others, instead of waiting for somebody to take care of me."

He wasn't the least bit surprised that she would feel that way. It was just like her to consider others first. He also knew it wouldn't do any good to argue with her. He crawled out from under the wagon and then gave her a hand crawling out and getting to her feet.

Since he already had hold of her hand, he didn't let go of it as they went in search of those needing medical attention or some other sort of assistance.

They checked first on Simon Lash. Cornelius Russell already had taken the wagon-master's shirt off, cleaned the wound with some whiskey he carried—"Strictly for medicinal purposes, you know"—and wrapped bandages around Lash's torso.

"I'm fine," Lash insisted. "That bullet just plowed a little furrow in me. A few days and I won't even remember it happened."

Russell said, "You'll remember it for longer than that. You need to rest, Simon."

"The professor's right," said Preacher. "You won't be ridin' point for a while. But I reckon me and young Linford can take care of that."

"Do you know if Tom's all right?" Lash asked.

"Just headed to check on him now."

Preacher and Constance did so. The shooting had stopped completely now, and when Preacher scanned the countryside all around the wagon train, he didn't see any Sioux.

No *living* Sioux, that is. Plenty of carcasses were scattered around the plains.

Preacher and Constance were headed toward the lead wagon when Virginia Kemp climbed over the tailgate, dropped to the ground, and ran toward them.

"Help!" she cried. "Someone please help! Harrison is hurt!"

Constance caught hold of the panic-stricken woman's shoulders and stopped her mad dash. She said, "Where is he?"

Virginia gestured vaguely behind her. "In the wagon. He's been shot!"

"Come on," Constance said, keeping her voice calm and level. "We'll tend to him. I'm sure he'll be all right."

Preacher wasn't sure of that at all, but he knew of only one way to find out. With the two women trailing behind him, he headed for the lead wagon.

Wesley Kemp trotted up, carrying a rifle, just as Preacher arrived at the wagon. He appeared to be all right and confirmed as much when Preacher asked him.

"Your wife says your brother's been shot," the mountain man said. "I was just fixin' to check on him."

"Harrison!" Kemp exclaimed. "Where is he?"

"Inside the wagon," said Virginia. "Hurry!"

Wesley Kemp's expression hardened. "What was he doing here? The last I saw of him, he was fighting the Indians from horseback."

"He came to see if I was all right." Virginia clutched Constance's arm. "Please, help him!"

"Of course," Constance said. "Arthur, give me a hand."

Preacher lowered the wagon's tailgate so Constance could climb in easier. He saw Harrison Kemp sitting up with his back propped against the sideboards on the right. He was conscious, so that was a good thing, Preacher supposed.

Harrison's right hand tightly gripped his upper left arm. "I'm fine," he declared. "I tried to tell Virginia that I was just winged—"

"Why were you here at all?" his brother asked coldly from the open tailgate. "You abandoned your post, Harrison. You outriders were supposed to stay mounted in case of trouble and try to fight it off."

"I wanted to make sure Virginia was all right," Harrison

snapped back at him. "Where were *you*, Wesley? You abandoned her to the savages!"

"I'm the captain of this wagon train. It was my duty to check on the others and help anyone who needed it."

"We *all* needed help!"

Constance knelt beside Harrison and said, "Both of you hush. I want to see to this wound." She moved Harrison's hand away from his bloody sleeve. "Arthur, loan me one of your knives so I can cut away this sleeve."

Preacher handed her the knife he had taken from one of the Sioux who tried to kill him and told her, "Keep it. You're liable to need it while you're doctorin'."

"Thank you." She used the blade to slice Harrison's sleeve open, revealing two bloody wounds on his arm, a smaller one on the back and a larger one on the front. She asked, "Can you move your arm?"

Harrison grimaced as he lifted the injured arm. "Yes, but it hurts like blazes."

"That's good, though. It means the bullet didn't break the bone. I'll clean the wounds." Constance looked over her shoulder at Preacher. "You can go ahead and see about the others. When you find someone who needs medical attention, send them here or to Professor Russell's wagon. If they're hurt too badly to move, fetch one of us."

Preacher nodded and told her, "Don't forget to have that scratch of yours tended to."

"I won't forget, but I'm fine for now."

Preacher figured he might have to remind her of it later. He still wanted to find Tom Linford, though, so he went in search of the young scout.

He found Linford walking among the fallen Sioux,

gun in hand and ready to fire. "I'm checking for survivors," he told Preacher. "So far I haven't found any."

"Figure on puttin' 'em out of their misery if you do?"

"That's right." Linford glared. "Do you have a problem with that?"

"Nope. They done their dead level best to kill us, so they brought it on themselves. I've done the same thing more than once, just to make sure I wouldn't have anybody comin' up on my back trail. Probably be a good idea not to take any scalps or anything like that, though. That'll just rile the Sioux even more when they come back to gather up their dead."

Linford shook his head. "I wasn't intending to. Have you seen Mr. Lash?"

"He's in Mr. Russell's wagon. Got a bullet crease in his side." At the look of alarm on Linford's face, Preacher went on hurriedly, "Russell says he ought to be fine. Looked like it to me, too."

"Well, that's a relief. I didn't want another wagon-master killed before we even have a chance to deal with those outlaws." As if he realized how callous that comment sounded, Linford added, "Mr. Lash is a fine man, too, and has tried to help me, as well. Was anyone killed?"

"Don't know yet. I haven't come across any, but I'll be mighty surprised if we didn't lose anybody."

Preacher's hunch was correct. As he continued visiting the wagons, he discovered that four of the immigrants had died in the battle—three men and one woman. The woman had been married to one of the men who was killed, so their four children were left as orphans. Some of the other families in the wagon train volunteered to take them in. What would happen to them once they reached Oregon, Preacher didn't know, but at least for the time being, the youngsters would be cared for.

He was glad that no children had been killed. Digging those small graves was a gut-wrenching task, and in the past he'd been forced to do it more often than he liked to think about.

With the situation grim but under control for the moment, Preacher, Simon Lash, and Tom Linford met at Cornelius Russell's wagon to discuss their next move. In defiance of Russell's advice to rest, Lash was up and moving around, although stiffly because of the bandages bound tightly around his torso.

He said, "We should wrap up the bodies of the poor souls who were killed and put them in one of the wagons so we can move on. I'd like to get well away from this battleground before we make camp for the night. The rest of those Sioux will be coming back to reclaim their dead, and I don't think it's a good idea to be here when they do."

Neither did Preacher. That would be just begging for trouble.

"We'll lay those poor folks to rest later," Lash continued. "It's the best we can do."

"Should we see what Captain Kemp thinks about all this?" asked Linford.

Preacher and Lash exchanged a quick glance. "I don't believe Captain Kemp will argue with our decision," Lash said, "and I don't want to prolong the discussion, so let's get busy, shall we? Tom, scout the trail up ahead."

Linford nodded and started to turn away, then paused. "Mr. Lash . . . I'm sorry I led us right into that ambush.

I swear, I didn't see any signs that Indians were about to attack."

"Don't feel too bad about it, son," said Preacher. "I didn't spot the varmints, neither. When it comes to hidin' until they're ready to raise a ruckus, there ain't nobody better'n Injuns."

"Preacher's right," Lash said. "Don't worry, Tom. My trust in you remains as high as it ever was."

"Thanks, sir. That means a lot to me." Linford went to get his horse and carry out the wagon-master's orders.

Preacher said to Lash, "Maybe you trust that young fella, but I get the idea you don't much trust Wesley Kemp no more."

"I never placed a great deal of faith in the man's wisdom. He was elected captain because he's a persuasive speaker and he's wealthy, and people tend to follow that sort. But the unsavory clash with his own brother over his wife has influenced the opinion of quite a few people, myself included."

Preacher rasped a thumbnail along his jawline and said, "Here's somethin' else you might want to keep in mind about the fella. That bullet wound his brother got durin' the scrap with the Sioux . . . He was shot from behind. I got a good look at where the bullet went in, and where it came out."

Lash's eyebrows rose. "Do you mean to imply that Wesley Kemp shot his brother?"

"I don't know," Preacher answered honestly. "Probably won't ever be no way to know for sure unless Kemp confesses to it. The Sioux were on both sides of the wagon train, and bullets were flyin' ever' which way. But Kemp was nowhere around when his brother was shot, as far as

Harrison and Miz Kemp know, so he *could* have done it. The bullet holes in his arm didn't leave no doubt that he was shot from behind, though."

Lash shook his head. "I can't accuse the man over something like that."

"Ain't sayin' you should, just that we need to keep an eye on him."

"I already was," Lash replied. "And that's not going to change."

Preacher went to spread the word that the wagon train was pulling out. That allowed him to make sure Constance was all right before they got back on the trail. He found that she had asked Cornelius Russell to tend to her minor wound. She now had a bandage tied around her left shoulder so that it covered the deep scratch on her back. She still wore the torn, bloodstained shirt. Lines of weariness had appeared on her face, but they almost disappeared when she smiled at the mountain man.

"I'm glad we're moving on," she told him. "I'll be happy to get away from this place." A little shudder went through her. "All the killing, all those bodies scattered across the prairie . . . I want to put all that behind us."

Preacher was personally responsible for a lot of those Sioux corpses, but he didn't point that out to her. Instead, he just patted her uninjured right shoulder and said, "You did a mighty fine job of helpin' folks. This wagon train's lucky to have you along."

He felt that he was lucky to have made her acquaintance, too, but that wasn't the sort of thing he talked about. Instead, he went on about the work of getting the wagon train ready to roll. When he returned to the front, he saw Wesley Kemp on the driver's box of the lead wagon, sitting there stiff and sullen with the team's reins gripped in his hands.

"Where's your brother?" asked Preacher.

Kemp jerked his head toward the back of the wagon. "In there. Virginia insisted that he was hurt too bad to ride horseback, so one of the other men is using his mount and taking his place as an outrider. She's looking after him."

Kemp didn't sound happy about that, which came as no surprise to Preacher. He also didn't care whether Kemp was happy or not. He just nodded and said, "All right. We'll be movin' out soon."

He whistled, and Horse trotted up with Dog following. Preacher had checked on them already and found that they'd come through the battle all right. The big cur had some dark bloodstains around his mouth, so Preacher was sure he had taken care of some of the Sioux.

After swinging up into the saddle, Preacher stood in the stirrups and looked back along the line of wagons. Every vehicle had a driver. He spotted Simon Lash sitting on the driver's box of Cornelius Russell's wagon, next to the professor. Lash didn't look happy about not being in front of the wagons, taking the lead, but he was following Russell's orders—for now. Preacher figured that by the next morning, though, the Englishman would insist he had recovered enough to ride and take the point again.

Meanwhile, that responsibility had fallen to Preacher. He took off his hat, raised it above his head, and shouted, "Roll the wagons!" as he waved the hat to signal the vehicles ahead.

They were on the move again, leaving the grim and bloody battleground behind them.

Chapter 18

Staying out of the fight between the immigrants and the Sioux was one of the hardest things Jamie Ian MacCallister had ever done. When he heard volley after volley of gunfire drifting over the plains, every fiber of his being wanted to gallop ahead and charge right into the battle.

But doing so would have exposed his presence behind the wagon train and ruined the plan he and Preacher and Simon Lash had come up with.

Besides, he told himself, one man wouldn't make much of a difference in a ruckus of that size. It didn't really matter whether he was there or not.

If he kept telling himself that for long enough, he might actually believe it, he mused. But probably not.

For strategic reasons, though, he hung back, finding a place where he could bring his spyglass into play and watch the battle. He was far enough away that he couldn't make out too many details, but he saw the wagons and the haze of powder smoke hanging over them. He picked out a fast-moving figure he thought must be Preacher wreaking havoc among the Sioux attackers.

After a while, the Indians broke off the assault and fled. Some of the immigrants hurried around, and in a relatively short period of time, the wagons were rolling again, heading northwest over the trail that followed the North Platte. The surviving Indians had vanished. Jamie kept an eye out for them, thinking that they might double back, but the dust cloud raised by their ponies' hooves finally faded away and didn't reappear. The Sioux were finished.

Jamie mounted up and followed slowly as he pondered what the attack meant. Could that have been a Sioux campfire he had smelled?

Or was someone else out here on these vast plains?

Either of those things was possible.

Fort Laramie was a very welcome sight a week later, just as Preacher expected. Many of the immigrants whooped and hollered with excitement when the military compound came into view. It was the first sign of civilization they had seen in a long time.

During the week since the battle with the Sioux, the wagon train hadn't run into any more trouble. The Indians hadn't come back, those wounded in the fighting had begun to recover, and the weather had cooperated, staying hot and dry. The sun-baked trail was hard, and the wagon wheels rolled easily on it, slowed down only by the deep ruts carved into the earth by the passage of thousands of other wagons in the past.

Also, as Preacher expected, Simon Lash was back in the saddle the next morning after the Indian fight, ignoring Cornelius Russell's suggestion that he ought to rest more before resuming his duties. His handsome face was haggard, and he seemed a little weak from the blood he'd lost, but other than that he showed few ill effects from the injury and didn't allow it to slow him down.

After a few days, Harrison Kemp had taken to riding again, too, carrying his bandaged left arm in a sling. Preacher heard that Victoria tried to talk him out of it, claiming he was still too weak, but Harrison insisted. Preacher figured he mostly wanted to get away from his brother. Things were still pretty chilly between them.

Constance said that the scratch on her back was healing up fine. Preacher hadn't seen it, so he didn't know. He was willing to take her word for it.

Tom Linford had settled back down into his duties as scout and seemed to be more diligent than ever. He might still get taken by surprise again—with the threats they faced, it was almost impossible to avoid that possibility ever happening—but Preacher believed the likelihood of it was small.

While the wagon train was at Fort Laramie, Simon Lash declared that they would stop for several days to give the immigrants a chance to rest, carry out any repairs that needed to be made on the wagons, and replenish their supplies from the fort's stores. After the long haul from Independence, the livestock was badly in need of some rest, too.

Also, while they were there, Preacher and Lash met with the post's commanding officer to tell him about the clash with the Sioux.

The commander, a middle-aged colonel named Alonzo Wheeler, shook the mountain man's hand and said, "I didn't expect to see you back again in these parts so soon, Preacher. It was just last year you were here, wasn't it?"

"That's right, Colonel," Preacher said. "I'm goin' by Arthur these days, though, not Preacher. Most of the folks on this wagon train don't know who I really am. Simon does, though."

Wheeler shook hands with the wagon-master and said, "It's good to see you again, too, Mr. Lash." They were acquainted because Fort Laramie was a major stop on the Oregon Trail and Lash had brought plenty of wagon trains through here in the past. "What are you and this grizzled old reprobate of a mountain man up to?"

Lash smiled at the colonel's description of Preacher, then grew sober and asked, "Have you heard what happened at the Three Crossings of the Sweetwater?"

Wheeler frowned. "You mean the Devil's Crossing? That's all anyone around here calls the area anymore, since all those massacres have taken place there. Yes, I've heard, and I'd be very happy if the War Department ordered me to take a troop of dragoons up there and clean out that rat's nest. So far, unfortunately, that hasn't happened. My hands are tied when it comes to putting a stop to it."

"Well, ours ain't," said Preacher.

Wheeler's eyes widened. "That whole wagon train is just . . . bait for a trap?"

Lash grimaced and shook his head. "Not exactly, Colonel. I was engaged to lead them to Oregon before I heard about the outlaws plaguing the valley of the Sweetwater. I wasn't going to back out on that commitment, but I thought it wise to arrange for some extra help in case of trouble."

The colonel looked at Preacher and said, "He's talking about you."

"And Jamie," Preacher said. "Jamie MacCallister. You remember him?"

"Of course! I didn't see him when the wagon train rolled in, though."

"That's because he ain't travelin' with us. He's hangin' back a ways." Preacher smiled. "Sort o' like a guardian angel, I reckon you could say. A gun-totin' guardian angel as big as the side of a mountain."

Wheeler laughed. "Yes, that's a good description of MacCallister. I assume he'll warn you if you're riding into a trap?"

"That's the plan," Preacher said.

"I wish I could lend you a hand. But the best I can do is make you welcome while you're here."

"We appreciate that, Colonel," Lash said. "And I'll make sure that none of *my* people cause trouble for any of *your* people."

"No brawls in the sutler's store?" Wheeler grinned at Preacher. "That'll certainly be different for one of your visits."

"It ain't like trouble follows me around," protested the mountain man. Then he shrugged. "Well, yeah, sometimes it seems like it does . . ."

Not in this case, however, as the visit to Fort Laramie passed peacefully. The soldiers even gathered and waved farewell as the wagon train rolled out a few days later. All the immigrants seemed more enthusiastic and optimistic now, even the normally dour Jesse Willis, who grinned as he steered his plodding team of oxen.

Preacher sensed that things were still pretty tense between Wesley and Virginia Kemp, though. That situation might not improve.

However, Harrison Kemp's arm healed enough for him to discard the sling a few days later. His left arm was still stiff, but he could use it again and had no trouble riding.

At a place called Red Buttes because of the cliffs that overhung a great bend in the river, the North Platte curved sharply back toward the south. The wagons had to ford the stream here, but unlike the "mile wide and inch deep" quagmire they had crossed before, this far north and west, the river was small enough that it wasn't any trouble.

Once on the other side of the North Platte, they entered what Lash referred to as Rock Avenue, a dry, hilly stretch with no streams or waterholes until they reached the Sweetwater River. All the water barrels were full, though, and Preacher and Simon Lash knew the wagons could make it to the valley of the Sweetwater without running out of water, as long as they weren't delayed.

After traversing that semi-arid area, the sight of the greenery along the river as it wound through rolling hills brought whoops of delight from some of the immigrants. Preacher, Lash, and Tom Linford sat on their horses at the top of a rise as the wagons rolled past them and feasted their eyes on that welcome scene.

"I always enjoy reaching this point," said Lash. "From here we follow the valley of the Sweetwater all the way to South Pass. It's not difficult, other than . . ."

His voice trailed off as he frowned in realization of what he'd been about to say. Tom Linford finished the sentence for him.

"Other than the Devil's Crossing. That's what you were thinking of, isn't it, Mr. Lash?"

"That's right," the wagon-master agreed. "It's been a challenge at times, even under good conditions. All the other times I've been through there, however, it was called simply the Three Crossings or the Triple Crossing. This business of the Devil's Crossing . . ." Lash shook his head. "I hope that soon there'll be no further cause to refer to it in that manner."

"You and me both," Preacher said. "Come on, fellas. Let's go take a look at the river."

They rode down the gentle slope with Dog trotting along beside them. When they reached the Sweetwater, the big cur bounded into the brush, no doubt in hot pursuit of a rabbit or prairie dog.

Although the river's overall course ran almost due west, it twisted and turned along the way like a giant green snake crawling through a mostly gray, brown, and rocky landscape. The grass that grew on its banks would be welcome graze for the stock, and the trees, even though they were fairly short, would provide some shade for the immigrants, especially during stops, and plenty of firewood.

Simon Lash reined in, leaned forward in his saddle, and sighed as he looked at the river. "This is beautiful country, my friends," he said as the others halted beside him. "So is Oregon. It's more like my homeland, actually, with all the rain they get out there. But if I had to choose one or the other to make my home now, I believe it would be here."

"This isn't very good country for farming," Linford pointed out. "It's too dry except right here along the river. And there aren't enough trees for logging or anything like that."

"Plus, the fur trappin' business has just about dried up," added Preacher. "You might could hunt buffalo, but I don't see how there'd be much money in that."

"Perhaps one could raise cattle," Lash suggested. "There's grazing land even away from the river, if one didn't try to have too large a herd."

Preacher rubbed his chin, frowned in thought, and shook his head. "Maybe," he allowed, "but it seems like a mighty hard way to make a livin'."

"Most things worth having *are* difficult." Lash leaned his head toward the line of wagons lumbering toward them. "That's why all those people are willing to risk such a long, grueling, dangerous trek just for the chance to make a new start." He turned his horse. "We'll camp here for the night, even though it's early enough we could make a few more miles. All the living creatures in this group could use a bit of rest."

Preacher couldn't argue with that.

By this point, the band of Sioux that had attacked them was far in the rear, so he didn't expect any more trouble from them. They were too far south to worry much about the Blackfeet. Other bands of Sioux might be in the area and could take offense at the wagon train's encroachment, but Preacher didn't think it was likely.

No, the biggest threat from here on out ought to be the outlaws who had massacred the wagon train being led by Ethan Prescott, as well as others for which they had lain in wait. If the gang ran true to form, they wouldn't strike until the wagons reached the Devil's Crossing—but there was no guarantee of that.

The immigrants greeted the decision to make camp beside the river with happiness and relief. The hard journey across the waterless wastes between the North Platte and the Sweetwater had sapped some of their enthusiasm. The cool shade and the cold, clear water restored them.

That evening, Preacher ate supper with Simon Lash, Tom Linford, Constance Bradley, Roscoe Lomax, Edmund Farrington, and Cornelius Russell. Preacher enjoyed the company with its talk and laughter and the good food Constance had prepared.

Later, though, he got restless as Lash, Lomax, Farrington, and Russell sat around smoking pipes and continued their desultory conversation with the other men. He said to Constance, "I can help you clean up if you want."

"Oh, heavens, no, that's not necessary," she told him. "I can take care of this. You just sit and talk to the other fellows."

"I was thinkin' more like I'd take a turn around the camp. I know Simon's got guards posted, but it won't hurt nothin' for me to have a look, too."

"Of course not." She put a hand on his arm. "I enjoyed this evening, Arthur. I wish there could be more like it."

"You never know," said Preacher. "Maybe one of these days."

"Should I cling to that hope?" she asked with a smile.

"Well, I wouldn't squeeze it too hard . . ."

Constance laughed, leaned forward, came up on her toes, and brushed a kiss across Preacher's cheek. "I'll keep that in mind," she promised as she stepped back.

Preacher chuckled as he turned to walk through the ring of wagons and into the shadows that had gathered quickly once the sun went down. Dog appeared from somewhere and paced alongside him.

He was challenged a couple of times by guards and had to sing out and tell them who he was. When he asked if anything was going on, they assured him that the night had been quiet and peaceful so far. Preacher hoped it stayed that way.

They pushed out a little farther from the wagons. Preacher listened to the night noises. That was second nature to him. He noticed when all the furtive little sounds abruptly went silent. He didn't believe that he and Dog were the cause.

That would mean something—or some*body* else— was moving around out here in the darkness. Preacher put his hand on Dog's head. The big cur stopped instantly and stood rock-steady beside him. A moment later, an almost inaudible growl came from deep in Dog's throat.

Then Preacher spotted a shape moving, nothing more than a deeper patch of darkness shifting through the shadows. He and Dog stood there and watched as the man—Preacher was pretty sure the shape was male— slipped closer and closer to the wagons. Whoever it was, he was alone, so Preacher didn't figure he was much of a threat. Silent as phantoms, he and Dog followed the lurker anyway.

The man went to one of the wagons and climbed inside. For a moment out there, Preacher had thought that maybe he had stumbled over Harrison Kemp again, returning from an illicit rendezvous with his brother's wife. Recently, however, Harrison had been sleeping under the wagon belonging to one of the other single men. This shadowy figure had gone to a different wagon, and it wasn't the one belonging to Wesley Kemp, either.

Preacher didn't know which immigrant went with every wagon, but when the group made camp earlier, he had taken note of where several specific vehicles were. So he knew who owned the wagon in which the shadowy figure had disappeared. Preacher had no doubt that was who he had caught slipping back into camp from some mysterious errand.

"Reckon now I've got one more good reason to be keepin' an eye on you, Jesse Willis," he whispered into the darkness.

Chapter 19

Even though the rest was a short one, part of a day and that night, it seemed to do the immigrants a great deal of good. Once again there was a sense of excitement and anticipation in the air as the wagons rolled out the next morning.

Within a few miles, that enthusiasm was heightened even more when a huge, symmetrical mound of rock beside the trail came into view ahead.

Tom Linford, who had been scouting ahead, rode back and told Preacher and Simon Lash, "There it is. Independence Rock!"

"And by my reckoning, this is the second of July," said Lash. "We're two days early, lads."

Traditionally, wagon trains bound for Oregon tried to reach Independence Rock by the Fourth of July, because if they did that, it was a sign that they would make it to Oregon while the weather was still good. That was the most widely accepted story, although Preacher had also heard the claim that the rock got its name because most of the wagon trains departed from Independence, Missouri. He didn't figure it really mattered, because now the big mound was known mostly for the fact that it was covered with names.

Thousands of travelers had passed by here, and a significant number of them had either carved their names into the rock or written them using paint, axle grease, or charcoal. The elements erased many of those names, but others dating back more than a decade were still there, proclaiming to anyone who saw them that those people had been daring—and lucky—enough to make it this far on the long journey to Oregon.

"Are you plannin' to stop and let people sign their names on there?" Preacher asked Lash.

"Of course," replied the wagon-master. Lash smiled. "It would be tempting fate to deny them the opportunity to leave their mark."

"The Devil's Gate is only a few miles on up the trail," said Linford. "They'll probably want to do the same thing there."

Lash nodded. "Yes, I know. It keeps their spirits up. That's always a good thing."

"And there's a place in the Devil's Crossing," Linford went on, "where immigrants have written their names." The young scout's face was bleak as he added, "I wrote all the names I could remember there, before I left them all behind."

Lash's voice was gentle as he said, "You hadn't told me that, lad. I'm glad you did. It was a fitting tribute to them."

"Not really. They never made it that far. Almost . . . but that doesn't count."

"It counts for something," Lash declared. "Everyone who has dared to pick up their lives and move west has contributed to the growth of this country, whether they reached their destination or not."

"That's right," said Preacher. "You can never have too many folks with gumption, no matter where it takes 'em."

Linford nodded slowly and said, "I hope you're right, both of you." With a forced smile, he went on, "These folks are going to be happy they've made it this far, that's for sure."

"Why don't you go tell them what happens next?" Lash suggested. "Let them know we've reached another milestone. Those milestones will come much more often on the second half of the journey."

With a more genuine smile, Linford turned his horse and jogged off toward the wagons. Lash watched him go and said quietly, "I hope someday that young man will put all of his demons behind him."

"I reckon that depends some on whether or not those demons are still lurkin' at the Devil's Crossin'," Preacher said.

Several times while following the wagon train, Jamie had caught a whiff of smoke at night. He knew now that someone other than the Sioux war party was stalking the wagons. It might be some other group of Indians, but he didn't really believe that. He was convinced the watcher was one of the outlaws, keeping track of the wagon train and waiting for a signal from whoever was the gang's inside man among the immigrants.

Now that the wagons had reached the valley of the Sweetwater and would be at the Devil's Crossing in a few more days, Jamie figured it was time to close in and find out as much as he could.

When he smelled the distant campfire again, he went to his horse, which he had left saddled for just this possibility, and swung onto the animal's back. He nudged the horse into motion and followed his nose.

The scent grew stronger, then faded with a slight shift in the wind, but Jamie was able to pick it up again and continued tracking it back to its source. He had been south of the Sweetwater River when he started, but he had to cross it, his horse's hooves splashing quietly in the hock-deep water, and then angle toward the northwest.

The Granite Mountains lay in that direction, and on the other side of them, the Shoshone Basin. Beyond the basin were the Absaroka Mountains. It was rugged, untamed country into which few white men other than fur trappers—and outlaws—had ever ventured. From what Jamie had seen of it, this might make good ranching country someday, if the Indian threat ever settled down.

For the time being, it was a good place for outlaws to establish their hideout. Nobody was likely to stumble over them by accident, that was for sure.

Jamie slowed his horse as the smell of wood smoke grew even stronger. He stopped and gazed ahead of him, his keen eyes searching for a tiny glow or a pinprick of light that would tell him where his quarry was camped. He hadn't reached the mountains or even the foothills yet, but off to the west, he could see them looming darkly in the faint starlight.

No sign of a campfire, though. Whoever had built the fire had done a good job of concealing it. If not for a vagrant breeze carrying the smell to Jamie, he never would have known that anyone else was out here.

He dismounted and let his horse's reins dangle. The horse was well-trained and wouldn't go anywhere. Jamie slipped ahead on foot. Despite his size, he could move almost as quietly as Preacher when he wanted to. Tonight, he definitely wanted to. He didn't know what he was going to find.

Away from the river like this, there wasn't much brush, just low grass. He saw a dark line at the top of a slight rise ahead of him, though, and figured those were bushes of some sort. The smoke smell was pretty strong now, so he dropped to hands and knees and crawled up the slope, taking off his broad-brimmed hat and flattening onto his belly just before he reached the top.

Jamie inched up the rest of the way until he could part the vegetation, which he now recognized as staghorn sumac. He peered through the gap and saw that the slope fell away sharply on the far side into a wide hollow lower than the level of the surrounding terrain.

That was how the man sitting beside the fire had been able to keep the flames hidden. The fire was small enough that it didn't cast much of an orange glow into the sky, so it wasn't likely to be spotted that way, either.

The man sat so that Jamie couldn't see his face except for a small slice of profile. He had long hair falling around his shoulders, but the broad-brimmed hat sitting on the ground to one side told Jamie that he was white, not Indian. So did the shirt with suspenders crossing it. No Indian would have dressed like that.

On the far side of the fire, a picketed horse cropped at some sparse grass. The saddle lay on the ground not far from the man, along with a blanket. Jamie knew the stranger intended to use the saddle as a pillow and roll up in that blanket, probably as soon as he finished the cup of coffee he was nursing along with an occasional sip.

As Jamie watched, the man reached down at his side, picked up something, and tipped it over the tin cup. Jamie heard a faint gurgle. So that wasn't just coffee in the cup, after all.

After a few more minutes, though, the man finished his whiskey-laced drink, wiped out the cup with a rag, and stowed it away in a pack with some other gear. Then he threw dirt on the fire to knock it down to embers and stretched out to sleep, just as Jamie expected. Within minutes, he started snoring.

It took a man with guts to travel alone and sleep out here in the middle of such a vast wilderness where there might be wild animals and wilder Indians. Of course, Jamie was doing the same thing, but his natural modesty meant he never thought of himself in that manner. Relying on his own skills, wits, and luck was just commonplace to him.

Jamie eased back down the slope until he was far enough away to stand up and walk again. He put his hat on and returned to where he had left his horse and led the animal away from there. He needed to find a good place to hole up for the night so that he could get some sleep, too.

Then, come morning, he would pick up that hombre's trail and see where it led him. Maybe this was a wild-goose chase and the man camped over yonder in the hollow didn't have anything to do with the outlaws who had been attacking wagon trains.

But Jamie didn't believe that for a second.

* * *

The Devil's Gate was only a few miles farther along the trail from Independence Rock. The immigrants had had a fine time inscribing their names on the huge rock mound. More laughter and jocular comments filled the air as they did the same on the steep walls of the sharply cut notch.

It was another milestone, and a dramatic one, at that. The Sweetwater River flowed through the narrow gorge its waters had etched into a granite ridge over thousands of years. The gorge was too narrow and rocky for the wagons to follow it, but as luck had it, the ridge petered out a few hundred yards to the south, so after the brief stop, all the wagons had to do was swing around that end of it and then turn back north to follow the river again.

Independence Rock and the Devil's Gate were miles behind them by the time they stopped and made camp late that afternoon. Split Rock, another distinctive notch in a high, rocky ridge was visible ahead of them, especially with the brilliant reddish-gold arch of the sunset behind it. Preacher knew the wagon train would be heading directly toward it for several more days. It was a landmark they could steer by, even if they hadn't had the rutted, unmistakable trail left by the thousands of vehicles that had come this way before them.

Preacher had continued to check every day for Jamie's signal but hadn't seen it. He didn't know if Jamie was still back there somewhere, or if some mishap might have befallen him. Preacher didn't believe that anything short of death would keep Jamie Ian MacCallister from doing something he'd said he was going to do, so he was confident that Jamie was still watching over them . . . but it would have been nice to see some concrete proof of that.

He'd also been watching Jesse Willis without being too obvious about it, but the man hadn't done anything else suspicious. It was entirely possible that the night Preacher had seen him skulking around, he'd been returning from answering the call of nature. Might not be anything sinister about his actions at all.

Preacher was just finishing up supper with Constance, Simon Lash, and Cornelius Russell when shouts rose somewhere else in the camp. Lash set his coffee cup aside and said, "That sounds like trouble."

"Sounds like a fight to me," said Preacher as he rose to his feet. "Reckon we'd best go see."

Russell started to get up, too, but Lash motioned him down. "Stay here, Cornelius," he said.

Russell settled back down on the keg he was using for a seat and said, "You're right. I wouldn't be much good at stopping a fight."

Preacher remembered how the professor had battled against those Sioux and wasn't so sure Russell was right. From what Preacher had seen, the former teacher had a core of steel when it was called for.

He was confident that he and Lash could handle whatever this ruckus was, though.

More people were shouting now. Preacher could tell that they were calling encouragement to whoever was mixed up in the fracas. They saw a knot of immigrants around a spot on the other side of the circle and headed for it.

"Step aside," called Lash. "Let us through, please."

He had to raise his voice and ask again before he was heard over the tumult. Then some of the members of the crowd looked over their shoulders and stepped aside to allow him and Preacher through.

Somehow, Preacher wasn't too surprised when he saw Wesley and Harrison Kemp going at it again. Harrison hadn't fully recovered from the wound he had suffered in the battle with the Sioux, so his left arm was still a little stiffer than the right. Preacher could tell it was bothering him as he watched the brothers throwing punches at each other. Harrison tried to use his left arm to block the blows, but he was only partially successful. Several of Wesley's punches got through and hammered Harrison in the body.

Harrison was doing some damage of his own, though. He was a little bigger and had a slightly longer reach. He landed a looping right on Wesley's jaw that slewed the older brother's head to the side. Wesley staggered back a step. Harrison roared in anger and charged him, obviously intending to bull Wesley off his feet.

Wesley twisted out of the way, however, and stuck out his leg. Harrison tripped over it and fought to keep his balance but went down anyway, tumbling into a nearby campfire with his arms pinwheeling. He bellowed in pain and anger as the burning wood scattered and sparks flew in the air.

Now it was Wesley's turn to charge in and try to take advantage of an opening. He raised his foot and tried to stomp his brother's head. Harrison flung his hands up, caught Wesley's foot just in time, and heaved, causing Wesley to fall over on his back.

"Reckon we ought to put a stop to this before one of

'em gets lucky and kills the other one?" Preacher asked Lash.

"I suppose. Where is Mrs. Kemp, do you think?"

Preacher had already noticed that he didn't see Virginia Kemp anywhere around the battle. "Maybe she just couldn't stand to watch it no more and climbed inside the wagon. Havin' to spend all her days around those two must be mighty frustratin'."

"Yes, I'd think so."

Harrison scrambled onto hands and knees, then went after his brother. His face was smeared with ashes from the fire, as were his clothes. He barely looked human as he dived on top of Wesley and hooked his hands around the older brother's throat.

Lash started forward. "We'd better step in before Harrison chokes him to death. I'm sure he would regret it once the deed was actually done."

Preacher moved alongside Lash, but neither of them had a chance to close in on the Kemp brothers, because at that moment a gunshot roared somewhere close by, the deafening report silencing the enthusiastic crowd as its echoes rolled away across the prairie.

Chapter 20

Preacher and Lash looked toward the Kemp wagon. Virginia Kemp had stepped out from behind it. She held a revolver in both hands. Preacher recognized it as a Colt Navy. He figured it was the same one Wesley Kemp had been packing lately. Wesley wasn't wearing a gun belt at the moment.

Virginia held the gun so that its barrel angled up toward the sky. However, she lowered it and aimed at her husband and brother-in-law as they lay on the ground. Harrison, startled by the shot, had let go of Wesley's throat. Wesley gasped for air as he tried to catch his breath.

"I ought to just shoot the both of you and put an end to this," Virginia said into the shocked silence that followed the gun blast.

"Virginia, put that down," Harrison told her in a shaky voice. "You don't want to hurt anybody."

"Are you so sure about that, Harrison? How else am I going to end this constant battle between the two of you and ever know peace again? Even when you're not trying to kill each other, the hate you both feel is almost suffocating!"

As if to confirm his wife's words, Wesley Kemp cursed bitterly and pushed a hand against his brother's chest. "Get off me, blast you!" he said.

Harrison rolled off and sat up. Wesley pushed himself onto an elbow and glared at Virginia as he went on, "This is all your fault! You could have had him if you wanted him that bad. But you chose me! You can't go back on that now. You're my wife. Nothing will ever change that!"

"The vows said until death do us part," Virginia reminded him. The words sounded especially ominous, coming as they did over the barrel of a gun with a few wisps of powder smoke still curling from the muzzle.

Simon Lash stepped forward, his right hand half lifted, and said, "That's quite enough, Mrs. Kemp. I know you feel justified in your anger, but I don't believe you really want to shoot anyone, let alone your husband or his brother."

"I just want them to leave me alone and stop fighting over me."

"And so they shall. Why don't you ride on one of the other wagons for a while, until things calm down? The rest of the way to Oregon, if need be."

Constance had followed Preacher and Lash. She stepped forward now and said, "You can travel with me, Virginia. I'd enjoy the company, and I could certainly use someone to spell me at the reins now and then."

The Colt Navy sagged in Virginia's grip. "I . . . I'm not sure I could drive a wagon . . ."

"Of course, you can. If I can, you can, too. I'll teach you."

Wesley Kemp had caught his breath. He climbed to his

feet and snapped, "Wait just a minute here! She'll stay with me, and no one has a right to say otherwise."

"She'll still be your wife," said Lash, "but if she rides with Mrs. Bradley, you and Harrison won't have a constant reason to clash." His voice hardened a little. "And as the wagon-master of this train, I do indeed have the right to make decisions regarding everyone's safety. I believe it will be better all around to follow Mrs. Bradley's suggestion."

"But I'm the elected captain!"

"So you are. But again, as the wagon-master, I can overrule you in matters such as this."

Wesley looked like he was going to continue arguing, but Harrison, who had also stood up, stepped forward and said, "That's all right with me as long as it's what Virginia wants to do."

Wesley sneered at him and said, "That's Mrs. Kemp to you. Don't forget it."

"I'm not likely to," Harrison said grimly.

Virginia lowered the gun the rest of the way and looked conflicted. She asked Constance, "Are you sure you want to make that offer?"

"Of course. Like I said, I can use a hand."

"Well, then, maybe it would be a good idea. For a few days, anyway. Just to see how things go."

"I forbid it!" Wesley Kemp bellowed. "I'm the head of this family, and my word is law!"

"Legally, you may be right," Lash allowed, "but we're a long, long way from civilization, remember. And if you force me to go along with what you want, Captain Kemp, I won't be responsible for what happens. Your wife *might* take matters into her own hands, as she's just made clear is a possibility."

Wesley Kemp stared at his wife and said, "You'd shoot me? Really?"

"I . . . I . . . Oh!" Virginia exclaimed in frustration. She threw the gun on the ground at her feet. Preacher frowned worriedly for a second, but the weapon didn't go off. Virginia stepped around it and came toward Constance. "Thank you for your kind offer, Mrs. Bradley. I accept."

Wesley took a step as if he were going to intercept her and stop her, but Lash moved smoothly so that he was in the man's way.

"Let's allow the lady to do as she wants, at least for now, shall we?" The wagon-master's voice was quiet, but it was firm enough to make it clear that he wouldn't accept any more argument.

Wesley's face twisted in anger, but he didn't try to push past Lash. He cursed and then said disgustedly as he turned away, "Fine. I don't care anymore."

He stalked to the back of his wagon without looking at either his wife or his brother and climbed inside—but not before picking up the revolver Virginia had thrown on the ground.

Constance put an arm around Virginia's shoulders and led her away. Lash raised his arms and his voice and addressed the crowd, saying, "All right, ladies and gentlemen, please go on about your business. There's nothing more to see here."

A few of the immigrants grumbled, but most moved off to gossip about the family drama they had just witnessed. Preacher heard the avidness in their voices and knew that enjoying other folks' misery was just part of human nature. Not the prettiest part, either. Thankfully, that wasn't all there was to being human.

Roscoe Lomax came up to Preacher and Lash and said, "I was tendin' to Mr. Farrington's teams. What'd I miss? Somebody get shot?"

"Not this time," replied Lash. "I don't know what the future holds, though."

"Don't reckon any of us do," Preacher said.

Jamie hated to abandon his surveillance of the wagon train, but Preacher was with the wagons and he had every confidence in the mountain man. Besides, locating those outlaws was the real reason he had come along on this journey to start with. He believed following the man he had observed the night before gave him the best chance of that.

So the next morning, he was about half a mile behind the long-haired hombre as the man entered the foothills of the Granite Mountains. The range ran parallel to the Sweetwater Valley, and from its heights, it would be easy to keep track of where the wagons were. The dust cloud raised by the wheels and the hooves of the teams was clearly visible a couple of miles to the south.

Jamie's years of experience and natural cunning made it possible for him to follow the stranger without being seen. He took advantage of every bit of cover he could find and never allowed himself to be skylined. Every now and then he lost sight of his quarry and had to pause for a while until he spotted the rider again. The man stopped occasionally to rest and water his horse, too. Jamie also stopped at those times, not wanting to get too close and run the risk of being spotted.

Jamie had been through here before, but several years had passed since then. Despite that, he had a good idea where they were going. Once he had ridden over a trail or even through an area, he never really forgot it. He saw the notch in the mountains up ahead and remembered it was called Split Rock. Once the wagon train was past it, the Devil's Crossing would be only a day away.

The outlaws could be lurking anywhere in this region, Jamie realized—if they were around at all.

When the immigrants made camp that evening, their cooking fires were clearly visible to Jamie from his position on higher ground in the foothills to the north. After so many weeks with no one to talk to except his horse, he briefly felt the pull of wanting to be around some of his fellow human beings again. Like most veteran frontiersmen, being alone didn't really bother Jamie, but it was good to associate with people every now and then. Even the most solitary mountain men had enjoyed the yearly rendezvous.

That would have to wait, however. Tonight, Jamie made another cold camp, ate an unsatisfying supper of jerky and water from his canteen, and after resting for a short time, he left his horse there and went in search of the stranger's camp.

It didn't take him long to detect the wood smoke scent. The smell was even stronger than usual tonight. The fella must feel pretty confident that he was out here alone, mused Jamie. He followed the scent easily.

The trail led to a small canyon that meandered through the foothills. A couple of bends would be plenty to conceal the flames. Jamie stayed near the canyon's rocky wall on the east side, which rose about a dozen feet above his head. The canyon itself was forty feet wide.

Brush clumped along the base of the wall. Slabs of rock that had broken away from it in ages past littered the ground as well. Jamie had plenty of cover as he drifted through the shadows and closed in on the stranger's camp. When he was near enough to hear the campfire crackling, he took off his hat and edged his head past the next bulging outcrop of rock to risk a look.

The stranger sat on one of those small stone slabs, in front of which he had built his fire. A coffeepot sat at the edge of the flames. Jamie smelled the coffee brewing and licked his lips.

Tonight, the stranger sat so that the orange glow of the fire washed over his face, and Jamie could see it. The man had blunt, coarse features, and a close-cropped beard covered what looked to be a pugnacious jaw. In the fire-light, his hair and beard were reddish brown, with a few touches of gold. He was a big man, with broad shoulders and long, muscular arms. A revolver rode in a cross-draw holster on his left hip. What looked like a long, heavy-bladed hunting knife was sheathed on the right side. A Sharps carbine leaned against another rock, within easy reach. The stranger had the look of a man who could handle just about any trouble he ran into.

Jamie figured there was a good chance he might put that theory to the test, sooner or later.

He pulled back around the outcropping and put his hat on again. Now that he knew where his quarry was camped, he could fetch his horse and move up to a spot where he'd be able to stay hidden and keep an eye on the canyon mouth at the same time. He didn't want the big stranger slipping away without him knowing about it.

He had taken only a couple of steps when something thumped against the crown of his hat, bounced off, hit the brim, and bounced off again, this time to the ground.

Jamie knew instantly what it was. A pebble had fallen from the top of the canyon wall and struck his hat. The question was whether it had come loose on its own, as sometimes happened . . .

Or if someone had knocked it down from up there.

That thought flashed through Jamie's mind, and he reacted just as quickly. He leaped forward, twisting toward the canyon wall and palming out the Walker Colt at his hip. If he'd jumped like that and it turned out there wasn't anything above him, he might feel a little foolish, but better that than being ambushed.

As he moved, a dark shape launched from the rim and plummeted toward him. Jamie's swift instincts had carried him out of the way, though. Instead of landing on top of him, the would-be attacker missed completely and crashed to the ground. Jamie back-pedaled more and covered the man with the Colt as he groaned.

Whatever was going on here, it was bound to have alerted the bearded man Jamie had been trailing. He was liable to come running around that bend any second now, gun in hand. Jamie was ready for that, too.

But he couldn't look in three directions at once, and when he heard boot leather scrape on the rim above him, he knew he wasn't out of trouble yet. Not hardly. He jerked the Colt up and tipped his head back so he could see. Another dark shape loomed and blotted out some of the stars.

This time, Jamie didn't have a chance to get out of the way. The man who had just leaped from the top of the canyon wall slammed into him feetfirst, driving him to the ground. A boot heel landed hard on Jamie's right shoulder, making that arm go numb. His fingers refused to work. The Colt's butt slipped out of them.

"Get him!" a man's deep voice called urgently. "Get the big son of a buck!"

Jamie would match his strength against any one opponent. He had won battles where he was outnumbered three to one, sometimes even four to one. This attack was worse. Half a dozen men leaped into the canyon from the shallow rim and swarmed around him. He made it to his feet and swung his left arm in a sweeping blow, hitting at least two of them. The impact shivered satisfyingly up his arm.

The next moment, somebody landed on his back. The weight staggered him. The man wrapped his legs around Jamie's waist and clutched his neck, howling, "I got him, I got him!"

That triumphant yell became a screech of pain as Jamie reached back, grabbed the man by the hair, bent forward, and heaved. The attacker went flying over his head before Jamie realized his right arm had started working again.

His gun was somewhere on the ground, and he didn't have time to look for it. A fist came out of the darkness and landed squarely on his jaw. The punch packed enough power that it staggered him.

"Grab him and hang on to him!" that deep voice bellowed. Jamie wondered fleetingly if it belonged to the man he'd been trailing. The fella had seemed big enough to go with a voice like that.

Somebody else tackled him from behind. Jamie kept his feet, but the man clung stubbornly to him. Another man had hold of his left arm. A third gripped his right arm. Jamie couldn't shake any of them off.

A blow exploded in his midsection. He grunted in pain and would have bent over, but the men holding him prevented that. Again and again, big, hard fists hammered into him until it seemed that a huge ball of pain had engulfed him.

The man started in on his face then. Jamie's head jerked from side to side, driven by the force of the brutal blows.

When he was a younger man, he could have taken on all of them, he thought fuzzily. He could have beaten them now if not for the big bruiser doing most of the damage. Jamie would have been pretty evenly matched with him, one on one. With five or six more men against him, they were just too much.

"Dadgum, Zeke!" gasped one of the men holding Jamie. "You're gonna kill him!"

"No, I'm not," replied the deep-voiced man, confirming that he was the one who'd been slamming those fists into Jamie. "I just don't want him giving us any trouble while we take him back to the boss."

He had walked into a trap, thought Jamie. The outlaws had a man watching the wagon train—this man called Zeke—but they also had somebody watching the watcher. And *that* man had spotted Jamie. They had lured him on until they had him where they wanted him, and he had fallen for it.

Zeke hit him again, then said, "Let him go and step back."

"Are you sure about that?"

"Do what I told you, blast it!"

The hands fell away from Jamie. He swayed but caught himself. He was going to try to throw himself at Zeke and grapple with the man, maybe get his hands around the varmint's throat . . .

Before he could do that, Zeke clubbed both hands together, swung his arms, and smashed Jamie in the face with a terrific blow that sent him flying backward, right into the deepest darkness he had ever seen.

Chapter 21

Waves of heat beat against Jamie's face. A garish red glare penetrated his closed eyelids. Those were the first two things he grew aware of as consciousness returned to him.

If he didn't know better, he would have said that he was waking up in hell.

He kept his eyes closed, not wanting to announce to anyone who happened to be looking at him that he was awake. His head throbbed with every beat of his heart. He ignored that pain and took stock of himself instead.

Slowly and carefully, so that no one would notice, he tried to move his arms and legs. He couldn't. He was tied hand and foot. His arms were pulled behind his back and his wrists lashed together so that he lay in an awkward, uncomfortable position.

He was lying on rocky ground. The way the sharp places poked at him added to his discomfort. By now he had figured out that he wasn't in hell but rather was lying fairly close to a large campfire. The sounds of men's rough voices talking and laughing among themselves confirmed the theory that had formed in Jamie's mind.

The outlaws had taken him prisoner, and he was in their camp right this very minute.

Somewhere not far away, a man said, "I don't think that big ol' codger is ever gonna wake up, Zeke. You killed him that last time you walloped him."

"Naw, he's alive," replied deep-voiced Zeke. "I made sure he was breathing before we tied him up and slung him over his saddle. It's just that when I hit somebody, he stays hit for a while, by grab!"

Jamie heard footsteps approaching him. They stopped, and a second later a boot toe thudded into his ribs. He couldn't hold back a grunt of pain.

"Wake up, mister," Zeke said. "It's time for you to tell us why you've been skulking around after me like that."

Jamie wasn't going to tell him anything of the sort, didn't even want to acknowledge that he was conscious. Then Zeke went on, "Somebody throw a bucket of water in his face." Jamie didn't see any need to suffer that indignity, so he stirred and let out a groan.

"Never mind," said Zeke. "He's coming around."

He kicked Jamie again for good measure. Jamie opened his eyes and glared up at the man. In the firelight, he got his best look so far at Zeke. He was indeed the big, bearded man Jamie had been following for the past few days.

Zeke put his hands on his hips and returned Jamie's glare. "You'd better speak up," he warned. "The only reason you're still alive is because I'm curious. It'd be simpler just to kill you. Then we wouldn't need to worry who you are or what you're doing out here."

"If I satisfy your curiosity, you blamed sure won't have

any reason to keep me alive any longer," rasped Jamie. "How dumb do you think I am?"

Zeke chuckled. "Dumb enough to get caught. Not much question about that." He hunkered on his heels so he could get a better look at Jamie. "What's your name?"

The odds were that none of these outlaws had ever seen him before, but some of them might recognize his name, thought Jamie. It didn't seem like it would be a good idea to give it to them, so he said the first thing that came into his mind.

"My name is Smith. Shawnee Smith."

The Shawnee were the Indians that had attacked his family, many years ago when he was a youngster, and made him a slave for quite a while. He would never forget that terrible time in his life, but he might as well get some use out of the experience, he told himself.

"Well, I never heard of you, Shawnee Smith."

Jamie snorted in contempt. "I probably never heard of you, either."

That touched a nerve in Zeke. He reached out and gripped Jamie's chin, digging his fingers in painfully on each side of the jaw.

"My name's Zeke Connelly," the big man growled. "You won't forget it the rest of your life . . . because that's not going to be very long!"

He gave Jamie's chin a hard shove, then straightened to his feet.

"I'll let the boss know you're awake. You'd better answer his questions, if you know what's good for you."

"That's a problem," Jamie said as he raised his head as much as he could. "I never did learn to pay much attention to jackals howling."

Zeke Connelly just sneered and turned to walk away.

Jamie sagged back and took advantage of this opportunity to look around. The other outlaws weren't watching him closely.

From where he was, he saw about a dozen men gathered around the large campfire that still sent waves of heat against his face. He could tell that other campfires were burning around the place, though. He heard them crackling. That meant the gang could number three dozen men or more. Probably more.

The ones closest to him were typical hardcases: lean, wolfish, beard-stubbled hombres who looked like they would kill a man just as easily as saying howdy to him. One on the other side of the fire caught Jamie's eye in particular.

That man sat with his back propped against a rock and his legs stretched out in front of him, booted feet crossed nonchalantly at the ankles. He wore canvas trousers, a white shirt with a buckskin vest over it, and a flat-crowned black hat that was tipped forward far enough to conceal all of his face except for a strong jaw and a wide mouth. A pair of gun belts crisscrossed at his narrow hips. A small buckskin bag hung from a rawhide thong in the open throat of his shirt. Indians carried medicine bags like that, but so did a lot of white men, including Preacher. The other men were joshing with each other and passing around flasks and jugs, but this one sat aloof.

That made him seem more dangerous to Jamie, despite his casual, even drowsy attitude. Jamie would be willing to bet that he was watchful under the lowered hat brim, not asleep.

While he had the chance, and now that he wasn't

pretending to still be unconscious anymore, he twisted his arms back and forth as much as he could, trying to work some slack into the bonds around his wrists. He knew he wasn't doing much good, though. Whoever had tied him had done too professional a job of it.

While he was occupied with that, he realized that Zeke was coming back. Another man followed him. The second man was burly and barrel-chested in the firelight, although not as big as Zeke. He was older, too, with a beefy face, white hair under a black hat, and a bristling white mustache.

He stopped alongside Zeke and looked down coldly at Jamie. "This is the fella who's been trailing you?"

"That's right."

"Good-sized gent. But too old to be much of a threat, I'd say."

Jamie said, "You're a fine one to talk, mister. From the looks of it, you're older than I am."

The boss threw back his head and laughed. "Yeah, maybe so. All right, so you've still got the bark on you." He grew serious. "What I want to know is why you've been following my man Zeke here for the past few days?"

"I haven't been following anybody," Jamie declared. "Your *boy* Zeke just happened to be going the same way I was."

Zeke's rugged features tightened at the insult. He put his hand on the butt of his gun and started to step forward. "Maybe after a pistol-whippin', that mouth of yours won't be so loose."

The boss put out a hand to stop him and said, "Don't let him put a burr under your saddle, son." He turned back to Jamie. "You told Zeke your name is Shawnee Smith."

"That's right."

"I never heard of any Shawnee Smith."

"Have you heard of everybody west of the Mississippi?"

The boss grunted. "Maybe not, but I've been out here a long time. Most of the top men, I've met or heard of. But you're a stranger to me, friend, and I don't like strangers poking their noses in where they don't belong." He raised a hand to forestall whatever Jamie was about to say. "Don't try spinning that yarn about how you just happened to be going the same way. We've been keeping an eye on you, and we know that's not true. And then tonight, you came creeping up on Zeke's camp like you were fixing to ambush him. Can't blame us for not believing you."

Jamie locked eyes with the man for a moment, then shrugged as best he could, tied up as he was.

"I don't cotton to talking in this position. Either cut me loose or at least somebody help me sit up. You want the truth, I'll give it to you, mister."

"Somehow, I still have my doubts." The boss shrugged, too. "But I reckon I see your point. Proud man doesn't like having a bunch of folks looming over him. Is that pride I see on your face, friend?"

"Proud enough not to grovel, if that's what you mean," snapped Jamie.

The boss motioned to some of the men gathered around the fire. "Pick him up and set him on that rock."

Zeke began, "Boss, are you sure you want to—"

"If I didn't want to, I wouldn't be doing it, would I?"

Zeke wasn't going to argue with that. He crossed his arms over his chest and scowled at Jamie as several outlaws grasped his arms and lifted him. They left his wrists and ankles tied as they positioned him on a slab of rock that was farther away from the roaring campfire. That gave Jamie some welcome relief from the heat.

The boss stood in front of him, pushed back the long coat he wore, and said, "All right, mister, let's have it."

"You're the bunch that's been looting those wagon trains coming through these parts, aren't you?"

Zeke cursed and reached for his gun again. "He's some kind of lawman—"

"Lawman!" Jamie exclaimed. "Call off this pup of yours, mister, or I'll whip him with both hands tied behind my back! Lawman . . . The word puts a bad taste in my mouth. I never packed a badge in my life."

The boss rubbed his chin, frowned in thought, and said, "He sounds like he's telling the truth about that part, anyway." He paused. "You don't expect us to just admit to such as a thing as you've accused us of, do you?"

"Don't you understand by now?" Jamie shot back. "I want to throw in with you."

"Why in blazes would we agree to that?"

"I reckon you could use me," Jamie said with a scathing note in his voice, "considering that it took this big galoot and half a dozen others to bring me here. And they were only able to do that because they took me by surprise. In a fair fight, I might've beaten the whole bunch of them. I damn sure could handle any one of them."

He was looking right at Zeke Connelly as he said it.

Zeke's face darkened with anger, just as Jamie expected. He clenched his fists.

But the boss said, "Settle down, Zeke. Don't you see that he's just trying to goad us into turning him loose? Although I'm not sure what good he thinks that would do him. There are forty of us and only one of him."

"Yeah, but it's that one"—Jamie nodded toward Zeke—"who kicked me while I was down. I don't like that."

"Go ahead and turn him loose," said Zeke. "I don't care. I'm not afraid of him. Let me have him and I'll kill him this time. He's just been lying to us anyway."

"I'm not so sure about that," the boss said slowly. "If you really do ride on the wrong side of the law, mister, who have you ridden with in the past?"

Jamie knew he would be running a calculated risk by naming names. There might be someone among the gang who would know he was lying. But he could tilt the odds in his favor, if his brain worked fast enough.

"Hector and Ulysses Gilbert," he said, naming two notorious thieves and murderers who had roamed the Missouri Ozarks twenty years earlier with a gang just as unsavory as they were. "Abner Hammond, from back in Pine Bluff, Arkansas. Seminole Jessup, down in Indian Territory. Cougar Jack LeCarde in Kansas. Those names good enough for you?"

The boss let out a low whistle. "Those are some bad hombres you're talking about, Smith. Thing is, they're all dead now, and their gangs are busted to hell and gone. Nobody in our little group is going to be able to vouch for you."

"That's not my problem. I answered your question and told you the truth. You said it yourself, all those gangs scattered when the law finally caught up to the men running them. You blame me for lighting a shuck? Reckon I should've stayed and got strung up with the others?"

Zeke sniffed. "I still say he's lying."

Jamie looked straight at him and said, "That's because

you want somebody else to kill me so you won't have to answer that challenge I threw right in your face."

"You just keep pushing, don't you, friend?" the boss said. "All right, I'm going to give you what you seem to want so bad." Again he gestured to one of his men. "Cut him loose."

"That's more like it," said Zeke, grinning in anticipation as he rubbed his hands together.

"Just one thing," the boss went on to Jamie. "If Zeke here gets the best of you and decides to kill you, no one here is going to stop him."

One of the outlaws moved behind Jamie, holding a knife. The skin on the back of Jamie's neck prickled a little at having cold steel behind him like that, but he ignored it. A second later, he felt the blade sawing at the cords around his wrists. As they came free, he said, "Fair enough. But it goes the other way, too."

"A fight to the death," mused the boss. "Well, that ought to be entertaining, if nothing else."

Word of the impending battle spread quickly around the camp. Men left the other fires and came over to gather in a big circle. The man with the knife cut the bonds on Jamie's ankles. Jamie pulled his arms around in front of him, rolled his shoulders, and shook his hands to get some feeling back into them. Pins and needles stabbed into his feet as he stood up.

The outlaw he had noticed earlier, the compactly built two-gun man with the medicine bag around his neck, stood up and ambled off to the side where he could watch the fight without being in the way. Jamie frowned as something stirred in his brain, but he didn't have time to worry about it right now. Instead, he asked, "How's this fight going to happen? Knives, bare knuckles, what?"

Zeke flexed his fingers and said, "I want to tear you apart with my bare hands, old man."

"You're the one who was challenged, so I reckon it's your right to decide that," the boss agreed. "Bare knuckles it is. No holds barred." He nodded to Jamie. "If you actually rode with those ruffians you mentioned before, you ought to be used to things like this. Most of them liked a good brawl."

"That they did," said Jamie. "So do I."

He curled his hands into fists and moved forward. After being tied up like that, his legs didn't work quite as well as he would have liked, but he was getting steadier on them with every passing second.

The boss waved everybody back, giving the two fighters even more room around the blazing campfire. Jamie knew he would have to keep an eye on those flames, too. Zeke might try to pin him against them and use the fire as a weapon. That would be a sound strategy.

Zeke didn't appear to be much of a strategist, though. He bellowed and charged at Jamie like a bull, his big, mallet-like fists swinging wildly.

Chapter 22

Jamie darted aside, only to realize too late that Zeke's seemingly out-of-control attack was a feint. Zeke changed course with a nimbleness unusual in such a big man. Instead of trying to hit Jamie in the face, he sunk a hard left hook into his midsection.

The blow rocked Jamie but didn't stagger him. Since Zeke was within reach, he grabbed the outlaw's shirt front and swung him to the side. Jamie was a little taller and heavier and was able to throw Zeke off his feet. Jamie tried to dump him in the fire, but Zeke twisted agilely and avoided the flames. He rolled and came up quickly on his feet as Jamie went after him.

Jamie got a punch in, though, before Zeke could raise his arms to block it. The blow landed solidly on Zeke's bearded jaw and drove his head to the side. Zeke took a step back and Jamie bored in. He pounded a left to Zeke's sternum, whipped a right to his face again. Blood spurted from Zeke's nose and lips.

Zeke roared in pain and fury and threw himself at Jamie with surprising speed. He got his arms around Jamie's waist and rammed his shoulder against Jamie's chest. Zeke pushed hard with his legs. His weight forced Jamie backward.

Jamie tried to plant his feet, but Zeke was even more like a wild bull now. His rush knocked Jamie over. Pain shot through Jamie when he crashed down on his back with Zeke on top of him. The impact might have cracked some of his ribs. At the very least, they were going to be bruised.

But he didn't have time to worry about that, because Zeke was trying to get hold of his throat, while at the same time jabbing his knee into Jamie's belly. If Zeke ever locked his hands around Jamie's throat, that would be the end of the battle. He would choke the life out of his opponent.

Jamie hammered the side of his right hand against Zeke's left ear. Zeke grimaced and tried harder to get the stranglehold. Jamie grabbed his right ear and twisted. Zeke howled. Blood from his smashed lips spattered across Jamie's face.

Jamie bucked up from the ground. Zeke tried to hang on, but Jamie felt him slipping. Another violent heave toppled him off to Jamie's left. Jamie rolled right, ignoring the pain that stabbed through him, and came up on hands and knees. A few feet away, Zeke was doing the same thing. They reached their feet at the same time and stood there glaring at each other as their chests heaved. The brutal battle was taking a toll on both of them.

But Zeke was younger. He might have more stamina. Jamie didn't think so, but it was a possibility. He needed to end this fight as swiftly as he could.

Many of the outlaws gathered around to watch the

fight were calling encouragement to Zeke, but not all of them. Jamie wondered briefly if the big, bearded man had some enemies among the gang. Maybe not all of them were rooting for him to win. They might be willing to accept the newcomer—*if* he emerged victorious in this battle.

Jamie grinned. "Caught your breath yet?" he asked.

"Don't worry about me, old man," snapped Zeke. "Pretty soon, you're not going to be breathing at all."

"How do you figure? You're not putting that air to any use except running your mouth."

Zeke yelled a curse and charged again. Jamie didn't try to feint or dodge. He stood his ground, stood toe to toe with Zeke, and slugged away.

It was a lot of punishment to absorb, but the same was true the other way, too. Zeke was starting to look a little glassy-eyed after several of Jamie's punches landed on his head. Jamie mixed things up with some hooks to the body, but while he was doing that, Zeke managed to sneak in a right uppercut that rocked Jamie's head back and made the world spin crazily for a moment. Zeke followed it with a left, then another right. Jamie went over backward.

Zeke came in with his right leg raised to stomp. If his boot heel landed in Jamie's face, it would crush Jamie's skull like an eggshell. Jamie forced nerves and muscles to work and flung his hands up just in time to catch Zeke's foot. He yelled with effort as he held it back, then heaved and threw Zeke backward in a wild sprawl.

Zeke landed in the fire. That was pure luck. Jamie hadn't intended it. But he would take it. Zeke screamed and thrashed and fought frantically to get out of the flames.

He managed to scramble out of the fire, but by then Jamie was set and ready. As Zeke came upright, Jamie landed his hardest punch yet to the outlaw's jaw. The force of the blow twisted Zeke around, and he fell again into the flames, this time face-first. The way that he didn't try to catch himself showed that he was out cold.

The camp had gone absolutely silent now except for the crackling of the flames. Most of the outlaws hadn't expected Jamie to win this fight. They were shocked that Zeke had been defeated.

The stench of hair burning stung Jamie's nose. He stepped closer to the fire, reached down, and clamped his right hand around Zeke's left ankle. He backed up, dragging Zeke clear of the blaze. Zeke's clothes were on fire, but at a sharp command from the boss, several men broke out of their stunned reverie and dashed forward to slap out the flames on the burning garments. Another man ran up with a bucket of water and dashed it over the senseless form. Zeke shuddered but didn't react otherwise.

The boss gestured at Zeke and told his men, "Pick him up and take care of him. Get something on those burns."

While the outlaws were doing that, the boss turned to Jamie and went on, "I thought this was a fight to the finish."

"If I'd broken his neck, I wouldn't have lost a blasted second of sleep over it," Jamie answered honestly. "But I couldn't stand there and let him burn to death. It would have stunk up the whole camp, for one thing."

A grim chuckle came from the boss. "It would have, at that. But you didn't do yourself any favors by letting him live, Shawnee Smith. You'd have been better off putting a bullet in his head. Nobody would have tried to stop you."

"I don't have a gun," Jamie pointed out. "If I did, things might have been different."

The boss regarded him intently and said, "We didn't have a deal, you know. Nothing was said about how you could throw in with us if you beat Zeke."

"That was the impression I had."

"But it was just your impression." The boss shrugged. "Still, I'm not sure anybody else in the bunch could take Zeke, *mano a mano*, and that accomplishment ought to be worth something. I'll keep it in mind. While I'm thinking it over, you don't have to be tied up again. Nowhere you can go and not much you can do out here."

"Does that mean I get my guns and my knife back?"

"Don't push your luck," the boss advised him. "Sit down, have some coffee. I'll tell one of the boys to get you some food. After that fracas, you're probably hurting, so I reckon you can use the rest. Don't try anything, though. We'll be keeping an eye on you."

"Coffee and something to eat sound mighty good right now. So does taking a load off my feet."

The boss nodded and gestured toward the rock where Jamie had been sitting earlier. "Get to it, then."

As Jamie sat on the rock, enjoying the coffee and food that was brought to him, he took a better look around the camp. Three fires were burning, as he'd suspected. The boss had already said that the gang numbered forty men. Jamie didn't know if that was an exact count or an approximation. Under the circumstances, it didn't matter.

They were in a canyon similar to the one where Zeke

had been camped earlier, but it was larger, at least fifty yards from side to side, and the steep stone walls rose seventy or eighty feet and were too sheer to climb. A small creek meandered along the canyon floor, passing not far from the campfires. Scrubby trees and brush grew along it. The canyon curved at both ends after running fairly straight for a couple of hundred yards.

Jamie supposed this place was even deeper in the foothills of the Granite Mountains. It was handy enough for the outlaws to use as their headquarters while they plotted their next attack on one of the wagon trains passing through the Devil's Crossing. From here it was a day's easy ride to the site of the massacre Jamie had heard about, although it would take longer than that for the much slower moving wagons to reach it.

He recalled Preacher talking about how it was possible the gang scattered after committing one of their atrocities and only came back together when they were ready to strike again. Jamie could believe that, because there was no sense of permanence about this place. Enough trees grew along the creek that they could have built cabins if they wanted to, but instead he saw only a few tents. Some of the outlaws had simply spread their bedrolls on the ground.

He hadn't seen where they took Zeke Connelly to tend to his injuries, but a while later, the canvas flap at the entrance to one of the tents was pushed back and a couple of men emerged, helping a shambling figure between them. They started toward the fire. As they came closer, Jamie saw that the man receiving the assistance was Zeke. His hands were wrapped in bandages. A strip of white was bound around his head, too. His forehead and cheeks glistened with some sort of fat that had been rubbed on them to help with the burns. He appeared to be only half-conscious, but he was aware enough that from time to time he lifted the bottle he held awkwardly by the neck in one bandaged hand and took a long, gurgling swallow from it.

That whiskey was probably the only thing the outlaws had to dull the pain Zeke had to be feeling.

With his friends' help, he stumbled up and sat down on a rock on the other side of the fire from where Jamie sat. His head hung forward on his chest as if he were in a stupor. Slowly, though, it rose until he was gazing directly across at Jamie, and the light of hate in his eyes burned as brightly as those leaping flames between them.

He didn't do anything else, just sat there and glared and took a drink from the bottle every so often. Jamie returned the look, coldly and levelly.

Finally, the bottle of whiskey was empty. Zeke threw it into the fire, where it broke and caused a momentary flare-up as the residue inside the bottle ignited. Then Zeke struggled to his feet and stumbled away, heading back toward the same tent he had come out of a while earlier.

Jamie was watching Zeke go when a quiet voice said beside him, "Boss man was right. You should've killed him."

Jamie turned his head to look. He hadn't heard anybody come up to him, which meant the man who had spoken was light on his feet. Somehow, Jamie wasn't surprised to recognize him as the two-gun man he had noticed earlier. The hombre's hat was still pulled low, and his face was tipped so that Jamie couldn't get a good look at him. The tip of the quirley between his lips glowed orange as he inhaled.

"I never was much on killing men in cold blood," said Jamie. That was probably an unusual attitude for a hardened outlaw such as the one he was pretending to be, but he was too tired, and his ribs hurt too much, for him to care.

"Feeling like that might get you dead someday." The man's easy drawl was little more than a whisper.

"I'll take my chances. What's your name, mister?"

"They call me Absaroka."

"Because you're from those mountains?"

"Yeah, sure." The gunman drew in on the cigarette again, burning it down to a butt that he dropped at his feet and ground out with a boot toe. "Just watch yourself . . . Shawnee Smith."

Jamie stiffened. The way Absaroka paused before saying the name made it sound as if he knew it was false. But if he recognized Jamie, he didn't say anything else about it, just ambled away with his thumbs hooked casually in the crossed gun belts.

Jamie watched the slender form drift off into the shadows. He didn't believe for one second that he could consider Absaroka a friend or an ally—but at least maybe he wasn't an outright enemy like Zeke Connelly.

More than likely, all the other members of the gang would be happy to kill Jamie at the slightest provocation. But the fact that he wasn't dead yet meant he had a chance, at least, of becoming one of them. And if he became one of them, he might be able to discover their plans in time to get a warning to Preacher so the members of the wagon train would have a hot lead welcome waiting for the gang.

All he could do at the moment was wait and see how things played out . . . and try to stay alive.

That might prove to be the biggest challenge of all.

Chapter 23

By the next morning, Jamie was stiff and sore from the battle with Zeke Connelly, as he expected to be, but he could tell from the way he was able to move around that his ribs were only bruised, not broken.

One of the outlaws told him to help himself to food and coffee at the nearest campfire. The man seemed friendly enough. Several others spoke to him while he was eating breakfast. They complimented him on his victory over Zeke but stopped short of welcoming him to the gang.

Around mid-morning, the boss approached Jamie, carrying his gun belt with its holstered Colt and sheathed knife. "I reckon you might as well have this," he said as he held it out to Jamie. "I had a talk with Zeke, and he told me I ought to go ahead and give it back to you."

Jamie quirked an eyebrow in surprise as he took the gun belt. "Is that because he plans to throw down on me and wants it to be a fair fight?"

"With those burned hands of his, Zeke won't be throwing down on anybody for a while. And you've got him wrong, Mr. Shawnee Smith. Sure, he can be an arrogant son of a gun. Anybody as big and strong as he is usually winds up a mite full of himself. But he's got some common sense, too. He figures anybody who can whip him might be a good man to have on our side."

"Does that mean you trust me now?"

The boss snorted. "Don't go counting on it. I didn't get to be as old as I am by going around trusting folks. But like I said last night, there's not a whole lot of damage you can do out here."

Jamie ran his fingertips over the Colt's grip and said, "I could probably manage to kill you before anybody could stop me."

"Well, if it's that important to you, go ahead and try," the boss said with a grin. "You'd be dead about half a second later, so you wouldn't have very long to feel satisfied with yourself."

Jamie shook his head, stood up, and strapped the gun belt around his hips. "It's not worth it," he said. "I'd rather let you see that I just want to be part of your outfit."

"We'll get around to that . . . maybe. Meanwhile, steer clear of Zeke for a while. He may have agreed to let you stay alive, but that doesn't mean he's all that happy about it."

"Understood," Jamie said with a nod.

The boss went on about his business, whatever that might be. Jamie drifted over to the rope corral where the horses were penned up. He had assumed that the outlaws brought his horse along when they brought him here to their hideout. He was glad to see that he was right. The horse saw him, too, and came over to the rope fence to get his head scratched.

"Be patient, old son," Jamie told the animal, keeping

his voice low enough that he wouldn't be overheard. "We'll get away from these varmints sooner or later."

From there he ambled around the camp. He spotted Zeke talking to some of the other outlaws but, remembering the boss's advice, didn't approach him. Zeke noticed him, too, but other than a momentary glare, he didn't acknowledge Jamie's presence and went on talking to his friends.

Jamie looked for the slender, mysterious gunman called Absaroka but didn't see him anywhere around the camp. The boss might have sent him out to do some scouting, or he might have left on some other errand. Jamie hoped to get a chance to talk to him again and maybe find out more about him, especially why he seemed vaguely familiar.

The day dragged by with nothing happening. Jamie was glad for the chance to rest and recuperate. By that evening, the healing abilities of his iron constitution had started to take effect, and he was able to move around better.

Night had fallen and the campfires were burning, casting dark shadows around the canyon, when sentries called out that someone was coming. Jamie stood up from the rock where he'd been sitting as he heard a faint rataplan of hoofbeats.

He wasn't the only one to react to the news. Most of the outlaws left off whatever they were doing and gathered to greet whoever was riding in. Hands rested on gun butts, not because they were expecting trouble, particularly, Jamie knew, but because old habits were hard to break.

Everyone relaxed when the man who rode into the

firelight turned out to be Absaroka. The sight of him made Jamie understand what had happened. Zeke Connelly had been in charge of watching the wagon train, but with him so beaten up and burned, he couldn't handle the job anymore. Absaroka had replaced him, and now the young gunman was bringing a report to his fellow outlaws.

The boss, accompanied by Zeke, strode forward to meet him. As Absaroka reined in and swung down from his saddle, the burly chief of outlaws asked, "What did you find out, son? Did you get the signal from our man?"

Absaroka nodded. As usual, he was standing where Jamie couldn't get a good look at his face.

"Yes, he had the flap on the back of his wagon tied up on the right side today instead of the left. That means they'll be at the Devil's Crossing tomorrow . . . and that there's enough loot among the wagons to make it worthwhile to hit them."

So that was the signal, thought Jamie. Well, he had a signal of his own to send to Preacher, warning him that an attack would take place the next day.

The trick would be sending that signal without giving away that he was working with someone in the wagon train. It would be worth his life if he were caught.

But the lives of many others might be lost if he didn't succeed.

The boss and Zeke turned away from Absaroka, obviously pleased with the news the young gunman had brought. Jamie moved to intercept them and ignored the warning glare that Zeke gave him from under that bandage bound around his head.

"So you're going to hit a wagon train tomorrow," Jamie said bluntly. "Have you made up your mind whether you're going to let me come along?"

"I don't like it," Zeke said without waiting for the boss to respond first. "I don't trust you, mister. Not one bit."

"That's not your decision to make, Zeke," the boss snapped. "But it just so happens I don't trust you, either, Smith. You can't just ride in here and expect to be one of us a day later."

"I didn't ride in on my own," Jamie pointed out. "I was dragged in as a prisoner."

"Because you were sneaking around and not acting trustworthy." The boss shook his head. "No, you may be a good man, but you're not coming with us tomorrow."

"And you're sure not getting a share of the loot," added Zeke.

"But I'm willing to let you stay around for now," the boss went on. "A few of the men will be staying here to guard the place while we're gone. They can keep an eye on you, too. When we get back, we can talk about you being part of the next job . . . maybe."

That decision actually played right into what Jamie wanted, but he put a disappointed look on his face and said, "Well, all right . . . if that's what you've made up your mind to do."

"It is. And if you don't like it, well, I'm sure Zeke here can figure out something else to do with you."

Zeke's swollen lips twisted in a snarl. That made him grimace in pain. But he nodded eagerly and said, "I sure as blazes can."

Jamie shook his head. "Don't worry. I won't give you any trouble."

But in truth, that was exactly what he intended to do.

The only way out of the outlaw camp seemed to be by following the canyon in one direction or the other. But guards were posted at both ends when the gang rode out well before dawn the next morning, and Jamie knew he couldn't count on being able to slip past them. He figured they were all afraid enough of the boss and Zeke that they wouldn't dare relax on the job.

That left the canyon walls, which at first glance appeared to be so smooth and steep that they were unscalable.

During the previous day, however, Jamie had passed some of the time by studying those rock walls as intently as he could without making it obvious what he was doing. He thought he had found a place where there were enough little knobs and cracks in the rock that a man could climb to the top there—if he was lucky.

That was a mighty big if. He'd have had a better chance if he weren't so big and bulky. He wasn't made for climbing.

When that was the only way out, though, a man didn't have any choice.

He waited a while after the outlaws had ridden out, then drifted back to the canyon wall as silently as he could, pausing frequently to listen and look for any sign that the sentries had noticed his activity.

When he reached the wall, he turned to face it. He

stretched his right arm above his head, located the first little protruding rock he had picked out, and closed his hand around it. With his toe, he felt for the tiny crack that ought to be there.

Extending his arm like that made his bruised ribs hurt like blazes, but Jamie ignored that sensation. He took a deep breath and hauled himself up, then searched above his head for the next handhold.

It was slow, torturous going. Jamie measured his progress in inches, not feet. The rim seemed impossibly high above him, outlined sharply against the slowly graying sky. He had to stop and catch his breath occasionally, but that made things worse in a way because it meant his weight had to hang on his fingers and toes that much longer.

He was high enough now that if he slipped and fell, it would bust him to pieces, if not kill him outright. Minute by agonizing minute, though, the distance to the top decreased. When he reached the rim, at first he didn't realize he was there. He pawed futilely for the next handhold for several seconds before he figured out what was going on. Once he did, he pulled himself the rest of the way up and rolled over the edge to lie flat on his back. Every muscle in his body quivered from the incredible strain of what he had just gone through.

Jamie didn't know how much time passed while he recovered from the climb. Finally, he rolled onto his side, pushed himself to hands and knees, and then climbed wearily to his feet. He took a deep breath to steady himself and walked away from the rim with a firm stride.

The canyon had cut itself into a high, rocky plateau. The walking was easy enough. Jamie put a quarter of a mile between himself and the rim so the guards wouldn't be able to see what he was doing if they looked up, then he began gathering branches from the small, scrubby plants that grew here. He had lucifer matches wrapped in oilcloth in his pocket. He knelt and built a small fire.

As a thin column of smoke began to rise, Jamie took off his shirt and used it like he would a blanket to interrupt the smoke. He held it down, then let it go so the smoke rose in a distinctive puff. Six times, he did that.

If Preacher was watching, as he had promised to do early every morning about this time, he would know what the smoke signals meant.

Jamie kicked the fire out and walked back toward the canyon. He could have headed out on foot and tried to reach the Sweetwater River, maybe joined up with the wagon train, but he hated to leave his horse behind. What he ought to do, he decided, was wait around and see whether or not any of the outlaws returned.

First, though, he was going to circle around and try to find a way into the canyon without having to climb back down that rock wall. He didn't want to do that again. If he was careful enough, he might be able to take the guards by surprise and deal with them while the rest of the bunch was gone. In that case, he could get his horse and rifle and head for the Devil's Crossing, maybe hit the outlaws from behind and take them by surprise.

He sure wouldn't mind a chance to get Zeke Connelly in his gunsights.

It took Jamie a couple of hours to work his way around and down to the level of the canyon mouth. While he was doing that, he listened intently for gunshots in the distance, but so far, the morning had been quiet, which gave him hope. The sun was well up in the sky as he slipped closer to the canyon mouth. He had a pretty good idea where the guards were posted on this end. He thought he had at least a chance of taking them by surprise.

That hope disappeared when he heard a faint noise behind him and a split second later the unmistakable ring of a gun muzzle prodded him in the back. A quiet voice said, "Don't move . . . Jamie Ian MacCallister."

Chapter 24

Jamie stood absolutely still. Some men would be making a bad mistake if they got close enough to stick a gun in an enemy's back. They opened themselves up to the possibility of their would-be victim spinning around fast enough to avoid a shot and knocking the gun aside. Under different circumstances, Jamie might have tried that.

But he had recognized the voice that just spoke to him. It belonged to the young gunman called Absaroka. His instincts told him that Absaroka's reaction would be too fast for that tactic to be effective.

"Take it easy," he said quietly. "Don't go getting trigger happy."

"I never do," said Absaroka. "Lift your hands a little. I'll be happier if they're farther away from your gun."

Jamie raised both hands to elbow level. "I thought you were with the rest of the gang, Absaroka. You rode off with them, early this morning."

"Yeah, I did, but my horse went lame and I had to turn back. At least . . . that's what I told them. What I really wanted was to check on you. I couldn't believe Jamie Ian

MacCallister would allow that attack to go on without at least trying to warn the wagon train."

"That's the second time you've used my name," Jamie grated. "How in blazes do you know who I am?"

"We've met before."

That confirmed Jamie's feeling that Absaroka was familiar somehow. "Who are you?" he asked.

Absaroka hesitated before responding, "Come with me, away from the canyon."

Jamie decided to cooperate, not because he was afraid of the young gunman, but because playing along was the fastest way of finding out what was going on here. He turned and walked around the huge pile of rocks near the canyon mouth that he had been using for cover.

After a few minutes, when they were well out of view of any guard who happened to look out of the canyon, Absaroka said, "That's far enough." The gun muzzle went away from Jamie's back. "You can put your hands down and turn around."

"Thanks," Jamie replied dryly. He did as Absaroka said. The young man backed away from him, out of reach. The gun in his hand still pointed toward Jamie's belly, as steady as the huge slabs of rock by which they stood.

"You want to know who I am, Jamie Ian MacCallister?"

"The question did cross my mind."

Absaroka reached up with his left hand, loosened his hat's chin strap, grasped the brim, and took the hat off. That arm hung at his side as he stared levelly at Jamie.

A couple of seconds went by as Jamie got his first good look at Absaroka. The gunman had a handsome, strong-featured face with coppery skin, dark eyes, and high, flat-planed cheekbones. His mixed ancestry was obvious. He had spoken like a white man, but Jamie could see now that he was half Indian, quite possibly a member of the Absaroka tribe from which he must have taken his name.

The sensation of knowing his identity was stronger than ever, too, but the enormity of the answer that suddenly burst into Jamie's brain was almost more than he could grasp. He stared for a moment longer, then said in a half-whisper, "Hawk?"

Hawk That Soars, the son of Preacher and the Absaroka woman Bird in a Tree, drew in a deep breath that made his nostrils flare. He said, "I've promised myself never to use that name again, but . . . yes, that's who I am. Or who I was." His voice went flat and hard. "Hawk That Soars is dead. As dead as Butterfly, Eagle Feather, and Bright Moon. He's gone with them to their ancestors."

Jamie felt like somebody had taken an ax handle and slammed him in the belly with it. He knew those names. Butterfly was Hawk's wife, Eagle Feather and Bright Moon their children, a little boy and girl who had been happy and healthy the last time Jamie saw them, a couple of years earlier. They had been a very happy family, living with a band of Crow in the mountains not that far north and west of here, relatively speaking.

Jamie shook his head slowly. "Hawk, I don't know what you're talking about—"

"I told you, Hawk is dead. There's just Absaroka now. A gunman and an outlaw." The young man's mouth twisted. "A man alone."

"Blast it, you can't expect to just spring something like this on me and refuse to explain it! What are you doing with these outlaws and killers?"

"I told you, *I'm* an outlaw."

"You're not a murderer," Jamie shot back.

Absaroka, since that was what he wanted to be called, clapped the hat back on his head and tugged down the brim. "You don't know anything about me anymore, Mac-Callister. The man you knew is dead. Don't make assumptions about what I'm capable of."

"Don't forget, I know your father. I know the blood that runs in your veins."

The gun in Absaroka's hand came up a little. For a second, Jamie thought the young man was going to shoot him. But then Absaroka lowered the gun and, a second later, slid it back into its holster.

"We should go even farther away from here and talk," he declared.

"We should get after the rest of that bunch and help your pa and the others with the wagon train fight them off."

Absaroka stiffened. "Preacher is with the wagon train?"

"What do you think?"

Tense seconds ticked past. Then Absaroka said, "The two of you working together again . . . But it's too late. We could never get there in time. Did you warn them an attack was coming? Is that why you escaped from the canyon?"

Jamie didn't see any point in denying it now. "I did," he said. "I came back to get my horse, and to maybe take care of the guards and set up a warm welcome for the boss, Connelly, and the others when they get back. *If* they get back. I won't lie to you, it'll be just fine with me if they're all wiped out in the fighting. After the things they've done, I figure they've got it coming." He stared at Absaroka. "But I never figured that *you'd* have it coming, too."

"There's a lot you don't know, MacCallister."

Jamie grunted. "Tell me about it."

"I will . . . but not here. Not yet. There's work to do first. Stay here."

"Where are you going?"

For the first time, the shadow of a grim, humorless smile formed around the young gunman's mouth.

"To get your horse," he said.

Absaroka had left his mount a couple of hundred yards away in a little gully where it wouldn't be noticeable. He reclaimed the animal and then, with a glance at the cluster of boulders where Jamie MacCallister waited, he nudged the horse into motion and rode slowly toward the canyon mouth.

He hadn't gone very far into that opening when a guard stepped into view from behind an outcropping and leveled a rifle at him. Then the outlaw said, "Oh, it's you," and lowered the weapon. "What're you doin' back, Absaroka? Where are the boss and the rest of the fellas? Did something go wrong?"

"Only my horse," Absaroka answered the talkative outlaw. "He came up lame and I had to turn back."

The guard frowned. "Didn't look like he was lame when you came ridin' in just now."

"I rested him some along the way, and that seems to have improved his condition."

"Well, it's a dang shame you didn't get in on the fun." A shrewd look came over the guard's face. "Are you still gettin' a share? Me and the other three boys who got picked to be left behind are gettin' a half-share each, because we're guardin' the hideout and contributin' to the cause. But we don't need you here, so you won't really be carryin' any of the freight . . . No offense, mind you, just speculatin', you know? Be a shame if you was to come out with nothin' this time, seein' as how this was gonna be your first job with us and all."

"I'm not worried about that," Absaroka said. "I just want to put my horse up."

The guard gestured with his rifle. "Sure, go ahead."

"Where's the other guard? I don't want him getting nervous."

"About fifty yards ahead on the other side. Don't worry, I'll let him know you're comin'." The man turned, cupped his free hand around his mouth, and shouted, "Hey, Bailey, hold your fire! One of our own comin' in!"

Fifty yards along the canyon, a man moved from behind a rock and waved his rifle over his head to signify that he had heard the warning.

Absaroka rode on slowly.

He came to the camp and the rope corral where the guards' horses and the extra mounts were. Jamie's horse was there, too, cropping at the sparse grass with the others. Absaroka swung down, but instead of unsaddling, he picked up Jamie's saddle and blanket from where they lay, ducked under the rope, and approached Jamie's horse.

The animal eyed him warily and shied away. Absaroka spoke in a low, calming tone, speaking the words that Crow warriors used to keep their ponies from getting skittish. It worked, as the horse settled down and allowed Absaroka to put the blanket on its back, then the saddle.

The horse turned its head to look at him. He said, "Don't worry, I'm taking you back to your master."

The horse blew out a breath as if in understanding.

Preacher had always been able to communicate in almost supernatural fashion with the various stallions he had dubbed Horse. Maybe some of that ability had been passed on to his son . . .

Absaroka didn't allow himself to think about that for more than a split second. Then he tightened the cinches and grasped the horse's reins to lead it out of the enclosure.

He tied Jamie's horse to one of the small trees along the creek, where it would be handy if he needed it in a hurry. His own mount was tied there, as well. Then he walked toward the other end of the canyon.

As he expected, one of the guards moved out from the small cleft in the stone wall where he had been concealed. Absaroka hadn't spotted the second guard yet.

This man asked the same question as his compadre at the lower end of the canyon. "What are you doin' back, Absaroka? The attack get called off for some reason?"

"No, I had something else I needed to do."

The guard looked puzzled. "Oh? What's that?"

"This," Absaroka said.

His draw was so fast, his right-hand gun seemed to leap from its holster into his hand. The Colt rose and fell in a swift chopping motion. The unsuspecting guard, who had his rifle tucked under his arm, never had a chance to react before Absaroka's gun slammed into his skull. His knees buckled. He went down hard.

The next instant, a shot roared. Absaroka felt the wind-rip of the bullet's passage as it zipped by his ear.

The slug chipped splinters of rock from the canyon wall that stung Absaroka's cheek as they sprayed against it.

He whirled and fired, aiming as much by instinct as anything else. The canyon was wide enough that it was a long shot, but Absaroka's aim was deadly. The second guard, who stood on a narrow ledge about twenty feet up, dropped the rifle he had just fired and doubled over as the bullet punched into his guts. He pitched forward and turned over completely in the air before crashing to the canyon floor on his back.

Absaroka headed for the place he had left the horses, but he had taken only a couple of steps before a gun roared behind him. The bullet ripped his vest and shirt and drew a hot line of pain along his left side, just above the hip. It was enough to make him stumble but not fall. He twisted around and triggered a shot at the first guard, who had pushed himself up on his left hand and fired at Absaroka with the gun in his right.

Absaroka's bullet took him above the right eye and jerked his head back as it exploded out the back of his skull. The man flopped forward, dead before his face hit the ground.

Absaroka pouched the iron he held as he ran to the horses. He jerked their reins free, leaped into the saddle of his mount, and kicked it into a run toward the lower end of the canyon. He led Jamie's horse, holding its reins tightly in his left hand.

Having heard the shots, the guards at this end of the canyon were ready when they saw the young man galloping toward them. They might be confused about what was going on, but they had to figure that Absaroka had suddenly become an enemy for some reason. They lifted their rifles and opened fire.

Absaroka leaned forward over his horse's neck. The chin strap of his hat was taut, holding the hat on despite the wind tugging at it. A slug hummed past him as he closed the gap between him and the guards. He fired again and saw the man to his right spin off his feet.

A bullet from the man to his left tugged at Absaroka's vest as it went by, but it didn't find flesh. Absaroka twisted in the saddle and snapped a shot across his body as he flashed past. The final guard threw his rifle in the air as he went over backward, arms wide.

Then Absaroka was out of the canyon, heading toward the boulders where he had left Jamie. The big frontiersman ran into the open, gun clutched in his fist, obviously ready to take a hand in the fight if he needed to.

That wasn't going to be necessary. Absaroka might have made a mistake by assuming the guard he had struck down was out cold, but he was confident now that all four of the outlaws were either dead or soon would be.

No one would be left behind to tell the rest of the gang what had happened.

"Here," Absaroka called to Jamie as he tossed the older man the reins. "Let's get out of here."

"Sounds like a good idea to me," agreed Jamie as he swung up into the saddle.

"I reckon those guards figured out you were double-crossing them and took exception to it," Jamie said a while later while he and Absaroka rested their horses in some pine trees atop a ridge where they could keep an eye on their backtrail. Absaroka claimed he hadn't left anybody behind to come after them, but it never hurt to take some precautions. They had ridden hard away from the canyon, and now they were watchful.

"I would've left them unconscious and tied up, if they'd given me the chance." Absaroka shrugged. "They didn't play the hand that way."

"And if they're dead, that works out well for you. You can go back and rejoin the gang if you decide to. The rest of them will blame the guards' deaths on me."

"More than likely," Absaroka allowed. "But I doubt if I'll be rejoining them. I may be a killer, but I draw the line at slaughtering women and children."

"You let them ride off to do exactly that," said Jamie, his voice harsh with accusation.

Absaroka sighed. "I'm one man, MacCallister. There were forty of them. What was I supposed to do?"

"Maybe not throw in with a bunch of skunks like that to start with?"

"If I hadn't, it wouldn't have made one bit of difference what happens today. They would have gone after that wagon train anyway. The only thing is that now there are four less of them, overall."

"The four you killed." Jamie shrugged. "Yeah, I suppose you could look at it that way. But once you found out what their plans were, you could've left and warned those folks with the wagons."

"You already warned them," Absaroka pointed out. "Anyway, why would I do that? Until you showed up, I had no idea anybody I knew was connected with that wagon train."

"Your pa's riding with them."

"I didn't know that," Absaroka repeated, his voice tight with anger now. "You expect me to just ride around looking for opportunities to do good?" He laughed, but the sound held no humor. It was as cold and bleak as any laughter Jamie had ever heard. "After the way the world has treated me, MacCallister, I don't think that's going to happen."

"You still haven't told me that story," Jamie reminded him. "What happened to Hawk That Soars?"

"I told you, he died." The two of them stood there for a moment, trading glares, before Absaroka sighed. "You're not going to let go of it, are you? You've got your jaws clamped down just like that cur of my father's when he takes hold of something."

"Preacher's my friend. I reckon I've got a right to know what happened to his son and daughter-in-law and grand-kids."

Pain flashed in Absaroka's eyes, to go along with the anger he displayed. He jerked his head in a nod and said, "Fine. Let's sit down on that log over there, and I'll tell you the whole sad story."

Chapter 25

"You know what life was like for us," Absaroka said as he and Jamie sat a few feet apart on the trunk of a tree that had fallen sometime in the past, probably the victim of a windstorm. "Butterfly and I were happy there with Broken Pine and his people." He sighed. "With Big Thunder and all the others."

Jamie remembered. Broken Pine was the stalwart chief of the Crow band that had taken in Hawk That Soars. Big Thunder was the huge, simple-minded but good-hearted warrior who had been one of Hawk's best friends.

"What happened to them?" asked Jamie. "Were they attacked? The Blackfeet, maybe?"

The Blackfeet and the Crow were mortal enemies, had been for many decades. The tribes had a long history of raiding each other, including enslavement and wanton slaughter by the Blackfeet.

Absaroka shook his head. "No, something even worse. Sickness. Fever. It came on the people suddenly and claimed many of them. So many . . ."

"Your family?"

"The children died first." Absaroka's voice was hollow

with remembered grief. "After that, I knew Butterfly no longer had the will to live. Less than a week later, she . . . she . . ." He swallowed hard. "The fever took her as well."

For a long moment, Jamie didn't say anything. What *could* a man say in response to that? The only possible reply was the simplest one.

"I'm sorry."

Slowly, Absaroka nodded. He went on, "I thought about going into the mountains and climbing to the highest point I could find. Then I would throw myself off and join them in the world beyond that way. But every time I told myself to follow that path, I heard Butterfly speaking in my ear, telling me I couldn't do such a thing."

"I didn't know the lady that well," Jamie said, "but I've got a hunch that's exactly what she would have told you."

"Yes. So, despite the pain in my heart, I decided to carry on. But not there. Not with the Crow. There were too many reminders, too many things that were like a knife in my belly every time I laid eyes on them. Broken Pine and Big Thunder tried to convince me to stay, but I had to leave."

"They're still alive?"

"As far as I know. Big Thunder was sick with the fever but recovered. Broken Pine was fortunate and never fell ill." Absaroka let out another of those curt, humorless laughs. "Neither did I. Despite everyone around me dying, I was never sick. Not a single day."

Jamie sat there, hands clasped together between his knees as he leaned forward, gazing off into the distance. After a minute or so of silence, he said, "I'm as sorry as I can be about everything you've lost. But that still doesn't explain how you went from being Hawk That Soars to . . . this."

He nodded at the white man's clothing, the two guns, the pulled-down hat, the whole thing that added up to Absaroka, gunman and outlaw.

"There were two worlds available to me, the Indian and the white. If I was leaving the Indian world, I knew I had to turn my back on it completely. I trapped beaver and took the furs to Fort Laramie. They're not worth anything near what they once were, but I made enough money to buy white man's clothes. I cut my hair, worked at other odd jobs, and saved to buy these guns." Absaroka smiled thinly. "I suspected that I might have a natural talent for using them."

"Because of Preacher, you mean," said Jamie.

"That's right. Since he started carrying Colonel Colt's revolvers, he's become very good with them."

Jamie nodded. "Yeah, I've seen plenty of evidence of that."

"And I was right," continued Absaroka. "I practiced until I was good enough to earn more money."

"Gun work," Jamie said heavily.

"I hired out as a guide and guard," Absaroka snapped. "I wasn't an outlaw."

"Until now."

Absaroka glared at him. "I threw in with this bunch because I decided it didn't matter anymore. If I was going to be a gunman, I might as well go all the way and turn bad. I won't lie to you, MacCallister. When I joined up, I knew they were planning to loot a wagon train. I knew there might be killing. I was so bitter I didn't care." He drew in a deep breath. "I *thought* I didn't care."

"But when it came time, you discovered that it did matter to you, after all." Jamie nodded again. "Blood usually runs true, all right. You're Preacher's son."

"Don't remind me. He was nowhere around when my family died!"

"And what could he have done if he had been? He's not a doctor. He might be able to do some things that seem almost miraculous at times, but he's not a miracle worker when it comes to sickness. The only thing that might've turned out different if he'd been there is that he could have gotten sick and died, too."

For a long moment, Absaroka didn't say anything. Then one shoulder rose and fell in a minuscule shrug.

"You're probably right," he admitted. "That doesn't make it hurt any less."

"So what are you going to do now? Have you given up on the idea of turning outlaw?"

Absaroka stood up, stalked off several yards, and stood with his stiff back turned toward Jamie. Without looking around, he said, "Don't judge me, MacCallister. You've never had to go on after losing everything."

"You're wrong about that," Jamie said without trying to disguise the harsh note in his voice. "Preacher probably never told you about how my family was wiped out by the Shawnee when I was just a boy. I lost everything, all right, and they made me a slave, on top of that." He paused. "Or at least they *tried* to make me a slave."

Absaroka turned around at that and gazed at Jamie again. "So that's why you called yourself Shawnee Smith," he said.

Jamie's massive shoulders rose and fell in a shrug. "It was the first thing I thought of. I didn't have a clue that anybody in the gang might recognize me. And you still haven't answered my question, Hawk. Or Absaroka, if you insist. It may take me a little while to get used to that."

"I'd suggest you do get used to it, because I won't answer to that other name anymore. As for what I'm going to do next . . ." He lifted his head and peered off into the distance to the south, toward the Sweetwater River. "I think we'd better go see if we can find out what happened today at the Devil's Crossing."

Preacher continued to check for Jamie's signal every morning as the wagon train forged on past Split Rock and approached the Devil's Crossing. The lack of communication was both worrisome and reassuring. As long as the signal didn't appear, it could mean that the outlaws weren't going to attack the wagon train after all.

Or it could mean that Jamie was dead or disabled somehow and wasn't able to warn them that disaster was about to come crashing down on their heads.

Simon Lash called a halt a little early one afternoon and motioned for Preacher to join him as he rode toward Wesley Kemp's wagon. Tom Linford was on Lash's other side. The wagon-master told him, "Fetch the other leaders, Tom. I have to discuss the route with them."

"I know what you're going to tell them, Mr. Lash," the young scout replied. Grim lines appeared on Linford's face at the memory. "Mr. Prescott had the same sort of meeting with the men in the other bunch."

"I know, lad," Lash said quietly. "This moment was inevitable. And there's never been anything we could do except face it forthrightly." He paused, then added, "Perhaps it might be best if you didn't carry the word to Harrison Kemp, given the bad blood between him and his brother. Harrison seems to be the more reasonable of the two, and I don't believe he'll object strenuously to being left out of these deliberations."

Linford nodded and nudged his mount into a lope that carried him along the line of wagons. Preacher, who walked Horse easily alongside Lash, said quietly, "If those pilgrims choose the Deep Sand Route, it'll be safer for 'em . . . but we won't get a chance to spring a trap on those murderin' outlaws."

"And that's what we came for, isn't it? But at the same time, we have a responsibility to these people. They'll be running a great risk, too."

"They knew headin' west was gonna be dangerous. That's what they signed up for. And they got a good taste of it back when those Injuns jumped us. Folks who are willin' to take out across untamed country in the hopes of findin' a new and better life for themselves . . . well, those are the sort of folks who are willin' to fight for what they want."

"Most of the time, that's true," agreed Lash. His eyes narrowed as they approached Wesley Kemp's wagon. "However, I'm not sure the description fits each and every one of them."

Preacher grunted. He knew Lash was talking about Kemp. He couldn't disagree, either.

Preacher and Lash reined in next to Kemp's wagon. Kemp had brought the vehicle to a stop in response to Lash's signal, and all the other wagons had halted, too.

Kemp scowled. His wife was still riding with Constance

Bradley, his brother avoided him as much as possible, and he was surly as a sore-headed old bear most of the time. The clash with Harrison, and his wife leaving him, had brought out Kemp's true nature, Preacher suspected. The man's smooth façade had been exactly that, nothing but a front.

"Why are we stopping?" Kemp demanded. "We should be able to cover another mile, at least, before we have to make camp for the night."

"That's true, but there's an important matter to discuss," Lash explained. "That's why I've sent young Mr. Linford to fetch the other leaders of this group."

Kemp's expression darkened. "I was elected captain all the way back in Independence. I don't see why you and I can't decide anything that needs to be decided, Lash."

"The others have a voice in this, too, Mr. Kemp."

"Not my brother," Kemp snapped. "If you bring that traitor into this, I'll have nothing to do with it."

Preacher could tell that Lash didn't like Kemp's defiant attitude, but the wagon-master wanted to keep peace within the group if possible. Soon, they might have much bigger things to worry about than hurt feelings.

"I thought you might take that stance, which is why I told Tom not to invite the other Mr. Kemp to join us." Lash's voice took on a warning note as he went on, "It will certainly make the rest of the trip easier if the two of you can make peace between you, or at least agree to tolerate each other."

"That'll be up to Harrison," Kemp replied stiffly. "He's the one who transgressed. He and Virginia."

Preacher didn't know if any actual transgressing had

occurred, other than the sparking between Harrison and Virginia that he had witnessed. He didn't want to know. Getting mixed up in folks' personal lives held no appeal for him whatsoever. Unfortunately, as in cases such as this, it couldn't be avoided.

"You'll have to work that out yourselves," Simon Lash said. "Right now, we need to decide whether the wagons will continue to follow the river or swing south and take the longer way around."

"I don't want to make this journey any longer than it has to be."

Lash nodded. "I suspect the others will agree with you. But I'm going to give them their say."

Kemp just nodded and didn't respond otherwise. A short time later, Tom Linford returned with Cornelius Russell, Edmund Farrington, Stephen Millard, and Adam Gideon. Preacher noticed that Jesse Willis and Roscoe Lomax tagged along, too.

"Gentlemen," Lash greeted them. "I'll get right to the point. You've heard me speak of the Triple Crossing of the Sweetwater."

"The Devil's Crossing," Willis interrupted. "Isn't that what they call it now?"

Lash regarded him with a slight frown. "Are you a duly selected representative of the company now, Mr. Willis?"

"I'm a member of it," blustered Willis. "My skin's at much at risk as anybody else's."

"That's true," Lash allowed.

Farrington said, "Harrison Kemp suggested that someone should replace him in our little group. Jesse volunteered."

Preacher found that bit of news interesting.

"Very well," Lash said, nodding. "As I was saying, we've reached the point where a decision has to be made. Do we continue following the river, or do we swing south and avoid the three crossings less than a day ahead?"

"What do you recommend, Simon?" Cornelius Russell asked.

"I've taken wagon trains through both ways. Either will suffice to get us where we're going. Following the Sweetwater is shorter and faster, even though the river crossings can sometimes cause delays. The southern route crosses an area of deep sand, which makes for very slow going and is hard on the livestock."

"Which is safer?" asked Farrington.

Willis said, "We know the answer to that. There may be outlaws lurking ahead if we stick with the river."

"There could be danger anywhere we go," Russell said. "We've known that ever since we started out from Independence."

"That's true, Professor," Lash said. "There are degrees of risk, of course, but this is the frontier."

Preacher leaned over in the saddle, spat, and said, "No matter where you go out here, it ain't exactly safe. Chances are, it never will be."

Wesley Kemp asked, "How many weeks' difference are you talking about, Lash?"

"Two or three. Possibly more."

Willis said, "I'm willing to take more time if it means we don't get attacked."

Farrington pursed his lips. "But we don't have any guarantee of that." He looked around at the others and went on, "I believe we all understand the choice that's facing us. I say we follow the river and avoid the sand."

"Not me," said Willis. "I think we should go south."

Lash looked at Millard and Gideon. "You two haven't said anything so far."

Gideon chuckled. "I've been taking it all in and considering the arguments. I think we should follow the river, even if we do have to go through the Devil's Crossing."

"I agree," Millard said. "I don't want to waste that many days."

Jesse Willis said, "We're talking about a journey that takes months. What real difference does a few days make?"

"It makes enough of a difference to me," said Kemp. "I vote for following the river, too."

"As do I," Russell said.

Lash nodded and said, "That settles it. You're the only one who favors the Deep Sand Route, Mr. Willis. I'm sorry, but we're going to be following the river."

"And I don't suppose I have any choice but to go along with you," Willis responded with an angry glare.

"You can strike out on your own any time you want to," Kemp told him. "Nobody's forcing you to stick with us. But we're not going to wait on the other side of the hills for you if you decide to go all the way around."

"No, we can't do that," Lash agreed.

"Fine," Willis muttered. "But if we're attacked by outlaws, I want each and every one of you to remember that I warned you!"

"Reckon if that happens, we'll all have more important things to worry about," Preacher said.

Chapter 26

Preacher was up before dawn, as usual, the next day . . . the day the wagons would travel through the narrow valley where the terrain would force them to make three crossings of the Sweetwater River.

He had thought a considerable amount about Jesse Willis's actions the day before. By arguing against traveling through the Devil's Crossing, Willis had made it look like he couldn't possibly be the gang's inside man. But had that been a clever ruse? Maybe Willis had figured the other men would vote against the Deep Sand Route, which meant he could afford to vote *for* it without that having any effect on the actual outcome, just to make himself look less suspicious.

Or maybe he'd been wrong about the hombre all along and Willis was just an unfriendly cuss, Preacher told himself. All he knew for sure was that all this pondering wasn't his strong suit, so he gave it up in frustration.

Chances were, before the day was over, he would have the answers to his questions, one way or the other.

Coffee and bacon smells were starting to drift through the air and grayness had crept into the eastern sky when

Preacher walked out away from the wagons and the campfires. He stopped after going fifty yards and peered to the east, searching the heavens as they slowly grew lighter and the stars began to wink out.

Dog had come with him and sat on his haunches beside the mountain man. After a moment, Preacher murmured, "Ain't nothin' to see. Reckon we're on our own, old son—"

His words stopped short as he stiffened. There, a little farther north from where he had been focusing most of his attention, a small puff of smoke climbed into the sky, followed by another and another. It would take a man with keen eyes to spot the signal. Jamie MacCallister had been described as a man with the eyes of an eagle. Preacher was the same sort of man.

The signal was there, and that confirmed the outlaws would strike today.

Dog whined softly in his throat. Preacher knew that meant someone was coming, but the big cur didn't regard them as a threat. Otherwise, he would have growled. So Preacher wasn't surprised when Constance Bradley asked, "What are you doing out here by yourself, Arthur? I've seen you act like this on other mornings, when it's barely starting to get light."

Preacher turned to look at her. The light wasn't very good, but it was bright enough for him to see her slender form and the golden hair that framed her face. She was always a welcome sight.

"I reckon I was communin' with nature, I suppose you'd call it. That's a thing that people say, ain't it?"

Constance laughed. "I'm pretty sure it is, although I wouldn't think that you'd be the sort to do that."

"Why not?" he asked with a slight frown. "I've found that the fellas who spend the most time out here on the frontier are the ones who appreciate it the most."

She rested a hand on his arm and said, "You know, I never thought about it that way, but you're right, of course. You see wonders all the time, but you know not to take them for granted."

"I sure as shootin' try not to." He smiled at her. "And I've seen some wonders, right enough. Still do, sometimes. Like right now, maybe."

"Stop that. You're going to make me blush." She slid her hand up his arm. "Come on back to the wagons. Breakfast is just about ready."

Preacher was eager to tell Simon Lash that he had seen Jamie's signal at last, but he supposed that could wait until after breakfast. Based on everything that had happened in the past, the outlaws wouldn't strike until the wagons arrived at the Devil's Crossing. That wouldn't be until midday, so there was plenty of time to alert the wagon-master.

And Preacher didn't want to miss the opportunity to sit down and have breakfast with the beguiling Constance Bradley. A fella never knew when something might be his last chance . . .

Preacher, Simon Lash, and Tom Linford stood by themselves a short distance from the wagon train. Breakfast was finished, and the immigrants were hitching up their teams and getting ready to roll again, looking forward to being another day closer to the destiny that waited for them at the end of the Oregon Trail.

Preacher had just told the other two men about the signal from Jamie. Lash said, "You're certain about what you saw?"

"I ain't in the habit of makin' mistakes, especially when it comes to trouble."

"No, of course not," the wagon-master said. "I meant no offense, Preacher. So we have confirmation that the outlaws are going to ambush us today."

Linford asked, "Was Mr. MacCallister able to give you any idea where the attack will be?"

Preacher shook his head. "Hard to get that detailed with smoke signals. All we know for sure is that they'll be hittin' us. Outlaws tend to stick with what's been workin' for 'em, so that makes me believe they'll lay their ambush at the Devil's Crossin'."

"We'll need to be ready for them," said Lash. He sighed. "I need to call a meeting of the entire company."

"If you gather everybody around and the varmints are watchin' from somewhere up in the hills, they'll know that somethin's goin' on," Preacher warned. "They're liable to spook and steer clear of us."

"If that happens, then none of those innocent people will die," Linford pointed out, his voice tight. "I want a showdown with those outlaws as much as you do."

"More, I would imagine," Lash said quietly.

"That's right. But the closer we came to this spot, the more I've been worrying that we're in the wrong here. We can't take such reckless chances with innocent lives."

"The same thing's been botherin' me," said Preacher, thinking about Constance. "That's why we ain't gonna sit back and wait for the no-good skunks to hit us."

Clearly puzzled, Lash asked, "What are you talking about?"

Preacher tugged at his earlobe and then scraped his thumbnail along his beard-stubbled jawline. "I figure on ambushin' the ambushers. I'll pick nine or ten men I can trust. We'll drift off from wagons one at a time and ease on up into the hills. I'm bettin' that I can spot that gang before they're ready to attack, and we'll take the varmints by surprise."

"I'll come with you," Linford said without hesitation.

"As will I," Lash said.

Preacher said, "Nope, you're stayin' with the wagons, Simon. These folks need you leadin' 'em through those crossin's. And if the outlaws get past us, you'll need to rally everybody to fight 'em off." He nodded to Linford. "But I'll be happy to have you with me, Tom. You deserve a crack at 'em."

"The problem with your idea is that we don't know how large the gang is," Lash said. "According to Tom's eyewitness testimony, several dozen men were involved in the previous attack. If you have ten men, the odds will be four to one, if not worse."

"That's why I plan on takin' 'em by surprise. With any luck, we'll wipe out a bunch of 'em before they know what's goin' on. Also, I hope to find a place we can fort up where they can't root us out without losin' a whole heap more."

Lash considered for a moment and then slowly nodded. "Who else are you going to take with you?"

"Lomax, for sure. He's a fightin' fool. Maybe Harrison Kemp. He may be a darned fool for gettin' mixed up with his brother's wife, but he seems pretty cool-headed most of the time. I'll have to think about the others. When I settle on them, I'll talk to them durin' the mornin' and let 'em know what's goin' on and what I want to do. And I'll warn 'em to keep the whole thing to themselves for now. We don't want to spook the whole wagon train."

"All right," Lash said. "It seems that your plan is our best chance to protect the wagons and the immigrants but at the same time deal a smashing defeat to those brigands. You and the men who accompany you will be running the biggest risk, though, Preacher."

"That's fine with me," Tom Linford declared. "It'll be worth it for a chance to pay them back for what they did before."

To anyone watching, it appeared to be a normal morning as the wagon train got under way a short time later, the teams of oxen lumbering forward as they pulled the wagons along the grassy plains bordering the Sweetwater River. As far as most of the immigrants were concerned, it *was* a normal morning, although they knew they would be reaching the Devil's Crossing today and a sense of mingled anticipation and nervousness hung in the air.

Preacher and Simon Lash rode a hundred yards ahead of the first wagon. Tom Linford was even farther ahead, drawing out his lead until he was out of sight. After a while, Preacher dropped back with Dog trotting alongside him and approached Harrison Kemp, who was riding to the left of the wagons.

"Howdy, Kemp," Preacher greeted him.

"Morning, Arthur. Any trouble up ahead?"

"Not yet," replied Preacher.

Harrison frowned as if he'd caught the implication in the mountain man's voice. "But you're expecting some?"

"I'm fixin' to tell you somethin' because I need your help, but you got to keep it to yourself. Can't go raisin' a ruckus with the rest of the folks."

Harrison's frown deepened as he said, "Well, now you've really got me curious. What's this about, Arthur?"

"First off," Preacher said, "my name ain't Arthur. Well, it is, but that ain't what I've gone by for most of my life. But that ain't really important, either. What is, is what's waitin' for us at the Devil's Crossin'."

Quickly, Preacher filled him in on the previous attacks. Harrison had heard the rumors about those, like most of the other immigrants, but he hadn't known that Tom Linford was the sole survivor of one of those atrocities, or that the wagon train had a guardian angel watching over them in the form of Jamie MacCallister. His eyes widened as he soaked in all that Preacher was telling him, and his jaw hardened when Preacher said that he had seen Jamie's warning signal that morning.

"So you know for sure that we're going to be attacked?" he asked.

"If I believe Jamie, we are. And I trust that big fella with my life."

"Then we have to alert everyone—"

Preacher lifted a hand. "No, that'd just cause a panic. Those outlaws figure on jumpin' us . . . but I figure on headin' 'em off before they can do it."

"How are you going to do that?"

"With help from you and some other fellas like you."

Preacher went over the details of the plan he had come up with, telling Harrison to drift out farther and farther from the wagons and then when he was out of sight to circle ahead and rendezvous with Preacher, Linford, and the other men who would try to intercept the outlaws.

"How about it?" Preacher asked. "Are you game? It'll be a mighty dangerous job."

Harrison turned his head to gaze toward the wagons. Preacher wondered if he was looking for Constance's wagon, hoping to catch a glimpse of his brother's wife riding on the driver's seat next to the blonde.

"If you believe this gives us the best chance of protecting all those people, then I'm with you, Arthur. Or what should I call you?"

"Most folks call me Preacher."

Harrison looked surprised. "You're a minister?"

Preacher chuckled and waved a hand. "Naw. It's a long story. I'll tell you about it one of these days . . . if we come through this day alive."

Chapter 27

Preacher talked to Roscoe Lomax next. The big bull-whacker was excited to hear that they were in for a fight.

"It's blasted well about time," Lomax declared. "It's been so long since we tangled with those redskins that I've been gettin' a mite rusty."

"Well, you ought to have plenty of chances to knock the rust off today," Preacher told him. "Can you suggest a few other fellas who might want to join us?"

"I sure can. I been makin' friends all through the company, and I know several gents who like a good tussle. You want me to spread the word to 'em?"

"You do that. They'll have to get horses from the extra stock and drift away from the wagons one by one, not too close together. Those outlaws are bound to have a spy amongst the group, and we don't want to alert the skunk that we know what's fixin' to happen today."

Lomax nodded. "I'll make sure they understand. Where do you want to rendezvous?"

"There's a good-sized hill with a lot of trees on it, on the north side of the river overlookin' the Devil's Crossin',"

Preacher said. "We'll meet on top of it. Just keep your eyes open and stay out of sight as best you can. You don't want to blunder right into that bunch of thieves and killers."

"I blamed sure don't," Lomax agreed. "Don't worry, Preacher. I'll be careful, and so will the boys I talk to. If they ain't, I'll rip 'em apart from gullet to gizzard!"

"Save your rippin' apart for them outlaws," Preacher advised. He rode on, trying to be inconspicuous as he spoke to the other men he had selected as potential volunteers for this dangerous job.

None of them turned him down, and they all seemed to grasp the importance of proceeding in an apparently normal manner so they could take the ambushers by surprise. Feeling that he had done as much as he could to set things up and would have to wait and see how things played out, Preacher dropped back even farther, bringing up the rear until he judged the time was right to veer off and start circling wide toward the rendezvous point. Dog came with him, looking as eager for battle as the mountain man himself.

Preacher reached the thickly wooded hilltop late in the morning. The river was about half a mile away, sparkling in places where the sunlight slanted through openings between the trees that grew along its banks.

Tom Linford waited there for him. So did Harrison Kemp. Preacher nodded to them and said, "The other fellas ought to be here in a little while. Seen any signs of anything suspicious?"

"Not yet," replied Linford. "From the looks of it, we're the only people in a hundred miles."

"Yeah, but looks can be deceivin', as they say."

Preacher leaned forward in the saddle and gazed at the rugged landscape around them. "Could be almost anything hidin' out there, and if there is, we need to spot them before they spot us. So keep your eyes peeled, boys."

Over the next hour, eight more men arrived at the rendezvous one at a time, including Roscoe Lomax. That made eleven in all. Not much of a force to take on maybe forty ruthless outlaws, thought Preacher as he looked around at them. But a frontiersman generally learned how to work with what was available to him if he wanted to survive, and Preacher had been knocking around the frontier for a long time.

Besides, with luck they would have the element of surprise on their side. That automatically increased their chances.

Each man carried a rifle. Some had pistols, as well. Their faces were grim and determined. Lomax had picked men who weren't married, for the most part, but a couple of them had wives and kids they would be fighting for. He hoped they came through all right, but they knew what they were getting into. Like most men, they were willing to give up their own lives if they were battling to protect their families.

"You fellas stay here in the trees so you won't be spotted," he told them. "I aim to drift around and see if I can find those outlaws. When I do, I'll fetch you."

"What if we hear shooting?" Tom Linford asked.

Preacher smiled. "Then that's where the varmints will be, more than likely, and you can come a-runnin'. Just don't start blazin' away until you're sure I ain't in the line of fire."

The men nodded. One of them called, "Good luck," as

Preacher rode away. He would take all the luck he could get, the mountain man thought, but he was also relying on the skills and instincts he had developed during his long, hazardous life.

Within moments, he had vanished from the sight of Linford and the others, moving so soundlessly and without disturbing the vegetation that he almost might not have been there. Dog was just as much of a phantom, as the big cur ranged ahead of Preacher and Horse. The stallion placed each hoof carefully to make as little noise as possible.

Of course, such a large animal couldn't move through brush without making *some* sounds, but Preacher and Horse had worked together so often that each was like an extension of the other and seemed to know what the other was thinking.

Most of the time, Preacher couldn't see very well into the Sweetwater River valley from where he was, but occasionally he got a glimpse of the stream. After a while, he caught sight of the wagons as they rolled slowly westward, their white canvas covers bright in the sun, carrying the hopes and dreams of a lot of good folks.

Preacher spotted Simon Lash riding in front of the wagon train, straight in the saddle, peering ahead. It wasn't far to the spot where the hills would close in from both sides and force the wagons to cross and recross the river.

Dog suddenly reappeared and loped toward Preacher. The mountain man reined in and waited, but Dog stopped before reaching him. The big cur gave him an intent look and then whirled around to head off again. He paused after several yards and looked back over his shoulder at Preacher.

"I understand, old son," Preacher said quietly. "You've found somethin'. Go ahead and lead me to it."

He nudged Horse into motion. They followed Dog up and down a couple of hills. Then Dog stopped at the edge of a bluff and stood there stiffly, looking down at something beyond.

Preacher brought Horse to a stop and swung down from the saddle. He let the reins dangle and stole forward, taking off his broad-brimmed hat and dropping into a crouch. Anybody who caught a glimpse of Dog would mistake him for a wolf, more than likely, but Preacher didn't want their quarry spotting *him*.

He went to hands and knees, then bellied down and crawled forward to join Dog. He heard the soft growl coming from deep in the big cur's throat. He could see what had prompted the reaction, too, when he looked down into the narrow canyon that lay beyond the bluff.

Approximately three dozen riders had dismounted and appeared to be letting their horses rest. The men stood around in small groups, smoking and talking. They all wore long coats, and although their faces were uncovered at the moment, each man wore a bandanna looped around his throat and tied at the back of the neck, so it could be pulled up to conceal his identity.

That matched the description of the outlaws that Tom Linford had provided. Preacher had no doubt he was looking at the same gang. A few might be new to the bunch, but Preacher was confident many of them were the same ones who had carried out those earlier atrocities.

After a few minutes, a burly, barrel-chested hombre with

a red face and white mustache lifted his voice and called, "All right, this is long enough. Everybody mount up!"

The outlaws stepped up into their saddles. The older man, evidently their leader, took the point as they rode down the canyon. Preacher scuttled backward, standing up when he was well clear of the rim. He whistled softly to Dog and ran back to where he had left Horse.

He had tried to trace the canyon's route with his eyes while he was spying on the outlaws. He called on his memory, as well. Eight or ten years earlier, he had traveled through these parts. A lot of things had changed since then, but the landscape hadn't. The hills and canyons, the gullies and ridges, were still the same, and in his mind's eye, Preacher followed this canyon to the spot where it came out just east of the first crossing. If the outlaws charged out of there while the wagons were in the water, the immigrants would be sitting ducks.

That was what they'd done before. Preacher didn't see any reason for them to change their tactics now.

He mounted and heeled Horse into a run. There was no time to waste. By cutting through the hills at an angle, he, Tom Linford, Harrison Kemp, and the other men could get back to the canyon in time to intercept the outlaws before they reached the Devil's Crossing, but it would be close.

Preacher could move faster now that he was no longer scouting for the enemy. Horse lunged up slopes, bounded down hillsides, leaped small gullies. Dog ran flat-out to keep up. As they approached the wooded hill where they had left the others, Tom Linford emerged from the trees and rode hurriedly out to meet them, having heard Horse's pounding hoofbeats.

Preacher changed course, angling to the south. He jerked his hat off his head and waved it at the young scout, signaling that Linford and the others should follow him. Linford waved an acknowledgment and wheeled his mount. Preacher was too far away to hear him, but he knew Linford was calling to the other men. They burst out of the trees and strung out in a line as they galloped in the same direction Preacher was headed.

As their paths came together, Preacher slowed slightly to let them catch up to him. Tom Linford pulled alongside and shouted over the drumming hoofbeats, "Did you find them?"

"Yeah, I know where they are and where they're headed! We can cut them off if we hurry!"

"We're ready," Linford replied grimly. After all these months, after nearly dying, he was close now to having a chance to avenge what had been done to him, and to those he cared about.

Some of the men struggled to keep up as Preacher led them at a breakneck pace through the rough country in the hills. They kept trying, though, and didn't fall too far behind. Preacher studied the landmarks around them, casting his mind back to his last visit.

He spotted a narrow cut between two towering mounds of rock and rode hard into it with the others following. The cut twisted and turned and came out on a boulder-littered bench that loomed above the canyon where Preacher had seen the gang earlier.

At least, he *hoped* it was the same canyon. If he was remembering wrong, he and the others probably wouldn't get a second chance to stop the outlaws before they attacked the wagon train.

His hand slashed the air in a signal for the others to stop. As they dismounted, Preacher picked a couple of the men, cast about for a second for their names, and then said, "Ringling, Mathers, you'll be responsible for the horses. Keep 'em back away from the rim, out of the line of fire."

"I figured I'd get in on the fighting," one of the men objected.

"Well, you figured wrong. And if we wind up needin' these horses in a hurry, that makes you two the most important men in the bunch."

The one who had spoken up thought about it for a second and then nodded agreement. He and the second man took the reins and led the horses back to where the cut emerged from the rocks.

The other men carried their rifles and trotted behind Preacher out to the rimrock, where the mountain man picked out spots for them.

"Keep your heads down so that bunch won't spot you," he told them. "Try to aim at different targets, although you won't know for sure about that. Don't go to shootin' until I start the ball. Those of you with pistols, once you've fired your rifle, haul out those smoke poles and get to work. The range may be a little long, but we want so much lead flyin' around down there that some of it's bound to hit those varmints. The rest of you, reload your rifles as fast as you can and pour it on. I'd like to knock at least half of the skunks plumb outta their saddles before they know what's goin' on."

"How many are there?" asked Linford.

"I didn't take the time to count for sure, but I'd say around three dozen."

"So all we have to do is kill three of the devils each, and they'll be just about wiped out."

"Yeah, that sums it up pretty well," Preacher agreed. "Now spread out and get ready."

They did so, kneeling behind rocks and checking their rifles to make sure the weapons were loaded. Preacher studied the men's faces and could tell that they were nervous, but none of them looked as if they would crack under the pressure of the coming battle. However, it was difficult to be sure about things like that.

The one he had no doubts about was Tom Linford. The young scout looked like he was ready to jump down there into the canyon and tackle the whole gang by himself. Sometimes, such eagerness worked against a man in battle. Preacher hoped Linford would remain cool-headed once the shooting started.

Dog's ears perked up. He growled as the hair on his back rose. Preacher listened for a second and then said to the big cur, "Yeah, I hear it, too."

"What is it?" asked Linford.

"Horses comin'. A big bunch of them."

The men looked at each other. Their nerves tightened even more. Preacher could see that on their faces.

"Just wait for me to start things, boys," he told them. He took off his hat and knelt behind a boulder. Dog sat beside him, still growling softly. This was going to be strictly a gun battle, at least starting out, so he wouldn't be able to get in on the action. Preacher knew that frustrated his trail partner.

Then he stopped worrying about Dog and narrowed his eyes at the sight of the riders coming around in a bend in the canyon some fifty yards north of their position.

Preacher made sure his rifle wasn't where it would reflect any light toward the approaching riders as he edged his head to the side of the boulder to get a better look.

That red-faced, white-mustached hombre was still in the lead, all right, and the rest of the bunch was right behind him, strung out a little but not much.

Preacher was about to ease his rifle up to his shoulder when he heard Tom Linford's gasp from where the young scout was hidden a few yards to his right. His head jerked in that direction.

"What is it?" he asked in a harsh whisper.

"That . . . that man leading them." Linford's eyes were wide with shock as he answered. "That's Ethan Prescott!"

Chapter 28

Preacher drew in a sharp breath. "Prescott!" he repeated. "The fella who was leadin' that other wagon train you were with?"

Linford's voice was so thin and strained it sounded like he was being tortured as he replied, "Yeah, I . . . I thought he was dead, killed in the attack, even though I never found his body. I can't believe he's alive!"

"You know what that means, don't you?"

"I see him with my own eyes," said Linford, agonized by the betrayal he was witnessing. "He's leading that bunch. He . . . he must be the one behind the whole gang!"

"Yeah, I reckon," Preacher agreed. "He must've decided he was tired of pretendin' to be an honest man. That's why he had the gang hit a wagon train he was leadin'. That way when he disappeared, folks would think he was killed."

"And it worked," Linford said bitterly. "I never would've dreamed he was alive." The young scout lifted his rifle as his lips drew back from his teeth in a grimace. "But he won't be for much longer!"

"Hold on," Preacher said, his voice sharp with command. "Don't go to shootin' just yet. Let 'em get a little closer."

Linford's finger was tight on the trigger, but he didn't give it the last little squeeze that would fire the rifle. Instead, he jerked his head in a grudging nod that told Preacher he understood.

"Easy, easy," the mountain man said as the outlaws rode closer. He was talking to himself as much as to Linford.

Normally, shooting men from ambush went against the grain for him. These outlaws had proven that they were more animals than men, though.

Worse than animals, really. An animal might kill from madness if it was infected with hydrophobia, but Preacher had never known a four-legged critter to kill out of greed, or lust, or pride.

Only the two-legged kind did that.

Since he knew that Linford would be targeting Ethan Prescott, Preacher lined his sights on a man riding just to Prescott's left and slightly behind him, a brawny, bearded gent whose hands appeared to have bandages wrapped around them. Preacher didn't know what had happened to the man, but the fact that he was going along with the gang meant he could still use a gun. His position in the bunch led Preacher to believe he might be Prescott's second-in-command. If both of them were dead, the outlaws probably would be a lot more disorganized.

Preacher drew in a breath and held it. His finger curled around the rifle's trigger and was about to squeeze it when Dog suddenly growled. Preacher knew something was wrong.

A crashing volley of gunshots a split second later confirmed that.

He didn't know right away where the shots came from, but a bullet spanged off the rock next to him. Somewhere along the rim, a man cried out in pain. Preacher took the shot at his intended target anyway, but the man had already kicked his horse in the flanks and the animal leaped ahead just as the mountain man fired. Preacher knew he'd missed as soon as the rifle boomed and kicked against his shoulder.

Linford fired, too, and then grated a curse that sounded almost like a sob. Preacher could tell by that reaction that the young man had missed his shot at Prescott, too.

In the canyon below, somebody bellowed deep-voiced commands. The rataplan of hoofbeats rose into a roll of thunder as the outlaws charged ahead. Ragged shots came from the rim as some of Preacher's men still tried to do the job they had come for, but most of them were pinned down by the fire that came from behind them. Preacher caught a glimpse of one outlaw flinging his arms in the air and toppling off his racing horse, but as far as Preacher could tell, that man was the only casualty among the gang.

A cloud of dust rose in the air from the hooves of the galloping horses, obscuring the outlaws as they escaped. With the bitter knowledge that his plan had failed, Preacher set his empty rifle aside and whirled to face the new threat as his hands dropped to the holstered Dragoons on his hips.

He saw the sprawled bodies of Ringling and Mathers near the mouth of the cut, where they had been holding the horses. The gunfire had spooked the animals, and, with the exception of Horse, who was too well-trained to panic, they had bolted and now ran haphazardly along the bench.

Muzzle flame spurted from several guns inside the cut. Clouds of powder smoke floated near the opening. The outlaws had spotted them somehow, Preacher realized, and sent a handful of men to ambush them while the majority of the gang continued on its way to attack the wagon train. So what was happening now was a double ambush . . . or was that a triple ambush?

Preacher shoved away those whirling thoughts and concentrated on what mattered: killing the low-down skunks who were trying to kill him and his friends.

He sprang to his feet and called, "Dog! Hunt!" The big cur took off like a gray streak, weaving back and forth to make himself a more difficult target as he raced toward the cut where the would-be killers lurked.

Preacher charged after him, firing the Dragoons in an alternating fashion. The .44 caliber balls whipped through the air inside the cut. One man, clad in long coat, broad-brimmed hat, and bandanna like the rest of the gang, stumbled into view, clutching his stomach where he had been hit. He collapsed and didn't move again.

Tom Linford joined Preacher in the frontal attack. They spread out, zigzagging, and kept throwing lead even as the return fire sang past them. Preacher felt the wind-rip of a bullet as it passed close by his left ear.

Dog disappeared into the opening, and a moment later one of the hidden men began to scream. Preacher knew the big cur had found some prey.

As he and Linford reached the cut, two men jumped out at them, the revolvers in their fists blazing. Preacher fired both Dragoons at the same time. The bullets slammed into one outlaw's chest with such force that they picked him up off his feet and threw him backward. The gun he'd been holding sailed high in the air as it flew from suddenly lifeless fingers.

An instant later, the other outlaw crumpled as Linford fired. But the young scout stumbled, too, and had to catch himself with his free hand against the rock wall of the cut to keep from falling.

"Tom!" Preacher called. "Are you hit?"

"He just winged me," Linford replied. "Are there any more of them?"

Preacher followed the sounds of Dog's savage growls to the spot where the big cur was finishing the job of ripping out the throat of an already dead outlaw. Dog had torn him up good.

Quickly, Preacher checked the other three fallen outlaws. They were all dead, just as he expected. He didn't see any others, and the narrow cut had gone quiet except for the fading echoes of the gun-thunder from a few moments earlier.

"Go see how many of our boys are hurt," he told Linford. "I'll take a look on up the cut to make sure nobody else is lurkin' around. Come on, Dog."

Linford hurried to carry out the order while Preacher and Dog scouted for more enemies. Not finding any, they returned to the bench where the ambush had been set up—but had backfired on the men from the wagon train.

Linford was kneeling next to the bodies of Ringling and Mathers, who had been laid out on their backs. Roscoe Lomax, apparently unharmed, stood nearby with his rifle cradled in his arms.

Linford looked up at Preacher and said, "The poor devils probably never knew what hit them."

"More than likely," the mountain man agreed. "The

varmints took them out first, since they were the closest and the easiest shots to make. How about the others? Anybody dead?"

Linford shook his head. "A couple of men were hit, but not seriously." He nodded toward his own left shirt-sleeve, where blood had stained the cloth. "I just got nicked. Nothing to worry about."

"All right. We'll patch up the fellas who are hurt as quick as we can, and then we got to light a shuck outta here."

"What about these two?" asked Linford as he came to his feet, indicating the two bodies in front of him.

"I hate to leave 'em, even for a while, but we don't have time to bury 'em. We'll come back to get 'em when we can and take them back to the wagons so they can be laid to rest proper-like. First, though, we got to get after those outlaws." Preacher rubbed his jaw. "They sent those four fellas to ambush us so we'd be distracted and the rest of the bunch could slip past us . . . and it worked. They'll be well on their way to the Devil's Crossin' by now."

"And that's where they'll attack the wagon train," Tom Linford said, his voice hollow. "Ethan Prescott . . . and all the rest of those bloody-handed murderers."

Jamie MacCallister and the young gunman who called himself Absaroka were cutting through the hills when they heard gunfire coming from somewhere to their right. It sounded like it was a mile away, maybe more.

They reined in and Jamie frowned. "We're not far enough south for that to be coming from the Devil's Crossing," he said.

"No, the crossing is still ahead of us," Absaroka agreed.

"Maybe your friends ran into some trouble before they got there."

"They're not my friends," Absaroka said. "I told you, I made a mistake ever considering riding with them. That's why I helped you, MacCallister." He paused, then said, "Maybe we should go see about that shooting."

The distant gunfire had been furious for a minute or two, but now it was starting to dwindle away. Jamie shook his head and said, "Sounds like whatever the ruckus was, it's just about over. I think we should keep on heading for the crossing. We know there's likely to be trouble there, and those folks with the wagons will need all the help they can get."

"You're right about that." Absaroka nudged his horse into motion again, and the two men continued riding toward the Sweetwater River, making the best speed they could through the rugged terrain.

Simon Lash had been on edge all day. Under the circumstances, it was impossible not to feel the nervous strain of waiting to be attacked by outlaws. He hoped Preacher's plan worked. If the mountain man succeeded, the gang of thieves and killers would be routed, perhaps even wiped out.

But if Preacher failed, Lash and the people for whom he was responsible were going to be in deadly danger before the day was over . . . and most of them didn't even realize that, he thought as he looked back at the line of wagons from his position at the front of the column.

Late in the morning, the hills began to close in on both sides of the river, forcing the wagons to travel closer to the stream on the southern bank. Lash saw the steep, rocky slope crowding in up ahead and knew they had almost reached the point where the first crossing would have to be made. He turned and rode back to the lead wagon, signaling for Wesley Kemp to stop.

Kemp brought his team of oxen to a halt and looked at the wagon-master. "Is this it, Lash?" he asked. "Is this the Devil's Crossing?"

"Part of it," Lash confirmed. He turned in the saddle and gestured toward the river. "Up there a couple of hundred yards, we'll make the first of the three crossings. The Sweetwater isn't running high at the moment and isn't flowing exceptionally fast, so the wagons should be able to make it without much trouble."

It wasn't the river that held the danger; it was the swarm of human locusts that might descend upon them, intent on stripping them of everything of value, including their lives.

"There's talk that this is where several wagon trains have been attacked in the past couple of years," said Kemp. "Are we going to have trouble?"

"Everything certainly seems to be peaceful right now," replied Lash. "But you knew a journey such as this might be dangerous when you signed up for it."

"Maybe so, but I don't like the looks of this. The way these hills are crowding in, if anything happens there won't be any place for us to go."

In the heavy wagons pulled by lumbering teams of oxen, making a run for it wasn't really an option to start with, but Lash didn't point that out. Instead, he said, "You voted to follow this route, Mr. Kemp."

"I know that," Kemp replied irritably. "I still don't have to like it." He frowned. "You're friendly with that Bradley woman, aren't you?"

"Constance?" Lash was a little surprised by the question. "Why, yes, I'd like to think that we're friends. Why do you ask?"

"My wife's still riding with her. I just . . ." Kemp sighed. "I wondered if Virginia is all right, that's all."

"I saw her this morning, and she seemed fine."

"I wish she was up here with me, where she belongs. That way, if anything happens, I could protect her."

"I'm sorry things haven't gone smoothly for the two of you. I'm sure you can work all that out once you arrive at your destination in Oregon, however."

"What about my brother?" Kemp glared. "I haven't seen him all morning. Not that I was looking for him, you understand. But where in blazes has he gotten off to?"

Lash knew that Harrison Kemp was one of the men Preacher had taken with him to try to stop the outlaw attack from happening. But he said, "I'm sure Harrison is around somewhere. The outriders often drift a considerable distance away from the wagons, so that they can keep an eye on our surroundings and provide ample warning in case of trouble."

Kemp snorted contemptuously. "Harrison would run the other way if he saw any real trouble. So I guess that would be a warning, all right."

Lash didn't believe that Harrison was as timid as his brother claimed. If he had been, Preacher never would have picked him to go along on that mission to intercept the outlaws. But he wasn't going to waste time arguing with Wesley Kemp about it, so he said, "We'll rest the livestock here for a bit before getting under way with the crossing."

With a nod to Kemp, he rode on to deliver that news to the rest of the immigrants.

On his way to the front again after informing everyone, he stopped at Constance's wagon. Virginia Kemp was on the driver's seat next to Constance.

Not quite sure why he was involving himself in their marital squabble, Lash said, "Mrs. Kemp, your husband inquired about you when I was talking with him a short time ago. He expressed a desire that you would consent to ride with him again in the lead wagon."

"I don't care what Wesley wants," she responded stiffly. "If he was really that worried about me, he wouldn't act like such a hotheaded fool."

"What you do is up to you, of course." Lash touched a finger to his hat brim. "Ladies."

"Be careful, Simon," Constance called. Lash wondered if her feminine intuition was warning her that something might happen.

He was passing Cornelius Russell's wagon when the former professor lifted a hand to stop him. Russell knew about Preacher's plan. Lash had filled him in on it. He asked quietly, "You haven't seen or heard anything yet from our mountain man friend, have you?"

"Not yet," Lash replied with a grim look on his face.

Russell patted the shotgun that rested on the seat beside him. "I hope there's no trouble," he said, "but I suppose I'm as ready as I can be if there is."

"I hope we all are," Lash said. He waved in farewell

and galloped ahead to resume his position in front of the wagons.

The sturdy vehicles rolled forward again, and following Lash's directions, an obviously nervous Wesley Kemp drove his wagon into the river. Lash rode ahead of him, checking the bottom even though he knew it ought to be firm enough to support the wagon wheels.

Unlike the Platte, conditions here on the Sweetwater didn't really change that much over time. The stream bed was gravelly for the most part, and it held up well to crossings like this one.

Lash turned and looked back. Several more wagons had entered the river now. The water came up to their wheel hubs but no higher. The wagons weren't in any danger of starting to float. Lash reached the north bank and turned his horse to watch the wagons as he allowed himself to hope that this crossing was going to proceed without incident.

That was when enough gunfire erupted somewhere in the hills, not far away, that it sounded as if a small war had broken out.

Chapter 29

Simon Lash stiffened, sitting up straighter in the saddle as he jerked his head toward the sounds of battle. The shots came from the east, somewhere in the rocky hills north of the river. It was quite a violent clash, judging by the number of reports that filled the air.

Preacher and his force of volunteers must have encountered the outlaws, thought Lash. He could only hope and pray that the mountain man would be successful in putting an end to the brigands' plans.

But that was out of Lash's hands. He turned his attention to the wagons and saw that Wesley Kemp had hauled back on the reins and brought the lead wagon to a stop. Kemp was staring openmouthed in the direction of the gunfire. By stopping in the middle of the river, he had forced all the other wagons to come to a halt, as well.

Lash cupped his hands around his mouth and shouted as loudly as he could, "Mr. Kemp!"

He had to call the man's name a second time before Kemp broke out of his shock and fear at hearing the gunfire and turned his head to look toward the wagon-master. Lash waved his arm in an urgent motion.

"Mr. Kemp, keep going!" he ordered. "Get across the river! Quickly, now, quickly!"

Kemp shook himself like a dog shaking off water and then slapped the reins against the backs of his team. He bellowed curses at the oxen. The yelling probably didn't have much effect, but the sting of the leather got the beasts of burden moving again. The wagon lurched and rolled forward.

"Come on, come on!" shouted Lash as he continued waving his arm at the others, urging them across the river. He still hoped that Preacher would stop the outlaws' attack, but in case the mountain man failed, Lash didn't want those killers catching the wagons in the middle of the stream.

With water streaming from the legs of the oxen and the wheels, Wesley Kemp's wagon rolled out of the river onto the grassy bank. The next wagon in line was close behind it.

Kemp looked like he was getting ready to stop again. Lash brought his horse alongside the team and leaned over to grab hold of the harness on the left leader. As he tugged on it, he called to Kemp, "Keep moving! Just follow the river and don't stop!"

"What's going on here?" Kemp shouted with a frantic, almost hysterical edge in his voice. "Are we under attack? Is it outlaws? Indians?"

"We're fine," Lash told him as he rode alongside the wagon. There might be some truth to that statement. The shooting had tailed off to nothing. Perhaps Preacher and his men had emerged victorious. The mountain man might return and assure them that they had nothing to worry about.

Lash wasn't going to believe that until it happened, though. He went on, "We want to keep moving until we get past the next choke point, which is several hundred yards ahead of here. There'll be a long, granite bluff on your right. Beyond that is an open area where we can rest for a bit before the next crossing." Recalling previous trips through here, Lash added, "Don't stop to write your name on the bluff, as many have in the past. No time for that. Just keep moving."

"Why don't we have time? I don't hear any more shooting. What's going on? I'm the captain of this wagon train. I have a right to know!"

The questions tumbled out of Kemp's mouth. Lash ignored them. He was losing patience now. He barked, "Just do as you're told!" and turned to ride back along the line of wagons toward the spot where they were still crossing the Sweetwater. He didn't know if Wesley Kemp tried to argue more. He didn't look back.

Five more wagons had successfully forded the stream, and six were in the water now. But that still left sixteen vehicles lined up on the southern bank, waiting their turn. Lash glanced downstream. No sign of the outlaws.

"Keep moving, keep moving!" he called to the drivers. They were actually doing an excellent job, progressing smoothly across the river. Every time one wagon emerged from the water, another entered it. Lash wished he could hurry them up even more, but some things just couldn't be rushed.

Cornelius Russell's wagon rolled up the slight incline to the northern bank. Lash waved at the former professor, who looked tense but was handling his team well. Russell returned a curt nod as he concentrated on what he was doing and gripped the reins tightly.

Constance Bradley's wagon was two back from Russell's. On the driver's seat, Constance and Virginia Kemp rocked slightly side to side as the wagon jolted across the stream bed. Lash smiled and nodded encouragingly to them as they reached the northern bank and the wagon rolled past him.

The minutes seemed to drag by with maddening slowness as Lash watched the wagon train's steady progress across the Sweetwater. Finally, the last of the wagons was in the water, and he began to hope that they would all make it across without incident.

That hope vanished in an instant as he glanced downstream and saw a large group of riders rounding a bend. They were on the southern bank, which was easier going than the northern one at that point. As they galloped toward the wagons, Lash's keen eyes made out the long coats, the pulled-down hats, and the bandannas concealing the lower halves of their faces. This was the same gang of killers and thieves that had struck before, here at the Devil's Crossing.

"Move, move!" Lash shouted again as he waved his arm desperately at the last few wagons. "Get across and follow the others!"

That small open area where he had told Wesley Kemp to stop would hold all the wagons. They could draw some of the vehicles up into a line to serve as a buttress of sorts and take cover behind those wagons. If they did that, they might be able to hold off the outlaws for a while, at least until Preacher and the other men got back.

Assuming that Preacher and the other men were coming back and weren't all dead . . .

Simon Lash banished that thought from his head and pulled his rifle from the straps that held it to his saddle. The range was still pretty far, especially shooting from horseback at a moving target, but he wanted the outlaws to know that they were in for a fight. Lash steadied his aim and fired at an angle across the river, hoping that he would hit one of the two men riding in the forefront of the gang.

Instead, one of the other men riding slightly behind them jerked and sagged in his saddle but managed to stay mounted. Lash knew he had wounded the man. That was better than nothing, he thought as he pulled down the trigger guard, opening the rifle's breech to reload.

Lash's movements were automatic, born of years of practice. He didn't have to look at what he was doing or think about it as he slid a new cartridge into the breech. Instead, he glanced at the wagons to check on their progress. Only four vehicles were left in the water now. The others were on the northern bank, trundling as fast as they could along the trail beside the river.

As he lifted the rifle to his shoulder again, Lash was vaguely aware of little spurts of water kicking up in the stream. Those came from bullets, he realized. The outlaws were targeting the wagons still in the river. Anger welled up inside him. He took aim and fired a second time, but he couldn't tell if he hit any of the outlaws. Still holding the empty rifle in his right hand, he used his left on the reins, turning his horse so that his back was to the charging gang.

"Hurry, hurry!" he urged the drivers. One of the

wagons bounced out onto the bank. Another was close behind it. That left just two in the water.

The man driving the next to last wagon screamed and jerked halfway to his feet. He would have toppled off into the river, but his wife reached out from inside the wagon and caught hold of his shirt. She pulled on him so that he fell over the back of the seat and into the wagon instead. Then, with the innate bravery of pioneer women, she scrambled over the seat and reached down to grab the reins her man had dropped when he was hit. At this point, she probably didn't know how badly he was hurt or even if he was still alive, but she knew the most important thing was to keep the wagon moving. She slashed at the oxen with the reins and yelled shrilly at them.

Simon Lash admired her but had no time to dwell on it. Lead was humming all around him now. He hung the rifle on its straps and pulled his pistol. Triggering it toward the onrushing outlaws on the other side of the stream, he wheeled his horse into the edge of the Sweetwater. He hoped the barrage he was laying down would shield those final two wagons.

They made it out of the river, and the last vehicle turned to follow the others along the northern bank. Men on horseback swept past both sides of the wagon train and joined Lash in emptying pistols toward the outlaws. The outriders had been busy shepherding the wagons in their flight, as they were supposed to do, but now that all the wagons had made the crossing, the men were able to join Lash in trying to hold off the attackers.

Bullets flew back and forth in a fierce, deadly storm. A couple of the outriders cried out and fell from their horses, struck down by outlaw lead. But the stubborn resistance blunted the horde's charge. They slowed and began to fall back slightly.

Simon Lash knew that retreat wouldn't last. The outlaws were just regrouping and would attack again, probably within minutes, more determined than ever to slaughter the immigrants and loot the wagon train.

He would fight to his last breath to prevent that . . . but he knew in his heart that might not be enough.

Not without help that might not ever come.

As Jamie and Absaroka reached the edge of the hills, Jamie reined in, looked across the rolling, grassy plains, and saw a line of vegetation about half a mile away.

"Is that the river?" he asked, pointing to the growth.

"It must be," said Absaroka. He cursed. "We came out farther east than I intended. It's at least a mile to the Devil's Crossing."

"I thought Indians didn't cuss," Jamie commented with a grim smile.

"I've been around white men too much. Picked up your bad habits." Absaroka heeled his horse into motion again. "Come on. I don't hear any more shooting right now, but that doesn't mean that wagon train is out of trouble."

Jamie knew that was right. He galloped after the young gunman.

Preacher, Tom Linford, Roscoe Lomax, Harrison Kemp, and the other five men rode hard through the hills, paralleling the canyon used by the outlaws. If they could have gotten down into the canyon, they might have made better time, but the canyon wall was too sheer for horses to negotiate it. The riders had to travel around rock spires and through gullies and along razor-backed ridges where a horse's misstep could cause a bad fall.

Every delay gnawed at Preacher. They had come so far, traveled for so long, all with the aim of putting an end to the bloody depredations at the Devil's Crossing, and now it seemed they were on the verge of failure.

Judging by the anxious expression on his face as he leaned forward in the saddle, Tom Linford felt the same way, if not more so. Preacher had committed to this job out of a sense of right and wrong. Linford had personal scores to settle.

And now it was even worse for the young scout with the revelation that a man he had admired, tried to learn from, regarded almost as a second father, was really the mastermind behind the gang preying on the wagon trains. He would want vengeance and justice for that act of betrayal, as well.

Linford suddenly reined in and cried, "Listen! Do you hear that?"

Preacher checked Horse and lifted his head. The sound of shots came to his ears, enough of them that he knew Prescott's gang had reached the crossing and attacked the wagon train.

He wasn't the only one who understood that. Harrison Kemp exclaimed, "We're too late! They're going after the wagons!"

"It don't sound like we're too far behind 'em!" Preacher said. "Come on!"

The stallion bolted forward with the other horses thundering after him. Preacher had reloaded his guns before they started. He drew the right-hand weapon now and held it ready to dispense some of that vengeance and justice he had been thinking of a moment earlier.

With the outriders who had just driven back the outlaws for the moment, Simon Lash galloped along the narrow trail in front of the bluff where thousands of names were carved in the rock or daubed with charcoal or grease. Lash's spirits rose slightly as he realized the topography was going to help them. The entire gang couldn't charge them at once along this trail; there wasn't room for that. It would be easier to hold them off.

But that was only a short-term advantage. The hills to the north of the river weren't so rugged that men bent on murder couldn't climb into them and fire down into the little cup where the wagons were gathering. The gang could lay siege to them from there and pick off the defenders one at a time until there weren't enough left to withstand an all-out attack.

As Lash reached the open area, he looked around and saw that the wagons had stopped in a haphazard fashion. Spotting Edmund Farrington, he called, "Mr. Farrington! Pull your wagons up in a line right here!" He made a sweeping gesture with his arm to demonstrate what he meant. "We'll use them as a blockade."

"But they're loaded with all the goods I'm taking to Oregon!" Farrington protested. "Those men will shoot everything full of holes and ruin it!" Then he sighed and went on, "But all those crates will make good protection, won't they?"

"I'm sorry," Lash told him, "but none of those goods will mean anything to you if we never make it to Oregon."

Farrington nodded, then added, "I just wish Mr. Lomax was here to take charge of moving the wagons. I'll have to do it myself." He turned and started bellowing orders and curses at his men and the teams of oxen. Under other circumstances, such a tirade in his squeaky, high-pitched voice might have sounded pretty comical, but nobody in the wagon train was laughing today.

Lash dismounted and reloaded his rifle. He led his horse over to the area where the extra livestock was being kept and turned it loose, knowing that it wouldn't stray far from the other saddle mounts. He trotted back to the wagons and saw that the defensive line formed by Farrington's vehicles was shaping up. Once the wagons were in place, the merchant's drivers unhitched the teams and led them away. The men who had been serving as outriders, dismounted now, hurried up and positioned themselves behind the wagons with their rifles pointed back along the trail.

Lash frowned. The trail was empty now. The outlaws had pulled back out of sight. Surely, they hadn't abandoned their plans to loot the wagon train.

Lash walked back and forth behind the wagons and said, "Steady, boys. They'll be coming in a bit, I'm certain of that. Make your shots count."

Edmund Farrington, Cornelius Russell, Jesse Willis, Stephen Millard, and several other men hurried up, each with a rifle. Russell asked, "Where do you need us, Simon?"

"There's not room here for all of you," said Lash. "Go back to the other wagons and spread out among them. Make sure all the women and children are inside the vehicles and are staying low as much as they can, behind furniture or boxes of supplies, anything that will give them more protection." He looked around. "Where's Wesley Kemp?"

"Haven't seen him since we stopped here," Farrington said.

Willis grunted. "He's probably hiding in his wagon."

"Well, I don't suppose it matters," Lash said. "Good luck to you all, gentlemen."

As they trotted off, Lash noticed Constance Bradley hurrying toward him. He went to meet her, noting the worried expression on her face. She had plenty to be worried about, he thought. They all did.

In Constance's case, however, it wasn't just the outlaws causing her concern. She said, "Simon, Wesley Kemp came to my wagon for his wife."

"I can't blame him for wanting her with him at a time like this. I'm sure he simply wants to see to it that she's protected."

"She didn't want to go with him," Constance said. "He forced her."

Lash grimaced. The very last thing he needed to deal with right now was the personal drama between the Kemps. If they didn't defeat the outlaws, none of that would matter.

"I'll have to look into it later—"

"Kemp said they were going to take some horses and get out of here," Constance interrupted him.

That surprised Lash. "You mean he intends to abandon the wagon train?"

"That's what he said, yes. He told Virginia they weren't going to stay here and let themselves get killed."

"Well, so much for being elected captain," Lash replied with a wry shake of his head. "Sometimes those we choose to lead us prove less than worthy of our vote."

"I'm worried about Virginia. She and I have become friends since we've been riding together."

"I know, and I'm sorry, but there's nothing I can do about it now. Perhaps later . . ."

If there *is* a later, he thought.

"But for the moment," he went on, "you need to get back to your wagon and find a good place to take cover."

"All right, but I have a rifle, and I can use it if I need to."

"It may come to that," he said as he reached out and rested a hand on her shoulder for a second.

Before he could say or do anything else, one of the men crouched behind Farrington's wagons yelled, "Here they come!"

Chapter 30

L ash squeezed Constance's shoulder, resisting the urge to push her toward her wagon, and said, "Hurry now! Get under cover and take care!"

She nodded and turned to run. Lash went the other way, hurrying to join the men at the blockade.

He stood at the back corner of one of the wagons and peered along the trail that followed the bluff. The outlaws had crossed the river and were on the northern side now, riding four abreast, crowded onto the trail. The masked men in the front rank blazed away with the guns in their hands. Bullets thudded into the wagon bodies and ripped through the canvas covers to strike the piled-up crates inside.

"Open fire!" Lash called as the deadly missiles whipped through the air around them.

A thunderous wave of rifle, pistol, and shotgun fire rolled out from the defenders and scythed into the outlaws. Two horses went down, causing the riders crowding close behind to try to leap over them. Instantly, it was a bloody, flailing tangle on the ledge-like trail in front of the bluff.

But even though they had to rein in sharply, the outlaws who were still mounted continued blasting at the wagons. As Lash reloaded his rifle, he saw that there weren't as many in the gang as before. Only a dozen men had attacked along the trail, leaving the others unaccounted for. He knew the defenders hadn't killed that many, so there was only one logical place the rest of the outlaws could be.

Shots that suddenly rang out above and to the left of them confirmed Lash's hunch. Some of the killers had already climbed into the hills to the north. From up there, they had a good angle on the wagons.

"Take cover!" Lash bellowed at the men with him, then turned toward the wagons and waved his arms. "Look out above! Take cover!"

One of the men behind the wagon barricade cried out and lurched forward, arching his back because of the bullet that had just struck him between the shoulder blades. He fell against the wagon and then slid down it to collapse into the loose sprawl of death.

Lash swung his rifle to his shoulder and fired at a puff of smoke he spotted on one of the hills looming over the wagons. It was a snap shot but lethally accurate. One of the outlaws lurched forward and doubled over to clutch at his belly. His hat flew off as he pitched forward and tumbled down the slope in a loose-limbed fashion, finally disappearing into some brush.

"Take cover!" Lash shouted again as he crouched and ducked underneath the wagon next to him. He knelt there and reloaded, all too aware that slugs from the guns of the outlaws on the trail were still striking the vehicle. One of them chewed splinters from a wheel spoke only a couple of feet from his head.

He lifted the reloaded rifle to his shoulder and took a shot at the onrushing men. One of them toppled out of the saddle. That gave Lash a momentary surge of satisfaction, but it lasted only a split second before another bullet screamed past his head and caused him to duck instinctively. He reached for another cartridge for the rifle.

Another couple of men crowded under the wagon with him, seeking refuge from the sharpshooters in the hills. "Concentrate your fire on the men on the trail in front of us, lads," Lash told them. "We can't allow them to overrun us."

He wished he knew what was happening elsewhere with the immigrants. Under attack from two directions as they were, they had to be taking some casualties. He was worried about all of them but was human enough to be especially concerned about his friends, Constance Bradley and Cornelius Russell.

But all he could do was keep fighting and hope and pray for a miracle.

At the top of a rise, Preacher reined in and held up a hand in a signal for Tom Linford, Roscoe Lomax, Harrison Kemp, and the other men to stop. The gunfire was loud now and seemed close by. A ragged line of hills still separated the men from the river, though. Preacher recalled that the Sweetwater, and the Devil's Crossing, lay just on the other side of those hills.

He checked that recollection with Linford by saying, "Tom, the river lies just beyond those next hills, doesn't it?"

Linford frowned in thought for a moment before nodding. "I'm pretty sure that's right. From the sound of that gunfire, they ambushed the wagons from the slopes above the river."

"At least some of 'em did," Preacher said. "Wouldn't surprise me if the varmints hit 'em from two directions at once. But Simon's bound to have heard the shootin' from when we tangled with that bunch earlier, and with any luck, he hustled the wagons on across and forted up somewhere. That's what we got to hope for, anyway."

"Can't we get moving?" Harrison Kemp asked with a note of worried anguish in his voice. "People could be getting killed!"

"Yeah, but chargin' in blind usually ain't a good idea. We can do more good for the folks in the wagon train by takin' some of the heat from above off them. We'll see if we can't take the ones in the hills by surprise. We'll spread out in a line with, say, fifty yards between each of us, and head for the river, cleanin' out the rats as we come to 'em."

Linford added, "You saw the way they were dressed before, so you know if you spot anybody who looks like that, they're one of the gang. Don't hesitate when you come across them."

"Which means that gunnin' down skunks like that from behind ain't nothin' to lose sleep over," said Preacher. "Because they sure as blazes wouldn't hesitate to ventilate you if they got the chance, whether you were facin' 'em or not. In fact, most varmints like that prefer back-shootin'."

The men nodded in understanding. Some of them might hesitate anyway, simply because pulling a trigger and ending a man's life was a weighty thing to do. Some fellas found it easier in a face-to-face battle, where it was a matter of kill or be killed and no time to ponder things, and some were quicker to pull the trigger when they *couldn't* see their target's face. Every man was different, and so was every moment. But at least Preacher and Linford had let them all know what they were about to tackle.

They spread out as Preacher had ordered and moved forward. Linford was to the mountain man's right, Harrison Kemp to his left, and Roscoe Lomax beyond Harrison. Dog padded straight ahead, ears pricked forward, with a tenseness in the smooth play of his muscles that showed he was ready to spring to the attack as soon as he sighted any quarry.

The skirmish line started up a heavily-wooded slope. The growth was thick enough that within moments, Preacher could no longer see either Linford or Harrison. He heard them moving through the brush; with the possible exception of Roscoe Lomax, none of his companions had enough experience on the frontier to be able to travel quietly through such growth. But they weren't making a big racket, and the outlaws, with their hearing assaulted by the constant pound of gunfire, probably wouldn't notice any sounds the men made while approaching them.

That was Preacher's hope, anyway. He knew he and Dog would be able to account for some of the outlaws. He had waited long enough to turn the big cur loose, he decided. Quietly, he said, "Dog, hunt."

The sleek gray shape lunged forward into a run and vanished in the brush.

After a few more minutes of homing in on the sound

of one particular rifle, Preacher dismounted, left Horse's reins dangling, and stole ahead on foot, moving through the undergrowth like a phantom. He reached the top of the slope and came out on a large, relatively flat rock slab that hung beetle-browed over the narrow canyon through which the Sweetwater River flowed. A few scrubby bushes grew at the slab's edge. An outlaw knelt behind one of those bushes, sighting over the rifle he held to his shoulder.

Preacher moved closer and looked past the man into a rough half-circle of open ground on the river's northern side. The wagons had stopped there, and several of them were lined up in a crude barricade to protect the others from attackers on the trail beside the river.

But there was nothing protecting them from the outlaws who had climbed into these overlooking hills.

Preacher didn't see anybody moving around down there, but he did spot a few sprawled, motionless bodies: luckless folks who hadn't been able to get to cover quickly enough when the outlaw barrage came thundering down from above. But the others had taken shelter under the wagons and were putting up a fight. A pall of powder smoke hung over the cup surrounded on three sides by the hills.

Preacher took all that in with a half second's glance. The outlaws had to be dealt with one at a time, so he started by stepping closer, sliding his knife from its sheath, and with a sweeping thrust, driving it into the rifleman's back just before the man fired again. The weapon went off anyway as its wielder's finger pulled the trigger involuntarily. He had already jerked the barrel up, though, as Preacher buried the cold steel in his body, so the bullet screamed off harmlessly somewhere in the hills across the river.

Preacher looped his left arm around the outlaw's neck and jerked him back away from the edge. The man spasmed again, then went limp. Preacher pulled the knife out and lowered the corpse to the ground. As he wiped the blood off the blade on the dead man's long coat, he thought about tossing the body down the steep slope, then decided against it. That might warn the outlaws that enemies were among them, and it would be better to continue taking them by surprise as long as possible.

A sudden thrashing in the brush off to his right caught his attention. He heard a choked, gurgling cry. Preacher headed in that direction.

He wasn't surprised when he found Dog standing over the body of another outlaw. The man's throat was a bloody ruin. Crimson dripped from the big cur's muzzle.

"Good job, old son," Preacher told him. "Go find another of the varmints."

Dog glanced up at Preacher, then arrowed off into the brush again. The mountain man would have sworn that the cur had just grinned at him.

The shooting hadn't slowed. The outlaws were still pouring bullets down on the wagon train. Preacher moved along the rim, staying back so that none of the shots fired by the immigrants would strike him accidentally.

He hadn't gone very far when a man abruptly appeared in front of him. His garb marked him as one of the outlaws. He was muttering curses as he worked on a pistol that evidently had jammed. He and Preacher spotted each other at the same instant, and both men reacted swiftly.

Preacher's hand dropped to the Colt Dragoon revolver on his right hip. As the gun came up, the outlaw flung the weapon in his hand at Preacher's face as hard as he could. Preacher had to duck to the side to avoid the thrown gun. That delayed him just enough for the outlaw to launch himself in a diving tackle.

The man's shoulder crashed into Preacher's midsection and drove him over backward. They fell into one of the bushes that proved to be full of long, slender, surprisingly vicious thorns that ripped Preacher's buckskin shirt and clawed savagely at every inch of exposed skin. Several of them jabbed into his face, dangerously close to his eyes. Those thorns could blind a man.

He tried to hang on to his gun, but between the pain of the thorns and the impact from landing on the ground with the outlaw's weight on top of him, the Colt slipped out of his grasp. The man jabbed a knee in Preacher's belly and grabbed him by the throat. Strong fingers clamped on the mountain man's flesh like iron bars and started trying to strangle the life out of him. His thumbs dug hard for Preacher's windpipe.

The outlaw's face was only a couple of feet away as he leaned over Preacher. It was an ugly, lantern-jawed, beard-stubbled visage. The left eye had a grotesque cast to it, as well as a milky film. The man had to be blind in that eye, but he probably saw just fine with the other one. A leer twisted his mouth as he loomed over Preacher.

With his left hand, Preacher reached out and snagged one of the branches. Ignoring the pain as the thorns bit into his palm, he shoved the branch into the outlaw's face. The man screamed as one of the thorns speared his good eye. He let go of Preacher's throat so he could clap both hands over his face.

Preacher's right hand shot up in a slugging blow to the jaw. The outlaw fell back and to the side. He was still pawing at his injured eye, in too much pain and shock to be aware of Preacher scrambling up. Preacher plucked his knife from its sheath again and lunged forward. He came down on top of the outlaw and slammed the blade into the man's chest, aiming for the heart.

He found it. The outlaw bucked up from the ground, arching his back, and then sagged lifelessly. His hands slid away from his collapsed, ruined eye, which still leaked fluid. He didn't feel it anymore, though.

Preacher pulled his knife from the man's chest, wiped it off, crawled over him and out of the brush. He was bleeding in a dozen places from thorn scratches, including on his cheeks, but none of the wounds were serious. He must have looked a sight, though, with blood smeared over his face and hands.

For a second, a grim smile tugged at his mouth under the thick, salt-and-pepper mustache. Maybe he looked grisly enough that the next outlaw he encountered would hesitate for a second in shock. Preacher would take any such advantage he could get.

He had to reach back into the brush—carefully—to retrieve the Colt he had dropped. After checking the barrel for fouling, he pouched the iron, then had second thoughts and unleathered it again.

The next outlaw he ran into, he'd be ready to shoot the varmint without having to draw.

He wondered how Linford, Lomax, Harrison, and the rest of the men were making out. He hoped all of them were still alive and in the thick of the fight.

Chapter 31

Tom Linford had his gun in his hand as he followed a twisting, brush-choked draw that ran gradually upward. He heard regularly spaced shots not far in front of him and knew they had to be coming from one of the outlaws.

Linford thought about what he and Preacher had told the others about not hesitating to gun down any of the outlaws if they got a chance. During the battle at the Devil's Crossing the previous year, he had shot to kill, but that was in the heat of combat. Even after everything that had happened—the pain and loss he had suffered, the weeks of recovery, the months of being consumed by grief, anger, and the burning need for vengeance—he wasn't sure he could shoot a man in the back. Even an outlaw . . .

Unless the man was Ethan Prescott. After what Prescott had done, Linford figured he could shoot the crooked wagon-master anywhere, any time.

Right now, though, he wasn't going to be shooting anybody, he realized as he saw that the draw he'd been following ended in an almost sheer wall of dirt and rock.

A few roots stuck out of the dirt, and as the young scout studied them, he decided he would be able to climb the slope by hanging on to those roots. But he would need both hands to do it, so he holstered his gun.

Linford reached up, grabbed one of the roots, found a toehold, and pulled himself up. The slope actually inclined more than it looked like at first glance, so climbing it required an effort. The top was about twenty feet above him. He climbed steadily.

Despite his youth and being in good shape, he was a little winded by the time he reached the top. He pulled himself over the edge and then remained on hands and knees for a moment as he tried to catch his breath.

His head was hanging down a little as he drew air in and out of his lungs. That was a mistake, as he realized instantly when a booted foot appeared in front of his face. He hadn't even heard anybody walking up to him over the pounding of his pulse inside his skull.

Linford raised his head slowly and found himself peering upward into the barrel of a gun. Beyond it he saw a stern, red-bearded face. Linford recognized death in the outlaw's eyes and expected the gun muzzle to erupt in a blinding flash that would be followed by black oblivion.

Instead, surprisingly, the outlaw chuckled and said, "Thought you'd sneak up on ol' Hennessy, did you, boy? How many more of you are there out here? Tell me, and I won't kill you."

Linford didn't believe that for a second. The gun was cocked. The outlaw could pull the trigger in less time than the blink of an eye. And he would, as soon as Linford told him what he wanted to know.

Since his situation really couldn't get much worse this side of dying, Linford threw himself forward, powering his body with his feet as he drove his shoulder against the outlaw's legs. The gun boomed deafeningly loud, right over his head, but he didn't feel anything. Either the shot had missed, or else he just wasn't aware yet of how badly he was hurt.

Didn't matter. He was going to keep fighting.

Surprise was on his side. The outlaw stumbled backward. Linford reached up, grabbed the long coat, and hauled on it as hard as he could. With a startled yell, the outlaw toppled off his feet. Linford saw the gun barrel swinging toward him again. He batted it aside with his left forearm and drew his own gun with his right hand. Lunging forward again as he eared back the hammer, he shoved its muzzle into the hollow under the man's chin and pulled the trigger.

The gun's boom was muffled. The look on the outlaw's face and the way his eyes bulged out as the bullet tunneled up through his brain and exploded out the top of his head was a grotesque spectacle Tom Linford would never forget. Even so, he felt a surge of relief as the man sagged back, dead.

Linford pushed himself to his feet and stood there for a moment, trying to catch his breath. The air stunk of powder smoke and death, so he stepped around the outlaw he had just killed and moved on. His right arm hung at his side with the gun still in his hand. He wasn't going to holster it again until this fight was over, one way or the other.

* * *

Harrison Kemp knew he ought to be focused on what he was doing, since he might come face-to-face with a vicious killer at any moment, but it was impossible for him to force persistent thoughts of Virginia out of his mind. The sight of her beautiful face, the taste of her warm, sweet lips, the feel of her body's soft, swelling curves in his arms . . .

Those things kept coming back to him, filling his head with pleasant memories. He stopped where he was, just short of some trees, took a deep breath, and clenched his hand harder on the butt of the gun he held as he tried to banish those distracting memories.

After a moment, he blew out the breath and moved forward with renewed concentration to resume hunting the outlaws who were attacking the wagon train.

He had taken only a couple of steps when a rifle barrel protruded past one of the tree trunks ahead of him and a harsh voice called, "Drop that gun, mister, and keep right on coming this way."

Harrison knew that one of the outlaws had gotten the drop on him and would kill him if he surrendered, so he didn't do either of the things the man commanded. Instead, he flung himself forward, diving to the ground as he triggered wildly toward the sound of the voice that had just accosted him. Splinters flew from the trunk of the tree behind which the rifleman was concealed.

Harrison landed hard on his belly but kept his head up, cocked and fired the revolver twice more as the rifle roared and the bullet kicked up dirt near his head.

The outlaw who had been hidden in the trees reeled to the side, out into the open enough for Harrison to see him. A bloodstain bloomed like a crimson flower on the man's shirt. The man dropped the rifle and clawed under his long coat for the holstered gun he wore.

Harrison raised his Colt, steadied it by gripping his right wrist with his left hand, and fired again. This shot took the outlaw in the chest and knocked him over backward. His legs kicked a couple of times, and then he lay still.

Harrison's heart slugged in his chest and his pulse hammered wildly in his head as he climbed to his feet. During the earlier battle with the outlaws, and the Indian fight before that, there was a decent chance he had killed some of the enemy, but never up close like that, where he could see the face of the man whose life he was ending. He breathed hard a few times, blinked rapidly as reaction coursed through him.

Knowing what these men intended for Virginia and all the other innocent people with the wagon train, he would kill the outlaw all over again if he had the chance, Harrison realized.

With that thought in his head, he reloaded the chambers he had emptied in the Colt's cylinder and moved on in search of more enemies.

Roscoe Lomax wore a shaggy, buffalo hide coat nearly year-round, no matter what the weather. He was accustomed to it and it didn't bother him, even when it was hot. As he stalked through the hills, he swept the coat back on both sides so it would be easier for him to reach the gun on his right hip and the knife on his left.

When trouble came at him, though, it was so unexpected that he didn't have time to grab either weapon.

He was passing under a tree when he heard a faint rustling in the branches above him. He threw his head back to look up and saw a shape plummeting at him. The man crashed into Lomax a split second later. He weighed enough that the impact knocked the burly bullwhacker off his feet.

"He's down!" the man who had landed on top of Lomax shouted. "Come on, boys! He's down!"

Lomax heard rapid footsteps rushing toward him. He was a little stunned by being knocked down like this, but he was still able to reach up and grab his attacker by the neck. His sausage-like fingers closed hard, choking off the man's exuberant cries. Lomax flung him to the side like a rag doll.

But several other outlaws already surrounded him. Boot toes slammed into his ribs, belly, and head. Lomax flung his arms up over his head to try to protect himself and rolled hard to the side, crashing into several legs and bringing more men toppling down on him like falling trees.

Their weight pinned him to the ground for a moment, but he fought back, bucking and rearing, jabbing with elbows and knees, and hammering his bony fists into every face he caught a glimpse of. He battled furiously to make some room around him, then heaved upright and threw off his foes, scattering them around him like a grizzly bear shaking loose from a pack of wolves.

One of the men landed right in front of him but started to bounce back up instantly. Lomax lifted his foot in a kick that caught the man under the chin. The outlaw's head jerked back with a sharp crack. His eyes rolled up in their sockets. He collapsed as if all the bones and muscles in his body had turned to water. Lomax knew he had broken the man's neck.

Two men closed in on him from the sides and grabbed his arms. "Hang on to—" one of them started to yell.

Lomax brought both arms around in front of him and slammed the two men together. They should have let go of him instead of trying to hold him. Their foreheads clunked together with enough force that they bounced off each other and fell backward, out cold.

If he'd had time, Lomax might have stomped the life out of both of the varmints. But there were still two outlaws flanking him, and they must have realized that they didn't want to tangle with him hand to hand after all. They started backing off rapidly, hands pawing at their guns as they did so.

Lomax was no fancy shooter like Preacher. Usually, he could hit what he aimed at, but he was no great hand at hauling out a gun and getting to work with it in a hurry. So instead of trying to outdraw either man, he lowered his head and charged like a bull at the closest one, who happened to be to Lomax's right. The man yelled in alarm as he rushed his shot and sent the bullet screaming over Lomax's head.

Lomax plowed into the man and sent him flying through the air. As a bullet from the other man ripped past Lomax's right ear, he threw himself to the left, rolled when he hit the ground, and came up with the heavy Walker Colt in his hand. He thumbed back the hammer and let fly with a shot at the second outlaw. The man ducked but didn't seem to be hit. He raised his gun and cocked it again.

Lomax surged up and dived to the side again as the

outlaw squeezed off another shot. He felt the bullet tug on the flapping buffalo coat. Lomax got off a second shot with the Walker. This time the outlaw slewed to the side as the round tore through his left lung. He fell to his knees and coughed up bloody froth. But he didn't pass out. In fact, he managed to lift the gun again as he twisted back toward Lomax, who was already drawing a bead on him for another shot.

The thunderous report that filled the air didn't come from Lomax's weapon, however. Something slammed into the gun and knocked it out of his hand. The impact deadened that arm past the elbow. Lomax roared a curse and clutched the stunned arm to him as he turned his head and saw the man he had knocked down aiming at him for another try.

Lomax's left hand flew to his waist and yanked the long-bladed knife from its sheath. In a continuation of the same move, he threw it at the second outlaw just as the man fired. The knife struck the man in the chest and caused his shot to go wild. Lomax had put so much power behind the throw, even in that awkward position, that the blade sank nearly all the way to the hilt in the outlaw's body. He dropped his gun and pawed futilely at the knife's handle as he swayed backward and then fell over on his side.

A slug from the remaining outlaw's gun burned past Lomax's face. He turned and tried to use his left hand to pick up the gun he had dropped. He fumbled at it and glanced up to see the man leering at him over the barrel of the gun that was trained on Lomax's face. Lomax's eyes widened. There wasn't a blasted thing he could do to stop that outlaw from blowing his brains out . . .

A shaggy gray shape flashed out of the trees and streaked at the outlaw from the side. The man yelled as he saw the big cur coming and tried to jerk his gun in that direction, but matched against Dog's speed, he never had a chance. Dog sailed through the air. His wide-open jaws clamped on the outlaw's neck and took him down. The man thrashed, flailing his arms and legs as he gurgled. Then Dog's jaws closed with a crunching sound. The outlaw spasmed and slumped into stillness, dead as he could be with his throat crushed and bloody.

Without the pressure of having to fight for his life, Lomax was able to pick up the gun. He held it awkwardly in his left hand as he pushed himself to his feet. A few yards away, Dog gave the corpse's throat a last shake and then let go. He turned to look at Lomax.

The bullwhacker had always been afraid of dogs. He knew it didn't make much sense, but that was the way he felt. When he'd first seen this particular dog, he had taken it for a wolf. Even when he knew better, he had told Preacher to keep Dog away from him. Dog must have sensed that hostility, because he had never warmed up to Lomax, either. But the two of them had developed a grudging respect for each other and a truce of sorts. They just kept their distance from each other.

Now Lomax drew in a deep breath and rumbled, "I'm much obliged to you, you flea-bitten varmint." His right arm was starting to work again as feeling tingled back into it. He raised the arm and held out his hand. "I reckon I ought to pet you or something."

Dog bared his teeth.

Lomax dropped his arm and said, "Fine, we'll leave it the way it is. I'm still obliged to you."

With a chuckle evidently aimed at the bullwhacker's discomfiture, Preacher stepped out of the brush. "Are you all right, Lomax?" he asked.

Lomax flexed the fingers of his right hand and said, "Reckon I will be."

Preacher looked around at the sprawled bodies. "Wait a minute. Did you just kill five of the varmints?"

"Two," said Lomax. "Dog got one of 'em, and them two over there are just knocked out from when I whacked their heads together."

Preacher took a closer look and said, "Nope, they're dead, right enough. Looks like you busted their skulls."

"Huh," said Lomax. "I didn't realize they hit that hard. So, yeah, I reckon I killed four of 'em after all." He grinned under the thick beard. "Takin' on four outlaws single-handed and sendin' all of 'em across the divide, that's pretty impressive. Sort of like somethin' you'd do, I'd say."

"I ain't keepin' score," Preacher said. "But what I do know is that we've whittled down the odds considerable. Let's hunt up the rest of the fellas and see how they made out."

Lomax frowned. "I just noticed, I don't hear any shootin' anymore. Is the fight over? Are all the outlaws done for?"

"I don't rightly know," replied Preacher, "but I can tell you one thing. A few minutes ago, it sounded like all hell was breakin' loose down there at the Devil's Crossin'."

Chapter 32

Jamie MacCallister and the young gunman who called himself Absaroka followed the sound of guns through the valley of the Sweetwater. As the rocky slope on their right crowded in, the trail petered out and forced them to cross the river to the south bank. Sparkling droplets of water flew high from the splashing hooves of their mounts.

Once on the opposite bank, they rode hard for half a mile until, once again, the rugged terrain made it necessary for them to ford the stream. This was where the wagon train, which had been traveling on the southern bank to start with, would have made its first of three crossings.

Jamie didn't see any of the wagons, so he figured they had made it across before the outlaws struck. The loud booming and banging up ahead confirmed that. He and Absaroka galloped along the twisting trail until they rounded a bend and spotted a number of the killers up ahead. The outlaws had taken cover behind some rocks and were firing toward a line of wagons drawn up into a makeshift barricade.

As far as Jamie could tell, they weren't bothering to keep an eye out behind them.

They would live to regret that.

But not for long.

"That's them," Jamie said as he reined in. "Are you sure you want to take them on? We're outnumbered four to one, looks like, and some of those men might be friends of yours."

"I was never friends with any of that bunch," Absaroka said coldly. "Like I told you before, MacCallister, throwing in with them was a mistake. I realize that now."

Jamie nodded as he drew the heavy Walker Colt. He knew it was fully loaded and ready for him to get to work with it.

"Let's give them a little surprise," he said.

Absaroka pulled both of his irons from their holsters. "One thing," he said. "That's not all of the gang. I don't know where the others are."

Jamie nodded toward the rugged hills looming over them to the right. "From the sound of it, the rest of them are up there, shooting down at the wagons from above. We'll see about them when we're through dealing with this bunch."

A faint, grim smile tugged at the corners of Absaroka's mouth. "That sounds like a good plan," he said. Then he put his reins in his teeth, since both hands were filled with guns.

The two men charged along the trail that ran in front of the granite bluff. They held their fire as they closed in on the outlaws, not wanting to warn the men about this new threat any sooner than they had to.

Then one of the outlaws must have heard the swift

rataplan of approaching hoofbeats, because he craned his head around to look over his shoulder at Jamie and Absaroka. Jamie saw the man's wolfish features twist in surprise. The outlaw opened his mouth to yell a warning to his companions.

Jamie put a bullet right between those gaping jaws. The slug must have smashed the outlaw's spine before blowing a hole in the back of his neck, judging by the way he dropped like a puppet with its strings cut.

"Good shot!" Absaroka exclaimed.

Jamie just nodded. He knew the shot had been mostly luck. Anyway, he'd aimed at the outlaw's chest. But as any veteran frontiersman had learned, you took your good fortune where you found it.

The other outlaws, warned by the first man's bloody, unexpected death, whirled around to meet the attack from Jamie and Absaroka. A couple fired rifles while the others blazed away with pistols.

Jamie leaned forward in the saddle to make himself a smaller target—not that that did much good, as big as he was. But in a gunfight, a fraction of an inch might mean the difference between life and death.

Beside him, Absaroka guided his horse with his knees as he fired left, right, left, right, at the outlaws. A cloud of powder smoke rolled from the gun muzzles and whipped back around Absaroka as he rode, so that he almost looked like he was emerging from a fog bank.

Jamie felt as much as heard the bullets whipping past his head. He knew those leaden messengers of death were buzzing around Absaroka, too. But fate seemed to ride with them and shield them. Both men stayed in the saddle as they thundered along the trail toward the gang.

Bullets hammered several outlaws off their feet and sent others slumping back against the rocks they had been using for cover. Those boulders were no protection against the lightning strike from behind, though.

The hammer of Jamie's Colt clicked on an empty chamber, and both of Absaroka's guns fell silent an instant later. Both men holstered their guns, but they didn't break off their attack. There was no time to pull their rifles. Three of the outlaws were still on their feet, firing at them. Those shots went wild, because the men were spooked with the two grim-faced avengers bearing down on them. Their gun hammers snapped on empty chambers, too, as Jamie and Absaroka left their saddles in diving tackles.

Jamie seemed to have the wingspan of a giant condor as he spread his arms and crashed into two of the outlaws, dragging them off their feet.

Absaroka's shoulder drove into the chest of the third man and slammed him back against one of the boulders. That outlaw grunted in pain but had the presence of mind to chop at Absaroka's head with the gun he still held. The young man's hat had flown off when he dived from his horse, so there was nothing to soften the blow as the gun barrel thudded into the side of his head and skidded off, leaving a bloody welt above his left ear.

Absaroka staggered but managed to keep his feet as he tried to shake off the effects of the vicious strike. His left fist shot out in a jab that landed solidly on the outlaw's nose. Cartilage crunched, and blood spurted hotly over Absaroka's knuckles. The punch knocked the man's head back. It thudded against the boulder behind him. His eyes went glassy.

But only for a second. Then he lowered his head and charged into Absaroka. The two men grappled. Their feet got tangled up, and down they went, sprawling on the ground.

A few yards away, Jamie tried to seize the momentary advantage he had over his two opponents. He reached his feet first, and as one of the outlaws tried to scramble up, Jamie greeted him with a pile-driving fist to the top of the head. The man went right back down.

That gave the second man just enough time to grab Jamie around the knees and heave. Still slightly off balance, Jamie wasn't able to catch himself. He fell again. The outlaw grabbed a knife from his belt and lunged toward him, trying to bury the blade in Jamie's chest.

Jamie flung up his left arm to block the thrust, then grabbed the outlaw's wrist. His right hand closed around the man's throat. The two of them rolled over and over on the rocky trail, locked in this grim struggle to see whose strength would prevail.

The outlaw was a brawny, broad-shouldered man, but he was no match for Jamie MacCallister. Jamie wound up on top, which allowed him to bear down even more with his death grip on the man's throat. The outlaw must have sensed that he was on the verge of defeat, because his struggles grew more frantic. He bucked and writhed and kicked upward with both legs, trying to hook one of them in front of Jamie's neck and lever him loose. Jamie ducked his head to prevent that. The muscles in his back and shoulders corded and rippled as he brought to bear all the force he could muster.

The outlaw's eyes widened grotesquely as Jamie crushed his windpipe. His tongue stuck out of his gaping mouth. He bucked one last time, then went limp. The knife he'd been clutching slipped from fingers that no longer obeyed any commands and fell to the ground. Any spark of life remaining in nerves and muscles flickered out.

Jamie turned to see how Absaroka was doing and instead saw the man he had tried to hammer into the ground coming at him. With both hands, the outlaw had lifted a heavy rock over his head and clearly was about to dash Jamie's brains out with it.

Absaroka's vision and mental processes were fuzzy from the blow to the head, but he put up the best fight that he could. As he threw punches at the outlaw and absorbed punishment in return, the world grew even more hazy around him.

Suddenly, he was no longer the gunman who called himself Absaroka. Once again, he was Hawk That Soars, a young Crow warrior, wrestling and play-fighting with his friends in the days before he had ever known that the mountain man, Preacher, was his father.

He gripped the shoulders of the man with whom he did battle, planted his foot in the outlaw's stomach, and lifted him up and over, throwing him into a somersault that brought the man crashing down on his back.

But in Absaroka's mind, it wasn't an outlaw and killer he fought with, but rather another young brave. He rolled over, about to laugh in glee at his triumph.

Then the scene shifted abruptly. He was still Hawk That Soars, only now he was with Broken Pine's people.

Broken Pine, his good friend, and Big Thunder, huge, loyal, good-hearted Big Thunder. And Butterfly, so beautiful, the light of his life, the sun that rose within him, the night that soothed him with its tranquility. There were his children, too, those dear ones!

But why were they fading away, as if obscured by the smoke of a campfire drifting between him and them, fading until he could no longer see them? He cried out, asking to know where they had gone and why they would not come back to him.

There. There was the evil that had taken away everything dear to him. Hawk That Soars leaped on the monstrous thing taken flesh and began pounding it, pounding, pounding, trying to wipe out all the horror and loss . . .

Jamie was about to try to throw himself aside before the outlaw heaved the big rock at him, but before that could happen, a shot boomed somewhere not far away. The outlaw's upper body rocked back as a heavy caliber slug smashed into his chest. Momentum made his feet take another step, overbalancing him backward. He dropped the rock behind him and fell beside it as a blood-stain spread rapidly on his shirt front.

Jamie pushed himself to his feet, leaning on a boulder to do so, and looked around to see Simon Lash standing not far away. A wisp of powder smoke still curled from the muzzle of the Sharps that Lash held.

Jamie nodded to the wagon-master, who returned the gesture. The exchange was wordless and very brief but spoke volumes to two frontiersmen.

The sound of someone breathing heavily and fists

thudding against flesh made Jamie look around. He spotted Absaroka kneeling on top of one of the outlaws, hitting him in the face with rights and lefts, one fist and then the other. Jamie moved closer and saw that the man's face was a bloody ruin. Absaroka's hands were swollen and bleeding, too.

Jamie hooked his hands under Absaroka's arms and lifted the young man up and off the unconscious outlaw. Absaroka howled in fury and started to thrash around as he tried to get free. Jamie slid his arms around his chest from behind and lifted him off the ground.

"Stop it!" Jamie said. "Blast it, take it easy, boy! That fella's already out cold." Jamie took a second look. "Actually, I think maybe he's dead. Sure doesn't look like he's breathing."

Words spilled out of Absaroka, but they were in the Crow tongue, not English. Jamie understood most of them and knew that the young man was crying out for his lost family and friends. He didn't know what had caused those awful memories to well up inside Absaroka, but obviously for a few minutes he had been lost in them while he was beating that varmint to death.

Jamie wasn't going to lose any sleep over the outlaw, but he hated to see his old friend's son being tormented by the past. "Hawk!" he said sharply. "Hawk, snap out of it!"

Absaroka just thrashed harder. Jamie realized his mistake and went on, "Absaroka, settle down. It's all over, Absaroka."

Indeed, the battle seemed to have ended. No more shots rang out. Simon Lash moved among the fallen outlaws, checking to make sure they were all dead. Other people from the wagon train crawled out from under the vehicles and hurried around, trying to find out if friends or relatives were wounded.

Several men approached the cluster of boulders where Jamie and Absaroka had wiped out this bunch of would-be killers and thieves. Since Jamie hadn't been traveling with the wagon train, he didn't know any of them.

Lash took care of that, introducing Cornelius Russell, Jesse Willis, Stephen Millard, and the others. Then he said, "Gentlemen, this is Jamie MacCallister."

"Hey, I've heard of you," Willis exclaimed.

"As have I," added Russell. "Simon told us that you've been watching out for us, Mr. MacCallister."

"Wish I could've done a better job of it," Jamie said. Absaroka had settled down some, at last, so Jamie let go of him but was ready to grab him if he went loco again.

"I don't know this young fellow," Lash commented.

Jamie glanced at the two-gun man, who now stood there with a bleak, faraway look on his face. At least Absaroka seemed to be in control of himself again.

"He's called Absaroka," Jamie said. "We ran into each other, and he came along to give me a hand."

He didn't offer any other details about Absaroka's real identity or his brief membership in the outlaw gang.

"Then we're very obliged to you for your assistance, Mr. Absaroka," Lash said.

"Just Absaroka," the young man muttered, reminding Jamie of Preacher, who always objected whenever anybody called him *mister*.

"Somebody else is coming," one of the men from the

wagon train called excitedly. He pointed along the river trail.

Jamie turned to look and saw a group of half a dozen riders heading toward them. He recognized the man in the lead right away.

Preacher loped forward on Horse, with Dog trotting alongside them. As he came up and reined in, he swung down easily from the saddle before the big stallion had stopped completely, his movements as lithe and graceful as those of a much younger man. He caught Jamie's hand, pumped it, and slapped his other hand on Jamie's upper arm.

"Looks like you wrapped up this job, pardner," he declared. "When I heard all the shootin' down here a few minutes ago, I said to myself, that's ol' Jamie's work I'm hearin', that's for danged sure."

"And I'm betting you had something to do with those outlaws up in the hills giving up the fight," Jamie replied.

Preacher chuckled. "Yeah, they gave it up permanent-like, I reckon, mostly thanks to these fellas ridin' with me."

As he spoke, he glanced curiously toward Absaroka, then looked again, sharply, startled.

"That's right," the young gunman said, then added with no real affection in his voice, "Hello, Pa."

Chapter 33

Preacher took a step toward Absaroka and, in a shaky voice for the normally self-possessed mountain man, said, "Hawk?"

"Once, in another life, I was Hawk That Soars." Absaroka took a deep breath, squared his shoulders, and hooked his thumbs in the crossed gun belts as he stared defiantly at Preacher. "Now I'm just Absaroka."

"What in all the blue devils of Hades—"

Jamie interrupted Preacher by saying, "It's a long story."

"No, it's not," Absaroka contradicted him. "It's a short, simple, very ugly story. My wife and children fell ill and died. So did many of my friends. I've turned my back on that world. Now I live in the white man's world."

Preacher looked at Jamie, whose massive shoulders rose and fell in a shrug. There was nothing else Jamie could say. Absaroka had summed it up, all right.

Preacher reached out and put a hand on his son's arm. "Hawk, I'm sorry—"

Absaroka shrugged off the touch and stepped back. As

he did so, he stumbled a little. A woozy look came over his face. He shook his head, as if trying to clear cobwebs out of it.

Jamie gripped the young gunman's arm and said, "Steady there. From the looks of that welt on your head, you got walloped pretty hard. Maybe you'd better sit down on one of those rocks and let your head settle."

Absaroka nodded and said through clenched teeth, "Maybe for now." He didn't try to pull away from Jamie's grasp. Instead, he allowed the big frontiersman to help him sink onto one of the low boulders at the edge of the trail.

Simon Lash stepped up to Preacher and said, "This development comes as a complete surprise to all of us, Arthur." He smiled and went on, "Although I suppose there's no longer any reason to continue using that *nom de plume,* is there?"

"If you mean the phony name, I reckon not." Preacher looked at Absaroka and frowned. "I don't know what in blazes I ought to do, Simon. I ain't used to feelin' that way . . . and I don't like it. Not one blasted bit."

"At the moment, perhaps, you should just wait until the young man has recovered a little from his injury. In the meantime, you can help me check among the wagon train and see what casualties we've suffered."

"Yeah," Preacher muttered, "I want to make sure Constance is all right."

"The outlaws who circled around into the hills . . . you're sure they no longer represent a threat?"

"I'm sure," Preacher said. "There ain't a one of the varmints left alive."

* * *

"Arthur!" Constance Bradley said as she spotted Preacher and Lash coming toward her wagon. She finished tying a makeshift bandage around the wounded arm of a man sitting on the lowered tailgate, then turned and hurried to meet them. She threw her arms around Preacher and hugged him. Breathlessly, she asked, "Are you all right?"

"Yeah, I'm fine," he told her, not mentioning the shocking revelation he had just had. "How about you?"

"I stayed in the wagon and kept my head down, just like Simon told us to," she replied with a smile. "I'm not hurt."

"Well, that's the best news I've had all day, I reckon." Preacher looked around. "Where's Mrs. Kemp? Did she come through the fight all right?"

Constance stepped back and frowned worriedly. "Virginia is gone." She lifted a hand to forestall a startled exclamation from the mountain man. "No, I don't mean she's dead. She's not here. Her husband took her and fled just as the attack was getting under way. No one has seen them since."

Simon Lash said, "I was thinking about putting together a search party. Someone needs to locate the Kemps and let them know that it's safe to return."

Preacher nodded. "That's a good idea. I expect Harrison will want to go along and make sure his brother and sister-in-law are all right."

"Which might lead to more trouble, given their family

drama," said Lash. "But it can't be avoided. Will you lead the search, Preacher?"

"Sure."

Constance asked, "Why did Simon just call you Preacher, Arthur?"

"Well, as it happens, Arthur's my real name, but I ain't used it regular-like for a long, long time. Most folks out here on the frontier know me as Preacher. But we figured it might be best to keep quiet about that while I was travelin' with the wagon train."

"Because you suspected there was a traitor among us?" asked Constance, keenly making that deduction.

"Yep. Speakin' of which . . ." He looked at Lash. "Is anybody else missin' besides the Kemps?"

Lash shook his head and said, "I don't know yet. I need to go through the wagons and check on everyone. Once I've done that, perhaps we'll have our answer."

Preacher saw Tom Linford hurrying toward them, followed by Jamie and the young man now calling himself Absaroka. Preacher was going to have a hard time getting used to thinking of his son that way, he knew, just as it was going to be difficult to accept the fact that his daughter-in-law and grandchildren were dead. He was aware of an aching emptiness in his chest every time he allowed himself to think about that tragic loss—so he tried not to let himself think about it.

With a mixture of anger and excitement in his voice, Linford said, "He's not here!"

"Who isn't?" asked Lash.

"Prescott!"

Lash looked confused as he said, "Ethan Prescott, you mean? But he's dead—"

"No, he's not! He was the leader of that bunch of killers and outlaws!"

Quickly, Linford filled in the wagon-master on the discovery they had made. Lash was stunned, and that feeling was reflected on his face.

"I can hardly believe it," he said. "I knew Ethan Prescott. Not all that well, mind you, but he always struck me as an honest, honorable man."

Preacher said, "Based on what I've heard about the fella, maybe he was at one time, but 'most anybody can go bad. Sometimes for a reason you can understand, and sometimes it just seems to happen."

"We can't let him get away," Linford said. "We have to track him down and make sure he never tries anything like this again." He paused, took his hat off, and rubbed his hand over his face. "I checked all the bodies up in the hills," he went on, "and when we didn't find him up there, I figured he would be down here along the trail with the others. But he wasn't."

Jamie spoke up. "There's no sign of his second-in-command, either. Fella named Zeke Connelly. I'm thinking that the two of them sent the rest of the gang to attack the wagon train but hung back themselves, hiding out somewhere nearby. When it became obvious their bunch was going to lose, they cut and ran."

"We can't let them get away with it," Linford urged.

"We won't," Lash promised, "but right now there's a more pressing matter. Wesley Kemp and Mrs. Kemp have disappeared—"

"What!" The startled roar came from nearby. Harrison Kemp rushed up to them and grabbed Lash by the shoulders. "What did you say? Virginia's gone?"

Lash stepped back, firmly disengaging himself from Harrison's grip, and said coolly, "Please control yourself, Mr. Kemp. Your brother and his wife left before the fighting started. I'm sure they just went on up the river and they're fine. We're going to look for them and let them know that the outlaws were defeated, so they can return safely."

"But . . . but how . . . ?"

"Your brother took a couple of horses for them."

"So Wesley's a horse thief," Harrison murmured. "I'm not surprised."

"No one is going to hold that against him, under the circumstances. Now, if you'd care to come along with the search party—"

"You can't stop me," Harrison broke in.

"Don't intend to," said Preacher. "I'm leadin' the search party. Get your horse and come on."

Preacher and Jamie rode at the head of the little group that left the makeshift camp a short time later. Harrison Kemp and Tom Linford followed them, with Absaroka and Roscoe Lomax bringing up the rear.

Lomax had been reunited with Edmund Farrington, his employer and friend, and had been dismayed at the damage done to the freight wagons. He thought they ought to be able to salvage most of the cargo, however, and Farrington would have enough goods left to establish his store in Oregon Territory.

Simon Lash had wanted to come along, but Preacher had convinced him it would be best for him to stay with the wagons and supervise all the patching up of people and vehicles alike. Lash had agreed, grudgingly.

Preacher wanted to sit down and have a long talk with Absaroka, let him know how sorry he was for the loss that he'd suffered. Quietly, Jamie had passed on a little more of the information Absaroka had told him. Preacher still struggled with trying to comprehend the tragedy. Truly, it seemed senseless.

Unfortunately, senseless things happened all the time in life, and people struggled to grasp them, when actually, all they could do was keep going. The sun would come up in the morning, after all, and there were things to be done. The idea that someday everything might be clear and the world would make sense was a pretty thing to think about, but more than likely that was all it would ever amount to.

So Preacher rode on, following the Sweetwater River and looking for signs that Wesley and Virginia Kemp had passed this way.

He and Jamie spotted the hoofprints at the same time. Preacher dismounted, hunkered on the riverbank, and called Dog over to him. He let the big cur get the scent, then ruffled the hair on the back of his neck and ordered, "Dog, find."

Dog took off along the trail, nose to the ground. Preacher swung back up into the saddle, and the men followed as Dog led them.

Dog lost the trail where the two riders forded the river, but Preacher and Jamie, excellent trackers, the both of them, picked it up again on the southern bank. A few hundred yards ahead, a bluff with trees and thick brush at its base crowded all the way up to the river. The Kemps couldn't keep going that way, so Preacher figured they must have crossed the Sweetwater again, just as the wagon train would have to ford the stream when it reached this point.

Then his keen eyes caught a flicker of movement in the brush. He was about to say something when a shot roared out. The bullet whined over the men's heads as they reined to an abrupt halt.

"Don't come any closer!" a man bellowed.

Tom Linford leaned forward in the saddle and exclaimed, "That's Prescott's voice, I know it is!"

Preacher held out a hand to stop the young scout as Linford started to urge his horse ahead. "Hold on," he told Linford. "There's got to be a reason why he fired over our heads instead of shootin' one of us, and I want to know what it is."

Linford looked like he wanted to argue, but he jerked his head in a curt nod of agreement.

Dog was growling. Preacher said, "Dog, stay," and eased Horse forward a couple of steps. Jamie came with him. Preacher raised his voice and called, "I expect you've got somethin' to say, Prescott! Whatever it is, spit it out!"

From the brush, Ethan Prescott replied, "I want all of you men to turn around and ride away from here. Don't try to stop us, and don't come back!"

"Who's us?" Jamie called. "Is Zeke Connelly with you?"

A different voice replied in a mocking tone, "Well, if it's not Shawnee Smith! And is that . . ." Zeke suddenly sounded angry as he went on, "Absaroka! You damned, double-crossing, half-breed traitor!"

Absaroka remained stony-faced and ignored the outlaw's words.

Jamie said, "There are only two of you, Prescott, and six of us. You can't gun down all of us. Why should we turn around and let you get away?"

"Because there's more than two people over here!" replied Prescott.

That was enough to warn Preacher what was about to happen next. With a rustling of brush, Ethan Prescott stepped out into the open. His left arm was wrapped around Virginia Kemp's neck as he held her in front of him like a human shield and pressed his gun to her head with his other hand.

Chapter 34

"Virginia!" Harrison Kemp cried as he lunged his horse forward. Jamie reached out and snagged the reins as Harrison started past him. He hauled back hard and forced the horse to rear up. Harrison had to grab the saddle to keep from toppling off.

Virginia whimpered as Prescott forced the gun muzzle harder against her head. "Stay back!" he warned. "I don't have a whole hell of a lot to lose by pulling this trigger."

"I reckon you don't," drawled Preacher. "Ever'body along the Oregon Trail is gonna know what sort of skunk you really are, Prescott. Once word gets around, there won't be any place you can hide. Wherever you go, honest men'll be lookin' to ventilate you, just on gen'ral principles. So you might as well give it up now and take what's comin' to you."

"A hangrope, you mean? Or a bullet in the head?" Prescott laughed while he held the cringing young woman against him. "No thanks, mister. I'll take my chances. Now back off, all of you. I want you out of sight in two minutes, or I'll kill this woman, I swear it. But if you don't interfere, we'll let these two go a mile or so upriver. You got my word on that, too."

Harrison's horse had settled down. He was in control of himself, but just barely, judging by the wild look in his eyes. He called, "Wesley! Are you there?"

Without looking around at the brush, Prescott growled, "Go ahead and answer him."

In a frightened, unsteady voice, Wesley Kemp said, "Harrison, I . . . I'm here. Please do as these men say. They'll kill us—"

"You fool!" Harrison said. "You cowardly fool! You ran away instead of staying to fight, and now look what you've done! If anything happens to Virginia, it's your fault."

"Just . . . just do as they say . . ."

"That's enough palaverin'," Preacher declared. "Come on, boys."

"Come on?" Tom Linford repeated. "You mean we're going to cooperate with those murderers?"

Jamie said, "We don't have much choice. Two people's lives are at stake." He lifted his reins and turned his mount. Preacher did the same with Horse. With the two veteran frontiersmen crowding them, Linford, Absaroka, Harrison, and Lomax had to turn their horses and retreat along the riverbank, too.

Tom Linford said angrily, "You can't trust Prescott to keep his word. More than likely, he'll kill the Kemps when he doesn't think he has any more use for them."

"Of course, he will," Preacher agreed. "That's why we ain't gonna give him a chance to do that. But we got to gamble he won't get around to it before we have time to get ahead of 'em."

Lomax said, "I should've knowed you had somethin' up your sleeve, Preacher. You ain't the sort to just give up."

They had gone around a bend and were out of sight of the fugitives by now. Preacher looked over at Jamie and said, "You and me, right?"

"Sounds good," Jamie replied with a nod.

Preacher swung a leg over the saddle and dropped to the ground while Horse was still moving. He handed his reins to Lomax. Jamie did likewise, turning his reins over to Harrison Kemp.

"All of you keep moving," Jamie told the mounted men. "In fact, kick those horses into a run. We want Prescott and Connelly to hear all of them leaving."

"What are the two of you going to do?" Linford asked tensely.

"Cross the river on foot and be waitin' for them on the other side," replied Preacher.

"Then I'm coming, too. I have a score to settle with Prescott."

"Not this time, kid. This is the sort of job Jamie and me are cut out for."

Preacher's firm tone didn't allow for any argument, although Linford clearly didn't like being left behind. Neither did Harrison Kemp.

They seemed somewhat mollified when Jamie said, "Ride for a quarter of a mile or so downstream, and make plenty of racket doing it. Then you can come back up on foot. With any luck, Preacher and I will have dealt with Prescott and Connelly by then."

They had no more time to waste. Lomax rumbled, "Better do like they say, boys," and heeled his horse into a faster pace. The others followed suit, and as a result, the pounding hoofbeats echoed in both directions along the canyon where the Devil's Crossing was located.

Preacher and Jamie waded across the Sweetwater. The river, fed as it was by snowmelt, was cold, but they were tall men and it didn't come up much higher than their knees. They didn't have any trouble getting across. Dog half-swam, half-bounded through the stream and shook himself excitedly when he leaped out onto the northern bank.

The ridge on that side butted up against the river, making it impossible for wagons or even horses to travel on this side. Preacher and Jamie managed just fine, climbing to the top of the slope and then following the ridge west toward the spot where Prescott, Connelly, and their prisoners would have to cross. They used all the trees and brush they could find as cover to keep their quarry from spotting them.

They moved quickly, and within just a few minutes, they reached their destination. Hunkering in some brush, they parted the branches to look down at the river some fifty feet below them.

They had timed their approach well. Four riders were crossing the stream toward them, including Ethan Prescott, Zeke Connelly, and Wesley Kemp.

However, the fourth rider wasn't Virginia Kemp. She rode in front of Prescott on his mount, with his left arm clamped around her midsection. The fourth rider was familiar, though.

"Well, I'll be hanged," Preacher said.

"More than likely," Jamie agreed, "but why do you say that?"

"I know that other fella from Simon's wagon train.

That's Adam Gideon. He must've been the gang's inside man. I reckon he slipped off when the fightin' started, then ran into Prescott and Connelly when it all went bad and they were tryin' to get away. That horse he's on must be the one Miz Kemp was ridin' when they left."

Jamie nodded and said, "Makes sense. I take it you're surprised that fella Gideon turned out to be one of them?"

"Not really. I never knew him well enough to have any feelin's about that. He just sorta blended in with everybody else." Preacher grunted. "I reckon if you're gonna be a spy, that's a good quality to have."

"I'd say so. Well, we're outnumbered, officially, anyway. Three against two. Unless you think Kemp's likely to pitch in and give us a hand."

Preacher snorted contemptuously. "Not likely," he said. "Look down yonder, where they'll be comin' out of the river. The trail turns and goes right by that big rock."

"And that's where we need to be," Jamie said. "We'll tackle them from there."

"Sounds good to me. And the odds are even, if you stop to think about it." Preacher grinned at the big cur and went on, "Dog, you'll take that fella right there, the one on the last horse. Got it?"

Dog just let his tongue loll out and gazed with anticipation at Adam Gideon, as if he'd understood every word Preacher had just said. Preacher wouldn't have sworn that he didn't.

"I'll take Prescott," Preacher went on.

"And I'll take Connelly," Jamie confirmed. "He and I have a grudge against each other anyway."

"You'll have to tell me about that fracas sometime," Preacher said.

They slipped down to the massive slab of rock that jutted out toward the trail. The splashing of horses' hooves in the water covered any small sounds they made. They took off their hats and stretched out on their bellies, where their quarry couldn't see them, and followed the horses' approach by sound.

The splashing ended. The thudding of hooves on ground replaced it. Preacher and Jamie glanced at each other and nodded.

Then they surged up, poised for a split second at the edge of the rock to fix the positions of the riders below in their minds, and then sailed out in swift, diving tackles.

Prescott had time to yell a curse before Preacher smashed into him. Preacher didn't want to knock Virginia Kemp off the horse, but there was no way to avoid it. Better to risk a broken bone in the fall than let Prescott ride away with her.

They were close enough to the river, riding single file along the bank's edge, that Preacher, Prescott, and Virginia all went into the water with a huge splash. Prescott started fighting instantly, so Preacher didn't have a chance to see how Jamie and Dog were doing. He had his hands full with the burly, crooked wagon-master.

Prescott landed a wild punch on Preacher's jaw with enough force to drive the mountain man backward and under the surface of the river. Prescott lunged after him, trying to get his hands around Preacher's neck and hold him under the water until he drowned. Preacher writhed away and kicked Prescott in the chest. It was hard to see anything because of the water flying up around them. Preacher grabbed with his left hand, got hold of Prescott's shirt, and hammered a punch into his face. Prescott slugged back at him. Both men were choking and coughing from the water they had swallowed.

The battle went back and forth in the river with the combatants seizing momentary advantages only to lose them almost right away. From the corner of his eye, Preacher caught a glimpse of a soaking wet Virginia Kemp climbing out of the river and collapsing on the bank. Then Prescott's fist clipped him on the ear and he lost sight of Virginia as he turned his attention back to the battle.

Not far away, Jamie was engaged in a similar clash with Zeke Connelly. His dive had knocked Connelly into the river, too. The outlaw's burned hands didn't keep him from using them to sledge punches into Jamie's face and body. Jamie gave as good as he got, though. He had Connelly on the ropes, figuratively speaking, when his right foot slipped on one of the rocks in the streambed and shot out from under him. Off balance like that, he couldn't stay upright when Connelly bulled into him. Both men went under the surface.

Jamie didn't realize Connelly had gotten behind him until the man's arm looped around his neck and closed like an iron band. Jamie was bigger and outweighed Connelly, but the water nullified that advantage to a certain extent. Rockets seemed to go off behind Jamie's eyes as Connelly tried to choke the life out of him.

Jamie felt around on the riverbed until his hand closed around a rock the size of two fists pressed together. He brought it up and back, striking behind him. The rock thudded heavily against something. The pressure went away from Jamie's neck. He rolled over and pushed himself up, gulping down air when his head broke the surface.

Zeke Connelly was a few feet away, standing up in the water. Blood streamed from the cut on his head that the blow from the rock had opened up. But he had a knife in his hand, and his arm was drawn back, poised for a throw that would bury the blade in Jamie's body.

A gunshot roared, then another and another. Connelly staggered backward, doing a macabre dance in the river as bloodstains erupted on his shirt front. He dropped the knife and collapsed, floating on his back with his arms outflung as the water took on a red tinge around him.

Jamie turned his head to look and saw Absaroka standing on the bank, a gun in each hand. He figured he might have been able to dodge the knife if Connelly had thrown it, but at the same time, he was grateful the reinforcements had shown up when they did. He nodded to Absaroka to let the young gunman know he was obliged for the help.

A few yards farther upriver, Preacher dragged Ethan Prescott's limp form out of the water and dumped it on the bank. Tom Linford ran up, gun in hand, and asked, "Is he dead?"

"I don't think so," Preacher replied, breathing a little hard. "He put up a mighty good tussle, but he'd finally had enough."

Linford hooked a boot toe under Prescott's shoulder and rolled the older man onto his back. Prescott coughed wrackingly, spit out water, and opened his eyes to stare into the barrel of the gun Linford pointed at his face. For a second, he looked surprised and afraid, but then his beefy face twisted in lines of defiance.

"Go ahead and shoot, you blamed young pup!" he said hoarsely. "That's what you've been wanting for more than a year, isn't it? To even the score?"

For a second, Preacher thought Linford was going to pull the trigger. But then the young scout drew in a deep breath and lowered the gun as he said, "No, I'd rather see you beg for your life before you're strung up on a tree and left to rot."

Prescott pushed up on an elbow and shouted curses at Linford. Linford ignored them, holstered his gun, turned and walked away, shaking his head.

As he passed Preacher, the mountain man said quietly, "Maybe you should have gone ahead and shot him."

"No," Linford said, "I'm remembering a girl who wouldn't have wanted me to become a cold-blooded killer." His gaze locked with Preacher's. "But you'll see to it that he gets what's coming to him, won't you?"

"I sure will. And I'm not the only one. Jamie'll see to it, too, and so will Simon. I reckon we can have a trial before the wagons push on."

"A trial at the Devil's Crossing," said Linford. "Seems fitting."

Roscoe Lomax joined Preacher, Jamie, and Linford as Harrison Kemp ran past them and knelt beside Virginia, who was coughing and shaking. He pulled her up, embraced her, and held her tightly. Wesley Kemp sat on horseback not far away. He hadn't dismounted and gone to his wife, and he made no move to do so now.

Lomax nudged Preacher in the side and pointed to

another body floating facedown in the river. "Ain't that that fella Gideon?" the bullwhacker asked. "What's he doin' here?"

"Near as we can figure, he was workin' with the outlaws."

"Dog tore him up pretty good. He won't never double-cross anybody else."

Harrison helped Virginia to her feet. She sagged against him and didn't straighten until her husband called her name.

"Virginia," Kemp said. "Are you all right?"

She looked around at him, her wet hair tangled around her face, but didn't say anything.

"We can go back to the wagons now," Kemp said.

"No," Virginia told him, her voice weak from the ordeal she had gone through but, at the same time, strong with determination. "I'm not going back with you, Wesley. You've had . . . plenty of chances . . . to show you're not a coward. I'm staying . . . with Harrison."

Wesley Kemp looked like he was going to argue, but then lines of bleak despair settled over his face. He muttered, "If that's the way you want it," and turned his horse away as Harrison put his arms around Virginia again.

Standing apart from all this was Absaroka. Preacher started toward him but stopped when he saw the young gunman watching him with cold, empty eyes.

Jamie put a hand on his old friend's shoulder and said, "Later."

"Yeah," Preacher said. "Later."

Chapter 35

With everything that had happened, it was the next day before the wagon train forded the Sweetwater for the final time. Once again, Wesley Kemp was at the reins of the lead wagon, but Virginia was back with Constance Bradley. Harrison Kemp rode beside Constance's wagon and reached over to rest his hand on Virginia's shoulder for a moment before he peeled off to join the other outriders. She waved after him.

It wasn't long before all the wagons left the Devil's Crossing behind.

Also left behind were a dozen graves of those killed in the attack—and one more containing the body of Ethan Prescott, who had faced his fate stoically after a jury of immigrants empaneled by Simon Lash found him guilty of murder and sentenced him to hang. If Tom Linford was disappointed by that outcome, he said nothing about it.

Maybe the young scout had decided that vengeance wasn't always all it was cracked up to be, and it never changed what had gone before, Preacher thought. Or maybe Linford had just decided to put all that violence and tragedy behind him and face the future. Preacher hoped that was the case.

Lash had decided that Prescott deserved a decent burial because of the good things he had done in the past, the thousands of pilgrims he had guided safely over the trails to new homes and new destinies, before turning to evil.

The rest of the outlaws had either been left where they fell or had their bodies tossed into a ravine Preacher had found. They didn't deserve any more dignified fate than that.

After all the crossings were completed and the wagons were rolling easily through gentle hills, Preacher, Jamie, Simon Lash, and Absaroka rode to the crest of one of those rises and reined in to look out over the scene.

Lash said, "Are you sure I can't persuade you lads to accompany us the rest of the way to Oregon? There's some spectacular scenery between here and there."

"You know good and well we've seen just about all there is to see out here, more'n once," said Preacher. "And I reckon we'll see it all again, at least two or three more times. Ain't that right, Jamie?"

"That's the plan," Jamie said. "And with that gang of outlaws busted up, you shouldn't need us anymore, Simon. You've got a mighty fine scout there."

He nodded toward Tom Linford, who was pushing out ahead of the wagons.

"That's certainly true," agreed Lash. "I think Tom will have a long and illustrious career. As long as these wagon trains last, anyway. Although eventually, there will probably be railroads spanning the continent, and those days will come to an end."

"It'll be a while yet," Jamie predicted, "but I expect you're right."

"I'm a mite surprised ol' Roscoe decided to stay with you," Preacher commented. "Although once a bullwhacker, always a bullwhacker, I reckon."

"Not necessarily. He's talking about going into partnership with Edmund Farrington and starting a combined freight and mercantile enterprise in Oregon." Lash smiled. "I wouldn't be surprised if he winds up a business tycoon."

"That foul-mouthed grizzly?" Preacher chuckled. "Well, stranger things have happened, I reckon."

Lash grew serious as he asked, "You did say good-bye to Constance, didn't you?"

Preacher's forehead creased in a frown. "That's the hardest part about leavin'. She's a mighty fine woman. I'm just afraid that if I went the rest of the way to Oregon with her, I wouldn't want to leave when we got there."

"And you can't have that," Jamie said with gentle sarcasm. "Old fiddlefooted Preacher can't settle down with one woman."

The mountain man squinted at him and said, "I seem to recollect that you been hitched to the same woman for a mighty long time, and *you* don't stay home. You're always off gallivantin' around and havin' adventures like me."

"Not always. And even when I am, it's nice knowing I've got a place to come home to. You ought to try it sometime."

Preacher grunted and said, "Maybe I will," but he didn't sound convinced of it.

"But you *are* going to come back to MacCallister's Valley with me and have some of Kate's good home cooking, aren't you? Just for a spell before you meander on?"

"I wouldn't want to disappoint her, so I reckon I will." Preacher took a deep breath and turned to Absaroka, who hadn't said anything so far. "You're welcome to join us, if Jamie don't mind me speakin' for him."

"Not at all," said Jamie. "If Preacher hadn't asked you, I was about to."

Absaroka didn't meet their eyes as he shook his head. "I have places to go," he said.

"Where?" Preacher asked.

"Not here. Not anywhere that will remind me of what once was." The young gunman turned his head to gaze for a moment toward the northwest, where Broken Pine's village lay.

"You plan to keep on wearin' those two guns and huntin' trouble?"

"That's the white man's way, isn't it?" Absaroka asked with a faint smile. "And I'm a white man now and forever."

"Well . . . well . . . damn it!" Preacher sputtered. "You could ride with me!"

Silently, slowly, Absaroka shook his head. Preacher glared at him, but after several long seconds, acceptance began to settle over the mountain man's rugged face.

"I reckon everybody's got to follow their own trail," he said. "I always have . . . and you take after me."

"You could do worse, Absaroka," Jamie said.

The young man nodded. "Yes, MacCallister, I believe I could." He held out his hand. "I'm glad we met again."

Jamie gripped it tightly. "So am I. Good luck to you."

Simon Lash extended his hand. Absaroka hesitated, then took it, saying, "I'm sorry I ever considered joining that bunch, Mr. Lash."

"When the time came, you got it all sorted properly, lad," Lash assured him. "And if you ever want a job as a wagon train scout, I hope you'll look me up."

"I'll remember that," Absaroka promised. He leaned down from the saddle to scratch Dog's ears. "Good-bye, my friend."

Dog licked his hand and whined, then wagged his tail.

Absaroka straightened in the saddle, lifted a finger to his hat brim, and turned to ride away.

Jamie frowned at Preacher and said, "The two of you don't have anything else to say to each other?"

"It appears we don't," Preacher said as he watched his son ride away, down one grassy slope and then up another one, and then out of sight.

But Preacher thought that just for a second, right as he was going over that hill, Absaroka had looked back at him. Just for a second . . . before he was gone.

Preacher hoped his eyes hadn't played a trick on him. He wasn't as young as he once was.

Turn the page for an exciting preview!

Johnstone Country. Where Legends Are Born.

**Before he became known as "The Last Mountain Man,"
Smoke Jensen and his bride Sally were hardworking ranchers
on the Colorado frontier. This is a story of the early years.
When times were hard, tensions were high,
and guns were the law. . . .**

WHEN THE SHOOTING STARTS

For Smoke and Sally Jensen, the Sugarloaf Ranch is the American Dream come true. A glorious stretch of untamed land near the Colorado-Kansas border, it's the perfect place to stake their claim, raise some cattle, and start a new family. But when a man claiming to be an army colonel arrives in Big Rock—with a well-armed militia—the Jensens' dream becomes a living nightmare. This stranger calls himself Colonel Lamar Talbot. He's come to warn them about a looming war with the Cheyenne Indians. And only he can save them from a bloody massacre— by launching a counterattack that's even bloodier. . . .

Smoke and Sally aren't sure they trust him. They suspect the Colonel and his men are nothing more than brutal vigilantes with a hidden agenda of their own. But the Cheyenne war parties are a very real threat. The tribe's charismatic leader, Black Drum, is launching raids on local ranches, farms, and the railroads, too. Every day, the violence gets worse and the war moves closer— until it reaches the Sugarloaf Ranch. That's when Sally gets attacked. That's when Smoke grabs his guns. That's when the shooting starts—and the final battle begins. . . .

**National Bestselling Authors
WILLIAM W. JOHNSTONE
and J.A. Johnstone**

WHEN THE SHOOTING STARTS
A Smoke Jensen Novel of the West

Coming in June 2022, wherever Pinnacle Books are sold.

Chapter 1

"Hey, Buck! Buck West! Is that you, you old hoss thief?"

The loud, boisterous voice made Smoke Jensen come to a halt on the boardwalk. It had been a good while since he'd heard the name Buck West. When he stopped using it, he had figured he'd probably never hear it again.

But now here it was, coming from the mouth of the tall, rawboned man striding along the boardwalk toward him. The man's ugly face was wreathed in a grin. He wore a duster over canvas trousers, suspenders, and a flannel shirt. The brim of his battered old hat was turned up in front.

A holstered Colt swung on the man's right hip. Another revolver was stuck in his waistband on the left side. He had a lean, wolfish look about him that came from riding a lot of dark, lonely trails. Hoot-owl trails, some called them. Folks had started using the word "owlhoot" to describe the men who rode such trails.

Smoke had to search his memory for the name of the man who had just hailed him using that old alias. Sutcliffe, he recalled after a moment. Sort of a distinguished name for a gunman and outlaw. His nickname, Rowdy, fit him better. Smoke didn't think he had ever heard the man's real first name.

"Hello, Rowdy," he said, willing to be friendly as long as he could. "What brings you here?"

"Why, the same thing as you, I expect, Buck," replied Sutcliffe as he came to a stop and hooked his thumbs in his gun belt. "I heard that a fella name of Franklin was hirin' guns, so I come to sign on with him. This here is the town of Fontana, ain't it?"

That took Smoke by surprise. He frowned slightly and said, "You're a little behind the times. Tilden Franklin has been dead for almost a year. This is Big Rock. There's not much left of Fontana. It's fixing to dry up and blow away . . . like the memory of all the trouble that happened there."

Rowdy Sutcliffe cocked his head to the side and gave Smoke a quizzical stare.

"Franklin's dead?" he said. "Are you sure about that?"

"Pretty sure," Smoke said. He didn't add that he had been the one to hammer three slugs into the chest of the treacherous, would-be emperor of this valley.

Sutcliffe peered at him for a moment longer, then shook his head.

"Well, dadgum it. Seems like I'm always late to the party. Don't know why I didn't hear about that. O' course, I was down in old Meh-hee-co for a while, takin' my ease with the señoritas, so I weren't really payin' that much attention to what was goin' on up here in Colorado." Sutcliffe sighed. "I reckon I'm plumb outta luck." Then he brightened and went on, "Unless you got wind o' some other work for the likes o' you and me. Shoot, Buck West wouldn't be here unless hell was about to pop!"

"Sorry, Rowdy. I don't use the name Buck West anymore, and there's no gun work to be had around here. Big Rock has grown some since the railroad arrived, but it's still small enough to be pretty peaceful."

"Wait." A frown creased Sutcliffe's forehead. "Your name *ain't* Buck West?"

"That's right. That's just what I called myself for a while."

Back in the days when he had been riding the hoot-owl trails himself, searching for the men he had set out to kill. Men responsible for the deaths of several people he had loved . . .

"Then . . . what *is* your name?"

"It's Jensen. Kirby Jensen. Most folks call me Smoke."

Sutcliffe's eyes widened. "Smoke Jensen," he repeated. "Dang. I've heard that name, all right. Fella's supposed to be the fastest draw on the whole frontier. The fightin'est son of a gun anybody ever saw." He let out a low whistle. "And now, come to find out, Smoke Jensen is none other than my old pard Buck West. What do you know about that?"

Smoke shook his head and said, "We were never pards, Rowdy. We were just in the same places at the same times, every now and then."

Sutcliffe squinted now, instead of staring, as he said, "Well, that's an unfriendly sort o' thing to say. If I weren't such a forgivin' fella, I might take offense at it. Could be you're puttin' on airs, since you're really the high-an'-mighty Smoke Jensen."

"Never claimed to be high-and-mighty," Smoke replied

with a shake of his head. "Just another hombre trying to make his way in life."

"Looks like you've done all right for yourself," Sutcliffe said, sneering a little.

Smoke wasn't sure what the gunman meant by that. He certainly wasn't wearing fancy duds or anything like that, just common range clothes and a dark brown, curled-brim hat that had seen better days perched on his ash-blond hair. His boots still had a little mud clinging to them. The gun belt strapped around his waist and the walnut-butted Colt that rode in the attached holster were well cared for but strictly functional.

He looked like what he was these days, a hardworking, moderately successful rancher with a small but growing spread. He and his friend Pearlie Fontaine did most of the work around the place, with Smoke's wife, Sally, pitching in when she needed to. She was learning to ride a horse and use a lariat as well as most men.

Lately, there had been enough work to do that Smoke had hired a couple of extra hands, which had prompted Pearlie to start referring to himself as the foreman. The Sugarloaf—the name Smoke had given to the ranch—was still far from being the equal of some of the massive outfits in other parts of the state. Maybe it would grow to that point someday. Smoke hoped so.

One thing he knew for sure was that he never wanted to return to the bloody, dangerous, lone wolf days of his existence as "Buck West" . . . and Rowdy Sutcliffe was a living, breathing reminder of those days, standing right in front of him.

"It was good seeing you again, Rowdy," he said as he started to turn away. That was stretching the truth considerable-like, but he wanted to end this conversation as smoothly and efficiently as he could.

"Hold on a minute," Sutcliffe said as he raised his left hand slightly.

Smoke stopped, every muscle taut.

"Least you can do is let me buy you a drink," Sutcliffe went on. "For old times' sake."

Smoke hesitated, then nodded. What harm could that do? Maybe once he'd had a drink with Sutcliffe, the gunman would decide there was no reason for him to remain in Big Rock and would move along.

"Sure," he said. "Come on down the street with me to Longmont's. It's the best saloon in town."

"Longmont's," repeated Sutcliffe as he fell in step alongside Smoke. "That wouldn't have anything to do with Louis Longmont, would it?"

"Louis owns the place," Smoke said. "Are you acquainted with him?"

"Nope, just heard tell of him. He's supposed to be mighty slick with a gun and a deck of cards, both." Sutcliffe glanced around Big Rock's main street. "What's he doin' in a little wide place in the trail like this?"

Smoke thought the town had grown enough that it was more than a wide place in the trail, but he didn't waste the time or energy to argue that point. Instead he said, "Louis has put that part of his life behind him, just like I have."

Sutcliffe clucked his tongue and shook his head. "Smoke Jensen and Louis Longmont, both settlin' down. Never thought I'd see the day."

"Living like we used to can only have one end, Rowdy, and it's not a good one."

"I hope you ain't sayin' I ought to hang up my guns!"

Sutcliffe let out a bray of laughter. "That ain't gonna happen. I'll take my chances and keep on livin' like I want to."

"That's your choice," Smoke said solemnly.

"Damn right it is."

A slight air of tension remained between them as they entered Louis Longmont's establishment. Louis had told Smoke that eventually he intended to make the place as much a restaurant as it was a saloon, since he appreciated superb cooking as much as he did fine wine, a beautiful woman, a good card game, and a perfectly balanced gun. For now, however, it catered primarily to men's thirst for beer and whiskey.

Louis stood at the far end of the bar, a glass of bourbon on the hardwood in front of him and smoke curling from the thin black cigar in his mouth. He took the cheroot from his lips and used them to give Smoke a smile of welcome.

"Good afternoon, Smoke," the gambler said. "What brings you to town today?"

"Sally and I came in to pick up some supplies," Smoke replied. "She's over at the mercantile and doesn't really need my help right now, so I thought I'd stop by and say hello."

"I'm glad you did." Coolly, Louis appraised Rowdy Sutcliffe. "Who's your friend?"

Smoke didn't correct Louis's incorrect assumption that Sutcliffe was his friend. He said, "This is Rowdy Sutcliffe."

"You probably heard of me," Sutcliffe said with a confidence that bordered on arrogance.

Louis was about to inform Sutcliffe that he had no idea who he was, Smoke could tell. Before that could happen,

Smoke went on, "Rowdy and I met up a few times, a while back."

"Back in the days when you was usin' the name Buck West," Sutcliffe added.

Louis cocked an eyebrow. He knew most of the story of Smoke's background, although Smoke's laconic nature meant that prying it out of him hadn't been easy.

"Well, any friend of Smoke's is a friend of mine, as the old saying goes," Louis said. "How about a drink, Mr. Sutcliffe? First one's on the house."

Sutcliffe grinned and said, "I sure won't turn that down. I favor rye, if you've got it."

"Indeed we do." Louis crooked a finger at the bartender and told the man to pour Sutcliffe a shot of rye, then said, "What about you, Smoke?"

"I'd just as soon have coffee, if you've got it."

"We always keep a pot on the stove in the back room. I'm glad most of my customers don't have your moderate habits, Smoke. I'd go broke!"

"I like to keep a clear head."

Sutcliffe picked up the glass of rye the bartender set in front of him. He threw back the drink, wiped the back of his other hand across his mouth, and said, "Whiskey don't muddle me none. I draw just as fast and shoot just as straight, drunk or sober."

"I hope for your sake you're right, Mr. Sutcliffe," said Louis. "Being mistaken about a thing like that could have serious consequences for a man."

"You mean like he might get hisself shot?" Sutcliffe gestured for the bartender to pour him another drink. The apron glanced at Louis, who gave him a tiny nod. As the bartender splashed more rye in the glass, Sutcliffe snorted disdainfully and went on, "That ain't gonna happen. I know how good I am." He picked up the glass and swallowed the second shot of fiery liquor. "I know how good the fellas I have to face down are, too. Ain't none of 'em that can match me. Not even . . ." He thumped the empty glass on the bar and sneered. "Not even the high-and-mighty Smoke Jensen."

Chapter 2

Smoke kept his face carefully expressionless in response to Sutcliffe's challenging tone as he said, "I told you about that high-and-mighty business, Rowdy. I didn't set out to get any kind of a reputation—"

"But that didn't stop you from gettin' one anyway, did it?" Sutcliffe snapped. "Ever'where I go, people talk about Smoke Jensen and how he's the fastest gun there ever was. Bull!" Sutcliffe raised his left hand and pointed a dirty-nailed index finger at Smoke. "Don't forget, mister, I knew you when you was nobody! Just a snot-nosed kid packin' an iron like you know what to do with it. Hell, you ain't much more'n a kid now."

"I reckon I'm all grown up," Smoke said, his voice flat and hard. "I've got a wife and everything, and she's probably waiting for me, so I'll mosey on. I'd say that it's been good to see you again, but—"

"You ain't moseyin' nowhere," snarled Sutcliffe. "Not until I'm finished with you. Barkeep, put some more whiskey in that glass!"

Louis Longmont held up a hand to the bartender,

motioning for him to disregard Sutcliffe's order. He said, "Mr. Sutcliffe, I believe you've had enough."

"Why? Because I ain't paid for that second drink?"

"I don't care about that. It's on the house. But I think you should move on now—"

"I know all about you, too, you damn tinhorn," Sutcliffe interrupted without taking his eyes off Smoke. "You're supposed to be fast, too. But you ain't near as fast as me, and once I'm finished with Jensen, I'll prove it."

Smoke said, "You and I are already finished. You can still walk out of here, get on your horse, and ride away from Big Rock, Sutcliffe. No harm done."

"There's plenty o' harm! I been away so long, folks probably done forgot all about me." Sutcliffe's shoulders hunched a little. His right hand hovered near the Colt on his hip, ready to hook and draw. "But they'll remember, right enough, once word gets around that I'm the fella who killed Smoke Jensen. Then anybody who needs gun work done will be fallin' all over theirselves to hire me. Yes, sir, once I outdraw Smoke Jensen clean as a whistle—"

Smoke knew what the words pouring out of Sutcliffe's mouth were designed to do. They were supposed to anger him and prod him into drawing before he was ready, or else they would distract him, lull him into a split second of unreadiness when Sutcliffe abruptly made his move.

The rant didn't accomplish either of those things. Smoke just stood there stonily, and when Sutcliffe broke off and clawed at his gun, Smoke was ready.

The walnut-butted Colt appeared in Smoke's hand as if by magic. Rowdy Sutcliffe actually was pretty fast on the draw, even with two shots of rye whiskey burning in his belly, but he had barely cleared leather when Smoke's gun roared. And to tell the truth, Smoke could have shot him a little sooner than that, but he'd waited just to make sure Sutcliffe wouldn't realize his mistake and try to stop this.

The bullet slammed into Sutcliffe's chest, twisted him half around, and made him stumble backward against the bar. He would have collapsed if it hadn't been there to hold him up. A shudder went through him. Blood welled from the corner of his mouth. Still, he stayed on his feet, held up by a combination of rage, stubbornness, and being too dumb to realize he had only seconds to live.

With his left hand, he pulled the second revolver from his waistband. With a gun in each fist, he tried to raise them. Smoke shot him again, this time drilling a neat third eye in the center of his forehead. Both of Sutcliffe's guns thundered as his fingers spasmed and jerked the triggers, but they were pointed down and hammered their slugs into the sawdust-littered floorboards right in front of his feet. A cloud of powder smoke rose from the weapons, obscuring Sutcliffe's swaying form as if he were standing behind a dirty window, doing some sort of macabre dance.

Then the guns slipped from nerveless fingers and thudded to the floor, followed a heartbeat later by Sutcliffe's lifeless husk. He sprawled facedown and didn't even twitch.

Smoke shook his head and started reloading the two chambers he had just emptied.

"We both tried to talk him out of it," Louis Longmont said into the silence that gripped the room as the echoes of the shots faded away. Louis lifted the cheroot to his mouth and took a puff, then went on, "He simply wouldn't listen to reason." He looked like something had just occurred to him. "Were the two of you actually friends at one time, Smoke?"

"Not hardly," Smoke said as he slid the reloaded Colt back into leather. "He was just another two-bit gun-wolf. There are too many of them in the world."

"And they all believe it would be a wonderful thing to be the man who killed Smoke Jensen." Louis smiled humorlessly. "It must be a terrible thing to carry the hopes and dreams of so many around on your shoulders, my friend."

Around the room, the men who had dived for cover just before the shooting started were beginning to poke their heads back up. Louis waved the hand holding the cheroot to encourage them and raised his voice.

"It's all over, gentlemen. A round of drinks on the house!"

A short time later, as Smoke walked up to the Big Rock Mercantile, he saw an apron-wearing clerk loading sacks and crates of supplies into the back of the buckboard Sally had parked there earlier. Smoke's big, powerful black stallion, Drifter, was tied to a nearby hitch rail.

"Howdy, Smoke," the clerk greeted him. "Miz Jensen's inside, just finishin' up her business." The man placed the keg of nails he was carrying in the buckboard and then dusted off his hands. "Say, I thought I heard a couple of shots up the street a little while ago. You know anything about that?"

"You know me, Stan," Smoke replied with a smile. "I always try to steer clear of trouble."

"Uh-huh, sure. I just thought you might—"

"There was a little unpleasantness at Longmont's," Smoke admitted. He didn't see any point in denying what had happened. The story would be all over town in less than an hour, whether he wanted that or not. More than likely, it had spread quite a bit already.

The clerk let out a whistle. "How many of 'em did you have to shoot, Smoke?"

"Just one man. One stubborn, foolish man."

"Well, he should'a known better than to go up against Smoke Jensen."

Smoke didn't reply to that. When he and Sally had first come to this valley, not long after they were married, he had been determined to leave his gunfighting ways behind him. To that end, he had used a different name, one that people wouldn't associate with either Smoke Jensen or his previous alias Buck West.

Inevitably, though, the truth had come out, and by the time the ruckus with Tilden Franklin and his hired killers was over, everybody in these parts knew who he really was.

And as it turned out, that was a relief. Smoke never had liked secrets, and he was proud of his family name. Keeping quiet about it seemed almost like a slap in the faces of his father Emmett and his brother Luke, both of whom had died in the service of what they believed was right and honorable.

So, for better or worse, he would be Smoke Jensen from now on.

He stepped up on the store's porch and was about to go in when Sally appeared in the open doorway. She smiled when she saw him, and he was struck once again by just how beautiful this dark-haired young woman really was. She was pretty enough to take a man's breath away.

But there was a lot more to Sally Reynolds Jensen than just good looks. She was smart as could be, both in book learning and common sense, and possessed of fierce courage that wouldn't allow her to hesitate in the face of danger. In fact, Smoke wished sometimes that she was a little less courageous and more inclined to be careful.

If she'd been different, though, he might not have fallen so completely in love with her.

"Ready to go?" he asked her.

"I think so. I got everything that was on my list. Did you enjoy your visit with Louis?"

"It was all right, I reckon." He had lived through the shootout with Sutcliffe, so he couldn't complain too much about how the visit had gone.

The clerk was still standing on the porch. He said excitedly, ignoring the warning glance Smoke gave him, "Miz Jensen, did you hear the shootin' while you were inside?"

Sally looked at Smoke and raised her eyebrows. "Shooting?"

"I'll tell you about it once we're on the trail," he said, after scowling for a second at the clerk. The man cleared his throat, looked a little embarrassed, and retreated into the mercantile. Smoke cupped his hand under Sally's elbow and went on, "Let me give you a hand climbing up there."

She could have gotten onto the buckboard's seat just fine by herself, but she let Smoke assist her. Then she picked up the reins attached to the two horses in the team and pulled the brake lever out of its notch. Smoke untied Drifter and swung up into the saddle.

Sally waited until they were out of town and on the trail to the Sugarloaf before she said, "All right, what happened?"

"I ran into a fella I used to know a few years ago, back in the days when I was calling myself Buck West."

"An old friend?"

"No, but we weren't enemies, either . . . until he found out my real name and decided that we were."

Quickly, and without dwelling on the details, he filled her in on the deadly encounter. Sally listened in silence, but she wore a frown of concern.

He concluded by saying, "Monte Carson came down to Louis's place, took my statement, and sent for the undertaker. That's the end of it as far as I'm concerned."

Monte Carson was the sheriff of Big Rock, a former gunman himself who had been on the wrong side in the war a year earlier, until he realized that and threw in with Smoke. After that, with the founding of Big Rock, he had accepted the offer to become the new town's lawman.

"Does this man Sutcliffe have any friends or relatives who are going to come looking for you to avenge what happened to him?" asked Sally.

"Not that I know of, but honestly, I never really knew the hombre that well."

Sally sighed as she handled the team and kept the buckboard rolling along the trail while Smoke rode beside the vehicle.

"I know that by now I should be getting used to the fact there are men roaming around who'd like to kill you," she said. "Your past is what makes you the man you are, and I knew that when I married you."

"What I used to be doesn't mean that's what I'll always be," Smoke pointed out.

"No, but it's hard to get away from all the things that have happened to us, all the things we've done. Our history lingers, no matter what we do."

"That's like saying folks can't change."

"No, not at all," Sally argued. "But changing the way you go forward doesn't change everything you've done in the past." She paused, then went on, "Smoke, don't think I'm saying I regret marrying you. I don't, not one bit! I love you and I know you don't go around looking for trouble."

"But it seems to find me anyway, doesn't it?"

She smiled and said, "I suppose that's the way it is with some people. And honestly, I wouldn't change one thing about you, even if I could! Just let me hope that someday, peace will come to this land."

"It will. I'm sure of it." Smoke gazed off into the distance. "It may be a while before it does, though."

"Well, until then, I'm glad I have Smoke Jensen by my side."

"And I'm glad to have Sally Jensen by *my* side."

They smiled at each other and traveled on, but as he rode, Smoke couldn't help but think about the things they had said.

He truly believed that peace *would* come to the frontier someday . . . but there was still a lot of blood to be spilled before that could happen.